The Pirate's Conquest

Charlene J. Centracchio

Independently Published

North Providence, Rhode Island

ISBN: 979-8-9864153-2-1

Front Cover images by: The Killion Group, Inc. and Deposit Photos
Rear Cover images by: Deposit Photos

Book Cover designed by: Ramona Lockwood, Covers By Ramona

Revised second edition: 2022

Charlene J. Centracchio, Publisher
185 Chenango Avenue
North Providence, Rhode Island 02904
www.psychicimpressionslive.com
sunpsych3@aol.com

DEDICATION

In memory of my mother, Lucille, and my father, John, who taught the entire family the meaning of the words faith, hope, and courage.

CONTENTS

PREFACE 1

CHAPTER ONE.. 7

CHAPTER TWO 17

CHAPTER THREE 25

CHAPTER FOUR.. 31

CHAPTER FIVE 43

CHAPTER SIX 59

CHAPTER SEVEN.. 65

CHAPTER EIGHT... 69

CHAPTER NINE 81

CHAPTER TEN 85

CHAPTER ELEVEN.. 99

CHAPTER TWELVE 107

CHAPTER THIRTEEN 117

CHAPTER FOURTEEN 127

CHAPTER FIFTEEN 147

CHAPTER SIXTEEN... 155

CHAPTER SEVENTEEN.. 167

CHAPTER EIGHTEEN... 173

CHAPTER NINETEEN... 185

CHAPTER TWENTY.. 189

CHAPTER TWENTY-ONE.. 193

CHAPTER TWENTY-TWO 207

CHAPTER TWENTY-THREE 215

CHAPTER TWENTY-FOUR.. 229

CHAPTER TWENTY-FIVE...245

CHAPTER TWENTY-SIX...259

CHAPTER TWENTY-SEVEN 271

CHAPTER TWENTY-EIGHT 283

CHAPTER TWENTY-NINE...293

CHAPTER THIRTY 305

CHAPTER THIRTY-ONE 317

CHAPTER THIRTY-TWO 329

CHAPTER THIRTY-THREE..339

CHAPTER THIRTY-FOUR..349

CHAPTER THIRTY-FIVE 363

CHAPTER THIRTY-SIX 379

CHAPTER THIRTY-SEVEN 391

ABOUT THE AUTHOR...403

PREFACE

From a very young age, I have had an obsession with pirates. I was mesmerized by them, their ships, their lives and their travels. I would read anything and everything I could about them. I've watched pirate movies many times over and over again. Shortly after graduating from college, I began to work as a substitute teacher with the hope of achieving a full-time teaching job. Many times, teachers left work for the students, and I found myself having little to do, and quite frankly, I became bored. I decided that I would begin to work on a novel, so I took a blank notebook with me to the schools I substituted. The first day I opened the blank notebook I wasn't sure what I was going to write or how I would even start a book. However, the words just seem to flow from my mind to my hand and I wrote. Each day after that, I would read what I had written the day before and just pick up the pen and continue to write the story. I did not plan the characters, their names or their relationships with each other, or even the foreshadowing; it literally flowed from my brain to the pen and notebook. Possibly, I utilized my psychic ability and tapped into a form of automatic writing.

My closest friend at the time, Lady Ginger knew I was working on a book, a historical romance novel about pirates. She would ask me daily about my writing and then asked to read my handwritten novel. She would arrive promptly at six o'clock every night and read what I had written that day. She happily gave me permission to name one of the characters in the book after her. She was obsessed with the story and encouraged me daily to write. She wouldn't let me take a day off from writing. She pushed me towards the completion of the novel. Lady Ginger has always been and continues to be a true-blue friend.

Reflection is a very important tool that many industries utilize to make something better. One of the greatest aspects of being a self-published author is the freedom to make some necessary changes. Once I read my novel in print, I realized that two of my characters had the same first names. That name and another name were too similar. Some of the minor character names and a few secondary character names did not flow correctly or at least the way I had anticipated they would flow. Thus, I needed to make some adjustments resulting in this edition of the book.

My mother Lucille became ill in August of 1981; diagnosed with an undisclosed cancer on March 9, 1982. At this point the novel was written but not typed or copyrighted. She passed away on August 3, 1982, and I became driven to type and copyright the book. I did it. The typing was finished and the copyright was January of 1983. I knew she would have been very proud of my accomplishment. I know that my father was proud. I was determined at that point to become a full-time writer; however, the Universe and life had something else in store for me. My father was diagnosed with kidney cancer on December 20, 1983, and passed away on March 9, 1984. Yes, two years to the date that my mother was diagnosed with her cancer. I was the oldest of four children and we were basically left alone. Although many aunts and uncles helped us, the dreams of being a full-time author needed to be tabled. I had continued to substitute teach and finally, in March of 1987, I was hired as a high school social studies teacher. There was no time for creative writing because all writing was now geared toward crafting educational documents.

I had an amazing ride as an educator. I did it all from teaching to coaching to counseling and even planning large events such as proms as a class advisor. Because my creative side was bursting to come out, I was the drama director for approximately 11 years. I have had numerous accolades as an educator being a finalist in the late 90's for RI Social Studies Teacher of the Year to winning the Margaret Addis Award as a Counselor. I used my creative side in every aspect of education, yet something was missing for me. When I retired in 2010, I worked randomly for the school department, and I focused my free time on my psychic business and educational writing for colleagues across the state. The novel you will be reading shortly continued to sit in my basement.

The Covid 19 pandemic put everyone's lives on hold, including my teaching. I had been thinking about writing again and decided to go into my basement and pull out the book. Unfortunately, it would not scan because it was typewritten, so I had to type it all over again. My family waited about 39 years for this publication are about to get their wish and see it in print.

There are some people who must be thanked for proofreading and editing - Lori Borrelli, Inbar Goldmann, Jacqueline Grasso, Suzi

Grekin, and Melissa Thomas. Thank you from the bottom of my heart for the time and energy you invested for free in order to help me get this to where it needed to be for publication. A special thank you to cover designer Ramona Lockwood (Covers By Ramona) for being extremely patient and creative with my novel's cover. And thank you to Deposit Photos and The Killion Group for the photos used in the cover designing. My family is excited that this novel is now a reality. Finally, I know my parents are looking down, and I can hear my mother saying, "It's about damn time." My father is smiling from ear to ear and probably taking bets with others who have passed on as to whether or not this will become a bestseller. It is time to live the dream. Enjoy the book!

Part I: Timothy and Jennifer

(1848-1849)

CHAPTER ONE

Jennifer Weatherly gazed out of the porthole in her cabin watching the sea toss and turn in an endless fury as the large ship rocked back and forth, sometimes lost in the ocean. Jennifer's life seemed passive and remote compared to the young women she had met at Miss Lillian's School for Girls in Paris. Miss Lillian's School, according to James Weatherly, Jennifer's father, was to teach a proper young lady her manners, as well as to provide her with an education in English, French, Arithmetic, and History. Returning to London after a four-year absence, Jennifer Weatherly, at age seventeen, would be introduced to London's High Society. Her father would then arrange for some suitable young man to marry her.

Jennifer stopped staring out the porthole and walked to the mirror on the wall. She gazed into the mirror wondering if men really did find her pretty. Her eyes took in her handsome attire and the fine, delicate features of her face. Her eyes left the mirror as she glimpsed about her cabin wishing she had Lizabeth, her lady's maid with her to help her dress for dinner with the Captain. She sat on the edge of her bunk secretly wishing that they would dock before tomorrow. Oh, how she longed to see her cousin Stefan Weatherly, they were approximately the same age and had written to each other weekly since Jennifer had been away at school. Poor Stefan. He really did not have anyone except Jennifer and her father since both of his parents were killed in a riding accident ten years ago. She looked back into the mirror thinking to herself that school had not been that bad. After all they taught her how to fix her long auburn hair in the latest fashions and how to dress appropriately for any occasion. Tonight, she had decided that she would wear the emerald green velvet gown that she bought just prior to leaving Paris. It was of the latest fashion, yet more importantly it accented her eyes. She walked back to the porthole; the ship seemed to be rolling over the vast amount of water, rather than thrashing about as it had minutes earlier.

Another ship rocked in the water off the coast of Great Britain. Timothy Lockwood, a tall young man of twenty-eight, stood at the wheel of his ship looking out over the dark murky waters. His golden eyes peered out to the shore, as his mind raced back to the time ten years before, when he and his parents left England for America. Their boat was captured by a band of pirates; his parents were killed, and he was put to work as the cabin boy for Captain Mark Gregory, the most feared pirate of all time. Captain Gregory was not an easy man to please, but Timothy tried desperately to please the short, burly man with the patch over his left eye. Timothy did please Gregory when he and other pirates fought against an attacking ship, killing five people. Captain Gregory bestowed the name of Tim the Bloodthirsty, and gave him a reward, his own ship. Tim the Bloodthirsty and Timothy Lockwood were one in the same, yet while he was Tim the Bloodthirsty, he was feared by merchants and pirates, and when he was Timothy Lockwood, he was praised for his wealth and shipping endeavors. His ship, the *Moonlight,* flew two flags, an American flag when it approached the shores of any great port and a pirate flag when it was out in the open sea. He sailed the seas for five years as a pirate, gaining all kinds of wealth and notoriety as Tim the Bloodthirsty. The next three years he spent enjoying his wealth and capitalizing on his power in the Barbary States. White slavery had decreased considerably while he was in Morocco. The last two years, he spent in Providence and Newport, Rhode Island, introducing himself to many of Rhode Island's prosperous merchants, but most importantly introducing himself to Robert Gray, a sea Captain and fur trader, who had a dream of operating a shipping and trading company. Gray was in debt to Timothy for making his dream become a reality. Being accepted by Robert Gray was just the beginning. Timothy Lockwood would become the most respected man in Rhode Island.

During the ten-year absence from London, he kept an ongoing correspondence with Sir Robert Harrington, an old friend of his father's. Eleven years earlier, Harrington and Tim's father had an agreement that when Tim became established in America, he would return to London, be introduced to High Society and marry Laura Harrington. Now that Timothy Lockwood was an established shipping and trading merchant, he was going to London to claim his bride. Timothy smiled ruefully; he had no room in his life for one particular woman including a wife. However, he would honor his father's agreement and marry the woman. He would take her back to Lockwood, the large estate he was having built in Newport and deposit her there. The city of Newport had to be one of the most beautiful cities in the world, and he was sure that his bride would love Newport as he did. Timothy would make her understand that he had all intentions of keeping a mistress or two, and she could do the same, providing she was discreet. He estimated that by the time he and Laura returned to Lockwood, the construction of the large estate on the high cliff overlooking the sea would be complete. The *Moonlight* docked in the bay, bringing Timothy back to reality. Men scurried along the deck of the great clipper ship making sure it was securely docked. The crew went to work on various duties including slopping the decks and repairing the damaged rigging. While they were working on that, Timothy would arrange for the sale of his merchandise. It took several hours for the necessary arrangements to be made in regards to the goods he had carried to London. Returning to his ship, he found his men still hard at work. On his way to his cabin, he noticed a small clipper ship on the horizon. Timothy stopped and looked at the ship for a few moments, then he called his crew to a meeting about the cargo of the ship and how it was to be sold. Tim, during the meeting, told his crew that the return trip to Newport would be just that, a return trip. There would be no booties until after he secured his new bride in his home in Newport, then he and his men will go out for one last time before they all returned to a normal life with jobs being provided for everyone.

Timothy went to his cabin to clean himself up, putting on his finest apparel and rented himself a hansom cab to take him to Sir Robert Harrington's home. It was a rough ride, especially after a rain storm with the roads being over turned from the carriage wheels. The cab pulled up to the front of the door of the Harrington home, and Tim got out of the carriage and told the driver to return in three hours to take him back to the docks. He watched the carriage go down the road. As he pulled the door chime. A maid gasped as she looked at the man standing before her, tall, dark haired, topaz eyes with a deep golden tan, dressed in the best finery she had ever laid her eyes on. "Can I help you sir?" A nervous giggle escaped her lips.

He smiled and his eyes seemed to dance as he answered her question. "Yes, I'm here to see Sir Robert Harrington."

"Who shall I say is calling sir?"

"Mr. Timothy Lockwood," he answered, looking past her at the young woman hiding in the shadows. The maid escorted him into the sitting room, and the young woman in the shadows darted out of sight.

Harrington was short and stocky with gray hair and mustache. He walked briskly into the sitting room, "Tim Lockwood," he said extending his hand, "It is very good to see you after all these years."

"You too, sir."

"You must be anxious to see Laura. She has been told that you were coming," he said. "In fact, you must stay for dinner." He reached for the servant's cord and pulled the chime. Moments later, a maid appeared at the door, "Mr. Lockwood will be staying for dinner." His attention turned back to his guest, "So tell me, Timothy, how have you made all of your money?" he asked while chewing on a cigar. Timothy found his host's cigar chewing repulsive.

"I made my fortune by trading at sea for several years and then putting my resources into a shipping and trading company with my partner, Robert Gray."

"I see, interesting, I'm glad you decided to come and see Laura for yourself. I think you will be pleasantly surprised!"

The large oak doors swung open revealing the young woman who had been standing in the shadows earlier, "Excuse me, Mr. Harrington, but dinner is ready."

"Yes, we will be right there, Maggie." The young woman left as abruptly as she entered.

Harrington led the way to the dining room across the hall; he motioned to where Timothy was to sit. Laura Harrington made her entrance as soon as the men were seated, causing both men to stand. Harrington had been correct; Laura Harrington was no longer the demure sixteen-year-old blonde that he remembered. She was a gorgeous twenty-six-year-old woman. Her gold, satin gown was low but modestly cut, revealing the swell of her breasts, and the snug fitting gown left little to the imagination as it outlined all of her curves. She moved toward the table gracefully as she extended her hand to Timothy, his lips brushed her fingers, "Madam, you, I believe, are the most beautiful woman in the world."

"Why, thank you sir, and you are most handsome, more so than I remember," she looked at his curly dark hair, his gold flecked eyes and deep tan as she memorized his every feature. Timothy pulled out the chair for Laura reminding himself that this was a real woman and not some wench roaming the ports looking for a man to show her a good time.

When they finished dinner, Timothy asked if he could call on her the following day. Given permission to spend the day with her, he returned to his ship where he spent the entire evening dreaming of beautiful Laura. Morning came quickly, and by six o'clock, Timothy's boat was ablaze with men working; another clipper ship, one much smaller than his own, was just coming ashore.

Jennifer Weatherly finished packing her few clothes and books in the large trunk. Her father appeared to be late as she scanned the carriages parked near the docks. As her eyes caught sight of the ship to her left called the *Moonlight*, a tall, deeply tanned young man came out of the cabin and shouted some orders to various men. Obviously, the man must be the Captain. Just then, the man looked up, his eyes meeting hers for a fleeting moment until a voice called in the distance; bringing her attention to her father who was standing on shore waving his hands frantically. Hesitantly, she waved back before casting a glance to the other ship, but he was gone. As Jennifer moved towards disembarking; the men of the ship lowered the plank, so she could walk down to shore. While going down the plank, she gazed over her shoulder towards the *Moonlight*; he was there again, and he seemed to be watching her.

Timothy Lockwood's attention was on the young woman leaving the ship moored aside of his; a man on shore was yelling, "Jennifer, Jennifer." His golden eyes followed the man running towards the auburn-haired woman. She threw her arms around the older man, and then the younger man standing beside the carriage bore the brunt of her attention. "Father, Stefan, I'm so happy to see the both of you." Timothy continued to watch the little scene thinking to himself that younger man must be the young lady's fiancé or her husband. He turned and continued with his work.

"Jennifer, my daughter, you are absolutely beautiful, you look just like your mother did when she was your age."

"How is mother?" she asked her father.

"Well, I take it from what the doctors tell me; physically she is fine. Mentally, there is no improvement. The Bryant Sanitarium will continue to be her home for at least a few more years." Jennifer noticed the faraway look in her father's eyes; the way he spoke of her mother she might as well be dead.

"I had hoped that she would be well for my return," her voice trailed off, as they boarded the waiting landau carriage.

"We had all hoped that she would be well for your homecoming. So, tell me Jennifer, how was school?" asked Stefan, trying to change the subject.

"School? It was boring! My tutors at Weatherly taught me more as far as education is concerned. I'm sure I could have learned to fix my hair and dress just as well if I had stood home," she smiled, her sea green eyes sparkling with delight as she said, "Do we still have Olivia my Arabian mare?"

"Of course, why?" asked her father as the carriage rolled along the road to Weatherly, hitting as few bumps as possible.

"Stefan, if my father has kept Olivia, then you must still own Rogue."

"That I do, my dear cousin, but why all the questions about horses?" asked Stefan, his blue eyes twinkling, knowing and anticipating her answer before she even spoke.

"When we reach Weatherly, after I am settled back in the house, I wish for you to join me riding. I want to take my hair out of this ridiculous hair style, let it hang loose and be able to feel the wind blowing through it. I want to put on those old riding breeches and go riding like we did when we were young!" she laughed, "What do you say, Stefan?"

"Whatever pleases you, Jenny. I would like that, it would give us time to talk, however," he looked toward the angry expression on his uncle's face, "I think that your father would like to make a comment."

"My dear daughter, I do not think you should go riding."

"Why not?" she demanded.

"It is not proper for a young woman of your station to go cavorting around the country side in breeches."

"Really father, cavorting around the countryside is one thing, but riding around our land is quite another, and I will go riding," she stated firmly.

Her father's face turned red, "Damnation girl!"

"I'm not a girl; I'm a woman, and I want to go riding."

"Very well, you win, but Mr. Geoffrey Lyndon, your betrothed, is coming to visit later this afternoon, and I expect you to be presentable." Jennifer and Stefan exchanged glances, neither saying a word for the remainder of the ride.

Jennifer looked quietly out the window of the coach as it bounced over the pebbled road leading to Weatherly. In the distance, she could see the massive house, her home. Weatherly had been part of her father's family for years, and it had become part of her destiny; it was her destiny. The carriage came to an abrupt stop when Lizabeth, her nanny and lady's maid, ran from the front door to the road, causing the driver of the coach to stop the horses. "Miss Jenny, Miss Jenny, I did miss you!"

Jennifer was helped out of the carriage by Stefan, "And I you Lizabeth." Her eyes travelled past Lizabeth to Harris, the butler; she smiled, "I missed you too, Harris." The old man's eyes began to water as he smiled at her.

"And I missed you, Miss Jenny. Let me get your baggage." Harris carried the carpetbag, while Stefan and one of the new stable boys struggled with the large chest.

Lizabeth followed Jennifer up the stairs to her bedroom, "Missy, we have missed you. What's the matter with your father, he looks mighty angry?" Lizabeth hadn't changed in the fifteen years that Jenny had known her; of course, she put on a little weight, making her rounder than she had been since the last time Jennifer saw her, and her hair was a little grayer, but she was still as blunt as she remembered.

"He's a little upset, Lizabeth. You see, I wish to go riding with Stefan after I unpack these things, and I wish to take my hair out of this ridiculous hair style and wear a riding habit with boots and a whip and a hat. That is, if you have kept my riding habit." Jennifer busied herself with hanging out some of the dresses that were in the trunk.

"That I have Miss, but I don't think it will fit you because you have developed some since you left."

"The breeches and boots will surely fit. Go find an old shirt of my fathers for me to wear while I undo this horrendous hairstyle."

"Very well, Miss." Lizabeth hurriedly left the room to retrieve an old shirt of James Weatherly's.

Jennifer walked to the dresser and stared in the mirror. Carefully, she unwound the long hair, allowing the auburn curls to cascade down her back. She picked the gold brush up off the dresser and began to brush her hair. Jennifer went to the closet and began to look for her breeches. Finding the black trousers, she carefully tried them on. They were a little tight, but they would have to do. There was a knock on the door, and Lizabeth brought an old shirt for her to wear.

Jennifer motioned to Lizabeth to help her with the boots. Lizabeth helped her lady into the boots and then with the shirt. Jennifer dismissed her old nanny who had graduated to lady's maid before she left for school. She took one last glance around the room and then descended the long flight of stairs to the ground floor. Upon reaching the foyer, she turned to the left and placed two hands on the double doors of the sitting room and strode in. She hadn't realized that her father was entertaining. The older man looked aghast at his daughter's appearance and Stefan stifled a laugh. The older gentleman turned to his guest, "Sir Harrington, that is my willful daughter, Jennifer."

"It is a pleasure to meet you Miss Weatherly," he said kissing her lightly on the hand.

"It is a pleasure to meet you too, Sir Harrington," she smiled as she turned to Stefan who had remained seated, "Stefan are you coming riding?"

"Of course, Jenny," his attention now turned to his uncle's guest, "It was a pleasure meeting you, Sir Harrington." Harrington nodded his reply. Jennifer and Stefan left the sitting room arm in arm on their way to the stables.

Sir Harrington looked across the room at James Weatherly, who was pouring himself a drink, "Your daughter is a delight. I wish my daughter could be like her."

"Believe me, Robert, I wish my daughter was a frail woman without a mind of her own. I sent her to school because she was a disgrace to me. She doesn't care who sees her dressed that way!"

"James, I think she is charming. She will probably make a better wife for a man worth his salt than will my own daughter, Laura."

"Well, I plan to have her married shortly to Geoffrey Lyndon of Lyndon and Son Shipping," he said as he took a sip of his drink.

"My daughter's fiancé arrived last evening, Timothy Lockwood, formerly of Hampshire, now of Newport, Rhode Island, in the colonies."

"Lockwood, I once knew a man named Lockwood many years ago, Sir Thomas Lockwood, any relation?" asked James.

"Yes, it was Timothy's father, but he died shortly after leaving London ten years ago," replied Robert.

"What business is Lockwood in?" questioned James.

"Trading and shipping; he has become very prosperous in Newport. In fact, I am going to have a costume ball in honor of my daughter's engagement, and I would like your daughter and her fiancé to come. However, I think your daughter and my daughter should meet before the ball takes place," replied Robert, taking a sip of his drink.

Weatherly rose from his seat and walked to the windows where he tried to see Jennifer and Stefan, "I'll have my daughter invite her to tea the day after tomorrow."

"Thank-you. She worries me; she's so frail, and I think meeting your daughter will add to her life." He rose to his feet, "Now I must be going." James Weatherly walked his guest into the foyer and bid him adieu.

Jennifer stroked Olivia lightly on the nose. She reached into her pocket and gave the horse a small carrot, "Hey girl, do you remember me?" The horse whinnied as if she recognized her long lost master. Jennifer turned to Rogue, "Here's a carrot for you; I bet Stefan didn't give you any when I was gone."

Stefan interrupted her, "Of course I did; do you think I would let Rogue starve?"

"Of course not," she answered as she mounted Olivia and guided her out of the stables. Stefan followed on Rogue slightly behind her. He nudged Rogue with his knee, bringing the horse even with Jennifer's. "Do you remember when we would race to the large oak trees at the end of the field?"

"Yes, I do, but Jennifer, it's been a long time since you have been on a horse." Before he could finish his sentence, Jennifer and her mare Olivia, galloped away at full speed. He kicked Rogue and chased after his cousin. Jennifer and her horse jumped the fence with Stefan and Rogue on her heels. Trees, grass, sky all seemed to be whirling around her as she pulled on the horse's reins to slow down and finally stop. Stefan reached her a couple of minutes after she had dismounted and tied Olivia to the nearest tree. Stefan dismounted and tied Rogue, laughing, "You are still crazy, Jenny, you could have been killed back there when you jumped that fence!"

"Nonsense, Stefan, I knew perfectly well what I was doing," opening her saddle bag she continued, "I had Lizabeth pack us some bread and cheese."

"You think of everything, don't you, Jenny?"

She smiled, "Of course, sit here," she motioned with her free hand to the grass under the tree. Stefan sat aside of her as she handed him a hunk of bread and some cheese.

"Jenny, I missed you," he said as he bit a piece of the cheese.

"And I you, Stefan. Tell me, have you met this man father wishes me to marry?"

"Unfortunately, I have; his name is Geoffrey Lyndon. He is part owner of a large shipping firm, and he is a fop," replied her cousin Stefan.

"A fop! Father wishes me to marry a fop? How could he?" she ranted.

"Your father will not believe that the man is a fop. I had Geoffrey Lyndon thoroughly investigated. He gambles quite extensively, and it is my personal opinion that he wishes to get his hands on your inheritance and Weatherly so he can use that for his gambling ways," Jennifer listened intently as she nibbled on a piece of bread. Stefan fingered a piece of cheese before popping the morsel in his mouth. "I also found out that he has virtually caused his father to go bankrupt so," he paused, "his father encourages this marriage so he, too, will have access to the Weatherly fortune."

"Access to the Weatherly fortune? I will tell father I refuse to marry this Geoffrey Lyndon," she said as she stood to her feet.

"Jenny, your father is determined to marry you to that fellow. I'm afraid there is no way to get out of it," he said sadly.

"I will get out of this marriage. We have to put our heads together and come up with an idea." Jenny began to gather some wild flowers. Looking toward the sky for a moment, she prayed that some way, with God's help, she would get out of this sham of a marriage. "I think we should head back to the stables; after dinner tonight, we can discuss what we are to do about this Geoffrey Lyndon." They mounted the horses and rode back to Weatherly.

CHAPTER TWO

Timothy Lockwood knocked on the large oak doors. His eyes scanned the countryside surrounding the large estate. Laura Harrington would indeed make an ideal bride to bring home to Lockwood in Newport. She would be the talk of the city with every man turning his head when she walked down the street. The door opened, and the maid hurried him into the sitting room as she went to look for Miss Laura.

Laura looked at herself in the mirror. She adjusted one curl, so it fell lightly on her cheek; if she could pull off this deception, this mockery, she would have everything she always desired; wealth and power. The first thing she must do is to convince Timothy Lockwood that she is innocent of men and their ways. That first step would be the hardest! Her thoughts were interrupted by a knock on her door. Rising from her dressing table, she crossed the large bedroom and opened the door to the maid, "Mr. Lockwood is here to see you, Miss Laura."

"Tell Mr. Lockwood I will be down in a moment." Closing the door, she returned to the mirror taking one last look. The dress she had chosen for this meeting, the dark blue velvet with the white lace trim, added a touch of virginity. Laura left her bedroom hoping to make a grand entrance to the sitting room. Timothy was standing at the window oblivious to what was going on around him. Laura eased her way to him, "Mr. Lockwood."

He turned so that he faced her, "Please Laura, if we are to be wed in the couple of months, you must call me Timothy."

"Very well, Timothy, shall we go for a stroll in the garden?" she said taking his arm as she led the way out of the sitting room and into the large library to the doors leading to the garden. Laura casually looked over at Timothy Lockwood as they strolled through the garden wondering what kind of lover he would be, if he would be as good in bed as her current lover, Geoffrey Lyndon. She loved Geoff, and he loved her, but for economic reasons they were both betrothed to other people, but some day she would find a way to be with Geoff Lyndon.

Geoff Lyndon's carriage pulled into the Weatherly estate. He stared out the window totally involved in his thoughts as he looked at the large house. Within months that house, the power it meant, and the vast amount of wealth that went with it would be his. James Weatherly would have to be dealt with at a later date, perhaps slowly poisoning the man would suffice nicely. The carriage halted to an abrupt stop in front of the Weatherly home. Geoff Lyndon stepped carefully out of the carriage and walked to the front door, pulling the door chime twice. The door slowly opened and the butler stared at him. "Can I help you sir?"

"Yes, I'm here to see Mr. Weatherly and his daughter, Miss Jennifer Weatherly," replied Geoffrey.

"Follow me," Harris said as he turned. He disliked this man very much; in fact, it was more than dislike; it was hate. He led the way to the main parlor. Geoffrey Lyndon seated himself in the large chair in the center of the room. He looked around musing that the Weatherly wealth was abundant in this room; a Chinese carpet placed in the center of the room accented the Chinese furnishings. James Weatherly presented himself to Lyndon moments after Lyndon had helped himself to a glass of sherry.

"Well, Geoff, I see you have helped yourself," the older man stared coolly at him.

Geoff smirked, "Yes, I hope you don't mind."

"No, not at all. I suppose you have heard of Jennifer's return and wish to see her."

"Yes, that would be nice since I am to marry the young lady in a few months," replied Geoffrey.

Jennifer could not have made a grander appearance, as the doors were flung open, with Jennifer and Stefan laughing and joking with one another. Lyndon looked at the two of them, never guessing that it was Jennifer Weatherly he was staring at. The young woman, whoever she was, obviously had no morals if she paraded around in pants like a man, thought Geoffrey. Stefan's expression changed drastically from very silly to serious in a matter of seconds. Jennifer also stopped laughing as she gazed at the man standing in front of her; by her judgement, he was approximately thirty years old, blonde, thinning hair and grey-blue eyes.

James was shocked at his daughter and nephew's appearances. Jennifer was smudged in mud and looked like a common street urchin, and Stefan looked no better. Jennifer looked from the younger man to her father, "Father, I'm so sorry. I had no idea you had company." Now the younger man seemed appalled. Surely Weatherly must have another daughter, for this cannot be the Jennifer, he wishes me to marry, thought Lyndon. His thoughts were severed by Weatherly.

"Jennifer, you look like a common street waif, and Stefan, you are no better," grumbled James Weatherly. Geoffrey Lyndon placed his glass of sherry down on the table next to his chair. James had gotten to his feet causing Geoffrey to stand also, "Jennifer, this is Mr. Geoffrey Lyndon. Mr. Lyndon, my daughter, Jennifer, and of course you have already met Stefan."

Now it was Jennifer's turn to look shocked; slowly she offered her hand, but Lyndon politely declined, "Mr. Lyndon, it is indeed a pleasure to meet you."

Geoffrey smiled, his eyes narrowing, "As it is you, Miss Weatherly."

Jennifer smiled coolly, "Please call me Jennifer." Lyndon returned her smile and made a mental note of her icy green eyes. Stefan enjoyed watching his cousin bait this man.

James Weatherly broke the few moments of silence, "Jennifer, Mr. Lyndon will be having supper with us, so why don't you make yourself presentable while we discuss some business matters. Perhaps before dinner you can go for a stroll in the gardens."

"Yes, perhaps we will," she smiled once again, took a last fleeting look at Geoffrey Lyndon, turned on her heels and walked out of the main parlor. Stefan left the room minutes after Jennifer. He ran up the stairs bumping into Lizabeth.

"My dear, Stefan, where are you going in such a hurry?" questioned Lizabeth.

"To see Jenny," he stated, smiling.

"But you were with her all morning and part of the afternoon," said Lizabeth.

Stefan looked at Lizabeth, "Yes, but she just met her fiancé."

"Well then, Master Stefan, I must come with you to see what my lady thinks!" The two of them turned and climbed the remaining stairs together on their way to Jennifer's room.

Jennifer sat on the small divan and stared out the window. She thought to herself, "I will not marry Geoffrey Lyndon if my life depends on it! I must get out of this wedding no matter what the cost. I will not marry him, I will not!" Her thoughts were interrupted by a loud, frantic knock at her chamber door. "It is open, come in." As she turned to face the door, Stefan and Lizabeth hurriedly entered the room, closing the door tightly behind them.

Lizabeth laughed, "You mean to tell me that Geoffrey Lyndon saw you dressed like that? Your father must be outraged!"

Jennifer glared, "Yes, Geoffrey Lyndon saw me dressed like this, and my father is outraged!"

"You should have seen Mr. Lyndon's face when Uncle James told him that this was his daughter, Jennifer," laughed Stefan. Lizabeth looked back and forth from Jennifer and Stefan. She had brought up the two of them since they were small children. Now they were young adults who had a problem, yet they looked like the cat who swallowed a mouse.

"I refuse to marry that man," Jennifer said determinedly.

"Refuse you may, Miss Jennifer, but if your father wishes you to be married, there is nothing we can do," said Lizabeth firmly.

"No, Stefan, you and I must come up with a plan to put off this wedding for at least a year," said Jennifer, as she looked back and forth between her cousin and her maid.

"But Missy, if we succeed in putting off the wedding for a year, what will you do when the years is up and you must marry that man?" questioned Lizabeth.

Stefan, who had not spoken, answered Lizabeth's question. "You see, Mr. Geoffrey Lyndon and his father wish to gain access of Jennifer's inheritance and Weatherly. The only way they can do that is if Jenny marries Lyndon. Geoff Lyndon is a gambler and ladies' man; he has caused both he and his father to become nearly bankrupt. So, I'm sure Mr. Lyndon will press Uncle James for Jennifer's hand in marriage. If he can marry her within the next few months, he can dispose of his sorry state before the creditors come hounding at his door." Lizabeth listened intently as Stefan continued, "If we can postpone the marriage for one year, Geoff Lyndon and his father will become totally bankrupt, and Uncle James will not allow Jennifer to marry him."

Lizabeth sat quietly on the edge of the bed not saying a word, anger building inside of her until she could no longer hold it in, "So, he thinks he can take advantage of you Weatherlys, does he? I raised you and Jennifer to live like a king and queen and I will not let him destroy you or Weatherly!" Stefan and Jennifer giggled, "What's the laughing about?"

Jennifer put her arms around the old maid, "Oh, Lizabeth I knew you wouldn't fail me. Now we must come up with a way to stop this marriage for at least a year."

"Jennifer, at least six months we may be able to get away with it, but I don't know about a year," replied Lizabeth. The three of them sat in silence for several minutes; Lizabeth suddenly clasped Jennifer's hand, "Your father does not plan for your coming out until next month. Why don't you ask him if you can go on vacation before you marry?"

Jennifer interrupted Lizabeth, "A vacation? Father will never agree to that!"

"Now hear me out girl. Tell your father that you want to take this vacation now because after you are married, you will be too busy keeping house and being a devoted wife and mayhap giving him a grandson. Tell him that you want Stefan and me with you like when you were young for old times' sake," said Lizabeth.

"But where would we go?" asked Jennifer.

"Spain, Madrid," answered Stefan.

"That's a fine idea, Master Stefan! Madrid, Spain will take us several weeks to get there, and then we will spend a month or month and a half before returning. All in all, six months will have passed by the time we return," said Lizabeth.

"That still leaves six months," worried Jennifer.

"I know that, Missy, but no one will expect you to marry right on your return from abroad. We will set up the wedding for three months after your return," stated Lizabeth.

"Lizabeth, that is still only nine months, and Jennifer has to stall for at least a year," said Stefan.

"Let me finish young man. The day before the wedding is to take place, Miss Jennifer will plead illness. I will send for Doctor Warren," said Lizabeth.

"But if I am not sick, what good is Doctor Warren?" questioned Jennifer.

"Hush girl, we will tell Doctor Warren of your predicament and he will go along with us, I'm sure of it," said Lizabeth as she placed her hands on her hips.

Jennifer thought about Lizabeth's plan. Doctor Warren was a close friend of the family and would probably go along with anything they wished. There was one flaw however, "Lizabeth, really how long can I remain ill?"

"You can make off you're ill for a couple of weeks. Doctor Warren will say that you should wait for a month or month and half so you won't chance a relapse. By the time the wedding takes place, Mr. Lyndon will be bankrupt, and there will be no wedding!" grinned Lizabeth.

Jennifer hugged Lizabeth, "If we can pull off this plan of yours, I won't have to marry Lyndon."

"Now, Missy, you and Master Stefan had better get dressed for dinner." Lizabeth and Stefan left Jennifer's room.

Jennifer locked the door and walked into the wash room. Removing her clothing, she stepped into the tepid water to wash the sweat and dirt from her body. The water was lightly scented with lilac, which would perfume her nicely. Her wash room was decorated with the finest wicker from India; the large porcelain tub came from China as a gift from one of her father's many friends. She reached for the large blue towel resting on the wicker lounge behind the tub. Standing once again, she wrapped the towel around her body, so it would absorb the water until she could find her dressing gown. Leaving the wash room, she paddled across the Persian rug to her closet; opened the door, and reached for the white silk dressing gown. Letting the blue towel slide to the floor, she put on the dressing gown. Crossing the room to the dressing table, she sat on the small stool. Looking in the mirror, she decided that something must be done with her long, auburn hair; pulling it away from her face, she stared at herself in the mirror. She thought to herself that it would look nice if she tied it with a ribbon to match her gown. Crossing the room once more, she went to the closet to pick out her dress for dinner. Choosing a dark green satin dress with a white ruffled trim, she began to dress for dinner.

Stefan chose a sky-blue waistcoat to accompany dark blue trousers; he wondered if Jennifer would pay much attention to Lyndon. She would have to in order to not upset her father. Jennifer would have Lyndon in the palm of her hand by the end of the evening; he was sure of it.

Jennifer left her bedroom and walked down the hall passing the guest room on her way to the stairs. Hesitating at Stefan's door, she knocked. Stefan opened the door to see his cousin standing before him, "Jennifer, I was just thinking about you."

"Stefan, do you think father will approve of this dress?" She turned around letting him view the dress fully. Jennifer Weatherly, at seventeen, had matured beautifully.

Stefan smiled, "It is perfect!"

"Well then, accompany me to the sitting room where I am to entertain my fiancé," a note of sarcasm was in her voice.

Stefan guided her down the stairs to the sitting room, opening the door for her she; walked into the room. Startled, Geoff Lyndon took in the view of the young woman that stood before him. He licked his lips, reminding Jennifer of a wolf ready to jump his prey. Raping her with his eyes, he wondered about the softness of her flesh. Jennifer blushed uneasily.

"Jennifer, you are most beautiful," said Lyndon.

"Thank you, Mr. Lyndon, perhaps you would like to stroll in the garden, for it is a beautiful June evening," said Jennifer.

"Yes, that would be nice if your father approves." Geoffrey had to make the right moves where James Weatherly was concerned.

James Weatherly looked up from his newspaper, "Yes, that would be a fine idea. Jennifer, before you go, you must invite Laura Harrington to tea tomorrow. I promised her father that you would, and it completely slipped my mind. Geoffrey Lyndon stared blatantly at James Weatherly with mention of Laura Harrington's name. His expression did not escape Jennifer, who wondered if there was something going on between the two.

"If you would excuse me Geoffrey, I'll write a note to Miss Harrington, so Harris can send someone with it this evening." Jennifer left the room to attend to the note.

It was obvious to Stefan that Lyndon did not like him and the feeling was mutual. Jennifer returned within minutes. Lyndon and Jennifer went for a short walk in the garden. Lyndon was cordial to Jennifer, yet there was something about him that she disliked immensely. Dinner came and went quickly, with Lyndon leaving just after dinner. Jennifer walked him to the door and watched him ride away before returning to the warmth of the house. James Weatherly came out of his library, "Jennifer, what do you think of the man?"

"He's very nice; I think he'll make a fine husband." Not really, she thought, but why argue with her father now. Let it wait until she asks him if she could go away, "I'm going to my room father, I'll see you tomorrow morning."

Her father kissed her lightly on the cheek, "Good night, my daughter."

"Good night, father." She turned and walked up the stairs to her bedroom. Stefan was waiting at her door.

"Jenny, it's about time. I've been pacing this corridor for ten minutes."

"I'm sorry, but I thought it proper to wait until he left," she said.

"Sorry, you are right after all. When the two of you were in the garden, did he try to convince you to get married soon?" questioned Stefan.

"No, but I'm sure he will when he finds out about my trip," she smirked.

Stefan rolled his eyes trying to be serious, "What will you do then?"

"I will politely refuse and tell him that it is very important that I take a trip. Now, if you will excuse me, Stefan, I'd like to go to sleep; it has been a long day." She opened the door to her bedroom.

"Goodnight, Jenny." Stefan said.

"Goodnight." Closing the door behind her, she prepared for bed. Sleep came quickly, for she was exhausted.

CHAPTER THREE

Dawn appeared shortly after six-thirty in the early evening with the twilight fading away. Birds were chirping by seven o'clock, and small animals scurried on their merry way. The Weatherly household had been in a flurry of activity since six, as the maids cleaned and prepared for Jennifer's guest, Laura Harrington.

Jennifer awoke around nine o'clock to a loud knock. Lizabeth brought her breakfast and prepared a bath. Jennifer was famished; she had not really eaten all that well the last few days. A pot of hot tea warmed her chilled bones; the hot buttered muffins were just as she remembered them, and the eggs, she decided, must be fresh from the coop. After eating, she sunk into the hot bath and began to bathe herself. The water had a refreshing lavender fragrance. She could have laid in that bath forever, but she had to dress before eleven when her guest was due to arrive for an early lunch.

Laura Harrington arrived exactly one hour late. Jennifer was in a rage over her guest's carelessness to arrive at a luncheon late. The moment Jennifer laid eyes on Laura Harrington; she knew that she would dislike her. Laura was wearing a dark green muslin gown with gold trim. Her blonde hair was piled neatly on her head. Jennifer noticed that for someone who was supposedly of good station, Laura's dark green muslin gown was not in the best condition. Perhaps she was one of those rich who did not like to show exactly how rich they really were. Laura made a quick assessment of Jennifer Weatherly; the girl's beauty was astonishing for someone only seventeen; it was quite obvious that the girl reeked of money. Her gown was of the finest silk, probably from China, and her hair was constructed in one of the latest fashions from Paris.

During the lunch and the hour and a half later, Laura Harrington wished Jennifer Weatherly was ugly, self-centered and penniless. Jennifer Weatherly, on the other hand, thought to herself that someone like Laura Harrington would definitely have to be rich even if she didn't dress rich. She was arrogant, self-centered and not to mention, vindictive. However, both girls were cordial to each other; the meeting ending with Laura extending invitations to Jennifer, her fiancé Geoff Lyndon, her cousin Stefan and a guest of his choice, and her father, to a costume party to be given at the end of the week. Jennifer accepted without hesitation, and Laura Harrington left her home.

Laura spent the afternoon thinking about something to wear. Perhaps one of her mother's fine old gowns would do nicely, and she could go as a Princess. Yes, something that would turn everyone's head and make Geoffrey Lyndon extremely jealous. Laura went to the attic and searched for one of her mother's gowns to wear. The attic was dusty and filled with cobwebs. The trunks that once belonged to her mother were covered with a thick dust. Striking a match, she lit the lantern so she could see better. The extra light scared the small critters that lived in the attic, causing them to scurry every which way to hide from the brightness. Years ago, Laura would have been frightened by a rat, but since her family's financial losses, rats were now common in their household. Her father had just enough money to feed the servants and herself; there was no money to buy rat poison. This party caused her father to sell the last piece of land that he owned, so she wanted to look perfect. Spying an old trunk set way back in the corner of the attic, she decided to start with that one. The trunk creaked open, revealing gowns of the finest satins, silks, and velvets. Laura found a white satin gown with a scoop and a full skirt with long, puffed sleeves trimmed in white velvet. Looking further into the trunk, she found a cape in pale blue velvet, lined in white satin to match the gown. The old trunk proved to be a gold mine in that it yielded both the dress and matching cape. Leaving both articles on the top of the open trunk, she moved to another trunk, which, when she opened, revealed slippers of all kinds and colors. After trying on a slipper for fit, she chose the dainty white satin slippers to match her gown. Thinking to herself, she put the gown against her body and vowed that she would be the belle of the ball. Jennifer Weatherly would not give her any competition at the costume party because everyone will be staring at her fine costume. A maid suddenly appeared at the door of the attic startling Laura.

"Excuse me, Miss, but this here note came for you." Laura took the note from the young girl's hand, dismissed her, and read it. *"My dearest Laura, the days have been long since I have last seen you. I have met my fiancé, Jennifer Weatherly"* so have I she thought, *"You, my dear, are far more beautiful, and I long to see you before your party. If you can, please meet me at our place at six. G.L."*

Our place, the words pieced her heart; the place was an empty house on the outskirts of her father's land. In the days when they were extremely rich, the house was for servants. Now, it was boarded and closed for the most part, but she and Geoffrey used it as a secret meeting place. Laura quickly gathered the party costume and ran to her room, tossing the garments on the bed, she looked into the mirror, adjusting her hair and her clothes. Quietly, she slipped down the stairs to the foyer and took her cloak out of the closet. Maggie watched quietly from her dark corner in the foyer; it appeared that Miss Laura was going out to meet someone. Laura looked nervously around, making sure that no one saw her get her cloak. Feeling successful, she slid past the quiet Maggie and out the rear door. Maggie ran into the kitchen and looked out the window to see Laura running across the grounds, past the stables, to the former servants' quarters. Laura stopped in front of the door, looked casually around, and then disappeared into the house. Maggie continued to look out the window for several minutes until she saw a horse and rider come up to the old quarters. The man getting off the horse was not Timothy Lockwood but Geoffrey Lyndon. What would Miss Laura have to do with that vile man? Maggie took her shawl off the hook in the kitchen, gathered her basket, and went outside to collect eggs for the morning meal. The chickens were kept behind the old servants' quarters, which would enable Maggie to slip in the rear door without being discovered and hear what was going on between Miss Laura and Mr. Lyndon. Maggie quietly slipped in the rear door, walking toward the voices. The voices grew louder as she got closer.

"Geoff, how could you send a note like that to my house, suppose one of the servants read it?

"Do servants normally read your messages?" he asked sarcastically.

"No," Laura replied.

"Well, then you have nothing to worry about. No one saw you leave the house, correct?" Geoff asked her.

Laura sighed, "No, my father is getting a tour of my fiancé's ship and then they are coming back here for dinner."

"I note a hint of sarcasm in your voice; don't you like your fiancé?" Geoff asked.

"He is handsome, but he isn't you. We both know that we have to play by the rules," said Laura.

"Yes, I must marry Jennifer, and you must marry Timothy; however, the rules can be broken today," Geoff's voice had become thicker as he reached for her. Pulling her close to him, his lips came crashing down on hers. Shocked with the game these two people were playing, Maggie dropped her basket. Geoff pulled away from Laura, "What was that?"

"Probably a rat," replied Laura, as Maggie picked up the basket and held her breath for fear of being discovered.

"Are you absolutely positive that no one saw you leave the house?" questioned Geoff.

"Yes, my father is due home around seven-thirty, and the servants are preparing dinner." Taking his hand, she led him to the old bed, "Come now, we don't have much time, take me now, so I can get back to change for dinner." Her hands worked quickly on his shirt and trousers.

Maggie had heard and seen enough; she had to get back to the house before the other servants questioned her whereabouts. Sneaking out the door, she quickly gathered the eggs and ran all the way back to the large house.

Mary, the cook, was preparing dinner, "Child, what's wrong with you, you look like you saw a ghost?"

Maggie tried to gain control of her breathing, "I," she hesitated, "I thought I saw a big animal out there."

"Set yourself down a moment child," said Mary. Maggie sat in the chair by the large table, "When you catch your breath you can tell me what kind of animal you saw outside and help me with supper."

A few moments went by, and Maggie said, "I didn't see an animal, I thought I heard something in the woods, and it scared me."

"Probably a bird," replied Mary, "Peel some potatoes." Maggie went to the potato bin and began to peel the potatoes and help with the evening meal.

Sir Harrington and Timothy Lockwood came an hour later. Maggie set the table and was sent to get Miss Laura. Maggie set out to fetch Miss Laura; she knew one thing; Laura Harrington did not deserve the fine gentleman that sat in the study with Sir Harrington.

Laura had just gotten in the house shortly before she heard her father's carriage pull up; she ran up the stairs to prepare for dinner.

There was no time for a bath now; she'd have to wait. She had just finished dressing when Maggie appeared and said that dinner was ready. Laura looked once more in the mirror before going downstairs; Timothy and her father rose when she entered the room. Timothy walked to the door, kissed her hand lightly and escorted her to her seat. Supper consisted of mutton soup, leg of lamb with browned potatoes, and fruit for dessert. They sat at the table discussing the coming costume ball.

"What will you be going to the ball as, Laura?" questioned her father.

"Well father, I have a costume picked out, and I want it to be a surprise," replied Laura as she turned to Timothy, "Timothy what will you be coming as?"

Timothy grinned, "Since you won't tell me what you are going to be, then I, too, will keep my costume a surprise."

Laura laughed lightly, "Very well, we will surprise each other."

Timothy turned to his host, "Who will be at the party, Sir Harrington?"

"James Weatherly, his nephew Stefan, and his daughter Jennifer and her fiancé, Mr. and Mrs. Richard Swenson and their son and daughter-in-law, Count and Countess Caprese of Venice, Italy, the Earl of Kent and his lovely family, some of our relatives from Liverpool and Manchester. I'm afraid none of them are involved in shipping, but they all would be interested in the United States," replied Robert Harrington.

Laura straightened in her seat, "No, father, you are wrong. Geoffrey Lyndon is a ship builder."

"I stand corrected, Mr. Lyndon is Miss Weatherly's fiancé; he and his father own Lyndon and Son Shipping Company," Sir Harrington replied as he took a sip of his brandy.

Timothy became curious, "Ah, they build ships, but are not involved with shipping other than that?"

"No, they just build ships; I don't even think they have ever been on one of their ships," laughed Sir Harrington.

"Perhaps, I'll commission them to build me another ship before I return to Newport. Speaking of ships, I must be getting back to mine." Timothy rose from his seat, "May I have permission for Laura to escort me to the door?"

"Certainly," replied Sir Harrington.

"Laura," she rose from her seat and took Timothy's extended arm. They walked into the foyer, hesitating at the door, "May I kiss you goodnight?" Laura blushed, shaking her head yes. His lips touched hers lightly; pulling away, he said in a husky voice, "I've got to go." Laura knew instinctively that she aroused his desire but she had to the play the part of the naïve, virginal girl.

"Will you be coming by tomorrow?" she asked shyly.

"No, I have business to attend to; I won't be able to see you until the party," Timothy replied.

"Okay, I wish that you could come, but I understand," she replied, trying to sound as a girl smitten with her fiancé.

He opened the door, went down the stairs, turned as if he wanted to say something, waved, Laura waved back; he got in his carriage and drove off. Laura closed the door and went upstairs to her room. Lighting a candle, she began to undress for bed, forgetting completely about the bath she intended to take. Her mind traveled back to Timothy Lockwood's kiss; if she could fool him now, she could play out this charade while they were married. Perhaps Geoffrey could continue to be her lover; of course, he would have to get Jennifer Weatherly to agree to move to the colonies, but she was sure he could do so. Slipping between the cool sheets, she quickly fell asleep.

CHAPTER FOUR

Jennifer laid in her bed deciding that the best way to make Geoffrey hate her would be to conduct herself in a manner of which he would disapprove. Having decided this, she quickly rose, ate and dressed; by eight-thirty in the morning, she was holding a conference in her father's library. Lizabeth and Stefan gathered around the large, oak desk. Jennifer stared across the desk at the two of them, "Lizabeth, Stefan, good morning," she smiled, "I have an exceptionally good idea concerning this party tomorrow."

Stefan noticed the devilish twinkle in his cousin's eyes. "What type of a plan do you have working in that devious little mind of yours?"

Jennifer smirked, and her eyes had that mischievous look about them, "Well, I was thinking in terms of costumes."

"What type of costume would you like to wear, Missy?" questioned Lizabeth.

"I was thinking in terms of either a lady pirate or a harem girl," replied Jennifer.

Stefan began to laugh uncontrollably as Lizabeth's mouth fell wide open; composing himself he said, "Jenny, I think that is a bit scandalous."

"Miss Jennifer," Lizabeth said, using her name versus Missy which was her term of endearment for Jennifer, "What would your father say? He'd never let you leave the house in either of those costumes."

Jennifer began to outline her costume plan, "That is where the two of you will come in to play. Stefan, his date, Geoffrey Lyndon and father will all be waiting for me to come downstairs. Stefan will convince father that Geoffrey and I would come later as soon as I was finished dressing. Lizabeth, your job will be to keep Geoffrey in the drawing room" she paused, "this will enable me to get my cloak out of the front closet and put it on before Geoffrey can see my costume."

Lizabeth shook her head, "It won't work, Miss Jennifer, why would you be late in changing into your costume?"

"I'll go out riding late that afternoon and return after Geoffrey and Stefan's date get here; that way, it would be easier for Stefan to convince father to leave," replied Jennifer.

"Jenny, why would you want to wear a costume that will shock the guests at the Harrington Party?" questioned Stefan.

"I was hoping that it will also shock Geoffrey, besides it will be fun. Now Stefan, I need you to accompany me to the wharf," said Jennifer.

Stefan's eyes opened wide, "The wharf? Are you out of your mind?'

Jennifer looked at him calmly, "No, I decided to be a lady pirate, and I need a costume. What better place to get a costume than at the wharf?"

"That is a dangerous place for a woman, Miss Jennifer," said Lizabeth.

"Lizabeth, this is none of your concern!" The old woman was hurt by Jennifer's anger, "I'm sorry Lizabeth, it's just that my nerves are wearing thin, it is the pressure of having to marry Geoffrey Lyndon." Turning to Stefan, she said, "Stefan will you come with me to the docks?"

"If it is what you want, I'll go," Stefan reluctantly agreed.

Jennifer smiled, "Good, the carriage is waiting."

Stefan shook his head, "You were so sure that I would say yes that you have the carriage waiting?"

"No, whether you said yes or no, I was still going to go. Lizabeth, if father comes home from his office and asks where I am, tell him that I went out with Stefan, and we didn't say where we are going." said Jennifer.

"Very well, Miss," Lizabeth left the library and set out to do her chores.

Stefan looked at Jennifer, "You are really going to go through with this?"

"Yes, let's go," Jennifer stood up and left the library with Stefan at her heels. Opening the closet door, she took out her shawl and Stefan's waistcoat. The two of them left the house and got into the carriage, commanding the driver to take them to town.

Jennifer did not say anything for a long time; she hoped her plan worked. Staring out the window as the carriage hobbled on the road, her mind traveled back to the day she came home. She wondered if that boat was still docked at the wharf. What was the name of that ship? The *Moon*? No, that wasn't it. *Moonstar*? No, that wasn't it either. Moon, Moon, Moon what?

"At least it will be dark when you get to the party in such an outrageous costume," said Stefan.

Jennifer was pulled out of her thoughts, "I'm sorry Stefan, what did you say? I wasn't paying attention."

"I said at least it won't be broad daylight when you leave the house with such an outrageous costume," said Stefan.

"The *Moonlight!*" she blurted out remembering the name of the ship.

"The *Moonlight*? Jennifer, what are you talking about?" questioned Stefan.

"A ship that I saw when I came home. I was trying to remember the name," replied Jennifer.

"What for?" questioned Stefan.

"No reason, if it is still in port, maybe we can ask there for my costume," she replied.

Stefan shook his head, "Whatever you want."

Jennifer's mind floated back to the *Moonlight*, perhaps she could get to meet the Captain. She remembered the tall, tanned man, and she wanted to see him again. Counting the days on her hand, she realized that he had probably set sail again, and she would never see a dream Captain for the rest of her life. Staring out the window, her thoughts came back to the present, as she watched the busy streets. The carriage came to a stop in front of the wharf. Stefan was the first one out of the carriage; he helped Jennifer down and told Jothan, the driver, to wait. Jennifer's eyes scanned the docks, spotting the *Moonlight*, she turned to Stefan, "There," she pointed, "that is the ship I was telling you about. Let's check with the Captain of that ship first."

"Whatever you wish," Stefan took Jennifer by the arm and led her to the ship.

Timothy Lockwood stood on deck talking to his first mate when he saw Jennifer and Stefan walking toward his ship. George, the first mate, followed his Captain's gaze, "Pretty little woman, ain't she Captain?"

Timothy's eyes were focused on her, "Yes, most beautiful."

"Looks like she's coming toward the *Moonlight*," said George.

"So, she does. Hello there," Timothy flashed a brilliant smile, his teeth gleaming against the dark tan. Jennifer felt as though she wanted to collapse at the sight of him.

"Hello," Stefan answered, as he led Jennifer up the gangplank, "My name is Stefan Weatherly and this is my cousin Jennifer."

Timothy remembered seeing the two of them a week before, and he also remembered the name in that they were invited to the party at the Harrington's, "How do you do Miss Weatherly? Mr. Weatherly, what can I do for you?" Now he looked at Stefan figuring that the young man must want something and just dragged his very pretty cousin along.

"It is not for me, Captain, but for Jennifer. Perhaps it would be best if she explained," responded Stefan.

"Very well, Miss Weatherly, what is it you wish from me and my crew?" Timothy asked.

"Captain," she hesitated, "I don't even know your name."

"So sorry, Captain Timothy Lockwood, of Newport, Rhode Island at your service, Miss."

"Captain Lockwood, I was invited to a costume party and I want to go as a lady pirate. I was hoping that you might be able to provide me with a costume."

"Miss Weatherly, how old are you?" questioned Timothy.

Taken aback, Jennifer retorted, "What does that matter?"

"I was just thinking, that you must be sixteen or so and that you should be looking for a husband. You certainly won't get one dressed as a lady pirate; the only thing you will succeed in doing is to ruin your reputation," replied Timothy.

"I'm seventeen, and the man whom I am supposed to marry, I hate. And at this point, I really don't give a damn about my reputation," exclaimed Jennifer.

Timothy's eyes twinkled, she was even more beautiful when she was angry. "Why did you agree to marry him?"

"I didn't agree; my father arranged it. Please, Captain Lockwood, I'm willing to pay for my costume," Jennifer said placing her hands at her waist.

"No need to pay, my first mate will go get a pair of trousers and a shirt from my cabin boy," Timothy turned to George, "Would you do that for me?"

"Aye, Captain," replied George. Jennifer watched the man hobble away.

"What happened to his leg?" questioned Jennifer.

"He was injured in a fight with pirates," Timothy answered coolly.

"Pirates? Real pirates?" Jennifer said excitedly.

Timothy laughed; Stefan was angered by the man, "Mr. Lockwood, what is so funny?"

"It appears that your cousin thought pirates existed in literature only," replied Timothy, watching Jennifer blush, casting her eyes to the deck, "Miss Weatherly, I'm sorry I laughed."

Jennifer looked up from the deck, "It is alright, Captain."

"No, it isn't, I was rude; please the two of you must be my luncheon guests. I have the best cook in creation, and I'll even fill you in on pirates, especially a lady pirate that I once met," replied Timothy.

Jennifer looked at Stefan, "Can we, Stefan?"

"Why not! You are hell bent on being a lady pirate, so you might as well learn what pirates are like," replied Stefan.

"Go tell Jothan that we will take a hansom carriage back when we are through," Jennifer said, and Stefan left the ship to tell Jothan he could go home.

George, the first mate, returned with some of the cabin boy's clothes, "Here ye are Cap'n."

Timothy took the clothes from George. "Tell the cook that we have two guests for lunch." George nodded and left to do his chore. Timothy turned to Jennifer, "Miss Weatherly, here are the clothes you wished. I hope that you succeed in what you are planning to do."

"I'm sure I will. Captain, tell me, do you ever take passengers on your ship?" questioned Jennifer.

Timothy replied, "Occasionally, why?"

"I was wondering if you were interested in taking a young woman, a lady's maid, and a young man to Spain. They are willing to pay a very high price for the voyage," replied Jennifer.

"When will I be required to take these people to Spain?" questioned Timothy.

Jennifer eyed Stefan coming up the gangplank, "As soon as it can be arranged."

Stefan reached the two of them in time to hear the Captain ask, "Are these people running from something?"

"Yes, Captain, we are." replied Jennifer.

Stefan stared at his cousin and then at the Captain, "What are you talking about?"

"Arranging passage to Spain aboard my ship, Mr. Weatherly," said Timothy.

"Jennifer," Stefan said harshly, "I thought we were not going to discuss this until everything was set?"

"I'm sorry, Stefan, I just thought it wouldn't hurt to ask," replied Jennifer.

Now Timothy began to wonder about the two people that stood before him, what were they running from? What were they running to? "I think the two of you had better tell me what is going on before I agree to take you anywhere."

Jennifer stared at him. She did not intend to tell the Captain of the ship why she was going to Spain, but she had slipped, so now she must tell him, provided he promised not to breathe a word of what she or Stefan would tell him. "Is there some place where the three of us can talk without being overheard?"

"Yes, my cabin, follow me." Timothy led the way to his cabin below deck. Opening the door of the cabin, he motioned to Jennifer and Stefan to sit at the table. Jennifer and Stefan walked to the table and sat down, while Timothy shut the door. "Would either of you like something to drink?"

Stefan replied, "No."

"No thank you," answered Jennifer.

Timothy sat down, "I think the two of you had better tell me why you have to go to Spain, who are you running from, what you're running towards, and how long do you have to get away from England?"

Stefan turned to Jenny, "I think that you had better tell him what you know, and then I will tell what I know."

"Very well, I'll start from the beginning. I have just come home after being at school for four years. When I arrived home, my father told me that he arranged for me to marry a man named Geoffrey Lyndon." Jennifer bit her lip.

Stefan interrupted her, "Mr. Lyndon has a questionable reputation that my uncle refused to believe."

"What type of reputation?" asked Timothy.

"Before Jennifer came home, I had the man investigated and found out that he is on the verge of bankruptcy; he gambles quite extensively and has been known to pay homage to Madam Celeste's." Stefan assumed that a Captain of such a large ship would know about places such as Madam Celeste's.

Timothy questioned, "Did you bring this information to your uncle?"

"Yes, but he refuses to believe it," replied Stefan.

Jennifer interrupted Stefan now. "My father has set the wedding date for late September; that is why I have to go to Spain."

"What is in Spain?" questioned Timothy.

"My family has a large villa in Madrid that we can stay at while we attempt to postpone the wedding," replied Jennifer.

Timothy's eyes bore into Jennifer's. "Aren't you going to tell someone that you are going to Spain?"

Her bluish-green eyes widened, "Oh yes, I am going to tell my father that I promised a friend from school that I would visit them in Spain; plus, I am going to tell him that I need to take this trip before I settle down. You see, I plan to tell him that I am going to give him lots of grandchildren; therefore, I cannot wait for this trip until after I am married, I must go now."

"What will you do if your father refuses you?" questioned Timothy.

Stefan looked at Timothy, "Her father has never refused Jennifer of anything in her entire life."

Jennifer reached across the table, placing her hand lightly on Timothy's arm, "Please say you'll help us."

Timothy looked from Jennifer to Stefan; Jennifer's hand was still resting on his arm. Her eyes had the look of desperation in them. How could he help them? He himself was to be married within a month. But Jennifer touched him more than he could ever imagine any woman could affect him, even Laura. This woman-child who sat across the table from him, stirred his desire, and her plea was deafening to his ears, "My first response to you would have been no, in that I would feel like I was aiding in some sort of scheme, yet I see the fear and desperation in your eyes and I must say yes." Jennifer smiled, removing her hand from his arm. "I just hope I can postpone my own marriage until I return from Spain on this voyage of mercy. When do we sail?"

"We will sail as soon as I ask my father for permission. I would say, if all goes well, we will sail by the end of June," replied Jennifer.

"If the tide is right, we will sail. If the two of you would excuse me, I must see to it that lunch is served." Timothy got up from his seat and walked to the door.

"Excuse me, Captain," Timothy turned to face Jennifer and Stefan as Stefan continued, "You must promise that you will not say anything to anyone concerning this voyage until the wheels are set in motion."

"Don't worry. You have my word." Timothy left the room to check on the lunch.

"Stefan I'm glad we picked this ship. Now we only have to get father agree to the trip."

"Don't worry about the trip Jennifer, your father will agree," replied Stefan.

"I'm not worried." Jennifer gazed around the Captain's cabin. To the far left sat a large oak desk covered with papers, maps and charts. Opposite the desk was a large bunk with a trunk at the base of the bed. The room was relatively neat except for the desk. To the side of the desk was a bookcase filled with books. From where Jennifer sat, she could not make out the titles but presumed they had to do with the shipping or perhaps his business.

Stefan was also taking note of the Captain's quarters. A large sword hung over the desk, and a small gun was sitting on the third shelf of the bookcase. He wondered if they had been too fast to let this stranger in on their secret, but it was too late now, and they had to take their chances. Glancing around the room, he spied another rapier; its handle was most unusual. It was carved in ivory. Stefan had heard a story recently about a man who had a sword with an ivory carved handle, if he could just remember what it was that he had heard. His thoughts were interrupted by Timothy's entrance to the cabin. "Lunch will be served in a few moments. Perhaps you wish to wash before you eat?" His gold flecked eyes were piercing Jennifer as he spoke.

"Yes, Captain, I would like to wash my hands if it is not too much trouble," answered Jennifer.

Timothy walked over to the door. When he opened the door, a young boy, not even fourteen, appeared, "Gideon, get fresh towels and some hot water for Miss Weatherly." The boy did not say a word as he turned and went on his errand.

Jennifer stared after the boy. Stefan turned to Timothy, "Captain, I noticed the rapier with the carved ivory handle. I was wondering where you got it?"

Jennifer's attention was drawn to the rapier and then to Timothy, "It is most unusual. It was given to me as a token of peace from a Berber King."

"A Berber King? Really, Mr. Lockwood, do you expect myself and Stefan to believe a story like that? Why, everyone knows that Berbers are just a myth," said Jennifer.

"My dear lady, I did receive the sword as a gift from a Berber King. He is a good friend, and he saved my life many years ago. Berbers live in the Barbary Coast area, and I understand that there are some living in both Europe and the Americas." There was a knock on the cabin door, "Come in."

Gideon walked into the room carrying a large wash bowl of hot water and some fresh towels. He placed the bowl on a small table near the bed. He turned to face Timothy, "Will that be all, Captain?"

"Yes," replied Timothy.

"Then I will bring lunch for you and your guests." Timothy nodded yes to the boy, Gideon, who quickly and quietly disappeared.

Jennifer walked to the bowl and called over her shoulder, "Do you have any soap?"

Timothy walked across the room to a small cabinet at the base of the bed. Opening the cabinet, he retrieved a bar of soap and handed it to Jennifer. His hand touched hers for a moment as she took the soap from him. She proceeded to wash her hands and then dry them. Stefan was next and was closely followed by Timothy. Gideon reappeared with a large tray and began to set the table, placing the dishes neatly on the table. He then returned with the food. Timothy helped Jennifer to her seat and then he and Stefan sat. The first course was a tasty French onion soup with fresh bread. During the soup, Timothy chatted about pirates to give Jennifer an idea of what they were like. Both Jennifer and Stefan were captivated by the young Captain.

Jennifer tasted the meat. It was something she never tasted before, "Captain, what kind of meat is this? It is very good."

Timothy replied, "I believe that is lamb, although I am not sure. You see, I never question my cook. The only thing I am concerned with is that it tastes good. Hervel, my cook can make an old shoe taste good if you let him."

"With the way this tastes, Captain, I'm sure he could. In fact, you should let him give lessons. I'm sure our cook could learn a few things, don't you agree, Jennifer?" asked Stefan.

"Yes, but she could probably teach Hervel some things, too!" Jennifer's remark, although innocent, caused the men to laugh, "What's so funny?"

"Nothing, just eat," Timothy answered, trying to control his laughter. The young woman did not catch the same meaning that the men caught. Jennifer Weatherly was a refreshing young woman.

Jennifer watched Timothy and Stefan closely during the rest of the meal; every once in a while, they would laugh. Timothy Lockwood excited her. Why couldn't her father have engaged her to someone strong like him rather than that fop Geoffrey Lyndon? Perhaps Mr.

Lockwood would decide not to marry after all. Maybe he could find her attractive. She wondered if she knew the person Mr. Lockwood was marrying.

"Jenny, what are you thinking about? You have a faraway look in your eyes?" questioned Stefan.

"Oh," she blushed, "I was just thinking about the pirates the Captain told us about."

"Pirates fascinate you, Miss Weatherly?" questioned Timothy. She was like a young child in her curiosity, and Timothy reminded himself that she was a mere seventeen.

"Yes, would you tell us about the lady pirate that you met?" said Jennifer.

Timothy began his story, "Her name was Season. She owned her own ship called the *Sea Witch*. She had fiery red hair with black eyes. She was most popular by the outfits that she would wear, tight fitting breeches and a loose-fitting shirt tied at the waist. I met her in Java on my last voyage there several years ago. She was seeking revenge against the man who raped her, vowing to take down every one of his ships. Along the way, she has destroyed not only his ships but also those of another man, Justin Rafael, the owner of the Dutch Shipping and Trading lines."

"How did you meet her?" questioned Stefan.

Timothy sighed, "She attacked one of my ships. She almost destroyed us until we surrendered to her, and she told me her story and how she got into piracy." Timothy changed the truth slightly, after all, he couldn't tell them what really happened.

Jennifer stared across the table at Timothy, "How did she get into piracy?"

Timothy's eyes sparkled with merriment, "The man who raped her, held her captive for one year on one of his ships. He had other women captives who had been on the ship for more than a year. One of them, Yvonne, was determined that she would learn about running a ship, so she followed the men around all day asking questions and learning. When Season was brought to the ship, Yvonne was impressed with her harsh tongue and her ability to survive. Yvonne knew that she couldn't take over the ship alone, so she asked the other women if they would be willing to learn to run a ship. Season jumped at the chance and helped Yvonne convince the other women that they could learn and finally be free. It took them one year to gain enough confidence to overthrow the ship. Once they disposed of the men, they sailed into Java and made that their home base. Season and Yvonne share Captain's duties, and the other women take care of everything else; there are no men aboard."

Stefan was amazed that a group of women could command a ship and almost destroy a ship run by men, "Captain, are you telling us that a group of women almost destroyed your ship?"

Timothy looked Stefan in the eye, "Yes I am, Mr. Weatherly. You are too young to realize this, but what I am going to tell you, you had best remember. Never, never underestimate a woman, especially a woman who has been broken by men, a woman who has to scratch, claw, and exist on very little to survive. That, Mr. Weatherly, is a woman who can taste sweet revenge before she even has it, and that woman's revenge will be brutal, more brutal than you can ever imagine. Remember, a woman can take much more pain than a man, and she will continue to if it means staying alive."

Stefan realized that he could not reply to Timothy Lockwood's statement. He also realized that if he tried and failed, he would look like a fool. Jennifer was shocked by what the Captain said; perhaps it would be wise if she remembered his advice as well. "Stefan, I really think we should be going; if you would get my shawl, please," she turned to the captain, "Captain Lockwood, thank you for the most enjoyable afternoon. It was very educational where pirates are concerned. You seem to know a great deal about the subject. Thank you for lunch and the clothes." Stefan handed Jennifer her shawl as she continued, "I will return your cabin boy's clothes."

"There is no need, Miss Weatherly, Gideon is well provided for on this ship; he can do without one shirt and a pair of pants," responded Timothy.

Jennifer smiled, "Thank you again, Captain Lockwood, you have been most helpful."

"It is a pleasure to aid a woman as beautiful as you, Miss Weatherly," said Timothy.

Stefan smiled. He wondered if Captain Lockwood was attracted to Jennifer, as much as she was obviously attracted to him. "Captain, you will be hearing from either Jennifer or I concerning the voyage to Spain. Once the plans are set, we will notify you."

"I will wait for your word on the matter." Timothy escorted Jennifer and Stefan to the main deck and watched them leave the ship. He wondered what Jennifer Weatherly would look like in a lady pirates' outfit. He liked her; she had a vitality, a spirit about her, something which his dear fiancé lacked. Perhaps with the voyage to Spain, he might convince Jennifer Weatherly that he was the right man for her. He could call off his marriage to Laura Harrington. Jennifer Weatherly was the type of woman who he could respect, admire, and love, yet she was also the type of woman who once possessed by a deep ambition, would not give up until she acquired that ambition. He turned and went back downstairs to his cabin. He had some paperwork to finish before the party at the Harrington's tomorrow.

CHAPTER FIVE

The afternoon of the costume party Jennifer had decided that she would go out for a ride on Oliva, her horse. She timed it so she would arrive at the front door of her home at the same time as Geoffrey. He was as usual disgusted by the fact that she reeked of sweat, horse odor and was just returning from a ride. He glared at her as she said, "Oh my, I must have lost track of the time. Tell my father and Stefan to go on without us." Jennifer breezed past Geoffrey leaving him standing in the foyer. She grinned as she climbed the stairs. Her plan was working perfectly. Once in her bedroom, she sank into the hot tub that Lizabeth had prepared for her. Her mind wandered as she took her time. She really didn't want to get out of the tub but knew that Geoffrey must be getting angry having to wait for her.

Geoffrey poured himself another drink, his third. Jennifer Weatherly was a spoiled brat, and he was glad that he had made a deal earlier that day. Soon he would be a fairly rich man and with little trouble, he would be getting the money he desperately needed. Jennifer came into the sitting room with her cloak already on, "Are you ready Geoffrey?" she asked smiling.

"I've been ready," he snapped. "It's about time you are ready. Let's go." He grabbed her roughly by the arm and pulled her out the door.

Sir Robert Harrington had to sell some of his last parcels of land in order to have this party for his daughter and to impress his daughter's fiancé, Timothy Lockwood. Deep down, he knew that his selfish daughter did not deserve this party, but she had asked him, and he could not refuse.

Laura Harrington was in her room putting the final touches on her costume. Being the hostess of the party, she wanted to look her best; she wanted to be the most looked at woman at the party; she would make every man desire her, and she would desire every man. The princess of the party!

Robert Harrington grew impatient with his daughter, "Laura, hurry down; the first guests are beginning to arrive now."

Laura took one last look in the mirror; satisfied with how she looked, she ran downstairs to the foyer to greet the first of her guests, Mr. and Mrs. Richard Swenson, their son and his wife. Laura was pleased that none of their costumes could compare to hers; she showed them into the main sitting room which was highly decorated for the occasion.

The Weatherly carriage pulled up to the front of the house. James Weatherly was still grumbling about his daughter's timing of deciding to go horseback riding. Stefan and his date, Devon Forster, were dressed as a lord and lady. They were shown into the sitting room and given wine. Stefan wondered when Jennifer would make her grand appearance. He was sure all of the stuffy people at the party would be shocked and appalled. What would Uncle James say?

Laura looked around. Most of the guests had arrived except for her fiancé, and Jennifer Weatherly and her fiancé, Geoff Lyndon. She was pleased to see that no one outshined her costume; and she was sure that Jennifer Weatherly would not either.

Maggie, the young maid, answered the door to find a tall dark man standing in pirate garb. She instantly recognized him as Timothy Lockwood, Miss Laura's fiancé. She announced him, and the people gasped. Standing before them was a tall, deeply tanned man dressed in the most outrageous costume of the evening; bright red balloon pants tucked into black leather boots, a deep purple sash hung at his side, accompanied by a rapier with a carved handle of ivory; the white shirt made his tan seem even darker.

Stefan put his wine glass down on the table. Seeing Timothy Lockwood standing before him dressed as a pirate was a shock; seeing the rapier at his side jarred Stefan's memory. There was rumor of a pirate, a man feared by many, who had an ivory carved handle on his sword, but Timothy Lockwood certainly was no pirate, although at this moment, he certainly fit the bill. If he was that pirate, it could explain how he knew and understood pirates so well. Where was Jennifer? An hour and half had passed since Stefan arrived at the party; she should have been here by now.

Timothy Lockwood was hustled around from guest to guest by Laura. The men all commented on his choice of costume, and the women were all captivated by his charm. Many of the men made reference to the rapier, how unusual it was, how there was a rumor of a pirate with one similar to his. Timothy was neither frightened or alarmed by the men. With none of them involved in shipping, they could never guess that he was Tim the Bloodthirsty. Timothy smiled at the questions and then responded, "I assure you that I am not that infamous pirate. The rapier was given to me as a token of peace from a Berber King."

Sir Harrington said, "I didn't know that Berbers existed."

Timothy looked at his host and knew that he had to keep his composure, "I did receive the sword as a gift from a Berber King. He is a good friend, and I saved his life many years ago. Berbers do exist, and they live predominately on the Barbary Coast, and I also understand that some live-in other sections of the world such as Europe and the Americas."

Jennifer and Geoff Lyndon arrived at the Harrington party one hour and forty-five minutes late. As soon as they got into the house, Jennifer asked the maid if she could freshen up before she went into the sitting room. Maggie showed Jennifer the way, and Geoff went into the sitting room. Laura was impressed with his costume; it was very original. He was dressed as a vagabond.

James Weatherly called from the other side of the room, "Mr. Lyndon, where is my daughter?"

Geoff Lyndon replied, "She'll be along in a moment, Mr. Weatherly."

Jennifer walked into the sitting room wither her cloak still on. The butler asked, "Would you like me to take your wrap, Miss Weatherly?"

"Yes, please," replied Jennifer. Timothy Lockwood could not wait to see the expressions on the faces of the guests. Stefan wondered if Jennifer had really gone through with what she had planned. The butler waited until Jennifer had undone the fasteners of the cloak before he removed it from her shoulders. Gasps filled the room while James Weatherly sat down in the nearest chair. How could Jennifer do something like this? How could she appear in public dressed that way? She had put the family to shame. Stefan was shocked but not as shocked nor surprised as his uncle. He quickly refilled his wine glass and downed the liquid.

Laura Harrington was appalled; Jennifer Weatherly had captured everyone's attention with her revealing costume. She moved toward Timothy, "This is terrible," she whispered, "she looks like a common wanton, a street urchin, a disgrace to her family. Don't you agree?"

Timothy had been staring at Jennifer since she appeared in the room. Her costume was shocking to people who had never seen a lady pirate, and no, she didn't shock him, "Quite contrary, Laura, I find this most amusing."

"Amusing! Look at her father, her cousin, and her fiancé; the color has drained from their faces." She looked up at Timothy who was smiling, "You find this funny?"

Timothy looked down at Laura, "No, I told you amusing."

Jennifer began to look around the room. Her father was white as a ghost, "Jennifer Weatherly has ruined my party," said Laura tapping her foot in pure outrage.

Never taking his eyes from the beautiful and seductive young woman across the room, Timothy said, "Don't be foolish, this will blow over."

Geoffrey wasted no time in approaching Jennifer, "You have ruined me, Miss Weatherly."

Jennifer's green eyes became cold and icy, "What I wear is no reflection on you. If you don't like it you don't have to marry me."

Geoffrey was angry, "People are staring at you."

"Let them stare; they will get over it." Jennifer looked for Stefan. She wondered what he thought. She had to admit that wearing a man's breeches and shirt tied tightly at the waist was a little daring. Jennifer made her way over to her father. "Father, do you like my costume?"

"I find it revolting! Now I understand why you were so secretive about your costume. If I had known, I would have never allowed you out of the house," James said, tersely.

"I'm sorry father. I wanted to be different." Jennifer had not wanted to hurt her father, but she had to do this to try to push Geoffrey away.

"Actually, my dear daughter, you are not that different," James said.

Jennifer's eyes widened, "What do you mean?"

"A gentleman is dressed in almost exactly the same garb; and he caused quite an uproar when he entered," replied James.

"Where?" questioned Jennifer. Her father pointed across the large room. Jennifer followed her father's finger. The man stood with his back to Jennifer. He was dressed in red balloon pants and white shirt, a deep purple sash hung at his side accompanied by a rapier. Suddenly, the man turned, and Jennifer gasped.

"What's wrong, my daughter?" questioned James.

"Nothing. I thought I knew the gentleman. Excuse me, I must speak to Stefan for a moment." Timothy Lockwood's gaze met hers, his golden eyes burned through her. Jennifer walked toward Stefan and Timothy as if in a trance. The man was the one she had seen on the docks the day she had returned and then when she and Stefan had gone to look for the costume at the wharf. Her body seemed to tingle from the excitement of seeing him at the party. Why couldn't her father have engaged her to a man like him? "Captain Lockwood, don't say anything my father is watching. Stefan make introductions as if we are just meeting."

James Weatherly watched his daughter from where he was sitting. He saw Stefan make introductions, and the Captain kissed his daughter's hand. His lips felt like fire on her hand, forever leaving their mark thought Jennifer, "Stefan where is your date?"

Stefan retorted, "She had too much wine and decided to lie down for a little while."

"Good, I want you to accompany me onto the terrace so we can talk." She looked at Timothy, "Captain, I want you to follow us out in five minutes, can you do that?" questioned Jennifer.

"Most certainly," replied Timothy, as he pulled himself up to his full height. His gold flecked eyes were perusing Jennifer as he noticed Laura making her way over to them. Jennifer had noticed as well. "I once knew a lady pirate."

Jennifer smiled, "Really, you must tell me about her, Captain."

Laura had reached them just as Jennifer had finished her sentence, and she moved quickly towards Timothy. "Yes, you must tell me about her, dear." She hadn't been oblivious to the fact that the attraction between Timothy and Jennifer was electrifying.

Laura purposefully placed her hand intimately on Timothy's arm. Jennifer's green eyes glazed over with annoyance. Timothy's eyes moved between the two women as he began to speak. Laura quickly grew bored with the story and was quite sure that Timothy had made up every word as a crowd had gathered around to listen to him. Jennifer, however, hung on every word of the tall Captain until Geoffrey made his way through the crowd and pulled her away for a dance. A young gentleman interrupted the dancing and asked Jennifer to dance with him. She took his hand as he whirled her around the dance floor. Timothy watched her; he liked her; she had a vitality, a spirit about her, something which his dear fiancé lacked. Jennifer Weatherly could be the type of woman who could never be tamed. That he could sense because of the recklessness of her nature as he had personally witnessed here this evening. He took Laura by the hand, and they joined the dance floor. He noticed that both Jennifer and Stefan were at the refreshment table as Geoffrey approached to dance with Laura. Timothy made his way to the refreshments, smiling at Jennifer and Stefan.

Jennifer said quietly, "Make sure no one sees you leave the room, especially my father."

Timothy said, "Not a problem."

Stefan took Jennifer by the arm and led her out to the terrace. Timothy continued to mingle with the guests. Excusing himself, he slipped into the foyer and out the front door. Making his way around the large house, he reached the terrace, scaring both Jennifer and Stefan as he crawled out of the bushes. "Captain Lockwood, you scared me to death!"

Timothy replied, "I did not mean to; I hope the lady forgives me."

"Of course," Jennifer blushed, "I wanted to tell the both of you that I plan to ask my father about the trip in the morning."

Geoff Lyndon had noticed the disappearance of his fiancé, her cousin, and the Captain. Laura excused herself. As the hostess, she wanted to move around the room. Geoffrey made his way towards the doors to the terrace, which were slightly open. Hearing voices on the terrace, he moved closer to the doors and looked out. Jennifer, Stefan, and the Captain were discussing some matter, but their voices were muffled, and he could not make out what they were saying. The three of them moved toward the path leading to the gazebo. Geoffrey went outside as soon as they disappeared behind the trees. He circled around and hid in the bushes, so he could hear what they were saying.

Timothy said, "Miss Weatherly, this was a good idea. If we had stayed on the terrace someone might have disturbed us."

"I realized that Captain; it is very important that no one hear what we discuss. It is also very important that you realize that you cannot tell anyone that Stefan and I have hired you to take me to Spain," said Jennifer.

Timothy looked at her, "I understand completely."

"The reason I asked the two of you to meet me out here is that I have come to a decision. If my father refuses me this trip, I will come to your ship and we must sail quickly before anyone discovers that I am gone." She looked at Stefan, "I'm sorry Stefan, you will not be able to come with me if it comes to pass."

"But your father will ask where you went," replied Stefan.

"I've thought of that also; you will tell my father where I went as soon as you get word that the *Moonlight* has sailed. I must get away from that vile Geoffrey Lyndon; I despise him." Geoffrey had heard enough. Jennifer Weatherly would pay for this. If he couldn't marry her, he would kidnap her and hold her for ransom. She would be sorry that she ever met him.

Timothy could not help being in awe of this woman-child; she had guts, "I think we should return to the party before we are missed."

"Jennifer and I will return and then you had better return the same way you left. Come Jennifer," Stefan took her by the arm, and they returned to the party.

Timothy Lockwood made his way back to the front door with his thoughts on Jennifer Weatherly, who began to look more and more appealing to him every time he met her. She was more beautiful than Laura, in that, hers was a natural beauty; Laura's was painted on. Slipping in the front door, he was caught by Laura, "Hello," he smiled.

"Where have you been?" she demanded.

"I felt like some fresh air. It is a little stuffy in the sitting room; perhaps you should have the maid open some of the windows," replied Timothy.

"My father wishes to see you in the library, right now," said Laura sternly.

Timothy nodded to Laura and walked across the hall to the library; he knocked, "Come in." Opening the door, he strode in the room and stood before the desk Robert Harrington sat behind, "Please, Captain, sit down."

Timothy sat, "What did you wish to see me about?"

Harrington looked the captain in the eye, "Captain, the wedding to my daughter."

Timothy said flatly, "The wedding may have to be postponed."

"Why?" questioned Sir Harrington.

"I may have to make an important voyage within the next few days. I'm not sure exactly when I will be leaving," replied Timothy. He wasn't about to tell Harrington that he met someone far more interesting than Laura.

Harrington needed this wedding to take place, "Then we will have the wedding before you leave so you can bring Laura with you."

Timothy stood up, "No, this voyage could be a dangerous one in that I will be travelling for someone of great wealth. I have been vowed to secrecy, and I will not break that confidence. Laura could be hurt if she travelled with me." Hurt yes, but not physically, she would be hurt emotionally.

"Very well," said Sir Harrington, "I will trust your honor in this matter. Have you told Laura?"

"I plan to tell her this evening," replied Timothy.

Sir Harrington rose, "Perhaps you better go find her."

"Yes, if you would excuse me," Timothy rose, and Robert Harrington nodded to him as if he was dismissing a servant, which infuriated him.

Laura Harrington had gone to her room and was followed by Geoffrey; he told her everything he had overheard. "How could she say those things about you?" she purred.

"Simply, she doesn't love me the way you do. You must help me," replied Geoffrey.

Laura sighed, "I will do anything you want."

She looked very appealing to him sitting on the bed, but he had more important things on his mind, "I plan to kidnap Jennifer Weatherly and keep her at the servants house for a couple of days until I can get her away from London."

Laura's eyes widened, "When will you do this?"

"Tonight," replied Geoffrey,

His answer stunned Laura. "Tonight? But someone will see you, unless you get her into the foyer and out the rear door."

"That, my dear, is exactly what I plan to do." Geoffrey walked toward her and touched the curl at the base of her neck, "Perhaps we can see each other tomorrow."

"Yes, tomorrow, after you get rid of Jennifer Weatherly," replied Laura.

"I'll leave here first and then you come down. If anyone asks where you've been, tell them you were resting, the excitement of the party exhausted you." Geoffrey quietly left her room and made his way downstairs to find Jennifer.

Stefan, his date Devon, and her father were all leaving soon. She needed to find Geoffrey to tell him that she was going home with them. Geoffrey had just reached the bottom of the stairs when he saw Jennifer approaching him with her cloak in her hand, "I've been looking all over for you."

"I was looking around this house, I thought I would get some ideas for when we build our home, or buy a house. Come with me I want to show you this kitchen, which I think would be ideal for us." Taking Jennifer by the hand, Geoffrey led her to the kitchen. Jennifer sighed, once inside the kitchen. He let her wrist go, "Do you like this arrangement or would you prefer something different?" He paused, "Look at this table, would you like something similar?"

"I really do not think that this is very important, really we can do this another time," responded Jennifer as she turned her back to him, gazing out the window, she felt his presence close to her but said nothing.

Within a split-second, Geoffrey covered Jennifer's mouth with his hand and dragged her toward the old servant's house. Jennifer fought him, kicking, and clawing at him. She tried to open her mouth so she could bite his hand, but the pressure of his hand was too much against her mouth. When they reached the old servant's quarters, he loosened his grip on her so he could open the door. In that few moments she sunk her teeth into his hand as hard as she could, until she tasted his blood. He pulled her up the stairs and flung her to the floor, "You little vixen; you will pay for this!"

Jennifer sat on the floor dazed from hitting her head when he threw her. It was dark, and she could not see him, she could only hear his breathing. It seemed like he was far away from her; she began to crawl, trying to reach the door. Geoffrey turned in time to see her passing by a window where the moonlight was streaming into the room. He pounced on her. "You thought you were going to get away, well I am going to tie you and keep you here for a few days." He gagged her, and then tied her hands and feet. Geoffrey picked her up and carried her to the bed, "You should be comfortable now. I have to return to the party before they discover we are both missing." He turned and left her in the dark. Jennifer's head was spinning. What was wrong with her? She had to get away. Suddenly, she passed out from the pain.

Geoffrey made his way to the back of the house. Once inside, he looked at his hand; Jennifer's teeth had found their mark in the palm of his hand. The blood was drying into a crusty surface. If he kept his hand in his pocket, no one would notice. Making his way into the sitting room, he was stopped by Stefan Weatherly, "Where is Jennifer?"

"I was about to ask you that. I've been looking for her," Geoffrey replied.

Stefan looked him in the eyes, "She went looking for you an hour ago."

Geoffrey frowned, "I haven't seen her. Maybe she left."

Stefan was nervous because Geoffrey didn't really seem to care that Jennifer was missing, "She wouldn't do that without telling someone."

"We must search for her then. Tell your uncle to have Mr. Harrington group the men together and we will search the grounds," said Geoffrey trying to sound concerned.

Stefan and Geoffrey approached James Weatherly, who was talking with Laura and Timothy, "Uncle, excuse me."

"Yes Stefan," turning to face his nephew, he saw Geoffrey, "Where is Jennifer?"

"We don't know sir; she seems to be missing," replied Geoffrey. Timothy's heart began to beat faster. He felt the color drain from his face, but he could not explain his reaction. He searched Stefan's eyes for some clues, but found none.

Laura came to Geoffrey's aid, "Jennifer went home; she said she wasn't feeling well; she said to say her goodbyes for her, but it must have slipped my mind."

Timothy's stare was frightening, "You let her family and fiancé worry for nothing? Really, Laura, if you were less concerned about yourself, you might begin to think about other people's feelings."

Laura was angered by his remark. Of course, she was concerned about herself; after all she was more important than anyone in the world. "Apologize to me for your reprimand," demanded Laura.

Timothy glared at her. "I will not say I'm sorry; in fact, I'm leaving.

"But I thought we were going to discuss our wedding," whined Laura.

Stefan spoke before Timothy could answer Laura, "If you would excuse us, we are leaving. Good evening, Captain, and Miss Harrington.

"Yes, goodbye, I hope you enjoyed yourself this evening," replied Laura petulantly.

"We certainly did; please tell your father we said goodnight, and I am sorry about my daughter leaving so early," replied James Weatherly. The Weatherlys and their guests left the Harrington sitting room, leaving Laura and Timothy alone.

Laura was upset, "You have insulted me in front of my guests."

"I really don't care," replied Timothy, as he poured himself a glass of wine.

"You are rude, and I don't even know why I like you," said Laura, acting like a child.

Timothy stared at her, "I'm beginning to wonder what I see in you, my dear."

Laura began to tap her foot, "How dare you! A lot of people thought I was the belle of the ball tonight; they liked me."

"They were only being nice. You know as well as I do that Jennifer Weatherly was the person who became the center of attention the moment she walked through those doors," Timothy replied dryly.

Deep down, Laura knew he was right. She sat down on the sofa. Jennifer Weatherly stole her party! Timothy enjoyed seeing the color drain from Laura's already pale face. She looked up at him and pleaded, "Please say you're sorry."

"I'm sorry," he said it convincingly enough to keep her from crying. He sat down beside her, offered her some wine, and she drank it, "About the wedding," began Timothy.

"Yes," Laura said with anticipation.

"We have to postpone it," said Timothy.

Laura got to her feet, "Postpone? I will not postpone my wedding."

"You really have no choice." The cool tone of Timothy's voice alarmed her.

"Of course I have a choice; it is a wedding for the both of us," she said, very upset.

"Yes, that is exactly why it is being postponed until I come back from a very important voyage," Timothy replied.

"What voyage? Why can't I go with you?" questioned Laura.

"It could be dangerous, so I would not want you on that ship. As far as I'm concerned, we have nothing left to discuss, goodnight." Timothy kissed her lightly and left her standing in the middle of the room.

Laura smiled to herself. Won't he be surprised when he finds out that he won't be needed for Jennifer Weatherly's trip to Spain? She put out the lamp and made her way upstairs to her bedroom.

Jennifer drifted in and out of sleep, her head throbbed. She wondered how she could possibly escape from this madman. It must be nearing dawn she thought, as it seemed a little brighter in the room. Looking around the room, she saw a rat in the opposite corner, its beady eyes were fixed on her. She tried to loosen the gag around her mouth but couldn't. Suddenly, the door opened and Geoffrey Lyndon appeared, "Good morning, Jennifer. Did you have a nice sleep?" Perhaps he would untie her, she thought. "I know what you are thinking. You want me to untie you; well, my dear, I am not that stupid. You must be wondering what I'm doing here so early? I have to move you because when your family discovers that you never went home, they'll come looking for you, I'm sure. I'll bet you want to know what I told them," he laughed. "Well, it wasn't me. Laura told them you weren't feeling well and went home." He untied her feet, "That's so you can walk. Don't get any ideas." Pulling her to her feet, he led her out of the abandoned house and put her in a carriage. They seemed to drive for hours until they came to a stop. The carriage door opened, and he dragged her out into an open field. Geoffrey untied the gag around her mouth.

"Where are we?" she snapped.

Geoffrey answered, "We are on the outskirts of London."

"What are you planning to do with me?" questioned Jennifer.

"To tell you the truth, I was going to hold you for ransom; however, I met someone after the party last night," he paused, "He buys white women to sell to the people of the Barbary States."

"The Barbary States! Surely my father will give you more money than anyone who is willing to buy me as a slave," said Jennifer, trying to be strong.

"No, I have convinced the buyer that you are good lover and in good health. He's offered me several thousand for you." Geoffrey was quite pleased with himself.

"My father will double it." Jennifer knew her father would help her, if only she could scream. It would be a waste of voice; out here, no one would hear her.

Geoffrey shook his head. "I can't take that chance of arranging for ransom," responded Geoffrey as he continued, "If I did do that, I'll be apprehended within twenty-four hours. Selling you into slavery is a far safer course of action."

"No. You can't. Please let me," Jennifer pleaded with him.

Geoffrey grabbed her by the hair. "Shut up!" Taking the gag out of his pocket, he tied her again. Jennifer sat on the grass, bound like an animal. Stefan would help her; she knew he would. Her head still hurt; she felt herself dozing off again.

Stefan ate breakfast alone; his uncle had left for the office, and Jennifer was still asleep. Perhaps he should have Lizabeth check on her. Rising from the table, he went to find Lizabeth. He found her in the library dusting the tables.

"Good morning, Master Stefan," she said, as she wiped her forehead with her hand.

"Morning Lizabeth, did you see Jennifer when she came home last night?" Stefan asked.

"I was asleep when you came home, Master Stefan." She continued to move from table-to-table, dusting.

"She didn't come home with us. She came home about an hour before; she told Laura Harrington she was feeling ill," said Stefan.

"I'm sorry. I did not see her," replied Lizabeth.

"Would you go look in on her; she usually doesn't sleep this long," Stefan said.

"Very well." She left the dust cloth on the table, and the two of them left the library and headed upstairs. Lizabeth knocked on Jennifer's door, "Missy, are you in there?"

"Jenny, its Stefan, are you feeling well?" There was no answer; he turned to Lizabeth, "Try the door."

Lizabeth turned the knob, and the door opened; the room was empty, "She's not here."

"Check the bathroom; maybe she slipped and fell," said Stefan nervously.

Lizabeth opened the bathroom door; the room was empty, "She's not here either. Maybe she went riding?"

"Yes, that must be it. I'll go to the stables." Stefan left the room, ran downstairs, grabbed his jacket, and went to the stables with a feeling of foreboding deep in his heart. Upon reaching the stables, he ran directly to Oliva's stall. The horse was still there as were the other horses. She hadn't gone riding.

Lucas, the stable hand, was preparing to feed the horses. He looked up from filling the buckets with grain and saw Stefan, "You want me to get your horse for you, Master Stefan?"

"No, thank you. Do you know if Jennifer took Olivia out this morning?" asked Stefan.

"No, her horse is in the corral, been there since five this morning," replied Lucas.

"Are you sure?" questioned Stefan.

"Yes sir; you can take a look for yourself if you don't believe me."

"No, I believe you; I already saw Olivia in her stable. Thank you, Lucas." Stefan left the stables; he was beginning to think that Jennifer never reached home last evening. Reaching the rear door, he decided to call for a thorough search of the grounds and the house. He ran down the hall yelling, "Lizabeth, Lizabeth, where are you?"

Lizabeth appeared at the top of the stairs, "Master Stefan, will you calm down. What's the matter with you?"

"I can't find Jennifer. Check her room for the dark green cloak; I'll check the front closet." Lizabeth disappeared to check Jennifer's room. Stefan walked across the hall to the closet. Taking a deep breath, he opened the door. Nothing. Empty.

Lizabeth called from the top of the stairs, "Master Stefan, the cloak is not here."

"Lizabeth, come downstairs, I want this house and the grounds searched," said Stefan.

"Yes sir, I'll tell the rest of the servants." Lizabeth turned in a panic shouting for the house staff to assemble to search for Jennifer.

Stefan's mind whirled. Could her father have refused the trip to Spain? No, she would have told him. She wasn't planning to ask him last night. Where can she be? Laura Harrington said she went home early; could she have lied? Very likely. The last time he saw Jennifer, she was looking for Geoffrey Lyndon. Lyndon! Lyndon must have something to do with Jennifer's disappearance. The minutes ticked by, slowing turning into hours. Jennifer was nowhere to be found. It was time to contact James Weatherly and the police.

James Weatherly received a note telling him to return home as soon as possible. When he arrived, he noticed the police wagon in front of Weatherly. Stefan met him at the door, "What the devil is going on here?"

"Uncle, please come into the house." The two men walked into the sitting room. "This is Mr. Ownsby, he's with the police."

"What is going on here?" demanded James Weatherly.

Stefan said, "Jennifer never returned home last night."

"What are you talking about?" James Weatherly sat down in his favorite chair.

"Uncle, the grounds and the house have been searched, she is nowhere to be found," said Stefan nervously.

James Weatherly sat in silence as Mr. Ownsby said, "Mr. Weatherly, you are a very wealthy man, your daughter is an heiress, I've come to the conclusion that she's been kidnapped."

"Kidnapped," his voice was shaky, "I'll offer a reward."

"Mr. Weatherly, I think it is best that you wait until a ransom note is delivered," replied Mr. Ownsby, as James Weatherly's eyes filled with tears.

James Weatherly rose to get a glass of bourbon, returning to his favorite chair. Stefan approached his uncle, "Uncle," no reply, "Uncle James."

James Weatherly looked at Stefan, trying to find his voice," Yes?"

"I will be going to town soon; do you want me to post a reward with the newspaper?" questioned Stefan.

James looked at Mr. Ownsby, "Yes, just tell them that a reward is being offered to anyone who can shed some light on the disappearance of Jennifer." Turning to Mr. Ownsby he said, "Will that be agreeable to you?"

Mr. Ownsby said, "Yes, that should be fine. I must be going; I will show myself to the door." Ownsby rose and left the two men together.

Stefan looked at his uncle, "I will leave now and go to the newspaper."

"Stefan."

He turned to look at his uncle, "Yes?"

"Be careful; you are an heir also, I don't want the two of you missing. We don't know how some crazed individual's ideas can continue to affect us."

"Yes, sir, I will be careful." Stefan left his uncle sitting drinking his bourbon.

Stefan reached the city and went directly to the newspaper office to post the reward. Entering the building, he spied Timothy Lockwood talking to one of the clerks, "Mr. Lockwood, I didn't expect to run into you here."

Timothy turned smiling, "Well, Mr. Weatherly, it is a pleasure to see you again. Pray tell, is your lovely cousin with you?" The color drained from Stefan's face, which did not go unnoticed by Timothy. "Is something wrong, Mr. Weatherly?"

Stefan swallowed hard, "As a matter-of-fact, Captain, Jennifer never returned from the party last night and has disappeared. We believe that she has been kidnapped?"

Timothy frowned, trying to be as casual as he could in the newspaper office, "Kidnapped?"

"She is an heiress to a very large estate, Captain. I've come to post the reward."

"Post your reward sir, and then I would suggest that you and I talk." Stefan nodded and went to speak to the clerk. Timothy waited patiently for Stefan to conduct his business. Of all the damn luck! The girl disappeared under their very noses and to think that he wished to court the young woman made him angry, indeed. How dare anyone steal her when he hadn't even had the chance to do so himself!

"Excuse me, Captain," said Stefan, interrupting the tall man's thoughts, "I believe you wished to discuss something with me."

Timothy nodded, "Yes, let us walk along the street." The two gentlemen left the newspaper office together. Once outside, Timothy said, "Have you many enemies?"

"Enemies?" Stefan hesitated, "Well, not really unless somehow Geoffrey learned about the plan we made with you."

"Geoffrey?"

Stefan began to explain to Timothy about Geoffrey Lyndon's reasons for marrying Jennifer, most of which Timothy already knew. He concluded his explanation with, "I've had him investigated thoroughly," reaching into his pocket, he withdrew the papers and handed them to Captain Lockwood as he continued, "If you would read over quickly you will see that if anyone had the nerve to kidnap Jennifer, it was Lyndon. The man is desperate and devious."

Timothy briefly scanned the contents of the papers, but four words jumped out at him *'rendezvous with Laura Harrington.'* This angered him. He would be damned if he let that woman cuckhold him. He certainly had no intention to remain faithful to her, but to know that she already had a lover was disturbing to him, as her father painted a completely different picture of her. "Do you have the man's address?"

"Yes."

"Let me have it; I'll have some of my men follow him."

"But you need not be involved."

Timothy wanted to laugh; the Weatherly's had already involved him prior to the party at the Harrington's. "I want to help. My men can gain access to many of the places you told me about without causing a disturbance, and they also can scout around for someone who may have seen your cousin with Mr. Lyndon." Timothy paused, "I will come to Weatherly tomorrow."

"Thank you, Captain." The two men shook hands, separating on the docks near Timothy's ship.

CHAPTER SIX

Timothy Lockwood returned to his ship, going directly to his cabin where he poured himself a glass of bourbon. His anger at his so-called fiancé was mounting; he opened the door to his cabin; he bellowed, "George." The man appeared within seconds, "I want you to alert the men that they are to watch for a man named Geoffrey Lyndon." He handed George a list of Lyndon's favorite haunts and the man's home address, "I want to know where he is at all times."

"Aye-Aye, Captain." George left the cabin to inform the men of their respective jobs.

Timothy sighed as he poured himself another bourbon; it was best that he left his men to do the necessary work; after all, there was no need to draw any unwanted attention to himself. He laughed; if the British authorities realized that one of the most prized pirates was sitting in their harbor, they would be on him, and he would see the gallows or Newgate. And that was not in Timothy Lockwood's plans for the near future. Pouring himself another drink, he paced around the cabin, thinking and drinking. He kept going over the facts: Jennifer had gone to look for Lyndon and disappeared; Lydon claimed he was looking for Jennifer. Laura said Jennifer went home early because she was feeling ill. That is what didn't make sense. Jennifer was fine when they had come in from the terrace. Laura lied; his eyes narrowed dangerously when he thought of Miss Harrington; she lied and now he knew exactly why. She was Geoffrey Lyndon's paramour and for that she would pay also. He put his drink down on the table and walked to his bunk, removing his belt, boots and shirt in order to lie down. It had been a long day, considering the fact that he had been up all evening making arrangements to sell the stolen merchandise that was aboard his ship. His mind kept going over the facts; did someone overhear them on the terrace? The only possible person who could gain anything by kidnapping Jennifer would be Lyndon. Come to think of it, Lyndon did look a bit haggard after he suddenly appeared claiming he was looking for Jennifer. Timothy closed his eyes, the bourbon taking its toll as sleep came quickly. His dreams taunted him. The first part of the evening he slept peacefully; the second part of the evening, his dreams were filled with the beautiful auburn-haired Jennifer begging him to help her, make love to her and telling her everything was going to be alright. He tossed and turned in agony as he awoke to a pounding on his cabin door. He blinked open his eyes, "Yes, who's there?"

"Gideon, sir."

"Just a minute," he answered as he rose from his bed and stumbled over to the door, unlocking it.

Gideon brushed past his Captain, setting the breakfast tray on the table, "Would you like anything else Captain?" Gideon turned toward Timothy as he spoke.

"Yes Gideon, I want some hot water and a hansom cab."

"Yes sir." Gideon bowed as he walked out the door.

Timothy sat down to the large breakfast waiting for him. Thick slices of ham, eggs and hot coffee looked excellent. He really did not feel like eating, yet thought he had better, for he did not know what time he would be returning to the ship. Gideon returned after the Captain had finished eating and set up the wash bowl on the table aside of the bed. Timothy washed after Gideon left and went to his desk, picking up the paper Stefan Weatherly had left with him last evening. The small piece of paper contained the address of Geoffrey Lyndon. Putting the paper in his pocket, he turned to the bookcase. taking the gun. Holding the gun in his hands, he stared at it for a moment, his mind returned to a time before when he used the gun to save a woman's life....

Season and Java. A time he remembered well. Season, her flaming red hair and dark flashing eyes, had seduced him, making him curious. He wanted to know her, all of her and he did for the six months he lived on the *Sea Witch*. The *Sea Witch*, was one of the most beautiful clipper ships he had ever seen. He had been stretching the truth when he told Jennifer and Stefan that he was captured. It was true, he and his men were captured, but they were captured because he was Timothy the Bloodthirsty, and Season and her crew needed help. Yvonne, her partner, had left the ship to get married to someone she had known previous to her pirate days.

Season sat quietly in the cabin of her ship. She needed someone to teach her about navigation because that had been Yvonne's job. The *Sea Witch* had been moored for weeks with the hope that the *Moonlight* and her Captain, Timothy the Bloodthirsty, would come into port. Season had heard the tales spun about Timothy, calling him the most feared pirate of all time. It was said that he could get his ship through any storm. He was known to navigate and get through inlets that other ships had met with their death trying to get through the coral. This man, she hoped, would pull into port any day, and when he did, she would capture him.

Days had passed when a young boy who worked for Season appeared at the door. "The *Moonlight* is here."

"The *Moonlight*," she repeated in a whisper, "Go to the ship, find out if the Captain is aboard and get me a description of him. A complete description, do you understand?"

"Yes, Season." The small boy turned to leave the cabin.

"Gideon," turning to face her, as she continued, if you have to, ask him for a job."

"Yes." Gideon ran from Season's cabin and raced down the docks toward the *Moonlight*. When Gideon reached the ship, the men of the *Moonlight* were all leaving the ship and going into the city to socialize with the local women. Gideon approached an old man, "Excuse me sir."

"What do you want boy?" grumbled the old man.

"I want to talk to the Captain about a job," replied Gideon.

"A job? What can a small boy like you do?" questioned the old, stocky, short man.

"I can do anything, really. I need a job; my mother is alone now since my father left. She can barely manage for herself," Gideon stammered, "I mean us."

"Well, you'll have to talk to the Captain about a job; follow me," said the old man's name, Gideon would later learn, was George. He hobbled as the young boy followed him to the captain's cabin. George knocked and opened the door. Gideon had never seen a Captain's cabin so grand before, and the Captain sat at a large oak desk looking at some maps. George said, "Cap'n, this here young lad would like to see you about a job."

Timothy stood up and faced Gideon, "You are awful young to be looking for a job, aren't you?"

"No sir, well yes sir, but my mother needs the money, sir. My father left us sir, and I thought that if I got a job, I could send home my pay to my mother and…"

Timothy interrupted him, "Slow down, so you need this job because your family doesn't have any money?"

"Yes, sir," said Gideon.

"Can I meet this mother of yours?" Timothy wondered if a mother existed or if the child was just lying to him.

"Yes, can I bring her here in an hour or two?" Gideon was excited, his ruse had worked.

Timothy nodded yes, "Since your mother and yourself are so poor," his golden eyes twinkled, "perhaps the two of you would like to join me for dinner?"

"Yes, that would be nice, sir."

"Very well; you bring your mother, and I'll have the cook prepare us some food," said Timothy.

"Thank you very much, sir." Gideon ran out of the cabin, off the ship and towards the *Sea Witch*. When he reached the ship, he told Season what had happened. Within an hour, Season was dressed in a shabby old dress, and her crew was ready to take over the *Moonlight*. Inside the cuff of her dress lay a small packet of laudalum, to be used on the Captain. It was enough for him to pass out.

Timothy found the woman most attractive, yet he thought she was much too young to have a child about Gideon's age. They drank wine, the Captain swallowing his in gulps. The drug finally took effect, and the Captain passed out. Gideon and Season moved him to the bed and tied him securely. Season went to the window with the lamp, her signal to her crew. The women dressed like men boarded the ship and waited for their prey. By daylight, the Captain woke to a vision of Season, dressed like a pirate with a sword at her belt. She informed him with a small laugh and a smirk that he and his crew had been captured by the Captain and crew of the *Sea Witch*. Timothy's head spun; the room seemed to be going around in circles causing him to realize that he had been drugged.

Once he had finally come to, Season explained what she wanted from him. Impressed Timothy agreed to help her on the condition that if they ever met on the sea, each would leave the other alone unless they were being attacked or needed help. Upon the agreement of truce, Timothy helped her learn about navigation, including navigating the most dangerous waters. He lived on the *Sea Witch* for six months, teaching Season how to read maps, how to navigate dangerous waters, how to find ports that were neutral as far as pirates were concerned and how to make her own maps.

Timothy had wanted her from the moment he laid eyes on her but restrained himself because of the story she told. He decided that he would wait for her to come to him and when she did, he would teach her how to love and please a man. Season later admitted to him after an evening of lovemaking, that she, too, had been attracted to him since the first time she had seen him. Three days after, the *Moonlight* set sail for the Barbary Coast. Timothy had said good-bye to Season the day before when the *Sea Witch* set sail for an unknown destination.

The *Moonlight* was a much faster clipper ship than the *Sea Witch*. Within twenty-four hours, the *Sea Witch* was spotted and to her left was a large Dutch Shipping and Trading vessel. The large Dutch ship appeared to be taking over the *Sea Witch*. The *Moonlight*, under Timothy's command, raced towards the *Sea Witch*, pulling alongside her. The crew of the *Moonlight* boarded the *Sea Witch* from the right and fought aside the women of Season's crew. Timothy looked for Season and found her.

"So, Season, we meet again," sneered Justin Rafael, the tip of his sword at her throat, "Only this time my dear, you will die."

Timothy shot the small gun hitting Rafael's hand and causing the sword to fly from his hand crashing to the deck. The second shot found its mark, killing Mr. Justin Rafael instantly....

Timothy's mind returned to the present, it was strange that he thought of Season and that incident now. He tried to remember the date of that year; it was somewhere around eight years ago, that would be 1841. Timothy walked to his desk opening his drawer for the bullets. He realized that if he had to, he would use that same gun on Lyndon without hesitation.

.

CHAPTER SEVEN

Geoffrey paced back and forth in front of Jennifer's limp body. Where was this man that he was supposed to meet? He was late! His attention was drawn to Jennifer, he would love to possess her completely but he couldn't take the chance. If he did and the man found out, he wouldn't get his money and he needed that money.

Jennifer moaned as she opened her eyes, it was getting late. She closed her eyes and prayed, "Dear God, please help me. Please let Stefan figure out where I am." They should be looking for her she thought. She lay still, not wanting Geoffrey to know she was awake, if only there was some way to escape. In the distance she heard a carriage. Hope.

Hope faded quickly as Geoffrey muttered, "Finally," he nudged Jennifer with the toe of his boot, "Wake up." She opened her eyes and stared coldly at him, "Well, Miss Weatherly, the man is almost here." A carriage rolled to a stop in front of them, a large burly man with tattoos climbed off the carriage.

"Is this the woman?" he slurred.

"Yes," replied Geoffrey, "Do you have the money?"

"Let me look at her first."

Lyndon untied the gag, the man pulled her to her feet by her hair; he smelled like rum and sweat, causing Jennifer to become nauseous. She closed her eyes wishing she was having a nightmare, yet knowing she wasn't dreaming. She opened her eyes as the man poked at her. He was chewing tobacco, the saliva dripping from his mouth as Geoffrey asked, "Well, do I get my money?"

The man spit a wad of tobacco out at Jennifer's feet, then wiped his mouth with the back of his hand, "Yeah, Lyndon, she sure is a fine specimen." He reached into his coat pocket and handed Lyndon a roll of money.

Jennifer had remained quiet through the entire ordeal. Her eyes widened at the sight of the money. She spoke for the first time, "Sir, would you mind if I said something to Mr. Lyndon, before we leave?" She knew it was useless trying to fight what was happening to her with this man.

"Why, the little lady has a voice! So, you want to say something to him before we leave," he said as he chewed on his tobacco.

Jennifer said, "Yes."

"Sure, say something to Mr. Lyndon."

"Geoffrey, you are the lowest of all men, you care nothing of people, only for money. Someday you'll pay for what you've done to me, and I swear you'll pay with your life." Geoffrey slapped her across the face; she felt the sting of his fingers but refused to yield; she would not give him the satisfaction of crying in front of him. "I hope you rot in hell!" The big burley man took her by the arm and motioned for her to go. She looked at him, "One more thing please." She turned to Geoffrey, spitting in his face. The big man laughed as he pulled Jennifer toward the waiting carriage. Geoffrey watched as she was put on the carriage before leaving.

The big man sat across from Jennifer in the carriage. He stared at her wondering why she was dressed in trousers. He'd have to get her something to wear for the ship. Jennifer looked at him thinking that perhaps she could convince him to let her go. "Sir, please let me go. My father will repay you handsomely. He's very wealthy."

He smiled, "Miss, it is not my choice to let you go. It does not matter to me how much money your father has. We can get much more for you in the Barbary States. Much more than what we gave Lyndon. No more talking, or I'll have to gag you again."

She shook her head yes, as she turned to look out the window of the coach. The man fell asleep after a while. Jennifer recognized the wharf and the *Moonlight*; she wondered if Mr. Lockwood knew she was missing. The ship was completely dark except for one light at the top of the ship. The carriage came to a rocking halt, awakening the man who sat across from her. "Well, I see we're here. Now listen to me gal, we are getting off the carriage, one word out of you and you'll be dead. You understand?"

"Yes," replied Jennifer.

"No, I don't trust you after what you said to Lyndon. I'm going to gag you."

"Please, no," but it was too late as he put the gag back on her and pulled the hood of the cloak over her head as he led her out of the carriage to a ship.

Geoffrey Lyndon, was headed for the nearest whorehouse and gambling establishment now that he had money in his pocket. He thought to himself, by this time tomorrow, Jennifer Weatherly would be long gone, on her way to the Barbary Coast.

Jennifer found herself in the hold of the ship with thirty-five other women of various ages, shapes and sizes. She wondered if any of the women had been of the same station as she; looking around the room, she began to doubt it; for the most part, the women looked like they were either poor or trollops. Of course, she herself looked no better, dressed as a lady pirate. Her stomach growled; she had not had anything to eat in over twenty-four hours. The other women were lying down on the grimy floor, but Jennifer vowed she would not sleep lying down. Sleep did not come easily nor quickly.

Morning came faster than normal, and Jennifer found herself wanting to go topside for a breath of fresh air. The air in the hold smelled like urine and vomit. Many of the women were vomiting, causing Jennifer to realize that they must have set sail sometime during the night. She turned her head not wanting to watch and prayed to God that she either die before she reached the Barbary States or was taken off this godforsaken ship. Breakfast was served to the women by the cook and a couple of the men; it was sort of slop, a mush, a grey gruel, which tasted as bad as it looked. Days passed when Jennifer noted that some of the women were being treated much better than the others. They were given clean clothes to wear and were allowed to go topside for fresh air. They also ate their meals upstairs. Jennifer questioned some of the other women and found out that the reason these women were being treated better is that they had sold their bodies to the crew in exchange for these things.

CHAPTER EIGHT

Mr. Ownsby had returned to the Weatherlys to inform them there was no trace of Jennifer at the Harrington estate. He waited patiently in James Weatherly's library for forty-five minutes. James Weatherly sat in the sitting room with his nephew and Captain Lockwood. Stefan spoke quietly, "Uncle, both Captain Lockwood and myself believe that Geoffrey Lyndon had a hand in Jennifer's disappearance."

"I can't believe you, Stefan. I've known the Lyndon family a long time, and I just don't think he would have anything to do with Jennifer's disappearance."

Stefan looked at his uncle for a moment. Reaching into his pocket, he withdrew some papers and handed them to his uncle. "These papers are proof of what I've been telling you. I took the liberty of hiring a private investigator who got this information. After you look at the papers, I would suggest you listen to what Captain Lockwood has to say."

James Weatherly took the papers from his nephew and sat down to read them. Timothy Lockwood sat quietly, wishing he had just gone on ahead to Lyndon's home. James Weatherly looked through the papers; it was a detailed account of everything Lyndon had done in the past two months including various rendezvous with a certain blonde woman named Laura Harrington. James noted that Geoffrey Lyndon was indeed the questionable character that his nephew had been alluding to these past months. Even his financial situation was questionable, he owed money to every shop in town and practically everyone he did business with right down to the whorehouses he visited frequently. James Weatherly looked across the room at the tall Captain, wondering why was he so interested in these matters, "Well, Captain Lockwood, I trust you have read these documents?"

"Yes, I have, Mr. Weatherly," replied Timothy.

"And why, may I inquire, are you so interested in Lyndon and my daughter?"

"I met your daughter a few days ago; you see, I am the one who gave her the pirate's costume. I am also the person who agreed to take her to Spain in order to get her away from Lyndon. I found her to be most charming at the costume party. In fact, I did not think that your daughter would leave a party without bidding adieu herself," Timothy said, staring at James Weatherly.

James Weatherly looked at the man with the lion's eyes in astonishment, "What do you mean that you agreed to take her to Spain?"

"You can ask your nephew about that tonight or later on; I'm sure Stefan will explain. But all of this is neither here nor there; I came to tell you that Lyndon did frequent many of haunts last night, flashing what appeared to be a great deal of money," Timothy said.

"Mr. Lockwood, he could have won the money gambling," replied James Harrington.

"No, he was quite drunk and bragging that he sold a woman to someone. It is very possible that the woman could be Jennifer," Timothy's golden eyes were expressionless.

"Why would he sell Jennifer instead of asking for ransom?" demanded James Weatherly.

Timothy looked at Stefan and then at James Weatherly, "I have a theory concerning that."

James Weatherly was frustrated, "Well, speak up!"

Stefan had wished that he could tell his uncle this part, but both he and Timothy agreed it would sound better coming from Timothy. Stefan's eyes shifted to the floor as Timothy spoke, "With your daughter being only seventeen and unmarried, I am to assume that her virginity is still intact?" James Weatherly was shocked that this young man would talk of such a thing, but continued to listen as the Captain continued, "I'm sure that you must have heard the stories of young women being kidnapped and sold into slavery along the Barbary Coast."

Weatherly whispered, "Yes."

"Well, a young woman who still has her virginity can be sold for an extremely high price. I believe that Lyndon sold your daughter to some men who will resell her for a much higher price in the Barbary States. My crew found out that a ship set sail late last evening, and its destination is the Barbary Coast".

James Weatherly inquired, "But how do you know Jennifer is on that ship?"

"I don't," Timothy stated flatly.

Stefan looked at his uncle, "Captain Lockwood would like your permission to seek out Lyndon and see what he can find out."

James Weatherly looked at Timothy, "You have my permission, Captain."

"There is one condition Mr. Weatherly," replied Timothy.

James Weatherly's dark eyes narrowed as he questioned Timothy, "Which is?"

"I do not want you to tell the authorities about Lyndon; you let me deal with him," replied Timothy.

"You have my word," James extended his hand to the tall Captain. Timothy shook his hand firmly.

"Uncle, I would suggest you talk with Mr. Ownsby," Stefan said.

"Yes," James Weatherly rose from his seat and went to the library.

"Would you like a drink, Captain?" questioned Stefan after his uncle left the room.

"No, thank you, I have a couple of errands that I must take care of before I seek out Lyndon. I'll see myself to the door." Stefan stared after the Captain; he wondered if the Captain would see Laura Harrington now that he found out she was no better than some of the whores that could be found in every port.

James Weatherly found Ownsby sitting quietly in the library, flipping through a book. "Mr. Ownsby, I'm so sorry to keep you waiting so long, but I was in a business meeting that I just could not get away from. Can I get you something to drink?"

"No, thank you, Mr. Weatherly. I came to inform you that we have conducted a search of the Harrington estate."

James Weatherly had, by this time, positioned himself behind his desk in the soft cushioned chair, "Did you find anything?"

Ownsby replied, "I'm afraid not sir. Everyone there agrees that your daughter left the party ill."

"Are you sure that your men searched every piece of property on the grounds?" inquired James.

Ownsby nodded, "Yes, and we made a thorough search of the house. I must say that Miss Harrington was quite upset."

James said nonchalantly, "I will personally apologize to the Harringtons."

"We will continue with our investigation until we have searched the entire area," responded Ownsby.

"Thank you very much. As soon as you turn up something please let us know," James said.

"Perhaps you will receive a ransom note," said Ownsby.

"Yes, "James Weatherly rose from his seat and saw Ownsby to the door and then returned to the sitting room where he found Stefan, "Where is Captain Lockwood?"

"He said he had some errands to run before he went looking for Lyndon. What did Ownsby say about the investigation?" questioned Stefan.

"They didn't find any trace of her, and everyone there says she went home early because she was sick," James sighed.

"I think the Captain will find her," Stefan said firmly.

"Stefan, you seem quite impressed with this man, what exactly do you know about him?" questioned James.

"Not much, except that he once saved the life of a Berber King and warrior, which is where he received the ivory carved sword as a token of peace. So, if Jennifer has been sold on the Barbary Coast, perhaps Mr. Lockwood can get this man to help him find Jennifer." Stefan was sure of it!

They were interrupted by Lizabeth, "Did the authorities have any word on Miss Jennifer?"

"No," answered Stefan.

Lizabeth frowned. "If either of you wish to eat, dinner will be ready in a few minutes." She turned and left the room.

Stefan looked at his uncle, "Most of the servants have been quite upset over Jennifer. Perhaps you should keep them informed as we receive information."

"Yes, I'll have Lizabeth call the servants into the sitting room after dinner so I can tell them. Come, let's go have something to eat," replied James. The two men left the room together.

The carriage rolled quickly over the streets on the way to the Harrington estate. Timothy Lockwood was seething with anger; how dare anyone make a fool of him, especially a woman. Laura Harrington was not the virginal, innocent young woman she played herself to be, and now she would pay. He remembered that first evening they had met; he should have known her to be the whore she was when she appeared in the revealing gold satin gown. The carriage came to a stop, and he jumped off and ran up the stairs. He knocked loudly on the door until Maggie opened it. "Where is Laura?"

"She's not here sir; she went out." Maggie noted the anger in his eyes.

Grabbing Maggie by the arm, he dragged her into the main parlor, "Where did she go?"

"I'm not—please sir let go of my arm; you're hurting me!" exclaimed Maggie.

Timothy's grip loosened slightly, "Tell me, you're her ladies' maid, so you must know where she went."

"I don't know, sir," Those gold eyes that she had once admired were now full of hatred and anger; could it be that he had found out about Mr. Lyndon, Maggie wondered.

"Does your lady have a lover?" No words came to the young woman; the tears ran down her face, "Damn you, answer me right now!" demanded Timothy.

"I don't…" his grip on Maggie tightened as she hung her head and whispered, "Yes."

"Who is the bastard? Tell me." Maggie was crying uncontrollably now; Timothy slapped her across the face, "Pull yourself together."

"Please, Mr. Lockwood, I can't afford to lose my job," cried Maggie.

"I'll give you a new job, now tell me," demanded Timothy.

"Mr. Lyndon," she whispered. Maggie had wished for once in her life that she did not eavesdrop so often.

"Lyndon; I knew it!" Timothy released his grip on Maggie. She rubbed her arm, "I'm sorry, now where is your mistress?"

Maggie said, "She is expected home any minute. Sir, please don't tell her I told you."

Timothy walked over to the desk and scrawled a note to James Weatherly. Handing the note to Maggie, he said, "Get your things together, tell the driver to take you to the Weatherly estate. Give the note to Mr. James Weatherly." She nodded her head, "Is there anyone else in the house?"

"Just the cook sir, but she'll be takin' her nap soon," responded Maggie.

"Good, now be on your way." Maggie ran to her room, gathering a few things and left quietly, moments before Laura returned.

Laura was pleased with herself today; having found Geoffrey with a considerable amount of money in his pocket, she convinced him to buy her a new gown. She opened the door to the entry way, face to face with Timothy. She smiled, "Timothy, what on earth are you doing here?"

His eyes were burning with hatred and disgust, but he managed a smile. "I came to see you."

She removed her cloak and hung it over the chair, "Then you've changed your mind about the wedding?"

"No," he stared at her, she was dressed in new clothes.

"Then why are you here? If you haven't changed your mind, then we have nothing to discuss." Laura turned, leaving the entry way and went into the sitting room. Timothy followed her into the room, shutting the large oak doors behind him. "So, we are still postponing the wedding?"

"No, we are canceling the wedding," he said without any expression.

"Cancel? But all the arrangements have been made, you must mean cancel for the time being," Laura was visibly upset by this news.

Timothy remained firm, "No, I mean cancel permanently."

"Permanently, but..." her voice drifted off as tears filled her eyes. What would happen when her father found out? If what she suspected was true, she was pregnant with Lyndon's child. Laura was determined to make Timothy marry her; she had to pass off the child as his, "Did I do something to make you angry?"

"Laura, I'm tired of the games you play," Timothy stated in a low voice.

"Games? What are you talking about?" questioned Laura.

"You know very well what I'm talking about." The anger began to boil inside of Timothy, "Don't play the innocent with me Laura; it won't work."

Laura turned her back to him; could it be possible that he was on to her charade? How could he have found out? She felt his eyes burning a hole through her back as she turned to face him, "But I really don't know what you're talking about. Honestly, Timothy, tell me what I did to make you angry?" She fluttered her eye lashes and raised her hand to touch his cheek. He jerked his face away from her and grabbed her hand, "Timothy, really I..."

"Shut up," snapped Timothy, his gold flecked eyes stared into empty blue ones.

"You're hurting me; let me go," whined Laura.

"You slut!" Laura turned and slapped Timothy across the face; he didn't flinch.

Laura was now in a rage, "Get out of my house."

"Not until I get what I came here for," replied Timothy coldly.

"How dare you…" her eyes widened in fear as he approached her, "My father will have your head."

"Your father is no better than you, my little whore. Let's see how well you can perform." He smiled sarcastically, "How much does Mr. Lyndon pay you for your charms? I'll wager he pays you nothing."

"You bastard!" Laura cried out as she made her way to the door.

Timothy was too fast for her, catching her around the waist, he pushed her to the floor, the yellow eyes reminded her of a cat ready to strike its prey, "Remove the dress."

"No," Laura said firmly.

"Then I'll remove it for you." Seizing the gown, Timothy ripped it from her body exposing her breasts. She stood there in a semi-shocked state of mind. His lips came crashing down on hers, she struggled against him as she felt his manhood growing bigger against her thigh. His teeth bit her lips, neck and breasts. Her body disobeyed her, she wanted him as much as he wanted her, she knew he had drawn blood from biting her, yet she was enjoying it, "Now," she moaned.

"Not yet my sweet." Now it was Timothy who was playing a game, "What do you know about Jennifer Weatherly's disappearance?"

Panting, she answered, "Nothing."

Timothy's lip curved into a cruel smile, "But you do my little harlot, now where is she?"

"Geoffrey sold her to a ship bound for the Barbary Coast, now please." She shuddered as she arched her body to his hard thrust. This man with his brute force was pleasing her more than Geoffrey's tenderness could ever please her. He brought her to a climax that no other man could ever bring her again.

When it was over, he stood up, pulling his clothes together quickly. Reaching into his pocket he withdrew some money and tossed it at her feet, "Buy yourself a new dress."

"I don't want your money," Laura said quietly.

"Take it, although I must admit, it is a bit much, considering I've had much better whores," replied Timothy.

Picking up the money, Laura stood to her feet to face him, spitting in his face, "I'm not a whore!"

He wiped his cheek with his handkerchief before speaking, "On the contrary, my sweet, you just proved you were." Timothy walked out the front door, got in his carriage and left the Harrington estate for Lyndon's home. He thought of Laura as the carriage rolled along the countryside; he had used her more than he had ever used a woman in his life. He had tried to punish her the only way he could ever punish a woman, by using her brutally. What really angered him was that she didn't feel punished at all; she wasn't ashamed of what happened and she probably wished it could happen again. Some of the women he had been with in gentleman's clubs, had a better moral standard than Laura Harrington. She was nothing but a whore, one that belonged in the lowest section of the streets of London. He was glad that he had his way with her; she helped him release all of the tension that had built up inside of him these last few days.

His mind turned to Lyndon; it would be his turn to pay for what happened to Jennifer. She was so young, so innocent, and Lyndon had ruined that innocence. The carriage stopped in front of Lyndon's home. Timothy climbed out of the carriage, "I won't be needing your services any longer." Reaching into the pocket of his trousers he paid the man and set him on his way. He stood in the street for a couple of minutes watching the carriage until it was difficult to see. Knocking on the door, he waited. No answer. If Lyndon's affairs were in such a sorry state, more than likely he didn't have servants. Making his way to the rear of the house, he tried the back door. It was locked. He ran his hand through his thick black hair. In order to gain access to the house he would have to break-in. Taking the small gun from his belt he used the butt of the gun to break the glass of the rear door. Chipping the glass from the pane, he slipped his hand through to unlocked the door. Opening the door, he entered the house and began to look around. The house was completely empty of servants, and it appeared that no servants had stepped foot in it for weeks. He had never in his life seen a house more disorderly; pirates even lived cleaner than Lyndon. The furniture was very old and in poor condition in every room except the sitting room and the dining room. It was obvious to Timothy that these rooms were used for entertaining. Making himself comfortable, he poured himself a bourbon and sat in an overstuffed chair in the sitting room to wait for Lyndon. He waited a little over an hour.

Geoffrey Lyndon had returned home from spending the afternoon at Madame Celeste's. Timothy heard the key in the lock, and Lyndon entered the house. Timothy could see him from where he was sitting. Lyndon tossed his coat onto a chair in the hall and looked at his mail. Bills, warnings of creditors. While Lyndon was busy with the mail, Timothy moved to the doors of the sitting room where his presence would be hidden by the large doors. Lyndon walked into the sitting room and poured himself a drink, as the doors closed quickly causing

Lyndon to whirl around. Seeing the tall Captain frightened him, "How did you get into my home?"

Timothy looked at Lyndon in a way that sent shivers down Lyndon's back, "How I got in does not matter."

"Why are you here?" He knew the answer to the question before he asked. He was certain that the man standing in before him wanted to duel. Lyndon had never walked away from a duel in his life, and he wouldn't walk away from this one.

"I want some information," Timothy's topaz eyes glittered.

"What kind of information?" Lyndon placed the drink on a nearby table.

"What do you know about Jennifer Weatherly?" questioned Timothy.

"Nothing. I don't know where she is; the last time I saw her was at the costume ball," replied Lyndon.

Timothy's eyes blazed with hatred for the man standing before him. He pounced on Lyndon. The two men struggled on the floor until Timothy got a good grasp on Lyndon's neck, he repeated the word "liar" over and over again as he squeezed. Lyndon's eyes began to bulge, his face was turning purple, and the veins in his neck looked as if they were going to explode. Suddenly, Lyndon's eyes closed, and he seemed not to be breathing. Timothy's sanity returned to him, and he released Lyndon whose limp body convinced Timothy that he was dead. Timothy stood up and left by the rear door. Making his way to the street, he ran until he reached the center of the city. Slowing down to catch his breath he looked around; no one appeared to be watching him; he crossed the street and went inside a livery stable.

A small man with a heavy Irish brogue asked, "What can I do for you, sir?"

Timothy asked, 'Do you have any horses for sale?"

"No sir, we don't sell horses. Perhaps you would like to rent one, sir?"

Timothy looked at the man, "I, ah, no. I was looking to buy one. I'll take a hansom cab. Thank you anyway." Timothy looked up and down the street after leaving the livery stable, finally spying a hansom cab, he flagged it down. "Take me to the Weatherly estate, and the faster you get me there the more money you will get." The driver nodded. Timothy sat in the carriage thinking, Lyndon was dead. The thing that bothered him was the fact that he had killed Lyndon for a woman. He had never killed for a woman before, except Season, but that was different; he had a truce with Season; he had promised to help her if she was ever in trouble. But this was totally different. He had purposely set out to kill Lyndon after he received the information from Laura. He had the distinct feeling that he would kill again for Jennifer. Jennifer. What was it about this girl that caused him to react in this manner? Jennifer. Was she his destiny? Was it fate that brought them together and that ripped them apart? She was an emerald eyed lady, with enough spirit to drive any man crazy. He wanted to possess her soul from the moment he saw her on the docks. He had wanted her for himself from the moment he talked and planned an escape with her, the escape that wasn't meant to be. Now he would turn the Barbary States upside down in search of her; no man would stand in his way. If it took him until the end of time, he would find Jennifer; he would leave no stone unturned until he held her in his arms. The carriage stopped in front of the Weatherly home. Timothy paid the driver and walked to the front door.

Stefan had been waiting for the Captain ever since the pretty little maid had appeared at the door with the note. Seeing Timothy coming up the marble stairs, he opened the door, "Where have you been? Do you know what time it is? Did you get any information?"

"Stefan, slow down. Where is your uncle?" questioned Timothy.

"In the library. Then you do have some information?"

Timothy walked past Stefan, toward the library, "Yes, I do, and if you want to know what it is, I suggest you come into the library." Opening the library door, he startled James Weatherly.

James Weatherly was not used to people just coming into a room without knocking, but seeing it was the Captain, he said nothing except, "Did you find anything out?"

Timothy sat down in the chair in front of Weatherly's desk, "Yes. What I have to tell you is not pleasant, so I suggest that the both of you sit down, and shut the door." Stefan went to the open door and shut it. Everyone sat down; Timothy decided to spare some of the details, especially those of the rape. "It seems that Lyndon did kidnap Jennifer, but he doesn't have her now. He sold her to a ship headed for the Barbary Coast just as I suspected. That ship left port two days ago."

"How do you know that Lyndon was not lying to you?" questioned Stefan.

"I didn't get my information from Lyndon, I got it from one of his lady friends," said Timothy preferring to leave out Laura's name.

"Did you check it out with Lyndon?" asked James Weatherly.

Timothy's eyes were expressionless, "No, Lyndon is dead."

"Dead? You didn't…" James Weatherly's voice drifted off into silence. What kind of man was he dealing with? His daughter's safety was going to be in the hands of a killer; the thought was horrifying.

"That really doesn't make a difference. I came here to tell you about the information. I also came to tell you that I'm shipping out to-night for the Barbary Coast. I promise that within six months you will have your daughter back at Weatherly. I can't promise that she will re-turn the same way she left, but she will return." Rising from his chair he continued, "Now if you'll excuse me, I have to round up my men if we are going to ship out within three hours." Timothy turned and walked to the door, "One other thing, I will be taking a horse from your stables, which one shall I tell the groom to give me?"

James Weatherly was appalled and dumbfounded. This Captain comes into his home without being announced, shocks the family with news of Jennifer, says in a roundabout way that he killed a man and now says he's going to take one of the horses. Stefan answered, "Olivia, it was Jennifer's horse." Timothy left the room and headed for the stables.

CHAPTER NINE

George, the first mate, took the wheel of the *Moonlight* from Ben. The ship glided along the vast ocean, picking up speed as she moved. George thought about the last few weeks; he had never seen the captain in a vile mood. His mood became worse when they were thrown off course by a storm and had to pull into the port of LeHarve, France for two weeks of repairs. If it wasn't for the storm, they would have made it to the Barbary States in record time. Although they were two weeks behind schedule, the *Moonlight* was expected to pull into port within forty-eight hours.

The captain had taken to spending a great deal of time in his cabin; George had never seen the captain so possessed with an idea of reaching a particular port as quickly as he wanted to reach the Barbary States. George suspected that the urgency had something to do with the disappearance of Jennifer Weatherly, the pretty young girl who had come to the ship with her cousin to borrow something to wear for a costume party. Perhaps Captain Lockwood was getting a great deal of money for going on this voyage, but if that was the case, he would not have stayed in his cabin since LeHarve. He would have been on the decks pressuring the men to work harder; instead, he sent his messages through Gideon. It was as if the crew were running the ship instead of the Captain.

George worried about his Captain. Timothy had never neglected the crew like he had on this particular voyage. Gideon had told George that the captain spent a great deal of time praying, for what he did not know, but nevertheless praying. Praying! George had never known the Captain to be a religious man, nor had he ever seen him act so strangely.

The following morning, Timothy made his first appearance topside since leaving LeHarve. Saying nothing, he watched the men work and then sought out George. He found George still at the wheel talking with Caleb. "Caleb, take the wheel from George." Turning his attention to George he said, "Come to my cabin." Together, they walked side by side to the cabin, neither saying a word. Once inside the cabin, Timothy and George sat down at the table, "George, I asked you in here to tell you what is going on."

"Cap'n, you don't have to explain anything to me or the crew."

"No, George, you are my first mate, and I really think you should know what is happening and why we are going to the Barbary Coast."

"Captain, really you don't have to explain." George felt uncomfortable. Timothy had never told the crew why they were going to any port, although George could not remember the last time that he was in the Barbary Coast without someone saying why they were going to that godforsaken place.

"But you see, George, I have to. It is very important that the members of this crew know that we have to leave the Barbary Coast quickly and be ready to fight." He paused, "This voyage is to save Jennifer Weatherly; she was sold to a ship headed for the slave trade in the Barbary States. With all of our delays, we might have lost her; of course, this ship is faster than the one she is on, and I'm sure that they hit the same storm."

"I see, but what if she has been sold," inquired George.

"If she's been sold, we'll find her and kidnap her back. That is when we may have to leave the Barbary States in a hurry."

"I understand Captain. What do you want me to tell the crew?" George responded.

"Tell them that they should be prepared to pull out of port with a minute's notice." He paused, you can tell them that you or I will give them better details once we find out exactly where we stand," replied Timothy.

"Yes sir." George rose to leave the cabin.

"George, really put the pressure on, it is very important that we reach the Barbary States as soon as possible." George nodded and left the room. Timothy walked over to the ivory carved sword and picked it up. He fenced with himself in the quiet of his cabin. He knew he would have to be prepared to fight. After an hour of fencing with himself, he went up to the decks. "Ben, raise the pirate flag. From this point on, we are pirates."

"Aye, aye sir!" Ben hurried to please the Captain. Timothy looked around the deck and began to give orders.

"Cap'n, we've spotted a ship," yelled George.

Timothy went to where George was standing, "Is it a slaver?"

"Hard to tell; it's too far away."

"See if we can pick up some speed to get closer to the ship. If we can overtake her, we will," said Timothy.

"Yes, sir."

It was impossible to overtake the ship that was directly in front of them. The ship was too far away, and there would be no way to pick up any more speed. Although the *Moonlight* had gained ground, Timothy called off the chase. They would be in Barbary waters within the next couple of hours and before long on the shore of the Barbary States.

CHAPTER TEN

It had been weeks since Jennifer had seen daylight. One of the women who sold herself to the Captain convinced him that it was unhealthy to keep women locked-up in a place where there was no fresh air. The Captain agreed that the women could be taken topside an hour a day until they reach their destination. The men were not allowed near the women when they were on deck. They did stare at the women, especially Jennifer, for she was dressed as a lady pirate. The men wondered about her; if she was a lady pirate, she certainly wasn't putting up a fight about being on a ship headed for the Barbary Coast. Perhaps she had other plans when she reached the Barbary States; if she was a lady pirate, she would have friends in that area. Surely there would be trouble.

Jennifer looked out into the ocean; the waves rolled carelessly, as they crashed into the ship. Her long hair was matted, and it had been weeks since she had taken a bath. Her own body odor was making her ill. She closed her eyes as she leaned against the railing thinking of home, her father, Stefan and Captain Lockwood. She remembered the day on his ship when he talked about the lady pirate, Season. She smiled; that seemed like a lifetime ago. Jennifer was determined to escape, and she would once they reached the Barbary States. Her thoughts were interrupted by the only person she had talked to, her friend Heather.

"Hello, Jennifer," said Heather.

Jennifer looked at Heather; she was a frail, red-haired girl of fifteen, who had turned to a life of prostitution because her family needed the money. "Hello, Heather. I'm glad you came up for some fresh air. How are you feeling today?" Lately, Heather had been losing a considerable amount of weight. Her face had thinned so much that she appeared to have the look of death about her, which worried Jennifer.

"I'm feeling a little better since I left that smelly hold. What were you thinking of?" questioned Heather.

"Home," replied Jennifer with a distant look in her eyes.

"At least you have a home to think about," said Heather softly.

"You have a home Heather, maybe not as nice as mine, but you have a home." Jennifer's voice was flat; lately she had become depressed.

"I'm sure you were thinking about something other than home. When you were telling me, you had a special look in your eyes," said Heather.

"No, I was thinking of home," Jennifer replied.

"Jennifer, I think we have become close enough friends for you to tell me the truth. Were you thinking of someone special?" questioned Heather.

Jennifer smiled, "Alright Heather, I'll tell you. Yes, I was thinking of a man. A very tall man, with jet black hair, the eyes of a lion and a golden tan."

"Who is this man?"

"He's a sea Captain. He was visiting London before he returned home to the New World," replied Jennifer.

Heather was excited, "The two of you fell in love?"

"No, it's just a girlish dream, he was engaged to someone else. A very self-centered woman." Jennifer's voice had gotten hard; oh, how she hated Laura Harrington! Why wasn't she kidnapped instead of her?

"You don't like this woman?"

Jennifer stared at Heather, "No."

"Tell me more about the Captain."

"There really isn't much to tell; he was the most handsome man I've ever seen." Jennifer could visualize his face.

"How did you meet him?" questioned Heather.

"I saw him on the docks when I returned home from Paris. But I didn't talk to him that day...." Her voice drifted off as she remembered the day she spent with Captain Timothy Lockwood of Newport, Rhode Island, formally of London. His voice, his eyes held her captive for the entire afternoon. She wondered what it would be like to make love to him; she blushed.

"What are you thinking about? What really happened between you and that Captain?"

"Nothing," replied Jennifer.

The first mate yelled, "Back downstairs ladies."

The women shuffled back downstairs into the urine filled room. Many of the women had caught some kind of fever and died. Jennifer worried about Heather; she had been experiencing the same kind of symptoms as the women who had died. It was difficult to see after coming in from the bright sun, into the dark lower part of the ship. Jennifer and Heather sat side by side as they ate lunch. Lunch consisted of a hard bread, some cheese and wine. After lunch the vomiting began, many of the women could not keep their food down. Jennifer could not decide whether it was the fever that was killing them or the fact that they could not keep their food down. Fifteen out of thirty-six women had survived this far. Jennifer didn't know how much time was left, but she was sure that within the next week, they would be in the Barbary Coast. What then? She had to come up with a plan to escape. Then she would have to book passage on a ship for London, but she had no money. Jennifer was sure that she could think of something, and once she was back in London, she would get her revenge against Geoffrey Lyndon. A voice from the past had talked about revenge but who? She sat quietly for hours trying to think of who had talked about revenge; finally, it came to her: Captain Lockwood; what did he say? The words slowly returned to her, *'a woman can taste sweet revenge before she even has it and that woman's revenge will be brutal, more brutal than you can ever imagine. Remember, a woman can take much more pain than a man, and she will continue to, if it means staying alive.'* Jennifer sighed; with no money, she wondered if she would ever taste her revenge against Lyndon. Was she doomed to a life of slavery on the Barbary Coast? No! She would refuse to be a slave to anyone. Anyone who tried to make her a slave, she would destroy, she would pick them apart until there was nothing left. Whoever bought her when they landed in the Barbary States would regret that he ever met a woman named Jennifer Weatherly. She would escape from him, and when she did, she would take his money with her. But she would have to get him to trust her, trust her so completely that she would have become his confidant. She would use him for her own means, just as she was sure he'd use her. Jennifer would return to Weatherly. It might take her months before she did, but she would return. She looked at Heather who had fallen asleep. Soon, Jennifer was sure that they would be parting, but Heather would always occupy a special place in her heart. She hoped that the young girl did not fall into the hands of some mean man, although she was sure that Heather could take care of herself. Jennifer closed her eyes; soon she would get her chance for revenge. Sleep came quickly for her as did morning, when breakfast was served and the vomiting would start again.

The first mate appeared to make an announcement, "There will be fresh water for you ladies to bathe; we'll be landing within twenty-four hours." The idea of fresh water to bathe appealed to Jennifer.

The women were given cleaner clothes to wear after they had bathed. Jennifer was given a bright red skirt with a white blouse. Heather had been given a green skirt and a white blouse. The skirts fit the women snugly around the hips and the blouses were very revealing.

Twelve of the thirty-six women survived. All of the women had been chained and brought to the deck. Jennifer's eyes scanned the seaport; people were everywhere. Most of the women on the docks were dressed like the women on the ship. The men were dressed the way Timothy Lockwood had been dressed the night of the costume party. The sun beat down on the women as they stood at the rail. Jennifer heard a man discussing the women and how they would be sold in the marketplace. Her eyes darted to the east as she saw a ship approaching, another slaver she thought; it was too far to be sure. Jennifer had given up hope of being rescued; she had resigned herself to believing that no one would be coming after her. They probably were waiting for a ransom note, and there would be none. The chains on her hands were heavy, and the sun made her feel faint, but she was determined not to collapse. Occasionally, a cool breeze blew her hair, and the spindrift hit her face. The women had been chained outside for hours when the men finally returned to the ship. The women were brought back to the hold to eat. Jennifer felt hot and sticky from sitting in the sun for most of the day. She wondered why they had bothered to give them clean clothes if the women were still going to be held below. Her clothes were soaked with sweat, and the temperature in the hold must have been over one hundred. The hold was stuffy, making it difficult to breathe, especially for a couple of the women who had been suffering with shortness of breath all day.

The *Moonlight* flying her pirate flag arrived in the Barbary States' chief slaving port around midnight. Timothy had decided to go to some local taverns. The *Timbtu Inn* was a favorite among the pirates and slavers. It was a large establishment located closely to the open market. Timothy walked through the door with his hand resting on the hilt of his ivory carved sword. Many of the people stared at him, knowing him instantly. The place grew quiet as Timothy walked across the room to the bar and ordered a rum. He turned to face the crowd of people. Those who were still staring at him put their heads down. Timothy's golden eyes scanned the room; leaning against the bar, he guzzled the rum. A woman approached him, "Buy a lady a drink?"

Timothy grinned, "Only if the lady can supply me with some information."

She looked him over, wondering what kind of information he wanted, "Very well, I'll have a rum toddy." She sat aside of Timothy at the bar.

"Do you know if any slavers have come into port within the last seventy-two hours?" questioned Timothy.

She sipped her drink, wondering why the most feared pirate on the waters was interested in slavers, so she asked him outright, "Why are you interested in slavers?"

His eyes glared at her, "Just answer the question."

"Yes, some slave ships have come in."

"Have any of the women been sold yet?"

"Some yesterday," she replied.

Timothy looked at the woman, "Were any of them very young, about seventeen, with green eyes and auburn hair?"

"No, sir, yesterday they sold all women with either black or blonde hair."

Timothy pressed again, "Are there any other women to be sold?"

"Tomorrow, in the square, women from three separate ships will be sold. I don't know the time."

Reaching into his pocket, Timothy handed her two gold pieces, "Thank you for the information."

"Would you like to come upstairs?"

"I'm afraid not, I have some important matters to take care of."

"Maybe I'm not your type?"

"It has nothing to do with types, I think the gold pieces will take care of your time." Timothy rose from his seat and left the *Timbtu Inn*. The men and women stared at him; it had been a long time since Tim the Bloodthirsty was in Morocco, approximately eight years, in fact. Timothy walked through the streets and down to the docks. He walked for a long time looking at the various ships. So many of them could be slavers; it was too dangerous to board any of the ships tonight. As he continued strolling, his attention turned to a clipper ship similar to his own; he rubbed his eyes; he couldn't be seeing the *Sea Witch*. Memories flooded his mind of Season; he began to run towards the ship. His mind whirled in excitement as he began to go up the gangplank. He was stopped at the top by a woman he had never seen before; she said nothing but held him at sword point, "I'd like to see your Captain."

"What for?" the sword did not move from his stomach.

"I'm a personal friend. I knew her a long time ago," replied Timothy.

"What's your name?"

"Captain Bloodthirsty, Captain Timothy Bloodthirsty."

The woman's eyebrows raised; apparently, she recognized the name, she lowered her sword from his midsection, "Follow me, Captain." Timothy could have shown himself the way to Season's cabin, but he decided it would be best if he was announced. The woman led him through the dark ship towards the cabin he had known like the back of his hand. She knocked on the door, "Excuse me Cap'n, but a Captain Bloodthirsty would like to see you." The door opened slowly and a woman motioned for him to come into the cabin.

"Where's Season?" Timothy asked, bewildered.

The new Captain thought, Season had been right, the man was a sight to behold from the broad shoulders to the tapering of his waist and the piercing yellow eyes, "Captain, you're everything she said you would be; she told me that someday you would return."

Timothy's gold flecked eyes darted around the cabin; the maps he had drawn for Season were still hanging on the walls as well as the charts. The cabin itself had not changed at all except Season was not here; he felt strange being in the cabin without her; he looked at the tall blonde woman, "Where is Season, and who are you?"

"I'm Yvonne, I'm the Captain of this ship," she did not want to tell him but she knew she had to, "I'm sorry to tell you Cap'n, but Season is dead."

"Dead?" His throat suddenly became dry as he sat down at the small table, "How?"

Yvonne knew this day would come, but she had always thought it would happen in Java, not in the Barbary States, "In childbirth."

"Childbirth! Are you telling me that Season got married? When?"

"She never married. I was with her and she asked me to take over the ship. She knew she was dying," responded Yvonne, her voice cracking.

"But I thought you had married?"

"I did, but my husband ran off with another woman a couple of months before Season gave birth, so of course, I agreed."

Timothy wondered how old the child was and where it was, "What about the child?"

"The child is in Java," replied Yvonne.

"With the father?" questioned Timothy.

"No, with some friends of Season's." Yvonne wondered about this tall, lion-eyed man. Would he be a good father? A child really should not be brought up by a man who was a pirate. Of course, the child's mother was a pirate, too. She had promised Season if the captain ever returned, she would tell him about his son. "Captain Bloodthirsty, I…."

He interrupted her, "Please call me Tim."

"I think we had better talk about Season's child. She made me promise to tell you everything that happened to her after you saved her life. Can I get you a drink?"

"No, what did Season want me to know?" He had a gut feeling that Yvonne was about to tell him that he was the father of Season's child, but that was a little over seven years ago. Why wasn't he told before?

"I always thought that we would be sitting in the *Blue Dolphin* in Java when I told you this; I would have never dreamed it would be aboard the *Sea Witch* and in the Barbary States of all places." She paused not knowing how to tell him. If she was Season, she would bluntly tell him, and that is what she should do. She stared across the table at him, "The child is yours."

Timothy felt as if the chair had been pulled from under him. Season, beautiful Season, had died giving birth to his child. Yvonne had moved from the table to pour Timothy a drink. She set the rum down in front of him. He took the glass and gulped the liquid; his eyes searched Yvonne's face for more information. Yvonne, sensing his thoughts, walked to the desk, opened the third drawer and handed Timothy a letter, yellow with age. "Season wanted me to give this to you. I think it will explain everything that you want to know." Timothy took the letter from Yvonne's hand, "I'll let you read it alone. Please feel free to make yourself comfortable."

"Thank you." He watched Yvonne leave the cabin; his hands trembled slightly as he removed the letter from the envelope, '*Tim, by now Yvonne has told you that you are the father of my son. It took most of my strength to write this letter, you see I know I'm dying. I overheard the doctor say that I am fading fast.*' Timothy's eyes began to water as he continued to read, '*Our child was conceived the last time we spent together. I searched the Java waters and the Barbary Coast. I really wanted to tell you, but I couldn't find you. I named our beautiful little boy, Lion. I'm sure you are wondering why such a strange name. When I named the child, I named him for your eyes. Timothy, you have the golden eyes of a lion and so does your son. I want you to take him with you, teach him about the sea, ships and navigation. I want you to tell him who I was and make him understand the lifestyle I led. I'll say goodbye now, I love you because you are the only man I've ever trusted; please take good care of our son. All my love, Season.'* Timothy folded the note neatly and put it in his pocket. He poured himself another rum which he downed faster than the first. He went looking for Yvonne and found her standing at the rail of the ship. Her hair was highlighted by the full moon, she whirled around when she heard him approaching. He smiled brilliantly, "Did I scare you?"

Yvonne wished she had known this man when Season had, "No, you've read the letter?"

He joined her at the rail as they both looked out into the sea, "Yes." They were silent for a couple of minutes, "Were you with her...." His voice faded as he could not bring himself to finish the sentence.

"Yes, I was with her continuously the last two days of her life," replied Yvonne, somberly.

Timothy turned to face Yvonne, "Was she in much pain?"

Yvonne bit her lip, "That's hard to say, Captain; she never once complained of any pain. The fever made her delirious. I think she was in some pain. I could see it in her eyes."

Timothy ran his hand through his jet-black hair, looked towards the ocean and back to Yvonne, "Did she talk to you at all during her lucid moments?"

"She talked mostly of you. She told me how you had helped her, how you saved her life when Rafael was going to kill her." Yvonne's mind traveled back to those two days as she continued, "Sometimes she would just call out your name or Lion's. She would say, I love you Tim, and then she would cry." Yvonne looked at Timothy, she could see the pain in his eyes, "Perhaps, I shouldn't continue."

"No, please, I want to know," Timothy said softly.

"She said that you would come back to Java, that you loved it there. She said that you were the only man she ever trusted and that you could be trusted by anyone. The last twelve hours she just mumbled." Timothy looked out into the ocean; he could see Season's face etched in the water. In a couple of hours, it would be dawn; he had to go back to his ship to prepare his men. Yvonne interrupted his thoughts, "The *Sea Witch* will be pulling out of port tomorrow evening. We will be going back to Java; will you be coming with us?"

"I have to," Timothy paused, why not tell Yvonne what he was doing in the Barbary States. Perhaps she and her crew could help. "Would you be interested in helping me either buy or kidnap a woman?"

"Buy or kidnap a woman! I think you had better explain." Yvonne couldn't fathom that he would need to do either, as she believed women would fall at his feet.

Timothy filled Yvonne in on his life since leaving Java. He told her his real name, how he got into piracy and his shipping endeavors in Newport. He told her about Jennifer, how she had been kidnapped, how he had raped the woman he was engaged to in order to get information about Jennifer. Yvonne noticed that when he spoke of this woman, Jennifer, his eyes blazed with love and passion, yet she did not think that the Captain realized his love for the woman. He told her that he did not know how much she had been sold for, but he would attempt to buy her back, and if he couldn't buy her, he would steal her back. He asked Yvonne if the *Sea Witch* would be willing to back the *Moonlight* in case of trouble. Yvonne agreed without hesitation. She even planned to back him in the marketplace, although she did not tell him so. Timothy left the *Sea Witch* and returned to the *Moonlight*.

The sun rose brilliantly, surrounded by a red and purple haze. Timothy stood at the rail of his ship waiting patiently for the men that would accompany him to the marketplace. He stared out into the ocean and at the hot sun, thinking of last evening. George, Ben and Caleb approached Timothy, "Cap'n, are you are ready to leave?' questioned Ben.

Timothy turned to face his three men, "Yes." The four men left the ship, each man knew his job as they mingled through the crowd that had gathered in the marketplace. Timothy's height made him tower over most of the people in the crowd, and his presence at a slave auction caused a considerable amount of whispering and chaos in the mob. Women from the first ship were brought to the block in the middle of the marketplace. Timothy looked each woman over, no Jennifer. The first ship had forty women to sell, which took two hours. Timothy saw Yvonne out of the corner of his eye; making his way through the crowd, he stood beside her. The sun beat down on them for another two hours, as thirty women from the second ship were sold. Yvonne wiped her face with the back of her hand. Timothy felt the sweat trickle down his neck as he waited patiently for the women of the third ship to be brought to the center of the marketplace. As the women were being brought to the block, Timothy looked them over, a woman who bore a striking resemblance to Jennifer was with this set of twelve women. He could not tell if it was her, for her face was covered by her long auburn hair. The bidding on this particular group of women began. As Timothy pushed his way closer; he could not take his eyes from the woman with the auburn hair as he walked. He stopped as he reached the edge of the crowd. The auburn-haired woman was the last woman to be sold. She was dragged to the platform and told to take her clothes off, she refused, and she was whipped.

Jennifer could not have been more humiliated than she was, but she was determined not to cry or scream when they whipped her, tearing her clothes. The bidding had begun on her, and two men were bidding against each other. The stakes were getting higher, and there was something familiar in one of the voices. Jennifer did not know why but the crowd had become quiet, enabling her to listen to the voices of the two men. Slowly, she lifted her head; the crowd gasped at her beauty as her green eyes locked with the golden eyes of the man standing before her. She drew in her breath; Timothy Lockwood stood before her dressed as he was the last time that she saw him and he was bidding on her. Jennifer's mind began to wander; what if she wasn't bought by Captain Lockwood? The realization of what had happened to her these last few weeks finally struck her.

Yvonne looked at the young woman on the block; she was extraordinarily beautiful. She now understood why Timothy had been so anxious to find her; her beauty was astounding. The bidding continued, and the stakes went higher and higher. Timothy upped the bidding by five thousand pounds; the man bidding against Timothy could not afford the price and said nothing. The man in charge of the selling announced, "Sold to Captain Bloodthirsty." Jennifer's eyes widened as she stared at Timothy. Captain Bloodthirsty was the most feared pirate of the waters. A man unchained Jennifer as Timothy paid another man, then two men that Jennifer had never seen before took her by the arm and led her out of the square towards the docks. Timothy started to make his way through the crowd as Yvonne sought him out, "Captain," Timothy stopped and turned to see Yvonne, "Timothy, what you did in there was dangerous."

"I know. The locals don't like pirates buying the women meant for the Barbary States, especially ones that tried to get slavery abolished." He smiled thinking how it had been a strange turn of events.

Yvonne grabbed him by the arm, "Listen to me, I suggest that you and your men pull out of port within the next hour."

"Why?"

"I overheard some men discussing the fact that you deliberately added the five thousand pounds so that their master could not buy the woman. They are planning to cause you some trouble and steal the woman."

"They think they can steal her from my ship, do they?" Timothy grinned, "Well, they will have to put up a tremendous fight."

Yvonne shook her head as they neared her ship, "Pull out now, Tim; remember, you must go to your son in Java."

His eyes took on a saddened look, "You're right, I can't take the chance."

"The *Sea Witch* will back you up in case of trouble; you have my word."

They parted, each going to their respective ships. Timothy gave orders to his men that they would be pulling out within an hour and that the *Sea Witch* would be supporting them on their voyage to Java.

Jennifer had been put in Timothy's cabin by the two men. Gideon had appeared moments later with hot water, fresh towels and clothes. As he filled the tub, he said, "The Captain said to enjoy your bath. There are fresh towels on the bunk and clothes. I'm afraid that they are men's clothes, but that is all we have at the moment, miss." Gideon left the room. Jennifer walked to the bunk and picked up the towels to move them closer to the tub. She winced in pain as she began to remove her clothing. The white blouse was torn and stained with perspiration and blood. The blood had become crusty, the beginnings of scabs. Jennifer found the soap in the small cabinet near the base of the bed. She stepped into the tepid water and began to lather her body, scrubbing it until it was raw. She then began to wash the long auburn hair and rinse it with a pail of water that had been left aside of the tub. Stepping out of the tub, she dried her body with the towel and wrapped another towel around her long hair. She then proceeded to dress in the clothes that had been left for her. The arms of the shirt where much too long and the waist of the trousers too big. Jennifer unwrapped her hair and let it hang loosely down her back as she curled up on the large bunk. Sleep came quickly as she dreamed of the tall Captain.

Gideon returned to the Captain's cabin a few hours later with Jennifer's meal. He knocked lightly and did not hear a reply, he knocked again and still no reply. Slowly, he opened the door and peered in; Jennifer was asleep on the bunk. He set the tray down on the table and woke Jennifer. "I'm sorry to disturb you, miss, but your dinner is ready."

Jennifer moaned and stretched as she rose from the bunk. Gideon wanted to laugh, for she was a funny sight. "What time is it?" she yawned.

"Close to six o'clock, miss."

She sat at the small table as Gideon uncovered the food. The smell overwhelmed her, it had been weeks since she had eaten anything that had smelled so good, "Won't the Captain be eating with me?"

"No, miss. The Captain says you are to make yourself at home in his cabin, and you are not to go topside for at least twenty-four hours."

"But why?" questioned Jennifer.

"It would be dangerous at this time considering we are still in waters inhabited by pirates."

"Pirates. Is your Captain not a pirate?" Jennifer said sarcastically.

Gideon said nothing except, "Is there anything else I can get for you?"

Jennifer's emerald eyes pierced him, "Yes, I want some salve for my injuries, and I want to go topside to get some fresh air."

"You cannot go topside. I'll get the salve." Gideon left the room thinking that the Captain was going to have his hands full with this young woman.

Jennifer paced around the room for the next ten minutes. She began putting the pieces together, Timothy Lockwood knew so much about pirates because he was a pirate! Gideon reappeared and left the salve. Jennifer removed her shirt, applying the medicine to the welts on her shoulders. She winced as she rubbed the ointment into her bruises. Putting the shirt on again, she was determined to go topside after she ate the food that had been prepared for her; sitting down at the table, she scanned the food. Everything looked so good that she did not know where to start. The veal looked exceptional as well as the vegetables and potatoes. She filled her plate with food, eating until she felt overstuffed. When she finished, she piled the dishes onto the tray. Jennifer then walked around the cabin touching the wood and looking at the books. Going to the desk, she began to look at the map that was laying there in plain view. It appeared that a course for the ship to follow was plotted on the map. The realization that she was not being taken back to London frightened her; she followed the lines with her index finger; they were going to Java. Java, another pirate haven; she sat in the chair and stared at the map. Her hand rested on a neatly folded piece of paper. She picked up the paper and opened it, her eyes scanned the first sentences, *'Tim, by now Yvonne has told you that you are the father of my son....'* Jennifer recognized the name Yvonne; she was the lady pirate he had told her and Stefan about the day on the *Moonlight*. Her eyes scanned the remainder of the letter; it was signed by Season. Jennifer folded the letter and placed it back on the desk; perhaps she shouldn't have read it, for it was none of her business. She could not take her mind off the letter; the contents upset her, and she wondered if he loved this woman, Season? She walked to the door of the cabin and tried to get out, but the door was locked. Going back to the bunk, she lay down, trying desperately to put her life in order. Her immediate thoughts were of her present situation; she wondered if the Captain was planning to take her home to London at all.

CHAPTER ELEVEN

Timothy went to his cabin in the wee morning hours after he was certain that he'd have no problems from the Barbary Coast. He found Jennifer sound asleep in his bunk. His senses were dull due to his lack of sleep in the last few days. He stripped to the waist and looked at Jennifer; how he wished he could have had his own bed. He poured himself a large glass of rum and drank slowly, savoring every sip of the liquid. Taking a blanket from the trunk at the edge of the bunk, he sat in the overstuffed chair. He thought about what she must have been through these last weeks aboard a slaver. The chair, which was usually comfortable, was now the most uncomfortable chair in the room. He could not stand it any longer; he had to sleep in that bed. Jennifer was sleeping at the far side near the wall. The bed certainly was big enough for the both of them. Timothy slowly sat down on the edge of the bed so not to wake Jennifer; he laid down and covered himself with a blanket.

Jennifer woke several hours later facing the wall; yawning, she turned to find Timothy asleep aside of her; she felt herself flush a brilliant red. She stared at his muscular arms and the massive hairy chest as it rose and fell, realizing that if she moved, she would wake him. Timothy turned; his arm landing on her long hair. Holding her breath, she tried to move her hair from under his arm. The blanket had revealed more of his chest to her; causing her to become alarmed. She wondering if he had anything on at all. Suddenly, he murmured in his sleep; she had no idea what he said. Jennifer wanted to reach out and touch him but knew that he might wake if she did, thus causing him to get the wrong idea. She thought to herself that she wanted him to touch her; she wanted to know what it was like being loved by a man; she wanted to know what it was like being loved by this particular man. Perhaps she wasn't any better than the local trollops of London, but ever since she saw this man, she had set him as her goal. Imagine, setting a person as a goal; he stirred again, startling her. Jennifer closed her eyes, pretending to be asleep. Timothy opened his eyes and found himself facing Jennifer. God, she was beautiful. She lay there so peacefully. The golden eyes searched her face; she had a tiny nose, long reddish-brown eyelashes and a full, sensuous mouth. A mouth made to share a man's kisses. He had the urge to lean over and kiss that mouth, but he didn't want to incur her wrath. Jennifer knew instinctively that he was awake, his breathing had changed, and she could feel his eyes on her. Suddenly, the bed creaked, and she heard Timothy sigh as he got up from the bunk.

Timothy stared at Jennifer, he wanted her. He had gotten up from the bunk because he could smell her fresh clean skin, and he couldn't bear not touching her or feeling her smooth skin. He knew he would have to wait, for she was a lady and should be treated as one. He promised himself that he would not force her to succumb to his desires. He went to the chair where he had left his shirt and began putting it on. Jennifer opened her eyes for a moment as she stared at his back. Timothy turned to face Jennifer, "I see you are awake."

"Yes." She answered softly.

Timothy found himself in awe of her beauty, "Would you like some breakfast?"

She hadn't moved from the bed, "Yes."

"Is that all you can say is yes? I can see that you're going to be wonderful to talk to in the morning," remarked Tim.

"Why did you buy me?" She asked ignoring what he had just said.

Timothy finished buttoning his shirt, "I promised your father that I would bring you back."

"Would you have come after me if you hadn't promised my father?"

"Perhaps." Of course, I would have come after you my little one he thought. He walked to the door and rang the bell, Gideon appeared seconds later, "Bring me and Miss Weatherly some breakfast." The cabin boy nodded and went on his way.

Throwing the blankets off, Jennifer stretched and swung her legs from the bed. Timothy looked at her and laughed, her clothes hung from her body, "What's so funny?"

He grinned, "You."

She ignored him, "How long will it be before we reach London?"

"We're not going to London; we're going to Java."

"Java? Why are we going to Java?"

"I have some personal things that I have to take care of in Java, which can't wait."

Jennifer looked at him, "Don't you have to return to London for your wedding?"

"As far as I'm concerned, there will be no wedding when I return to London."

Jennifer felt as if she wanted to burst. Something evidently happened between him and Laura Harrington so that there would not be a wedding; she smiled. Her eyes locked with his for a moment, neither wanting to look away, "Will I be getting my own cabin?"

Timothy's eyes were blank, "No, you will be staying in my cabin for the duration of the trip."

"Really, Captain, a lady needs her privacy."

Before he could answer, Gideon appeared with a tray of food, "Captain, your breakfast." He quickly set the food on the table and left.

Timothy pulled out the chair for Jennifer and then seated himself across from her. He began eating and noticed that Jennifer wasn't eating, "Aren't you hungry?"

"You're a pirate; that's why you knew so much about them. You're one of them."

Timothy put down his fork and stared at her; the coldness of his eyes alarmed her, "Yes, I am, Jennifer, are you surprised?"

"Yes, I thought you were a respectable person and to find out that you're not...."

"Ah, but I am respectable when I am in London, Paris, or Newport. People know me as Captain Timothy Lockwood, successful merchant and businessman."

"But I heard the slave dealer call you Captain Bloodthirsty, who are you really?"

Timothy said, "I'm him, too."

"Tell me Captain Bloodthirsty, are you really planning to return me to my family, or are you planning to use me for your own means?"

His eyes twinkled, "In answer to the first part of your question, the decision of going back to your family will be entirely yours when we reach London. You may find that you won't want to return to the respectable life once you have tasted that of a pirate. In answer to the second part of the question, I will not use you for my own means, unless of course you consent."

The emerald eyes flamed with anger and burned with tears, "How dare you think that I will consent to anything you have planned."

"By the time we reach Java, I think you may change your mind. Now, finish eating."

"Never!" She was lying to herself, and she knew it, but she was determined not to give into this man's whims although the thought of the Captain loving her excited and frightened her at the same time. She picked at the food on her plate while Timothy wolfed his down.

Timothy thought about the beauty sitting across the table from him; he longed to touch and stroke her long hair. Would she ever consent to make love with him? Tim rarely waited for a woman to consent to making love with him; he usually took what he wanted, but she was different. Given time, she would probably want him as much as he wanted her; the hard part would be the waiting. But she would probably be well worth the wait, "Would you like to go for a walk around the ship?"

"In these clothes?" Jennifer asked.

"Well, you either go in those clothes or no clothes, you have a choice," replied Timothy, smirking.

"Some choice, but I'm dying to get some fresh air."

"Good." Standing up, he extended his hand for her to take, and led her out of the cabin.

Jennifer could smell the salt air that surrounded her from the moment they left the stuffy cabin. The men stared at the woman; even in men's clothes, she was a beauty. Some of the men snickered, knowing full well that she was sharing the Captain's cabin. One cold stare from Timothy, and they knew that they had overstepped their bounds. They distinctly got the message that she belonged to the Captain, and if anyone touched her, they would pay with their life. George noticed that the Captain seemed much happier since they left the Barbary Coast. Timothy led her to the rail of the ship; the two of them had not spoken to each other since they left the cabin. He had decided that she should be the first to speak, and she was, "For the first time in my life I realized how large the world really was when I was taken to the Barbary Coast and how mean people can really be." Her voice drifted off.

She was innocent. "I'm sorry that you had to go through something so painful. I just wish I could have been able to get to you before you left London," replied Timothy.

Jennifer, for the first time, realized that the tall Captain, a man who was known by many as a pirate, could care about something; that he was not the ruthless person she thought him to be, "Geoffrey Lyndon will pay for this, my father will have him hanged."

"Geoffrey Lyndon already paid for this," his voice was hard and cold; the hatred he felt for the man could not compare with any other hatred he had ever felt.

Jennifer looked at him, "What do you mean?" Is he in jail?"

Timothy's face was expressionless, "He's dead."

"Dead? How?"

"It really doesn't matter how; the point is that he will no longer cause you any anguish or any other woman any problems. Come, let me take you back to the cabin." He led her back to the cabin, "It is important that you don't leave the cabin, unless I escort you, no one else, do you understand?"

"Yes." He left her in the cabin to wonder about the conversation that had transpired between them on the deck. Who could have killed Lyndon? Perhaps it had been her father or even the Captain. Staying inside the cabin for hours on end would be torture, but she had promised to remain inside. Looking around, she decided that she would busy herself with some kind of chore. The clothes she had been wearing when she was brought to the ship lay neatly on a chair. She looked around for a needle and thread. The least she could do was repair the blouse and then wash the clothes out. Ringing the bell, she summoned Gideon, "Would it be possible to get a needle and thread, a piece of rope and some hot water."

"Yes miss, the Captain said you are to get anything you want."

"Thank you," replied Jennifer.

Gideon returned several minutes later with the materials she requested. She sat down on the bed and began to sew the tears in the blouse. Later, she strung a rope across two chairs for a clothes line and then washed both the skirt and the blouse, hanging them out to dry. Pleased with her handiwork, she began to look around the room for something else to occupy her time. She began to dust some of the furniture and make-up the room so that it had more of a woman's touch. She rearranged the books so they looked more orderly and then cleaned the desk.

Timothy returned hours later carrying a large roll of cloth, "Gideon told me that you asked for a needle and thread. This material has been sitting in the hold now for months, I thought maybe you would like it."

"Like it, I love it!" She threw her arms around him; their eyes met, and an awkward silence grew. Slowly, Timothy bent towards her, kissing her mouth. The material had fallen from his hands as he lifted her in his arms and carried her to the bed. He needed a woman and he'd be damned if he'd wait for this one. He had never waited for a woman in his life. Jennifer knew her feet no longer touched the ground, and she realized that she was being laid ever so gently on the bunk. She had been kissed before, but never like this; she felt as if she was melting in his arms. Her hands went to his hair, and his hands were on the sides of her face. His tongue searched the inside of her mouth, a moan escaping from her lips. Suddenly, he stopped, he stared at her; the emerald eyes were telling him to continue; her lips were parted and moist. He knew she was ripe for the taking yet had not anticipated that she would be giving herself to him this soon. Jennifer searched his face for the reason he had stopped; she wanted him to continue; she was experiencing a feeling that she had never experienced before in her life, and she liked it.

Timothy looked at her, in a husky voice he said, "I'm sorry, I..."

Jennifer cut him off, "Don't say you're sorry unless you don't finish what you started."

He looked at her in amazement; hours before, she said she would never give in to him, now she was telling him to continue, "Do you really want me to continue?"

"Yes."

His lust had subsided for the moment, he smiled, "I had better lock the door." Rising from the bed he went to the door and bolted it. When he turned around, he noticed that she had slid between the sheets. He went to the lamp and blew out the flame. The cabin had become completely dark. He returned to the bed removing his clothes, Jennifer had been removing hers also. He slid between the sheets and reached out for her; pulling her to him, his lips found hers. He kissed her long and hard, his tongue playing with hers; his hands traced the curves of her body. Her skin was so soft to touch; he ran his hands back up her body running his thumbs over her nipples, teasing them to greater heights. She could feel his strong muscular arms encircle her, his rigid member pressing against her stomach. She drew in her breathe. Her mind screamed that this was wrong. He moved from her breasts to her mouth kissing her. Timothy knew that it was important that she have as much pleasure in the act as he would have; he slowly descended on her body, nudging her legs open with his knee. He covered her mouth with his own to stifle her scream as he entered her. Suddenly her fear of what was happening caused her to try to pull away, to throw him off of her and instead she involuntarily arched her hips to his causing herself undo pain.

Jennifer felt as if her insides had been torn open, the tears slowly trickled down her face. Timothy began to move slowly at first so not to hurt her again. Gradually his thrusts quickened and her body matched his fervor. She arched her back, grinding her hips toward his, wanting more and more of him. Sweat covered both of their bodies as their lovemaking continued. Jennifer had never experienced anything like she felt at that moment. Suddenly, she moaned as a burst of energy inside of her drove her to arch her back and drive wildly against him, experiencing her first orgasm. At the moment she felt he had unleashed a passion within her, a thirst for him; she wanted him to never stop. Seconds later, his body convulsed as he exploded inside of her. Holding her to him, he rolled over, and Jennifer found herself laying on top of him. Both were breathing heavily, gasping for air, neither saying a word. Timothy had never experienced a virgin before who had matched his own intensity for the first time. Jennifer was a passionate woman, and now she would belong completely to him, for he had made her his. Their breathing returned to normal as they lay arm in arm, Jennifer dozing off from exhaustion bathed in perspiration and lust.

Timothy disengaged himself from her and slid out of the bed. He dressed quickly and went topside. He remained topside for several hours instructing his men and ordering a large meal for himself and Jennifer. He wanted to adorn her with clothes fit for a queen. He returned to the cabin and found her still asleep; he picked up the material and put it on the chair. She was sleeping on her stomach and he could see the broken skin from where the whip had struck her. Getting the salve from the table, he began to gently apply it to her wounds. She stirred, "Stay still while I put this salve on, I don't want these wounds to get infected." He continued applying the salve.

Jennifer turned over, her eyes meeting his as he continued to apply the salve to her shoulders, "Thank you."

Timothy got up from the edge of the bed and walked to the desk. Jennifer watched him open one of the drawers and remove a box. He removed something from the box and placed it back in the drawer before walking back to the bed, "Take this, I want you to have it." He placed a ring in her hand, she stared at the large emerald surrounded by diamonds, "It was my mother's. I want you to have it."

Jennifer placed the ring on her finger, "Thank you."

"I chose that one because it matches your eyes. You had better get dressed, I have arranged for a special dinner, and the food should be coming soon."

"Would you leave the room, so I can get dressed."

He laughed, "Really, Jenny? Not even three hours ago you and I were involved in the most intimate relationship a man and woman could experience, and now you want me to leave the room while you dress."

She looked at him defiantly, tilting her chin upward, "Yes."

"I've seen naked women before; you must get over this privacy thing. The two of us are sharing the cabin, besides I know what you feel like, and I promise I won't touch you."

"Captain, please leave the room."

She called him Captain, which infuriated him, "Look Jennifer, the food will be here any second, and if you're sitting in bed when Gideon comes, the whole ship will know that you and I slept together." Jennifer tugged at the sheet until she wrapped it around herself as she picked up her clothes and began dressing. Timothy's eyes went to the blood-stained sheets and thought about what had transpired between them. He was happy to know what had transpired between them. He was happy to know he had been her first lover, and he'd be sure that he was her last; he was determined to make her his forever. Jennifer finished dressing and quickly made up the bed moments before Gideon appeared with the food.

CHAPTER TWELVE

Jennifer stood at the rail of the *Moonlight*, beside Timothy after they had spent the morning fencing. He had convinced her that she should learn the fine art of using a rapier in case she ever had to protect herself. Timothy pointed to an island in the distance, "That is Java, our destination."

"How long will it be before we reach the island?"

"Approximately twenty-four or so hours."

She touched his arm, "Tim you still haven't told me why we are going to Java."

"I have some personal business that I must attend to; it is of no importance to you and there is no need for you to worry yourself about it."

Jennifer knew he wasn't ready to tell her yet; she wasn't sure if he would ever be ready, "What is Java like?"

Tim's eyes had a faraway look in them, "Java is beautiful. It is part of a large network of islands. There are coconut palm trees, bamboo, Jati..." his voice drifted as his mind turned to Season and his son, Lion.

"What's Jati?" questioned Jennifer, bringing him back to the present.

He looked at her, "Jati is a teak wood. The natives make some beautiful furniture out of it."

"Why didn't you just say teak wood?"

"Jenny, if you are going to Java, you must talk like the Javanese. Now, did you ever eat a mango?"

"No, I never ate one, but I've heard of them."

"Wait until you taste one. I bet you've never tasted anything like it."

"What other kinds of food do they have?"

"Bananas, coconuts, rice, sweet potatoes, soybeans, fish and other things. We can't really stay here as long as I would like."

"Why?"

"Well, first and foremost, I promised your father that I'd have you back within six months and secondly, if we get caught in monsoon season, we may not be able to leave the island for quite some time." Jennifer was quiet; she wondered if he would ever tell her about his son or the real truth about Season. Timothy's eyes stared out into the vast ocean, the last time he had sailed these seas he had conceived a child, now he was going back to claim that child. He wondered if the boy looked more like Season or him; after all, he knew the child had his eyes.

Jennifer also stared into the ocean, thinking back to when she was on the slaver. How she had vowed to make the man who bought her pay. She looked at Tim. She could never be that vindictive or mean to him, although she knew she had every right. He had taken from her the one possession that would have ensured her a happy and prosperous marriage, her virginity. She scolded herself for the thought; he didn't take it; she gave it to him. He never said anything about marriage, and Jennifer had no idea whether he intended to marry her or not. She did know that he had whet her sexual appetite and knew that she could not live without a man.

Timothy gazed into the ocean debating whether or not he should tell Jennifer about Lion before they reached Java. If he asked her to marry him after she knew the truth about his son, she may not want to marry him. He turned to her, "Jenny, let's go back into the cabin."

"Tim, it's nice and cool here, please let's stay here awhile longer."

He smiled, "I have some things to discuss with you, and I'd much rather discuss them in the cabin." Jennifer wondered if he decided to tell her about his son. Once inside the cabin, he let go of her hand, "Jenny, please sit down."

She sat at the table and Tim sat across from her. She noticed that his face had become serious, "What's wrong? You look so solemn."

He reached across the table and took her hand, "We need to have an important talk. I realized that you're only seventeen and that I'm older, not too much, but I am. I've been involved with a variety of women; I must admit to you that there has been at least one in every port that I can count on to serve me, if I need them."

Jennifer's eyes became glazed with tears, "Why are you telling me this?"

"Please listen; it's important to me. I've never been in love with any of them. I always promised myself that no woman would ever totally possess me until now." He squeezed her hand. "This is hard for me to say, but ever since the first time I saw you on the docks I couldn't put you out of my mind. Then, when it was my good fortune to meet you on my ship and form a comradeship, I knew then that I wanted you. In fact, if Geoffrey hadn't kidnapped you, I would have." Jennifer stared at him; what was he trying to say? Timothy continued, "Jennifer, what I'm trying to say is that I killed for you and would again if any man other than I tried to touch you." She was shocked. The pieces fit together. Timothy Lockwood had killed Geoffrey Lyndon because of her, "I want you. I want us to be married."

"Married, but…" her voice drifted off. The man she had set as her goal had asked her to marry him. Could she possibly marry him knowing that there were many women who had shared his bed, that he had killed a man, was a pirate and God knows what else?

"Jenny, I couldn't stand another man making love to you. I want you to be mine forever, throughout eternity." His eyes became warm and tender.

Jennifer rose from the table, walked to where Timothy was sitting and knelt at his feet. Looking up at him she searched the topaz eyes for some sign of love, but they were empty. He never said he loved her; he wanted her, but was that the same: Jennifer ran her tongue over her lips, "I love you Tim; I think I have ever since I saw you on the docks," she paused, thinking that if she married him, at least society wouldn't look upon her as a fallen woman, "and yes, I will marry you whether you are a pirate or a merchant, rich or poor."

Timothy bent over, taking her face in his hands and began kissing her, leaning over too far as he lost his balance, and the two of them crashed to the floor entwined in each other arms. Laughter was mixed with tears; Jennifer had never been happier in her life. Timothy scooped her up in his arms, put her on the large bunk and went to the desk to get the box from which he had taken the emerald and diamond ring. He handed her the box, "These are for you, Miss Weatherly."

Jennifer looked at him, her fingers felt numb. She slowly opened the box, gasping at the contents. It was filled with jewels, bracelets, necklaces, rings, broaches, diamonds, emeralds, rubies and pearls. "I've never seen such beautiful jewels before."

He smiled, "Just wait, this is only the beginning. When we get to Newport, you will be the envy of every woman. I'll buy you jewels fit for a queen and dresses that you would never imagine. They'll come from the best French designers. The house will be finished by the time we reach Newport, and we'll see it for the first time together. We'll have balls and summer parties, and I'll work at the shipyard for a few hours a day." Jennifer's head began to spin, everything was happening so fast. "And we will fill the house with children. We'll be the best family in Newport."

"Why can't we go back to London now, instead of going to Java." She questioned him, wanting to know if he would tell her about his son.

Timothy rose from the bed and walked across the room turning to face her he said, "I should have told you this before, the reason that we are going to Java is that I have a son, and he lives there."

"You've been married before?" She said, playing along as if she knew nothing of Season and Lion.

"No, I told you, no other woman has ever possessed me the way you do."

"What about the woman who gave birth to this child?"

"She's dead. Remember when I told you and Stefan about the lady pirate named Season?" Jennifer nodded her head, "Well, it really didn't happen the way I said it did. It is true that she vowed her revenge, and she did overtake my ship, but not the way I said. She took it by drugging me while my men were ashore. When I woke, she was in charge of my ship and my men. She wanted me to teach her about navigation and maps because Yvonne, who knew all of that, had gotten married. So, Season needed someone to teach her; it took six months to do so," he paused.

"Please continue."

"Jennifer, it had been a long time since I had a woman and we really didn't have any type of relationship until the last couple of months. When I left, I had no idea that I had sired a child."

"How did you find out?"

"I found out from Yvonne. When I followed you to the Barbary Coast, I went to the *Timbtu Inn,* which is a haven for pirates and slavers. After getting some information, I went for a walk on the docks and saw the *Sea Witch.* The *Sea Witch,* was Season's ship. So, I went aboard and met Yvonne for the first time; she told me about Season and my son, his name is Lion."

"What are you planning on doing with your son? Are you going to take him back to London with us?"

"I want to see him. For the time being, I want him to stay in Java. I don't want him to have the stigma of being a bastard, and I would have a difficult time explaining him to your father."

Jennifer leaned over and hugged him, "You are so sweet. I really think we should take Lion home with us. I'll treat him as if he was my own."

"You can accept everything I've told you without reservations?"

"Yes; I love you Tim." They kissed.

The *Moonlight* docked in Java on a sunny and brutally hot day. The men sprang into action securing the ship. Timothy appeared on deck with Jennifer at his side. Jennifer had wound her long auburn hair into a bun at the nape of her neck. The gangplank was lowered, and Timothy led Jennifer down to the docks. They were met by a tall, blonde woman, "Tim."

"Yvonne, this is Jennifer. Jenny this is Yvonne."

"How do you do, Jennifer?" Yvonne extended her hand.

Shaking Yvonne's hand, Jennifer said, "It's a pleasure to meet you."

Yvonne turned her attention to Tim. "I took the liberty of renting you a suite of rooms at the *Blue Dolphin*."

"Thank you," replied Tim.

"Perhaps Jennifer would like to buy some new dresses; there is a very nice shop on the main street."

Timothy looked at Jennifer, "Maybe we can go later, right now I think the both of us should get settled in and have something to eat. Yvonne, would you meet us for dinner in a couple of hours downstairs in the *Blue Dolphin*?"

"Certainly. Then we can discuss the reason you're here," answered Yvonne.

Yvonne walked Timothy and Jennifer to the *Blue Dolphin Hotel*. The *Blue Dolphin* was not what Jennifer imagined; the suite of rooms was quaint. The first room was a sitting room or meeting room, which would also serve the purpose of a dining room. It was furnished with ornately carved chairs and a large table in the center of the room. Jennifer walked to the first door to her left and opened it; the room was empty, except for a large tub in the center and a chaise lounge in the far corner. The next room was a small bedroom with a single bed; Jennifer smiled to herself. Yvonne certainly had thought of everything. Jennifer was sure that Yvonne knew about her when she rented the rooms. Little did Yvonne know that Timothy and she shared the same bed; closing the door, she went to the next room. This last room was a large bedroom. The bedspread was a pale-yellow print, and the curtains matched. Jennifer walked to the open window; the view was breathtaking; she could see the *Moonlight* from the window. Timothy came up behind her and placed his hands around her waist; she leaned against him and sighed.

"It's beautiful, isn't it?" Tim's eyes glistened as he looked out over the ocean.

Jennifer turned towards him, "You were right; I do like it here."

Timothy's eyes bore into her, "Would you like to take a bath before we meet Yvonne for dinner?"

The idea of hot water against her body was inviting. She smiled, "Yes, that would be nice."

"I'll have them bring up some hot water and you can take your bath while I run a couple of errands," he kissed her.

"Too bad we didn't have time for other things," Jennifer smiled.

"What kind of a woman did I turn you into?" he asked, grinning.

"Your lover for the time being, later, your wife. Now, go get that water sent up here."

"I'll see you in an hour or so." He left the bedroom and went downstairs to order the water.

Tim left the *Blue Dolphin,* heading for the dress shop Yvonne had mentioned. Jennifer would be needing several dresses for her stay in Java, and when they got to France, he would buy her more. Finding the shop was easier than he had expected. He selected several light cotton dresses made for the weather. The first was a scoop neck pale yellow dress, the second was a pretty blue and white print, the third a lavender dress with long sleeves and the final, a dark green with lace trim. The woman who owned the shop was surprised that a man would take so much time and pleasure in selecting women's clothes; it was as if he was buying for a princess, with the way he felt the cloth and pawed over the dresses. Next, he went to the ladies undergarment section and bought several articles of undergarments and some pretty white lacy nightgowns. He then picked out a red satin robe and two shawls, one white and the other green. The young woman who worked at the store packaged everything he had bought, and paid for the merchandise in cash with some extra for her time.

Jennifer had finished with her bath, wishing she didn't have to dress in the dirty old thing she was wearing when she had come into the *Blue Dolphin*. Timothy returned and placed the packages on the table in the sitting room and went to the bedroom. Jenny sat in the chair looking out the window. "Jenny, I have surprise for you."

"You're back!" she exclaimed.

"Yes, come on into the sitting room." He led her by the hand into the sitting room. Jennifer could not believe the number of packages on the table.

"What is all of this?"

"They are for you; open them." His eyes twinkled with delight.

"For me? But I didn't…" She suddenly realized his urgent errand was for her, "You, bought all of this for me?"

"Come on, I'll help you carry them into the bedroom." Picking up the boxes, they carried them into the bedroom putting them on the oversized bed.

Jennifer began to open the boxes, pulling out the undergarments, she squealed with delight; Timothy laughed at her, "I love you, Tim."

He smiled, "There are more."

The next box she opened revealed the pale-yellow dress; putting it against her, she swirled to face Tim who had moved to the chair, "It's lovely." The third box revealed the lavender dress, the fourth the lacy shifts, the fifth the dark green dress, the sixth the blue and white print, the seventh was the shawls and the eighth the red satin robe.

"Do you like them?"

"I love them; which one would you like me to wear first?"

"With a sly smile he answered, "The nightgown and robe."

She blushed, "To dinner?"

He rose from his chair and bent to kiss her, "Who said anything about dinner?"

Catching her breath, she said, "But Yvonne will be waiting."

"Damn, I forgot all about her. We'll come back early; you can't imagine how much I desire you."

"Which dress?" She asked again, trying not to look at him.

He smiled; he knew she wanted him as well. "The yellow; it'll be cooler than the lavender because it has short sleeves. When we get to France, I'll get you some heavier clothes. I'll leave you to dress alone because if I don't, I just may attack you," he said with a grin. He went to the sitting room to wait while she dressed.

Moments later Jennifer appeared, "Would you fasten the back of this dress please." Timothy's fingers moved quickly over the buttons. She turned to face him, "How do I look?"

"Gorgeous. The most beautiful woman in the world."

Jennifer blushed, "Should we go see if Yvonne's ready for dinner?"

"Yes, let's go. It's the dessert I'm looking forward to." Jennifer smiled as he led her downstairs into the main dining room.

Yvonne had been waiting for fifteen minutes, when Timothy and Jennifer appeared. It was evident that someone had taken her suggestion to buy Miss Weatherly some clothes. Timothy and Jennifer walked over to Yvonne, "Tim, Miss Weatherly."

"Please, you must call me Jenny." She looked at Yvonne, who was dressed in a beautiful gown of pale green.

"Very well, I have reserved a table for us in the main dining room." Yvonne led the way and was followed by Timothy and Jennifer.

Once seated, Tim said, "Yvonne, you can say anything you want in front of Jennifer, she knows the whole story."

Yvonne nodded, "Do you want to talk now or order first?"

"Let's order, then we can talk." Tim summoned the waiter, "We'll start off with the roast lamb and the sweet potatoes and rice, then for dessert some fresh fruit and a bottle of wine."

"The name of the family that is taking care of your son is Van der Rhine, they are a very nice family and Roland Van der Rhine worked for Season and now for me. They are a good family, and I give them money from time to time for taking care of Lion."

"Have you told them that I am here?" questioned Timothy.

"No, I haven't had the time and besides, I need to know what you plan to do; are you going to take him with you, or will you come back for him?" asked Yvonne.

"I can't take him back with me now. I have to wait until I marry Jennifer, then I will send for him."

Yvonne was taken back. She had no idea Tim would marry the girl, "The two of you are to be married! My congratulations!"

"Thank-you," replied Jennifer. "Perhaps you can come to the wedding in London." Turning her attention to Tim, Jennifer said, "If Yvonne came to the wedding, she could bring Lion with her, then we could take him to Newport with us."

"That's a possibility, if Yvonne could come to London."

"I could probably come to London, but it would depend on when. If it's during the monsoon season, I wouldn't want to take the chance of coming," replied Yvonne.

Tim replied, "I don't blame you."

"Tim, while we are here maybe we can decide on a month for the wedding. Or at least an approximate time, so we can tell Yvonne," said Jennifer.

Yvonne smiled, "That would be ideal for me."

Tim looked at both women; it appeared that they had joined forces against him, both determined to pin him down to a date, "Alright, Yvonne, Jennifer and I will set a date and let you know before we leave."

After dinner, all three sat and discussed when it would be appropriate to let Tim see his son. Jennifer silently wondered to herself if the child looked like Tim and if eventually, he could accept her as his mother. Their small party disbanded, returning to their respective rooms.

Timothy sat in the sitting room writing a brief letter to his friend and partner, Robert Gray, while Jennifer prepared for bed. Jennifer picked up one of the lacy shifts. Putting it on, she looked in the mirror and blushed. It revealed more than it covered; the sides were slit high to enable freer movement and the neckline plunged deeply; she stood in front of the mirror gaping at herself. Timothy had entered the bedroom, a smile played along his lips. Jennifer turned, blushing, she recognized the smokey look of passion that had come over his eyes. His white teeth gleamed in the darkness of the room as he smiled at her. Her eyes drifted lazily over his tall frame; the white shirt was open exposing the broad, hairy chest to his thin waist. She saw that the muscles in his legs had tensed as he stood there quietly drinking in her beauty. He moved toward her with the grace of panther, stalking its prey; his arms drew her to him, their lips meeting, caressing each other. Lifting her, he placed her on the large bed; not taking his eyes off her, he quickly striped off the white linen shirt and his trousers. Jennifer's eyes widened; she had never seen him this swollen with desire. He came to her, removing the pretty lace shift, so his golden eyes could caress the curves and beauty of her body. Once again, their lips locked in a long passionate kiss, taking both of their breaths away. His arms held her tightly to him, her fingers massaged the upper portion of his back and neck. She moaned in pleasure as she felt him enter her, his hard-lean thighs against hers. He lay still for a couple of moments as if he wanted to savor every second of their coupling. Then he began to move, slowly at first, gradually picking up the speed. Jennifer's hands traveled to the base of his back, clinging to him, enjoying his pleasure as well as her own. Her hips met his in wild abandon, arching as he thrust. She wanted to take his whole being inside of her, to make him part of her as their destiny seemed fit. He whispered to her, urging her to destroy him with her love and in time perhaps she would bind him to her forever. Their bodies were drenched in sweat; Tim did not move from her, making Jennifer realize the full weight of his tall body. His deep golden eyes bore into her emerald ones. Jennifer noticed a softness there, a look she had never seen before yet deep inside she knew she would see that look again. He moved from her, yet still had her locked in his iron grip; he had not taken his eyes from her face. It was as if he was trying to memorize her beauty. "Jennifer, I'm sorry, I took you so quickly. Did I hurt you?"

"No."

"Are you sure? I really am sorry; I was thinking about my need and not yours."

She shook her head, "My love, you could never hurt me physically."

His hand rested on her hip, his fingers drew small circles tickling her, causing her to laugh. Her turquoise eyes danced with merriment and seduction as he pressed her body closer to his, her fingers played with the hair on his chest as he kissed her forehead, she had never known that such joy could exist.

CHAPTER THIRTEEN

Jennifer woke with Timothy's arms around her; he smiled, "Did you sleep well my little one?"

"Yes," she answered quietly, "What are you thinking?"

"I'm thinking that today, I will meet my son for the first time and that I feel guilty."

"Guilty? But why should you feel that way?"

His eyes took on a watered look of being far away, "I feel that I was responsible for killing his mother and eventually I will take him away from the family he has known and accepted and place him into a family that he will have to adjust to again."

Jennifer felt sorry for him; this situation was tearing him apart, "Tim," she said raising up on one elbow, "Let's get married now."

"Now? But I thought you wanted to have a proper wedding?" His eyes searched her face for an answer.

"It really isn't that important; besides it would be much easier taking Lion back to London with us, rather than having to return in a year's time to get him."

"Jenny, I haven't even asked your father for your hand in marriage."

"You haven't asked my father if you could take these other liberties."

He instinctively knew to what she was referring to; maybe it would be best if he married her in Java, considering that James Weatherly appeared not to care for him and possibly feared him after his escapade with Lyndon. He looked at Jennifer, "Are you sure you want to marry me in Java?"

"Yes, more than you can imagine."

"Very well, little one," he said rising out of the bed. Jennifer's eyes scanned the muscled body, hesitating on his strong muscular arms and broad chest. Timothy noticed her stare, "Do you like what you see?" Jennifer blushed, not wanting to speak, "I suggest you get up and get dressed, so we can find someone to marry us before we go to Batavia to collect my son." They were startled by loud knocking on the door. Timothy quickly put his robe on to answer the door, "Yvonne, what are you doing here so early?"

"There has been some trouble in Batavia early this morning."

"What kind of trouble?" his golden eyes became alarmed. Jennifer hearing the commotion donned her robe and went into the sitting room.

"The government of Batavia has been overthrown by a group of men. Women have been raped and murdered as well as all female children. The male children are going to be held for ransom to the fathers."

"Where are the fathers now?"

"It is the hunting season, many of the men are away on the hunt or are here in the city. The group is now pillaging the countryside."

Jennifer felt sick; her sea green eyes showed the fear she felt, "Tim, Lion is in the countryside of Batavia."

"I know." Turning his attention back to Yvonne he said, "Go to the docks and get my men."

"I already have; they are waiting downstairs with the crew of the *Sea Witch*; they are all ready, willing and waiting to save your son."

Jennifer had gone into the bedroom to braid her long hair, so it would fit under the hat and kerchief of a pirate. She looked through the clothes and found the young boy's clothes that she had worn her first days on the ship. She quickly stripped off her robe and donned the clothes; reaching for her rapier, she was startled by Tim, "And where do you think you're going?"

She turned to face him, "I'm coming with you."

"No, you're not; you're going to get the clothes together and go to the *Moonlight* where you will wait until I return," he said as he put on his pants and boots.

"Tim, surely if Yvonne can go, I can."

Putting on his shirt he answered her, "I appreciate your passion in this matter, but Yvonne and her crew are pirates; they can take care of themselves."

"And I cannot?" she questioned.

His eyes filled with anger, "Jennifer, I do not have time for an argument. You will do as I say."

She looked at him defiantly, "And what if I don't do what you want?"

"You'll suffer the consequences, and that is a promise. Now get your things together, and I will send Gideon up here to take you back to the ship." He stalked out of the room.

Damn him, she thought; how dare he tell her to stay put? She paced around the room like a caged animal until Gideon appeared. Jennifer said nothing as he took her to the ship.

Timothy, Yvonne and their respective crews rode through the countryside, finding many houses burned to the ground, women that had been raped, abused, left for dead, as well as crying children filled the countryside. Batavia, once a beautiful city of Java, was left in ruins by the group of mercenaries. Yvonne led the way to the Van der Rhine's home. Roland Van der Rhine died fighting to protect his wife and family. Timothy felt nauseous as he got off his horse and called inside the house, not hearing a sound. Yvonne walked past Timothy into the large country home to find Mrs. Van der Rhine laying slaughtered on the floor of the entryway. Yvonne turned her head from the gruesome sight. Two of the three Van der Rhine daughters were found, raped and murdered in the parlor. Tears ran down Yvonne's face as she turned to Timothy, "Tim, they had another daughter, but she's not on this first floor; I think we should look upstairs."

"What's her name?"

"Ramona."

Timothy shouted orders to his men to search the upstairs of the house; he felt as if had been sent to hell. He had seen destruction before, but never like this. Thank God Jennifer was safely on the *Moonlight*. George, the first mate appeared at the top the staircase, "Cap'n, we've found a young girl and a small child."

Timothy ran up the stairs two at a time, "Are they alive?"

"Yes, both are asleep in a hidden closet."

Timothy followed George into the large bedroom, which was in shambles, "How did you ever find a hidden closet, George?"

"When I came into the room and began to look around, I accidently knocked over that vase of fresh flowers. I heard a noise, and I turned around to see the wall open. Naturally, I went inside and found the two children sound asleep."

Yvonne had entered the room and went into the closet. Waking the two children, she carried Lion out; Timothy could see himself in the small boy, the jet-black hair and golden eyes. His attention focused on the young girl; she was about fourteen with black hair and violet eyes; she would turn into a beautiful young woman. "Ramona, you will be coming back to the *Sea Witch* with me; get your things." The girl moved slowly, numbly to the next room to get her clothes. Yvonne's attention turned to Tim, who was staring at the young child in her arms. "Tim, take your son with you, and get out of Java as soon as you can. I'll be leaving also."

Timothy took the small boy from her, "Where will you go?"

"It is evident that I can't stay here with my crew; I think we'll go to Ibiza and make it our home base. What will you do now?"

"I have no choice; I must take my son to London and later to Newport. Yvonne, I can't begin to tell you how much I've appreciated your help."

"Go. We don't have time to stand around thanking each other. Let's get out of here." The men and women who made up the crews of the *Moonlight* and *Sea Witch* left the Van der Rhine house, heading for the city with Ramona and Lion in tow.

Jennifer decided to go against Timothy's wishes. She paced around the cabin for an hour when she decided to leave. She had been on the ship long enough to know it like the back of her hand; quietly, she slipped off the ship to begin her search for Tim and Yvonne. She wandered around aimlessly taking in the breathtaking view of the beautiful lush green island. She saw a group of men in the distance riding as hard as they could; as they neared, she realized that they were not the crew of the *Moonlight*. Panic began to set in; her heart began to beat faster as she looked for a place to hide. Jennifer gazed longingly toward the *Moonlight;* if she made a run for the ship, she would surely be caught. She was trapped.

Timothy had returned to the ship with Lion and other members of the crew. Jennifer was nowhere to be found. Damn that girl. Could she have been that foolish to leave the ship when he told her not to? His blood boiled; he could kill her. Taking several of the men with him, he left the ship to look for the red-haired wench. Once inside the city, Timothy and the others split up. How could she do this? But that was a stupid question; this was typical of Jennifer. When she didn't get her way, she would try anyway. Didn't she learn her lesson yet? The last time she tried something like this, she ended up on a slave ship headed for the Barbary Coast. That damn fool! Didn't she realize that mercenaries would rape her over and over again and then murder her or worse, keep using her until she was dead. His heart felt as if it had been ripped out; if he found her he would surely kill her. He ran down alleys and weaved in and out of deserted buildings. He noticed that the mercenaries had already reached the city and were raiding stores and other establishments, probably for supplies.

Jennifer saw a group of men come down the alley where she was hiding in; her breath quickened, fear setting in as she looked around her. If she stays put, she would surely be found. Her only chance was to run. Thank God she didn't have on a skirt. She stood up and began to run as hard as she could with the men chasing after her. The hat she had been wearing fell from her head, and the long braids loosened. The men whooped and yelled, bringing Timothy's attention to the noises. He raced in the direction of the yelling and saw Jennifer running for her life, her hair flying wildly behind her. Seeing him, Jennifer screamed and collapsed. Timothy scooped her up in his arms as George and Ben appeared, swords drawn. Putting Jennifer down near a doorway, he drew his sword and began to fight along with his men; they were outnumbered five to three. Jennifer watched in horror as the men fought. Realizing that Tim's life was in danger, she stood up and reached for the hilt of her weapon. Tim was holding back two of the men, and a third was approaching him from the rear. Jennifer ran forward, her sword flashing back and forth wildly. She had forgotten everything Tim had taught her as she wielded the rapier, but found its mark in the man's back. With a sickening thud, he fell as she withdrew her sword. A wave of nausea overcame her, causing her stomach to feel as if she would retch at any second. Tim killed one of the mercenaries as George and Ben fought with the others. Timothy then turned his attention to the other man that kept coming, jabbing at him in quick movements. The man was skilled with a rapier; he had drawn blood on Timothy's arm several times. Seeing the red blood soak through Timothy's shirt, Jennifer regained her composure. With a wild yell, she ran forward, piercing the man's thigh and causing him to fall off balance. Moving quickly, Timothy took advantage of Jennifer's actions, and with one quick move, he sliced the man's throat and watched as the blood gurgled from the wound. He grabbed for Jennifer's hand as they ran back to the ship with George and Ben close on their heels.

Timothy threw Jennifer inside his cabin and locked the door, while he ordered his men to pull out of port. Anger raged inside of him. That damn fool almost got herself killed and him as well. As soon as they were safely out of port, he'd teach her a lesson that she would never forget. Timothy returned to the cabin about an hour after they had returned to the ship. Seething with anger, he opened the door. Jennifer sat curled up in the overstuffed chair reading. Striding angrily across the room, he pulled the book from her hands. The look in his eyes frightened her beyond words, "What the hell did you think you were doing today?"

She looked at him defiantly, "Looking for you."

"Looking for me? You can't take a simple order, can you?" Jennifer remained silent. How dare he talk to her that way? She stared coolly at him, "Don't give me that look, bitch, I won't stand for it."

"Who do you think you are, that you can order me around and talk to me like a common strumpet."

"You want to be treated like a strumpet? You got it, lady. I can't think of a better way to punish you for your behavior today. After all, I wouldn't want you to think that you missed something by not being caught by the mercenaries." His golden eyes glowered causing her to shrink in the chair, grabbing her by the hair he yanked her to her feet.

"Let go, Tim," she said calmly, her icy green stare piercing his heart.

He released her, "Take the dress off."

She held her ground, "I'm not your whore!"

"Those are harsh words for a seventeen-year-old, now do as I say or you'll have one less dress." Jennifer did not move. Timothy reached for the thin cotton dress and pulled; the material gave way, exposing her to the waist. "Now you will remove it?" The anger in his eyes bothered her; she was frightened of him. Gingerly, she removed what was left of the dress and stood before him naked and full of shame. He smiled; she deserved this and later she would thank him for it. "Get into bed."

"What are you going to do? Rape me after I saved your life?"

He removed his shirt, "Saved my life? I believe you have that twisted my little minx. If it wasn't for me, you would be at the mercy of those men."

"You think so, you insufferable bastard? I could have taken care of myself."

He slapped her across the face, the marks of his fingers stood out against the creamy skin, "Don't ever use that language again. Now get into bed."

"I asked you a question. Are you planning to rape me? Because if you are, you can save yourself the trouble because you did that before."

Timothy laughed, "Jennifer, I did not rape you; you seduced me, and you know it. You wanted me more than I wanted you." He lied.

Picking up a candlestick, she hurled it at him. It bounced off his muscular shoulder, appearing to cause him no physical pain; he pounced on her, and the two of them crashed to the bed. She fought him tooth and nail as he unbuttoned his pants exposing his rigid member. Jennifer held her legs tightly closed but to no avail, Timothy had her arms pinned over her head and his strength was unbearable as he forced her legs open and plunged deep inside of her. She wanted to cry out in pain but refused to give him the satisfaction of knowing that he had hurt her with that first powerful thrust. He bit her shoulder and breasts drawing blood; the tears welled in her eyes, and she couldn't hold back any longer as they rolled down her cheeks. His iron like grip crushed her to him as he moved deeper inside of her until she felt his warm seed explode, filling her insides. He rolled off her, his breathing uneven as he closed his eyes in anger. He hadn't meant to hurt her; she made him so angry that all he wanted to do was to hurt her. Jennifer pulled away from him, drawing the bedsheets up to her neck. Her body cried out in pain as she whimpered and cuddled in the corner of the bunk. Timothy moved from the bed, adjusted his clothes and left the cabin. He hated himself for what he had done to her. What was it with this woman? She had gotten under his skin like no other woman. This afternoon, when he had come back and found her gone, he hurt and he wanted her to hurt like he had, but his temper had gotten the best of him. She would never forgive him; he had seen it in her eyes. He wanted to rush back into the cabin and shower her with kisses, make love to her slowly and make the hurt go away, but he couldn't bring himself to do it.

George was startled seeing the Captain barking out orders. He certainly was in a foul mood. George noticed the dried blood on the Captain's cheek; what the devil happened in that cabin? He wouldn't dare ask Timothy, but he couldn't help wondering if the little slip of a girl was alright. He tried to put the thought out of his mind, yet the last time he saw the Captain in such a mood, the man had killed four men; he hoped the girl was alright. His fears were put to rest when he heard Tim tell Gideon to bring some hot water to the cabin for Jennifer to take a bath.

Gideon knocked on the door and entered with a large pail of water, which he proceeded to fill the tub with, "The Captain said that you wished to take a bath." He couldn't help noticing the imprint of a hand still on her face. One eye was turning a yellowish green; there was dried blood on the sheet that she covered herself with when he entered.

She managed a small, "thank-you," as she watched Gideon leave. Her body ached as she moved from the bed to the steaming water. She scrubbed as if trying to erase his lips that had caressed her hours before and that had just assaulted her moments ago. She began to cry until she was sobbing in the water while she scrubbed her body raw. She had been wrong about him, she hated him, if she could help it, he would never touch her again.

Timothy took his meals with the crew and spent most of his spare time with his son, Lion, who was a refreshing joy in light of the circumstances. He slept in the cabin that once belonged to George and converted it into a nursery for Lion. Several times, he caught a glimpse of Jennifer standing at the rail of the ship, looking forlornly out into the vast ocean. He had kept his distance; never once entering her cabin. If he needed something, he sent Gideon for it. But every time he saw her standing on deck, he was reminded of how much he desired her by the familiar ache in his loins. Soon they would get to the Le Harve; it had been weeks since they left Java, and when he got there, he would get himself a real woman, one who knew how to please a man, and he'd make damn sure that she was at least twenty-five.

The morning they reached Le Harve, Timothy sent specific orders with Gideon that Jennifer was not to leave the ship. They were stopping only to get fresh food and water. Jennifer went up on deck to find Timothy to scream at him; she couldn't take this treatment any longer. She felt like a prisoner on this godforsaken ship; she wanted to stand on soil. Finding Gideon, she ordered him to send the captain to her cabin when he came back to the ship. Gideon smiled, perhaps the little lady could get the captain out of the foul mood he had been in ever since they no longer shared the same cabin.

Timothy found a woman that appealed to him; he got as far as going to the room with her. She began to undress and stood before him in a chemise and pantalettes. He stared at her, trying to will himself to become excited, yet the tall, dark, sultry beauty did nothing for him. She approached him and began to unbutton his broadcloth shirt; his hands closed over hers, and he stared into her black eyes, "I'm sorry my sweet, but I just thought of something else I should be doing instead of this." He released her and withdrew ten gold coins from his pocket and pressed them into her hand, "Thanks."

"But we didn't do nothing." She pouted. How she longed to have this Captain make love to her; when he picked her over the other girls, she thought she would die. Now, after only a couple of minutes with him, he was leaving. Her English was not as fine as she wished, as she struggled with the words, "You don't like me?"

Timothy looked at her; certainly, she was use to men who were not interested in touching her, but just wanted to look, "It's not you, my petite, it's another woman that I just can't seem to get out of mind or my system," he said as he turned and left the room. Outside the door, he heard her crying. Damn, that was the second woman in the last month he had hurt, one more than the other. Damn Jennifer, that coppery hair and those fiery green eyes appeared nightly in his dreams. Sometimes, he woke in a cold sweat. Damn her. He left the establishment and began walking down the street. Passing a milliner's shop, he went in and purchased warmer dresses and a heavy cloak for Jennifer. Then he purchased some warmer clothing for himself and Lion.

When Timothy reached the ship an hour later, he brought all of the packages into his new cabin. Gideon had been watching Lion who was now sound asleep. Gideon looked up from the book he had been reading when Timothy entered the room, "Captain, Miss Weatherly would like you to come to her cabin immediately."

Timothy's heart fluttered, trying not to sound excited, he said, "Is there something wrong with her?"

Gideon had not expected this cold reaction, "No, but she said it was urgent that you go to her cabin as soon as you came back."

Timothy placed the packages on the bed, "Very well, Gideon, stay here with Lion. I bought him some warmer clothes." He left, so Jennifer wanted to see him, he mused with a smile. The thought of being in the same room with her excited him far beyond desire, but he must be careful to guard himself against a possible attack. Knocking on the cabin door, he waited, Jennifer opened it, "I understand you wished to see me?" He noted the expressionless green eyes.

"Would you come in, please?" There was something in his eyes, yet she couldn't place it.

Timothy walked to the table in the center of the room and sat down, "I trust you are well."

"Never better," she answered curtly. "The reason I asked you to come here is that I wish to change ships while we are in France."

The devil she would change ships, "Out of the question. I promised your father that I personally would return his precious daughter to him, and I keep my promises." The last part of the sentence was aimed at her.

Her face showed no sign or expression as to whether the words had sunk in; she wanted to spit at him, "Did you also promise my father that my reputation would remain untarnished? Because if you did, you have broken that one." She chirped bitterly.

Her words referred to the fact that they had enjoyed the physical aspects of marriage without the actual marriage, "I did not promise him that, and I seem to remember that we had this conversation before and quite frankly, I'm bored with it. Now, if there is nothing else, I have work to do."

She was angry, "There is one other thing; when will we reach London?"

"Two weeks."

"I can hardly wait until I get home."

"Then I see you've made your decision." He said coolly.

"What decision?"

His eyes twinkled mischievously, "The first day on this ship. I told you that you would have to decide whether or not you wished to stay on or return to your family. It appears the decision has been made, although I'm surprised at the choice." He left the room quickly, smiling to himself; as much as she might pretend to hate him, he had a feeling deep down that she didn't. She might not forgive him for his treatment of her when he was angry, but given time, the hurt would fade and she'd want him back. Whistling, he returned to the quarterdeck before going to his cabin.

Jennifer sat in the overstuffed chair, stunned. Damn him! He could still get to her after everything. Why did he have to be so attractive? How dare he think that she would choose him over her family! Her treatment since being on this ship had progressed from good to bad. He really must think that he's something; the only reason he whispered endearments to her was to seduce her deeper into his web. She would put him out of her mind once she reached London; there were plenty of eligible young men who would die to be her partner at a ball, and she would find a husband ten times better than the roguish Captain who cared nothing for anyone but himself. Her husband would have to be someone who was understanding of the trauma she had to endure at the hands of slavers and pirates.

CHAPTER FOURTEEN

Two weeks later, the *Moonlight* pulled into port. Timothy had come to the cabin earlier to give her the warmer clothes he had bought in Le Harve and to tell her that he personally would escort her to Weatherly.

Jennifer had packed her clothes and replaced the jewels Tim had given her. She sat on the edge of the bunk trembling; she wanted to tell Tim that she loved him, yet her pride stood in her way. It would be difficult to face her father, Stefan and Lizabeth; she had changed, and they would know.

Timothy knocked and entered the room, "Are you ready?"

The façade she had built up these last few weeks came to the surface, as she coolly said, "As ready as I'll ever be."

Timothy's eyes hardened. Taking her roughly by the arm, he led her out of the cabin. He had hired a carriage to take them to Weatherly. Neither said a word to the other during the half hour trip to the large estate. When the carriage pulled to the front doors, Jennifer noticed it was very quiet. Timothy helped her down from the carriage and rang the bell, as she smoothed out her clothes. Stefan answered, looking pale and drawn, seeing Lockwood and a tanned Jennifer. After months of not knowing whether the captain found her or not brought a look of relief to his face.

"Stefan, what's wrong?"

Finding his voice after a couple of seconds he said, "Thank God you made it in time."

"In time for what?" asked Jennifer.

"I'm sorry Jenny. Your father had a stroke this morning, and Doctor Warren says he won't make it through the night."

Tears came to her eyes, "I want to see him, where is he?"

"In his bedroom."

Timothy watched Jennifer run up the stairs, "I'm sorry, Stefan, he was a fine man."

"Please, Captain Lockwood, come into the study; there is something important I must tell you." Timothy followed Stefan into the study; it had been months since he had stepped foot inside the study. "Captain, I suggest you leave London at once."

"Why?"

"Sir Harrington is saying that he'll have you arrested for not honoring your responsibilities."

Timothy's eyes narrowed, "What responsibilities?"

"Towards his daughter and her coming child."

The blood rushed to his head as he raised his voice, "I will not marry that whore, who slept with everyone in London. Who the hell does she think she is?" questioned Timothy.

"Please, Captain, quiet down, or the rest of the house will hear you."

Timothy's eyes pleaded with Stefan, "You do believe the child's not mine."

"Yes, it's probably Lyndon's."

Timothy walked across the room to the liquor table, poured himself a large glass of rum and turned to face Stefan, "But Jennifer will never believe it." He swallowed a large mouthful of the liquid.

Stefan looked at him, "What does any of this have to do with Jenny?"

"I," he hesitated, "I wish I could tell you. The only thing I can say is to ask Jennifer."

"Ask her what?" Stefan questioned, noticing the pain in the Captain's eyes.

"Just ask her; it really is her place to tell you. I better get out of here." He put the glass down and began to leave the study.

"Wait, you haven't been paid for your services."

"Forget it; money is not important at the moment." He called back from the study door before leaving the estate to return to his ship.

Jennifer had gone to her father's room to find him unconscious. He looked so pale and old in the massive bed. She sat aside of him and held his hand; the tears trickled down her cheeks; she cried for both her father and herself.

When Timothy reached the *Moonlight,* he was surprised to find himself placed under arrest and taken to Sir Harrington's estate. He was brought by several constables into the main parlor in chains; Laura Harrington smirked. Tim felt disgusted at the sight of the woman; she was too far along to be carrying his child. Robert Harrington looked over the young man that had been brought to his home, "Timothy, not only am I appalled at your behavior, but also I was shocked at your disappearance." Timothy said nothing, but continued to stare hotly at Laura as Robert Harrington continued with his speech, "Now you will marry my daughter to give your child a name, or you will rot in Newgate."

Timothy said wryly, "That doesn't leave me much of a choice, does it?"

The coolness in Timothy's voice angered Robert Harrington; the man's eyes were full of hatred, which Sir Harrington decided to ignore, "You, young man, should honor your deeds. My daughter told me that the two of you had the relationship of marrieds because you were going to be married, but when she informed you of her predicament, you took off."

Timothy golden eyes angered, "That's a lie."

Harrington turned red, "Are you calling my daughter a liar?"

"Yes," Timothy's eyes never left Laura as he spoke, "The fact of the matter is your daughter never told me of her problem, but, of course, the last time I saw her we didn't have time for such trivialities, did we Laura?"

Laura turned a scarlet color, as she murmured a small, "No."

Timothy's attention returned to Sir Harrington, "So you see, Sir, I knew nothing and Laura try not to blush, you're far beyond that, don't you agree?"

She couldn't help to notice the anger in his eyes, as Sir Harrington said, "You will marry my daughter in two days. Do not attempt to escape, for you will be watched. If you escape, I'll hunt you down and you will spend the rest of your life at the Newgate prison, and I'll make sure that you're tortured."

Timothy knew that this must his punishment for what he had done to Jennifer. Punishment was one thing, but this could and would-be hell. The men who had arrested him released him from his chains. Somehow, he would escape before they had a chance to realize he was missing. He rubbed his wrists as he glared at Harrington and Laura,

"Considering you have made so many plans for my life, I wondered if it would be alright to continue with my normal business."

Harrington was pleased that Lockwood was being so cooperative, "Only if it does not take you from London."

"You can rest assured, Sir Harrington, that I would not leave your lovely daughter twice." The emphasis on the word lovely made Laura cringe. "Now if you would excuse me, I have work to do on my ship." He turned and walked briskly out of the Harrington home.

Jennifer sat by her father the entire night and well into the next day until he died, that afternoon. Stefan found her screaming and crying over her father's body. He led her to her bedroom, and Dr. Warren gave her a sedative. Stefan and Lizabeth tended to the funeral arrangements while Jennifer slept.

Timothy came to Weatherly to find a black wreath on the door. He instantly knew that James Weatherly had died. Knocking on the door, Lizabeth opened it and bade him to enter. Stefan appeared several minutes later, "Stefan, I'm sorry to hear about your uncle." He looked at the young man who was pale and looked as if he hadn't slept in days, "Where is Jenny?"

He spoke in a dry whisper, "Jennifer is asleep; the doctor gave her a sedative."

Timothy nodded, "The reason I came is to tell you that you were right. Harrington had me arrested and demanded I marry his very pregnant daughter tomorrow. I need to see Jennifer before I escape or rather attempt an escape."

"If you escape, where will you go?"

"Spain, maybe one of the islands in East Indies, I don't know for sure."

"What happens if you get caught?" questioned Stefan.

Timothy drew in his breath, "He's threatened Newgate."

"Why don't you marry her and then divorce her?"

"I am not the father of her child, and I refuse to be a sap and marry the girl to give her bastard a name." Timothy stated firmly, "Now what room is Jennifer's? I must see her."

Stefan could see that there was no stopping the angry Captain, "At the top of the stairs, turn right, and it's three doors down."

Timothy bounded up the stairs to Jennifer's room, his heart pounding so hard that it was deafening to his ears. He had no idea what he would say to her, good-bye, no that was too final. He reached her door and found his legs shaking like a newborn colt; taking a deep breath, he opened the door. Jennifer lay on the bed sound asleep; she looked so peaceful that he didn't want to wake her. Sitting on the edge of the bed he bent to kiss her lightly on the cheek. In her sleep, she murmured his name. He smiled; her heart was not as hard as he made it seem. "Jennifer," he said quietly as he shook her, "Jenny, wake up."

Her eyes fluttered open, her sight blurry from the drug, "What are you doing here? Get out, or I'll scream."

"Please Jenny, don't do this, I need to talk to you. It's very important."

"Couldn't you have waited until tomorrow, Captain," she snapped. The turquoise eyes flared with anger.

"Listen to me. I came to tell you that I'm getting married." He watched for the reaction on her face.

Her green eyes gave her away as they smoldered with anger, "To whom? You certainly move quickly."

He could tell she was still somewhat angry, "If I don't marry this woman, I'll spend the rest of my life in Newgate."

"Newgate." She repeated the name of the prison in awe.

"I need your help Jenny, you're the only one who can help me," he said as he came up with a brilliant idea.

"Really, Timothy, I see no way that I can help you, and why should I after," she stopped.

"After I treated you so badly," he looked intensely in her eyes, "I'm sorry. I was angry. Please listen to me, Jennifer; I'm in trouble, and you owe me a favor."

She swung her legs off the bed, not caring how she looked as she stood near the window. The moonlight was streaming into the room, outlining her body through the thin shift, "Owe you? I don't owe you a damn thing."

He smiled; she was so beautiful when she was angry. "Listen to me, you owe me your life; if it wasn't for me, you might have ended up a slave on the Barbary Coast or worse," he hesitated, "Dead."

"I'd probably have suffered less at the hands of whoever else might have bought me."

"Jennifer, I haven't treated you badly; I've given you clothes and anything else you needed; I treated you like a queen." He said quietly.

Her eyes penetrated his, "Except at night, when you treated me like…"

Timothy interrupted her, "Don't say it. Don't belittle yourself; you were a very beautiful naïve young girl, and I made you a beautiful young woman, and the truth of the matter is, you liked it as much as I did," he saw her eyes soften, and he knew he had her then.

She knew she loved him, and she would do anything for him. "Okay, what do you want me to do?" she asked meekly.

"After I left here earlier, I was arrested. Sir Harrington would like me, more than like me, has ordered me to marry his very pregnant daughter."

"Pregnant?" her eyes widened in surprise and then narrowed in disgust, "Oh, so now you're trying to get out of your responsibilities."

His eyes shimmered an angry glare, "Will you shut your damn mouth and listen to me? Laura Harrington is not carrying my child; I swear to you. Harrington said I have a choice, either I marry his daughter or spend the rest of my life in Newgate."

"What does this have to do with me?" Jennifer questioned.

"I need to buy myself some time; I want to escape, but I'm being watched. I thought if you went to the Harrington home and told them that we were married while we were at sea, I'm sure Yvonne could supply some papers stating that we were. If I am married to you, I certainly cannot marry that woman."

Jennifer began to laugh uncontrollably, "You really expect me to believe you, or better yet, pretend I'm married to you. Have you gone mad?"

"Jennifer, I'm begging you. It would be a marriage of convenience. I wouldn't ask to share your bed, of course we'd have to make some public appearances together to keep up the game until I can escape. Then you can resume your life."

Her eyes sparkled dangerously, "So, the fierce Captain, the pirate, Captain Bloodthirsty, is begging me to save his skin. For what you've done to me I should think Laura Harrington would be just punishment, whether you are the father of her bastard or not."

He grabbed her roughly by the arm, the golden eyes deadly, "Yes, I'm pleading with you."

"Let go of me," she said, smugly.

Instead of releasing her, he grabbed her other arm and kissed her long and hard. She responded to him, although she willed her body not to; why did he have to kiss her? Timothy released her almost as suddenly as he had seized her. "Don't say that you don't care for me, because as much as you say no," he paused, "your body betrays you and says yes."

He had her where he wanted her, and Jennifer knew it; she had no choice; he did save her life, "I'll go to the Harrington home with you tomorrow."

Timothy smiled slyly; he had won this round; eventually, she would come back to him, "In order to make this work, you must realize that I will move into Weatherly."

"Of course," she answered sarcastically.

"I will send a letter to Yvonne to have the necessary documents sent to me in case Sir Harrington wishes to check our story."

"I would really like to go back to sleep if you don't mind."

He swept her into his arms and carried her to the big four poster bed, "Sleep well, "he said as he placed the covers over her. Walking across the room, he turned and blew her a kiss, "Until tomorrow." He shut the door and went back downstairs to find Stefan.

Once Stefan realized the extent of Timothy's plan, he suggested that a personal friend, an attorney of the family, Mr. Spencer, would be able to get some legal documents stating that Jennifer and Timothy were married. Timothy agreed with Stefan that it might be better and more believable if he had the documents in his hand when he went to tell Harrington the news. Stefan promised to see Mr. Spencer in the morning and suggested Timothy spend the night at Weatherly.

The following morning, Stefan rose early and went to Spencer's office in town. Explaining the situation to Spencer, the attorney agreed to file the necessary papers, although he needed both Jennifer and Timothy's signatures as well as two witnesses. The men decided to return to Weatherly with the documents in order to get the signatures.

Lizabeth was shocked to find the tall Captain in Mr. Weatherly's study and went to wake Miss Jenny. Jennifer was already up and sick to her stomach. She decided it was from being upset about her father's death and last evening's happenings. She dressed quickly, choosing her dark blue velvet. Lizabeth breezed into the room, "Missy, that tall Captain is downstairs, and it appears that he spent the night."

Jennifer had been applying a light scent to her wrists as she turned to Lizabeth, "I thought he might have. He was here last night."

"In your bedroom? Miss Jenny, you are not supposed to have men in your bedroom unless he is your husband." Lizabeth was shocked, "Your father is not dead for twenty-four hours and you're turning into a real hussy."

Jennifer blushed, "Nothing happened. The Captain needed to ask me a favor. Something I could do for him considering he saved my life."

"What kind of favor might he have asked you?" questioned Lizabeth.

Jennifer was brushing her hair, she stopped, "That self-centered woman Laura Harrington is pregnant, and she says that it's the Captain's child."

Lizabeth retorted, "It could well be, considering he was engaged to the woman before he went to find you."

"Well, he says the child isn't his, and he had no intention of marrying her, so he asked me to tell Sir Harrington that we were married while we were away. It will only be until he can escape safely."

Lizabeth noticed something in Jennifer's eyes, it was only a fleeting look, a softness when she talked about the Captain, "You didn't really marry the man, did you?"

Jennifer shook her head, "Of course not!"

"Well, I don't like him. There's something about him that's sinister. I wouldn't trust him if I were you and I don't understand why you agreed to help him."

Jennifer looked at Lizabeth, "He's not a sinister man or mean." She lied. "Besides he saved me from a life of slavery, and I owe him."

Lizabeth narrowed her eyes, "You sure nothing happened on that ship?

Jennifer noticed that Lizabeth's eyes seemed to be looking into her soul, "Absolutely nothing happened; he treated me as if I was his sister." She lied again; she hated lying to Lizabeth, but it was for the benefit of everyone. She left her bedroom to Lizabeth who would tidy it up and went downstairs to find Timothy eating breakfast he rose when she entered the room; his topaz eyes swept over her, "Please don't stand on my account."

He grinned, "I see you are in a much better mood today." She glared at him, "Would you care for me to serve you my queen?"

"Stop with my queen; call me by my name, and I don't want breakfast. I'm not feeling well this morning."

"I'm sorry to hear it; I hope you'll feel better by the time we must go to the Harrington's to make our announcement."

"I'm sure I will be; thank you." She poured herself some tea and sat across from him.

"By the way, your cousin has agreed to help in this scheme and went to a lawyer, a Mr. Spencer, I believe, to get the necessary documents." Hearing the front door open, he said, "That must be Stefan."

Stefan and Peter Spencer walked into the dining room. Timothy rose as Stefan introduced him to Spencer, "Captain Lockwood, this is Mr. Peter Spencer. Mr. Spencer, Captain Lockwood."

Timothy extended his hand, "It is a pleasure to meet you. Thank you so much for aiding us in these matters."

"It's very good to see you, Peter."

"Jennifer, you are lovelier than ever. I was sorry to hear about your father. When will the funeral be held?

"Tomorrow." She answered quietly. "I'm very happy that you agreed to help the Captain."

"Once Stefan told me of the problem and the fact that the Captain saved your life, I'm sure your father would have wanted me to help." The old man took some papers out of his vest pocket as he continued, "The only thing we need is the Captain's signature, Jennifer's, Master Stefan and one other person."

Jennifer called Lizabeth, "Lizabeth, please sign the paper for me." Lizabeth nodded, as Timothy took the pen from Mr. Spencer, signed his name and handed the pen to Jennifer. She put her signature next to his and then both Stefan and Lizabeth signed.

Peter Spencer looked at the signatures, and then he, too, signed the document; handing the papers to Timothy, he said, "In the eyes of the law, you Sir, and Jennifer Weatherly were married in June of last year, secretly of course, before her abduction. When the two of you decide that it is safe for the Captain to leave, Jennifer must file for a legal divorce, or she will be unable to marry in London."

Timothy shook the man's hand, "Thank you; you have saved me from Newgate."

Jennifer had grown quiet; the realization of what Peter Spencer had said was a blow to her. She would have to get a divorce; she might as well have married him for real. She heard Spencer say, "If there is anything else I can do, just contact me."

Jennifer said goodbye and watched as Stefan showed him to the door, leaving her and Timothy alone, "Jenny, I'll be indebted to you for the rest of my life."

"I hope not. When do you want to go to the Harrington's? I say the sooner we get it over with, the better."

"If you are ready now, we can go."

"Fine, the sooner the better, I'll get my wrap." She breezed out of the room with Timothy looking after her with a grin on his face. Returning several seconds later, she looked at him, "Are you ready?"

"Yes," picking up the papers from the table, he stuffed them into his pocket, "Let's go."

Jennifer followed him into the hall and out of the front door. The ride to the Harrington estate was quiet. Jennifer thought of the last time she had been there and what had happened; in a way, she was happy that she agreed to this scheme; it would teach Laura Harrington a lesson. The carriage stopped at the door, and Timothy helped Jennifer down. He pulled the bell, and the two of them were shown into the sitting room. Sir Harrington and a very pregnant Laura entered the sitting room. Jennifer had to stifle a small laugh.

"Miss Weatherly, I was so sorry to hear about your father," said Sir Harrington.

"Thank you, Sir Harrington."

Seeing Jennifer, Laura flushed, "Yes, I, too, was sorry."

"How is it that the two of you arrived together?" questioned Sir Harrington.

"We often travel together Sir Harrington, "Jennifer smiled and took pleasure in her next sentence, "You see, we are married."

Laura turned a pale gray, and Sir Harrington exploded, "What do you mean you are married?"

Timothy sat back and watched Jennifer, she was enjoying herself, "It's true."

"I don't believe you Captain. If you were married why didn't you tell me so last night?" said Sir Harrington.

Jennifer said quickly, "That was my fault. I asked him not tell anyone until I told my father."

Timothy rose from his seat; his eyes twinkled, "I certainly couldn't go against my wife's wishes, could I?"

"When were you married, if you're married at all?" demanded Sir Harrington.

"In June," Timothy handed Sir Harrington the papers.

Laura's head began to spin, "You couldn't have married in June, Jennifer was missing then."

Jennifer turned towards Laura, "We married before I was kidnapped," Jennifer answered curtly.

Harrington handed the papers back to Timothy, "It's true."

Timothy smiled, "So you see, I cannot marry your daughter, I'm already married, and I can't have two wives."

"But my daughter is pregnant with your child," said Harrington, his voice becoming shaky.

Timothy's voice was flat, "That is what she said."

Jennifer chirped, "Sir Harrington, your daughter looks much too far along to be pregnant with Tim's child. Perhaps you should question her morals."

"Are you insinuating, young woman, that my daughter hasn't any morals?"

Jennifer stared at him coolly, "No, I'm telling you that she doesn't." Jennifer reminded Tim of a hen whose feathers had been ruffled.

Timothy decided it was time to step in, "What Jenny means is that I have considerable proof which proves your daughter is no different than an alley cat."

Harrington turned a bright red, while Laura fanned herself, "Get, get out of my house."

Timothy took Jennifer by the hand and led her out of the front door. Inside the carriage, they laughed. Since the night he had attacked her, she had been cold toward him; now, her emerald eyes showed a warmth as she laughed, "You were wonderful."

"So were you!" she exclaimed. "What were you talking about when you said you had enough proof to prove she wasn't any better than an alley cat?"

"Actually, your cousin Stefan has the proof," he paused, "written proof. Miss Laura Harrington was heavily involved in a very close relationship with a certain Geoffrey Lyndon."

"Lyndon and Laura? I don't believe it." She was surprised; she knew that Lyndon wasn't a saint, but she never thought that Laura would be involved with him.

"Jennifer, I think that we should have some sort of reception. The word of our supposed marriage will spread like wildfire. Of course, it will have to be a reasonable time after your father's funeral." The excitement in his statement made Jennifer realize that she was bound to this man, for how long, she did not know. She grew quiet for the remainder of the trip home.

Timothy sat in the study, gazing out the window; it was early; the sky dark, dismal as if it would rain. He thought of the funeral today; the weather just made it more depressing. Most of his clothes had been moved to Weatherly along with his son, Lion. He didn't know how long he could take the pressure of being in the same house with Jennifer. Didn't she know what she did to him? His room was next to hers; just knowing that drove him wild with desire. Many times last night he thought of her; he wanted to enter her bedroom but stopped himself; he wanted her to come to him. He heard her crying when he woke this morning; he had wanted to go and comfort her but decided against it. Now, he sat quietly in the study, angry at himself for not going to her.

Jennifer had cried herself to sleep and kept waking at various times during the night. She cried not only for her father but also for herself, her torment. When she rose, she went immediately to her bathroom; her stomach rumbled as she broke into a cold sweat. "My God, what is wrong with me?" This was the second morning in a row that a wave of nausea overcame her, and she threw up. She washed her face with cold water, her body shaking uncontrollably as she made her way back to the bed. She got into the bed and pulled the covers up high. Several minutes later, Lizabeth appeared, "Time to get up."

"Lizabeth, I didn't sleep well last night, and I don't feel that well. My father's funeral isn't until eleven, I'd like to have an extra hour or so."

"What's wrong with you?" Lizabeth said as she approached the bed, "You're so pale."

"I'm sick to my stomach. It must have been something I ate last night," she answered thoughtfully.

"But you hardly ate anything at all. Are you sure nothing happened on that ship?"

"No, nothing happened. I'll be alright."

"Very well, I'll just lay out your dress and, in an hour, I'll come back to help you." Lizabeth busied herself preparing Jennifer's things and then left the room.

Jennifer tried desperately to remember when her last monthly came. She couldn't be pregnant; she searched her mind and realized that it was before they reached Java. That was well over two months ago, "Dear God," she thought, "Please, no." A light knock on her door made her jump, "Yes?"

The door opened, and Timothy walked in shutting the door behind him. He was dressed in a black broadcloth suit and white shirt; his black hair was neatly combed and the golden eyes shone, "I understand that you are sick again this morning."

He approached her bed as she said, "It's nothing, just something I ate."

Timothy stared at her as he sat down on the edge of the bed, "Jennifer, you and I both know that you hardly ate anything last night. You were sick yesterday morning and now this morning."

"It's because I've been upset, my father died..." she tried to avoid looking into his eyes.

Taking her face in his hand, he turned her toward him, the dark green eyes were briming with tears, his voice soft, he asked, "What's wrong green-eyed lady? Why are you so upset?"

"I'm upset about my father, I loved him…" her voice trailed off as he brushed a tear from her cheek.

"No, it's something more, I can see it in your eyes. Are you," he paused, he didn't want to offend her, "Are you carrying my child?"

She turned her head from him, "No," she answered in a small voice.

"Jennifer, look at me, tell me the truth."

She looked at him; his eyes were warm; did she see love there? He almost seemed as if he cared, "I'm not sure."

"Not sure of what?" his eyes searched her face for more answers. Jennifer's mind was racing. Why did she lie? Of course, she was sure, she had always been regular until now. It really shouldn't worry her; everyone thought she was married to the Captain; it would be quite natural for her to have a child. But what of Stefan and Lizabeth? She felt ashamed of her actions; how could she face them. Timothy watched Jennifer's face change in a range of emotions. "Jenny?"

He hadn't called her Jenny in a long time; she looked him straight I the eyes and said, "Yes, I'm pregnant."

"Are you sure?"

Her eyes lit as if they were on fire, "Oh, so now you doubt me?" She raised her hand to slap him, but he caught her.

Calmly, he said, "That would have been a terrible mistake." She looked at her lap, as Timothy continued, "I don't doubt you, Jennifer. I know that the child is mine. I'll take care of you; it's my duty, and I'll do it." He released her hand.

"I'm so ashamed; what will my cousin and Lizabeth think? Lizabeth has already asked me if anything happened between us on the ship, and I told her no."

"You're my wife; you have nothing to be ashamed of; you'll bring life to something that two of us created."

"I'm not your wife, Tim," she said quietly, remembering the plans they had made in Java.

"You could be if you wanted." The look she had noticed earlier returned, "If you don't want to marry, I'll just tell everyone that we were married in Java."

"But Lizabeth and Stefan believe that I went along with you yesterday because you saved my life."

"I'll tell your cousin that we were married, and we didn't want to tell anyone until later, after the funeral, but now your condition forces us to tell him and the rest of the staff."

"He won't believe you," said Jennifer flatly.

His eyes twinkled, "You don't know me well, do you, little one, I have a way with words. Your cousin and the servants will all believe me."

"Are you sure?" her eyes meeting his.

"They'll believe me; however, this will change things between us."

She looked at him wide eyed, "How?"

"We are going to share the same room."

"Never," she stated firmly.

"Do you want everyone to know that you're not married and are carrying my child?" questioned Timothy.

"No," she glared at him.

"Then you'll do as I say."

"Yes," she answered bitterly.

"Now get dressed and come down to the library, I'll assemble the servants and your cousin."

Jennifer took her time dressing. Damn Timothy Lockwood! Was he agreeing to save her honor just so he could share her bed again? She went downstairs to the library. Timothy had kept his promise. Stefan, Lizabeth, Harris and the others were gathered in the large room. Timothy motioned for Jennifer to come by his side, "I'm sure you must all wonder why I assembled you in the library." His eyes scanned the room, "The truth of the matter is, I really didn't plan to make this announcement until much later, but circumstances force me to tell you." He paused and looked at Jennifer, "Yesterday, Jennifer went to the Harrington estate with me; many of you believe that she did it because I saved her life. The truth of the matter is that I was not worried in the least; Jennifer and I have been married for months." His eyes watched the expressions on their faces; Lizabeth sat slowly in a chair.

Stefan was the first to speak, "Where?"

"In Java," replied Timothy.

Jennifer who had remained quiet, spoke for the first time, "Stefan the reason Tim gave you such an elaborate story the other evening was because I asked him to because I wanted to wait until a much better time. A time that would be respectable after my father's death. However, as Tim said, circumstances have forced us to tell you now."

"Lizabeth and Stefan both asked simultaneously, "What circumstances?"

She could tell that the two of them did not believe the story that was just told to them, but answered as if it was the most natural thing in the world, "I'm pregnant."

Harris broke into a warm smile as he crossed the room to hug her, "Congratulations, Miss Jennifer; you have picked a fine husband."

She smiled weakly, "Thank you."

Stefan stood in semi-shock; he did not believe them, although, they both seemed serious. If his uncle was still alive, he would have disapproved of such a match between the Captain and Jennifer. Although it was rumored that the Captain was extremely wealthy, Stefan approached the couple, "I must extend my sincere approval." Jennifer murmured a thank you, and Timothy shook Stefan's hand. Jennifer excused herself and went to her room to lay down before the funeral.

James Weatherly's funeral was attended by several noted dignitaries from London, some friends, the servants, Stefan, Timothy and Jennifer. Timothy held on to Jennifer at the grave service, and she turned to him for support. He wiped her tears away as all eyes were on the couple. A small reception followed with some food and drink, the smells making Jennifer more nauseous. The last guest had left, and Timothy went to the study to work. Stefan poured himself a drink, and Jennifer went upstairs to rest. Her mind went over the events in the last few months and concentrated especially on the past two days. She dozed on and off, her dreams filled with a golden eyed man, staring at her. She woke to find Timothy standing over her bed gazing down at her, "Jennifer, I think you and I need to talk."

"About what?" she glared at him.

"About us, about what happened between us."

Jennifer sat up, her hair tumbled around her shoulders, "Are you referring to the fact that our child was conceived in rape?"

"Do you think it was rape?" he asked.

"What do you call it, Tim?" She asked defiantly.

"It was anger, I was furious at you for disobeying orders. It was as if I was blind by rage."

"Are you pleading with me again? You don't own me; no man will ever own me."

"We'll see?" The gold fleck eyes twinkled.

"What do you mean, we'll see?"

"Jennifer, when you come down from your high horse, I think you'll realize that you care for me much more than you are willing to admit at the moment." He paused, "And if you remember, I do own you. I seem to remember buying you from a slave block in the Barbary States for an enormous amount of money."

The green eyes flared, "You are so sure of yourself; you think you are the best in everything especially making love."

The topaz eyes were expressionless, "How do you know I'm not the best lover when you've had no others? I think I'll find myself a mistress, one who has spirit and fire. Perhaps you can get yourself a lover if you're not satisfied with me." He turned to leave and then turned back, "By the way, I will be sharing your bed this evening." And he left.

Jennifer threw her slipper across the room; it slammed against the door. Bastard, she thought. She fumed at the idea of him coming to her bedroom at night. She could scream; he thought he would take charge of the situation. She knew she was lost; everyone believed they were married, and it would look strange if he didn't share her room. She didn't want this child; she hated it and hated him. She rose from the bed and changed her dress to go downstairs.

Timothy sat in the library going over his ship's cargo papers. He thought about Newport for a few minutes. Lockwood should be completed by now, and he should return and tend to his shipping business. He thought that while Jennifer was pregnant, he should go back to Newport. He could leave her at Weatherly where she could be properly taken care of; his thoughts were interrupted by a light knock, "Come in."

Jennifer entered, "Dinner will be ready soon."

He rose from his chair, "Jenny, I'm glad you're here, please sit down."

"What? More discussion?" she snapped.

"Not quite, I've made a decision."

"You're not going to come to my room tonight?" her eyes brightened. Could it be possible that he changed his mind? Maybe he didn't want to sleep with a pregnant woman. Her thoughts disappeared as soon as he spoke.

"No, I will be staying in your room for the time being. The fact of the matter is I'm going home to Newport to take care of my shipping business. When I return from Newport, it will be your time," he paused, "After the child is born, we can decide what we want to do."

"Are you giving up piracy?"

"I haven't decided yet. I may and may not; it all depends on how I play my cards."

"How you play your cards concerning what?"

He smiled, a brilliant white flash of teeth against the deep golden tan, "You of course."

Jennifer chose to ignore the remark, "When will you be leaving?"

"Within the week."

"I see; well, if you would excuse me, I want to change for dinner," He nodded and watched her leave the library, shutting the door behind her.

Jennifer leaned against the wall, took a deep breath and continued to her room. Why did she feel this way? Her heart was telling her one thing and her mind another. Why was she so attracted to him when she should hate him? She sighed. Soon he would be leaving, and her life would be a little easier. She smiled and continued on to her bedroom to prepare for dinner.

The days passed quickly with Jennifer becoming angrier and angrier; she didn't understand why she was in such an outrage; in fact, she should be pleased. Timothy had come to her room as he said he would but did not lay a hand on her; it was as if she wasn't in the bed. He barely spoke to her unless they were in the company of her cousin and at that, the talk was idle. He was punishing her, and it should be the other way around; after all, he deserved to be punished. Now she must accompany him to the docks like a good little wife to see her beloved husband off on a long journey. She should refuse to go along, but they were being watched by Harrington's men. She dressed quickly, not wanting him to wait any longer.

Timothy was downstairs in the main sitting room watching Lion who was playing with a small toy on the floor. He was magnificently dressed in a beige broadcloth jacket and navy-blue pants; his tan had begun to fade, yet it still made him look like a bronzed statue.

Jennifer waltzed into the sitting room, "Are you ready?" Her voice cold and hard.

"Yes. I've been waiting for you. The carriage is waiting to take us to the docks."

"Fine, I'll get my cloak."

Tim watched her leave the room and yelled for Maggie, the maid he had sent to the Weatherly's from the Harrington home many months ago.

"Yes, Captain Lockwood?"

"Take my son up to his room. Mrs. Lockwood and I are going to the docks."

"Yes sir," she stooped in order to take the child by the hand. Ever since Captain Lockwood returned with his son, she had become the child's nurse, a job that she really liked.

Jennifer came back to the room with her cloak. Timothy helped her with it and two of them went outside to the carriage, where Harris was waiting to take them to the docks. The ride was quiet except for

Timothy whistling every once in awhile, making Jennifer nervous. They sat across from each other; her expression was one of boredom, which irritated Timothy. Jennifer noticed that his expression was blank, uncaring and at ease. He was always at ease and lately appeared to be indifferent in all matters except when they concerned his son. The carriage rolled to a stop, and Harris busied himself with the Captain's luggage. George waved from the upper deck of the *Moonlight*. Both Jennifer and Tim waved back. Gideon had come to get the luggage from Harris, who was now sitting at the reins. Timothy took Jennifer by the hand and led her away from the carriage and towards the ship. "Jennifer, I wish you could come with me."

"Do you?"

"Yes, I think you would love Newport. Maybe someday you can go there."

Blinking back tears which had come from nowhere, she said, "Yes, perhaps I will go to Newport someday."

He raised his hand to touch her hair; it was softer than he remembered; she stood perfectly still not wanting to encourage him. He looked at her thoughtfully, "Take care of yourself, green-eyed lady. Be very careful."

"I will," she said quietly, not wanting to take her eyes from his face.

"When I return, perhaps you'll have a change of heart." She said nothing. "If you find it in your heart to forgive me, things could be so much better. May I kiss you goodbye?"

Her eyes welled with tears as she nodded yes; he bent to kiss her, tasting her for the last time until he returned. He released her, "Goodbye Tim; good luck and Godspeed."

He smiled, "Goodbye, Jenny. Take good care of yourself and Lion." He turned and walked to the ship; she watched him until he was on the large ship and gave his orders. He turned and waved, reminding her of the first time she had seen him, as the *Moonlight* left port. She stood silently on the docks watching the ship for a few minutes before returning to her waiting carriage to go home to Weatherly.

When she got home, she had a visitor waiting in the sitting room. She opened the large double doors to find Laura Harrington sitting by the fire. "Well, Miss Harrington, what can I do for you?"

"Where is your husband?" The blue eyes were icy.

"The whereabouts of my husband are none of your concern."

"He's the father of my child; I demand to know where he is," Laura said angrily.

"I thought we already established the fact that you are much too far along to be carrying my husband's child."

"Your husband raped me."

Jennifer smiled, a sad, tired smile, "Really, Miss Harrington, get out of my home. I'm quite bored by all of your accusations Lizabeth!"

The maid appeared in the doorway, "Yes?"

"Show Miss Harrington to the door, and if she ever returns, see that she is not let in."

Laura Harrington stood up, "He did, you know." She turned and left the house.

Lizabeth returned to the sitting room, "Is there anything I can do for you?"

"No, I'm going upstairs to lie down. I haven't been sleeping well." Jennifer turned and left the room, leaving Lizabeth standing in the middle of the sitting room staring after her.

Once inside her bedroom, Jennifer undressed and looked at herself in the mirror. Her stomach was still flat, but soon her pregnancy would begin to show; she walked over to her closet taking out her white silk dressing gown. Putting on the dressing gown, she went to the dressing table, sat down and began brushing her auburn hair before turning down the covers.

The days passed quickly turning into weeks as Jennifer grew big with child. She spent many of her days reading or playing with Lion. Timothy had been gone for a couple of months now, and there hadn't been a word from him. She did receive a little note from Yvonne, telling her that she had settled on a small island off the coast of eastern Spain called Ibiza. Jennifer smiled when she read Yvonne's letter; she said that she would be coming to visit soon but could not give an exact date. Jennifer had read the letter over and over again, each time reminding her of happier times before and in Java.

Several days after reading Yvonne's letter, Jennifer became ill and the doctor was sent for; she was scared; she was bleeding lightly and didn't want to lose the baby. Dr. Warren came and examined her, shaking his head, he said, "Jennifer, you must stay in bed for the duration of your pregnancy. There is a very high possibility that you will lose the child." The tears streamed down her face. "I suggest that you contact your husband and let him know what has happened. As far as I can tell, you've strained yourself, which caused the problem." Jennifer nodded and closed her eyes. Bedridden for the next four and a half months would be torture.

Outside the bedroom, Dr. Warren said to Stefan, "I suggest you contact her husband immediately; if she loses this baby, we could lose her."

"Lose her? What do you mean?"

"Stefan, it will be touch and go; I didn't want to alarm Jennifer, but her health is in danger. She could die."

"Die?" He was dumbfounded, the only person he could ever really talk to might die.

"Stefan, you mustn't let her know; pretend that everything is fine and for God's sake find her husband, and get him back here."

Stefan nodded his head, and showed Dr. Warren out.

CHAPTER FIFTEEN

Timothy had been in Newport over a month. Robert Gray had been running the business well, Timothy could not believe the figures in his account. On his first day in Newport, he went to see Lockwood. The carriage pulled up to the large front doors and he walked-in, with Robert Gray closely on his heels. "Robert, the house is magnificent. "

"Yes, I'm pleased with the way the men have worked so hard, but I expected you to have your bride Laura with you."

Timothy smiled, "I'm not getting married."

Robert's eyes were questioning, "Tim, I thought that was your plan."

"Originally it was, but Miss Harrington had other plans. However, I did meet a young woman while in London."

"Is she from a good family?" questioned Robert, as he and Timothy went outside to walk around the grounds.

"Yes, a very good family. In fact, she's an heiress."

"So, you've made the necessary steps of courting her."

"Sort of," Tim said evasively, "At the moment she's angry at me but she'll come around."

"Well, I take it you are not interested in any of the Newport ladies."

Timothy grinned, his eyes twinkling with delight, "I'm always interested in the ladies."

"I was hoping that you would say that. Come I'll tell you about this particular lady on the way back to town." Timothy followed Robert to the carriage and Robert said, "Tonight there is a party at my home, my cousin from Providence is coming; her name is Amanda Bowmen, recently widowed." Timothy knew what Robert wanted before he even asked, "I would appreciate it my dear friend if you would be her escort for the evening."

Timothy laughed, "Anything for my business partner. How old is she?"

"Twenty or twenty-one, I'm really not sure. Her husband was killed in a fishing accident in Galillee."

"Pretty?"

"I haven't seen her in years, though I am told that she is very charming."

The carriage rolled to a stop at the *White Horse Tavern and Hotel;* Timothy got out, "What time should I be at your home?"

"Seven."

"Well, seven it is; see you later." Timothy walked briskly by a group of women on his way into the *White Horse Tavern,* each one turned to look at him. His rooms at the tavern were small, not as spacious as the one's he had shared with Jennifer in Java. He had a small bedroom and sitting room. He took a long hot bath before dressing to go to the party at Robert Gray's home.

Robert was several years older than Tim, with grey eyes and a thick black mustache. He had grown up in the area, which proved immensely helpful to Timothy. Robert had been preparing for this party for months, it would be here that he would announce his engagement to the very small and delicate Molly Jencks. The guest had begun to arrive an hour earlier, including his cousin, Amanda Bowmen. Amanda was tall and lithe, her black, raven-like hair was coiffured in the newest fashion, and her gown was a red satin that would shock most of the people at the party with its plunging neckline. Timothy was one of the last to arrive. He was dressed in a beige broadcloth pants and jacket with a burgundy waistcoat. The black hair stood neatly in place as he was dragged off to meet his date for the evening. Robert introduced them, thinking what an exquisite couple they would make. Perhaps Timothy would change his mind. The woman was beautiful, Timothy thought. His gold-flecked eyes took in every inch of her form, the black hair, the violet eyes, the creamy skin from her neck to the slopes of her breasts. The sight of her aroused him so much that he felt like a school boy.

Amanda liked the man she saw standing before her; tall, muscular, tanned and his eyes. They were the most unusual eyes she had ever seen, they were topaz, which reminded her of a lion. "It is indeed a pleasure to meet you, Captain Lockwood."

"The pleasure is all mine, Mrs. Bowmen."

"Please, call me Amanda."

"You can call me Tim."

What was it that she saw behind those well-hidden eyes of his? Lust? Desire? "I understand that you're planning to live here."

"Yes, I'm having a house built."

"I'm considering making the move from Providence to Newport. Newport has so much more to offer, don't you think?"

He couldn't help staring at her, she was sensuous, "Sorry, what did you say?"

"Don't you think Newport has much more to offer than Providence?" she asked again politely.

"I'm sure it does, although I really can't be a judge having never been to Providence. Would you care to dance?"

"Yes, that would be nice."

He took her hand, leading her to the dance floor unaware of the stares that were directed at them. They whirled across the dance floor for several numbers, moving closer to the terrace. Going outside for a breath of fresh air, they rested on a bench. He moved closer to her, his lips brushing her lips, which received him hungrily. In a few moments they were wrapped in each other's arms oblivious to their surroundings. Their breathing quickened as Timothy pulled away, his loins ached from desire, it had been a long time. "I'm sorry, I didn't mean to take advantage."

She smiled, noticing the effect she had on him, "Tim, you didn't take advantage; in fact I would like this to continue at my apartment in town."

Timothy was taken back, the woman was so forward, "Don't you think that might be scandalous for you? Perhaps it would be better if you came to my apartments?"

"Whatever you want," she purred.

"Come," taking her by the hand he led her back to the ballroom, where Robert was making his engagement announcement. Robert saw his cousin and Timothy enter the room from the terrace. Amanda's face was flushed. What the devil was Timothy up to? Timothy and Amanda crossed the room to congratulate Robert and Molly. Timothy extended his hand, shaking Robert's hand vigorously, he winked, "I'm pleased Robert."

Robert's eyes narrowed, "I see you and my cousin are getting along fine."

"Yes, but Amanda isn't feeling well so I thought I would escort her home."

"Of course; I'm sorry you're not feeling well, Amanda," he said turning his attention to her. Although he didn't know his cousin well, he had heard that she had a string of lovers behind her and would now make Timothy one.

"Yes, my stomach is upset, and I feel a little warm. I'm so grateful the Captain volunteered to take me home."

"Tim is gallant, that much I can say for him," replied Robert.

Taking Amanda by the arm, Timothy said, "Robert, a very nice party, I'll see you tomorrow." Robert stared after the two of them as they weaved their way out of the room.

Once inside the carriage, Amanda stared at the Captain, "You, sir, are so cool and calm. Are you always that way?"

He smiled, "Unless, someone makes me angry."

"I will remember to never make you angry," replied Amanda.

He moved closer to her, eyes shimmering with desire, "I like you Amanda; you are beautiful." His lips caressed hers. He wanted her now, but knew it would be best to wait. He knew her kind, out for a good time and a good time she would have starting with this evening. The carriage stopped in front of the *White Horse Tavern*. Timothy helped her down and led her upstairs to his rooms. On the way, he ordered a bottle of their finest wine and two glasses.

The wine was delivered, and they went into the bedroom with the bottle. Amanda smiled, "Are you married, Captain?" Timothy was startled, for the first time all evening he thought of Jennifer and the child she carried, his child, "Captain?"

Amanda's voice brought him back to the present, "In name only."

"Oh," she murmured.

"Don't worry, my wife is in London, she is staying with her family until the house is ready."

"Perhaps, I shouldn't stay."

"No, stay, I've had mistresses before. Perhaps you would like to be my mistress? You can have a house in Newport, money, fine clothes." He was so aroused by this woman that he wasn't thinking and realized what he was saying too late. Jennifer might decide to stay with him. What would he do with Amanda if she did? Amanda would be a nice diversion until then. He moved closer to her, putting his glass down and talking hers from her hand. His lips touched her finger tips sending shivers up and down her spine. His well learned fingers went to the rear of her dress, unbuttoning the buttons as he kissed her long, hard, seductively. Her well skilled fingers were unbuttoning his shirt moving it away from his body; she ran her fingers through the thick black hair of his chest. He pulled the dress down over her shoulders exposing the pink tipped nipples that were already beginning to harden. His mouth covered one nipple, sucking as if he was trying to draw milk, while his hand kneaded her other breast. He was driving her wild. Her late husband never pleased her like this man. Tim moved to her other nipple, pulling, sucking lightly, arousing it like he had the other. She couldn't stand it any longer; she pushed his head away from her; he caught her meaning. He rose and shed his clothes as she dropped her dress on the floor. He turned to face her, she gasped; he was massive; he frightened her. He came to her, taking her face in his hands, kissing her, his tongue searching. Lifting her in his arms, he placed her on the bed, covering her body with his. Her hands traced the muscles in his back as he followed the lines of her full, but thin body. Their lovemaking lasted over an hour, with Amanda brought to sexual heights she had never before experienced with neither her late husband nor her numerous lovers. Spent, they lay basking in sweat and lust, entwined in each other's arms.

That was how Timothy had spent his first day in Newport. Now, two months later, he realized he had made Amanda his mistress; buying her clothes, jewels and an apartment close to the specialty shops in Brick Market. Jennifer was a faint thought in the rear of his mind, usually surfacing while making love to Amanda. It was during those moments that he pleased Amanda far beyond what he thought he could please a woman. He liked Amanda, she was unlike Jennifer in that she was tall, sultry, and dark; whereas, Jennifer was small and petite.

The mail had arrived earlier during the day, but Timothy hadn't time to check it. Amanda passed by the table where the mail was and decided to look to see if anything was for her. Flipping through the envelopes, she came across a letter from Stefan Weatherly, addressed to Timothy which was marked urgent. Thinking Stefan, a business associate, she interrupted Timothy's meeting with several of the men from the *Moonlight* and Robert. "Excuse me Timothy, but there is a very important letter here, from a …"

Timothy cut her off, "Not now Amanda."

"But it's from London."

He looked at her, "Who is it from?"

"A Stefan Weatherly, it's marked urgent."

"When was it mailed?" His voice pressing.

She looked for the post mark, "Almost two months ago."

"Bring it here." She crossed the room and handed him the letter. Tearing it open, he unfolded the paper. *"Captain Lockwood, you must return to Weatherly at once. Jennifer has become seriously ill, there is a very high chance she could lose the baby and also her life. Dr. Warren suggested that we send for you. Jennifer does not know the seriousness of matter except that she must remain in the bed for the duration of her pregnancy. Come soon and Godspeed. Stefan Weatherly."* Timothy had become pale, his mind going back to Yvonne telling him about Season and now Jennifer?

George, who was sitting across from him, said, "Captain, is there something wrong?"

Timothy looked up, the golden eyes blurry as he fought back the tears that were forming, "Prepare for an immediate voyage to London; I want to leave within hours." Timothy dropped the note on the desk and ran out of the room, bounding up the stairs two at a time to get some sea clothing.

George, Ben and Gideon rose from their seats, George reached for the letter and read it. His eyes watered; the young woman he admired more than any other might die, "Damn, it's Jennifer."

Gideon stared at him; he, too, was fond of her, "What about her?"

George placed the letter on the desk, "She's very ill, the Captain will want to get there quickly; let's go."

"Who is Jennifer?" questioned Amanda.

George stared at her; it was obvious that the Captain never told her about Jennifer. Ignoring her question, he said again, "Let's go." Gideon and Ben were out of the door, with George close on their heels to round up the crew of the *Moonlight*.

Amanda stared at her cousin, Robert, "Well Robert? Who is Jennifer?"

"I honestly don't know who she is; he's never mentioned any relative or sister."

Amanda tapped her foot, "Well, I'm going to find out." Snatching the letter from the desk, she read that this Jennifer might die due to a possible miscarriage, but it gave her no clue as to who the woman was or how Timothy was involved with the woman. Could it be the wife he had mentioned? Timothy returned and took the letter from Amanda's hands, "Who is Jennifer?" she shrieked.

"Not now, Amanda. I don't have time for your theatrics." Turning to Robert, "Sorry Robert, but I have to go to London. Please take care of the business because I don't know when I can return. Start the construction of the new ship, the *Nightbird*." It was obvious to Amanda, that Tim cared much about this woman, Jennifer, so it couldn't be his wife. He said he was married in name only. Timothy had left the envelope on the desk which Amanda picked up as soon as Timothy left the room, putting it in her pocket for future reference. Robert left moments after Timothy, leaving Amanda to sulk in the study. Her hand went to her pocket, retrieving the envelope. The return address was clearly written in the left corner of the envelope. Going to the desk, she copied it on a piece of paper and disposed of the envelope.

CHAPTER SIXTEEN

Yvonne came to London in all her splendor. The *Sea Witch* had been renamed the *Sea Bird* in order to enter British waters without being seized as a pirate ship. Yvonne, herself had bought some fancy clothes to make her look like a lady in London Society. Giving her crew time to enjoy themselves in the city, she hired a hansom carriage and headed for Weatherly. She marveled at the sight of the massive stone house; someday, she hoped to have one as nice as Weatherly. She knocked on the door and waited; a tall, lanky old man answered.

"Can I help you, madame?"

"I'm here to see Jennifer and Timothy."

"I'm sorry, Mr. Lockwood is away, and Miss Jennifer is very ill."

"Ill?" she thought for a second, "Tell her Yvonne is here; I know she'll want to see me."

Harris showed Yvonne into the sitting room and went to get Master Stefan. Stefan appeared moments later, viewing a tall blonde woman, "I understand that you wish to see my cousin, Jennifer."

"That's right and who might you be?"

"Stefan Weatherly. Jennifer is very ill; she's not receiving visitors." This woman was very bold, he thought.

"She'll see me; tell her Yvonne is here, and she ain't leaving until I see her."

"Where do you know my cousin from?" he inquired because he couldn't imagine Jennifer knowing someone who didn't use proper English.

"The Barbary Coast and Java."

Stefan was shocked, "Did you meet her on the slave ship?"

"No, met through Captain Blo," She stopped and corrected herself mid-sentence, Captain Lockwood."

"Yvonne, I've heard the name before," he paused, "Alright, I'll tell Jennifer you're here; I don't know if she'll see you or not."

"She'll see me." Yvonne watched Stefan leave the room. She looked around the room, deciding to sit near the window.

Stefan returned moments later, "Jenny will see you." Yvonne rose and followed him to Jennifer's bedroom.

Jennifer smiled when she saw Yvonne, "Yvonne, it's good to see you."

"I didn't know you were pregnant." Yvonne said, shocked.

Before Yvonne could say something damaging, Jennifer said, "Stefan, Lizabeth, I wish to speak with Yvonne alone, I really don't need you here." Both left the room; Jennifer motioned for Yvonne to sit, "I got your letter."

"I didn't know that you and Tim got married."

"I must swear you to secrecy; everyone believes we are married, but in truth, we are not and probably never will be," her voice faded off on the last words.

"Never? Why?" Yvonne's eyebrows raised questioningly as she pulled the chair closer to the bed.

Jennifer sighed, "It's a long story; it really isn't important."

"Do you love him?"

"No, Yes, I don't know. I care for him. I'm having his child; I thought I loved him once. I was a foolish school girl who fell for the man who saved my life."

"He loves you; I know. I could see it in his eyes." Yvonne said.

Jennifer shook her head, "Maybe before, but he doesn't care anymore. I've been ill for two months and he hasn't returned from Newport." Her eyes brimmed with tears, "Yvonne, if he cared he would have come back. I'm sure he's met someone else, and that's why he hasn't returned."

Yvonne, sensing Jennifer's deep depression, decided to tactfully change the subject, "What exactly is wrong with you?"

"I have to remain in bed for the duration of my pregnancy because there is a chance I could lose the baby."

"I see. Is Lion here or with Tim?"

"He's here; I think he would like to see his Aunt Yvonne."

"I'd like to see the little one myself, and I don't want to tire you, so I'll be visiting from time to time."

"Yes, that would be nice; I don't see anyone other than the servants, Lion, the Doctor or Stefan, so I would be grateful if you came to visit."

"I'll try to visit every day; right now, I'll let you get some rest." Yvonne rose from her seat.

"Thank you for coming; tell my cousin to show you where Lion's room is, and if there is anything you need, please ask Stefan."

Yvonne smiled, "Sure, I'll see you tomorrow." Yvonne left the room to search out Stefan Weatherly, finding him in the sitting room that she had been shown into earlier, "I want some answers; what's really wrong with Jennifer, and exactly how serious is it?"

Stefan looked grim, "It is very serious, the possibility of her losing the child is very high; if she does, she could also lose her life."

Yvonne paled, thinking instantly of Season. Was Jennifer stronger than Season? Could she recuperate? "Does she know?"

"No, and you must promise not to tell her."

"I promise; can I see Tim's son?"

"Yes, come with me."

The days following Yvonne's initial visit to Weatherly made Jennifer happier in that she found a new friend in this pirate woman. Yvonne spent time with both Jennifer and Lion every day trying to make Jennifer somewhat less depressed. She found out from Stefan that he had sent an urgent message to Timothy almost three months ago, and nothing had been heard from him. Yvonne calculated that the letter must have reached him, and by now, he should have arrived in London. It appeared that whenever a woman really needed Captain Bloodthirsty, he was nowhere to be found. Yvonne was sure he would show up eventually; she hoped it would be before Jennifer's time. She refused to believe that Tim didn't love Jennifer any longer, no matter what Jennifer thought. She didn't know what had happened between them but was sure it was something that could be worked out.

Two weeks had passed since Yvonne arrived in London; her crew was becoming restless and Yvonne herself hadn't planned on staying for so long, but with Jennifer's illness and Timothy missing, she decided to stay until it was Jennifer's time. Jennifer had developed a high fever, which the doctor was concerned about; he felt that Jennifer must be watched twenty-four hours a day. Her fever must be brought down, or she would definitely lose the baby. Yvonne and Lizabeth took turns watching the delirious Jennifer, bathing her body with cold water in a futile attempt to bring the fever down. Four days had passed, and Jennifer's body temperature had remained the same. Yvonne and Lizabeth were exhausted. Doctor Warren came two to three times a day to check his patient, each time he said nothing but shook his head.

The *Moonlight* pulled into port three weeks later than expected; the Captain and crew looked haggard and half dead. They hit three major storms en route to London and were thrown off course by hundreds of miles. Timothy's hair was shaggy, and he hadn't shaved in two weeks. He had become thin and barely resembled the man who had left London months before; he rented a horse and rode hard to Weatherly. Tying the horse outside, he dashed into the house taking two stairs at a time. Lizabeth had just left Jennifer's room with a pan of water; she stared at Timothy, at first not recognizing him. Once over her initial shock, she realized it was Timothy and quickly moved out of the way as he burst inside of Jennifer's room. Yvonne turned to face him; words escaped her as she moved towards him, letting him see Jennifer over her shoulder. The topaz eyes teared at the sight before him. Jennifer lay on the bed, her eyes closed. She was very pale, very thin and he could hardly see her breathing. Yvonne had become a blur; in fact, he didn't recognize her until his senses returned. Yvonne looked at him angrily, as she whispered, "It's about damn time that you decided to come." Timothy said nothing but continued to stare at the bedridden Jennifer who looked as if death may take her at any second. "Every time a woman needs you," Yvonne continued, "You come too damn late." The tears that she had been holding in for weeks began to form in her azure eyes, one tear rolling down her cheek; her voice cracked from both exhaustion and fear as she said, "She might not make it." At that instant Jennifer let out a piercing scream that was heard throughout the house. Timothy and Yvonne ran to her bedside as she screamed again. The servants had gathered in the foyer and Stefan came running from the study. Lizabeth dropped her fresh bowl of cold water on the stairs and ran toward the room. Stefan was close on her heels and both burst into the dark bedroom. Timothy was bathing her forehead with cool water, trying to soothe her. Yvonne turned to face them, "The bleeding has started again and its's much heavier, send for Doctor Warren. Lizabeth, I want you to get a towel, soak it in cold water and bring it to me." Neither Stefan nor Lizabeth moved, "I gave you an order, do it." Yvonne screamed at the top of her lungs. Stefan ran downstairs to get Doctor Warren, and Lizabeth went to get the towel.

Timothy stared after them, realizing Yvonne had taken full charge of the situation. He continued to bathe Jennifer's face and shoulders. Lizabeth returned minutes later with the towel, Yvonne stripped the covers from Jennifer's naked body, startling Lizabeth because of

Timothy's presence. The bed sheets were covered in blood, Timothy felt faint. Yvonne ordered Lizabeth to hold Jennifer's legs up as she thrust the cold wet towel between them. The cold towel, Yvonne hoped, would shock Jennifer's body and possibly stop the bleeding or at least control it until the doctor arrived.

An hour later, Doctor Warren arrived, praising Yvonne on her fast thinking. The cold towel did shock Jennifer's system for the time being, but the bleeding would continue; however, it could be controlled by the same method. He shook his head, "There is nothing we can do now. She will lose the baby." He looked at Timothy, "I'm sorry."

Timothy finding his voice to speak for the first time since he burst into Jennifer's room said, "What about Jennifer? Will she be alright?"

Doctor Warren stared at Timothy for a few seconds, "It's hard to tell, the first seventy-two hours after she loses the baby are most crucial. Her fever must be brought down; if her fever is brought down, there is a good chance she'll survive."

"A good chance? You can't guarantee me anything more?" The gold flecked eyes searched the doctor's face.

"Everything depends on how well the bleeding is controlled. As it stands now, she might not make it through the night. She's lost a lot of blood, which has weakened her condition seriously. The women have been briefed on what to do, and they'll take care of her. There is nothing more I can do for her; only time will tell. She's young, so that is in her favor."

Timothy turned his attention to Jennifer, who lay motionless on the bed. He murmured, "Thank you," to the doctor and went to hold Jennifer's hand. He hated himself for becoming involved with Amanda; as soon as Jenny was well, he'd write a letter to Amanda and tell her that it was over between them. Why did he do it? He was so selfish; was Amanda just a release for the tension that had built up between him and Jennifer before he left? He hadn't realized how much this young woman meant to him; he would prove to her how much he loved her if it was the last thing he did in his lifetime. The important thing now was her well-being.

Lizabeth, Yvonne and Timothy took turns caring for Jennifer, yet Tim never left the room. She cried out several times during the night, her fever raging. Tim kept her bathed in cold water; he was exhausted but refused to leave until she regained consciousness. It had been twelve hours since she lost the baby, her fever continued to be high. Timothy paced around the room while Yvonne and Lizabeth changed the bed.

Jennifer had become very hot; Timothy placed cold wet towels over her body. Yvonne and Lizabeth went to rest for a while, leaving Timothy alone with Jennifer. He knelt by the bed rubbing his eyes, he touched her hand, "Jenny, I don't know if you can hear me, but you've got to fight for your life." He rested his head on the edge of the bed, his hand over hers. Tears trickled down his tanned cheeks; it was the first time he had cried since he was a small boy. He lifted his head, staring at her face; it was as if he was in a trance. He tried desperately to memorize every feature; he didn't want to lose her. He rose from his kneeling position and replaced the towels with fresh, cool ones. Yvonne returned hours later with some hot tea for him. He drank quickly not wanting to neglect Jennifer for a moment.

"Tim, why don't you go get something to eat and then go to bed."

"No, I don't want to leave her."

"I'll be here; look at yourself; you can hardly stand up."

It was true, but he was too worried about Jennifer than to care for himself, "Yvonne, what if her fever doesn't break before the seventy-two hours? There's not much time left, what four or five hours. If she dies, I don't know what I'll do."

"She won't die. Don't worry, the fever will break." She answered trying to reassure him. She, herself, was getting worried; if the fever didn't break soon, that meant infection set in; Yvonne didn't want to think of that possibility.

Timothy had become withdrawn, remembering the first night he made love to her and the last time. Would she hate him forever? He sat down in a large cushioned chair, watching Yvonne care for Jennifer. He was exhausted; he couldn't remember the last time he had slept. Closing his eyes for the first time in days, he drifted off into a light sleep. Yvonne sat by Jennifer for the next two hours, changing the towels. She noticed beads of perspiration on Jennifer's forehead, the fever had broken. Yvonne left the room to tell Lizabeth and Stefan. Timothy slept peacefully in the chair near the bed. He woke to a moan, looking around the room he realized Yvonne had left. Rubbing his yes, he gazed toward the bed at Jennifer. Another moan; he went to the bed, touching her hand, it was cool. The fever must have broken while he was asleep. He knelt by the bed, his hand on hers, her fingers moved. It was the first time her lifeless body had shown any signs of recovery. Timothy murmured, "Thank God."

Jennifer was regaining consciousness; she was parched, "Water," she said softly, her eyes still closed. Timothy poured a glass of water.

Jennifer's eyes fluttered open, seeing a strange man kneeling before her bed; yet, there was something vaguely familiar about him. The man lifted her head and put the glass of cold water to her lips. She drank slowly, he placed her head back on the pillow, putting the glass on the nightstand near the bed. Jennifer looked at the man. His eyes. Tim's eyes. "Tim," she whispered.

"Shush, don't try to talk. There'll be plenty of time for that later. You need your rest."

She squinted, he had changed, his hair was long and unkempt, he was thin and sported a full beard. He looked tired, "You look like you need a rest."

He smiled, "I said don't talk. I'll get Lizabeth to bring you some soup." He went to the door, opening it, bellowed, "Lizabeth, bring some soup." Lizabeth heard his yell all the way downstairs as did Stefan and Yvonne, who both came running. Tim greeted them at the door with a smile, "She's awake."

Stefan's face broke into a grin, the first time in days. Yvonne brushed past Timothy, going to the bed. Looking down at Jennifer she said, "Thank God! How do you feel?"

"Weak."

Yvonne shook her head, "That's to be expected."

Lizabeth came with the soup, sat down aside of the bed and proceeded to spoon feed Jennifer. Looking up at the crowd that had gathered in the room she said, "Stefan don't you have work to do?"

"I, uh, yes." He turned and left the room.

Lizabeth looked at Timothy, "Captain Lockwood, I dare say you need a bath, some hot food and a good night's rest."

"I'm not leaving," said Timothy sternly.

"Yvonne turned to him, "You're not going to be any good for her the way you look, go get some rest."

Timothy looked at Yvonne pleadingly, "I want to stay."

"I said get out; you can see and talk to her later," Yvonne said as pushed him out the door.

He sighed, the first thing he wanted was a strong drink, the second, a hot bath, and the third a soft bed. He went downstairs to the study and poured himself a glass of rum. Stefan was working at the desk. The liquid burned his throat all the way into the pit of his stomach. He refilled the glass. Stefan had been watching him, "You really care for her?"

Timothy turned to face him, "You sound surprised. I more than just care for her, I love her, more than I thought was possible for a man to love a woman."

"I love her too. I realized that while she was ill. She's my best friend, we've grown up together, she's like a sister. I didn't think you'd be good for her, but I was wrong."

Timothy gulped down his second glass of rum. "I do love her; I just didn't realize how much until now." He laughed, partly from exhaustion and partly from nerves, "You never really realize how much you care for someone until you are faced with the fact that you may never see them again. If she had died, I would have never forgiven myself for causing her so much pain. I should have never gone to Newport." He shook his head before finishing his drink.

"Nonsense, you had a business to tend to in Newport. You had been away from it for a long time; you needed to go back. How would you know that Jennifer would become ill? How did any of us know?"

"I should have never gone." Putting down the glass, he said, "I'm going to take a bath and go to bed."

"I don't know how you managed, Tim. You haven't slept in days."

He smiled, "I'm used to it. Talk to you later, Stefan."

"Tim, before you leave, can I ask you something?"

"Sure."

"Why don't you marry her?"

"I am married to her." Timothy answered, his face expressionless.

"No, you didn't think I would believe the story you told, did you? I may be young, but I'm not stupid; besides that, I know my cousin is attracted to you, and that on long voyages, certain things happen."

"Please don't say anymore, Stefan. I beg you to keep our secret until Jennifer decides whether or not she'll have me. Everything you said is true, but we had an argument before we reached London. It is too long to explain, but I was going to marry her. Good night." He left the room to go upstairs to bathe and sleep.

Jennifer slept peacefully through the night with Yvonne and Lizabeth taking four-hour watch shifts. Jennifer woke with a start. Yvonne was sleeping in the large chair; the sunlight was streaming through the window. She lay there, not wanting to disturb Yvonne.

Timothy woke, dressed and immediately went to Jennifer's room. Opening the door, he saw that she was awake, he smiled, "Good morning."

"Morning," she answered. He had shaved his beard, leaving a mustache and his hair was neatly combed.

"How are you feeling?" he asked.

"Weak, but okay."

"Are you hungry?"

"Starved."

"Good, I'll have Lizabeth fix us something to eat. How are you feeling this morning?" He asked, staring at her.

She looked at him, "Tim, you asked me that already."

"I'm sorry, what did you say?" he said still exhausted.

"I said, I was weak, but okay. I'm also a little tired. When did you return?"

"Four days ago. I would have been here sooner, but I had some weather problems."

"You don't need to make an excuse, the important thing is that you cared enough to come," replied Jennifer.

Timothy crossed the room, his eyes soft, "I do love you Jennifer, more than I can possibly express."

He embarrassed her, "I lost the baby."

"Yes, but we can have others," he said softly.

She touched his hand, "Tim, we're not married. Now we never have to be married."

He brushed his lips against her fingertips, "I want to marry you. Let me prove to you how much I care."

"I can't. Don't you see, if we were meant to be, I wouldn't have lost the baby. This is God's will." She smoothed the covers with her fingers.

He touched her hair, his hand taking her face, lifting her head, turning it toward him, "Kiss me, Jennifer. That will tell you whether we belong together or not."

What did she see in his eyes? Hurt, a certain sadness; she wanted to turn away but it was as if she was in a trancelike state gazing into his golden eyes. She moved closer to him, forgetting Yvonne was even in the room, her lips kissed his timidly. Timothy had decided to let her control everything that passed between them. Her second kiss was more forceful; Timothy responded the way he thought she would like. Jennifer pulled away, the sea green eyes misty, "You can be so gentle and yet so mean."

He was startled, "Mean?" He hadn't expected those words.

"Yes, you tear me apart, Tim. When you're here, you torture my heart. In all the months you were gone, even after Java, I became so confused."

"Confused? About what?"

"Whether or not you cared about me. Whether I cared about you. You hide your emotions so well; sometimes there is a something in your eyes; it's only there for a moment, and then it's gone." Jennifer replied.

"What about you? Do you care?" Timothy questioned.

"I, unlike you, am not capable of hiding my emotions so well. That scares me."

He laughed, "Jennifer, I'm not all that secretive where my emotions are concerned when it comes to you. The way I left Newport, what I put my crew through to get here, what I put Lizabeth and Yvonne through after I stormed into this house," he said, motioning to the sleeping Yvonne.

Jennifer asked again, "Do you really care?"

"Let me prove my love, green-eyed vixen. Marry me."

"Everyone thinks we are already married."

Stefan knows, I told him and swore him to secrecy."

"You told him! How could you?" questioned Jennifer.

"Shush, calm down, I just told him that we were not married although we had planned to be married. I also told him that whether we marry or not would be up to you." He paused, "Don't worry about the servants. I'm sure Yvonne and George would be more than happy to be our witnesses. They would never tell anyone. The consequences would be too great. After you're better, when you recover, what do you say?"

Jennifer hesitated, "I'm not sure."

His eyes hardened for a moment, becoming a deeper gold, "Make a decision, Jennifer, I won't pressure you. I'll ask you one other time when you're well. If your answer is still the same, I'll leave, and you won't have to worry about seeing me again."

She frowned, knowing she had hurt him, but could she trust him again. Timothy left the room to see to Jennifer's breakfast. Yvonne stirred, Jennifer smiled, "Good morning."

Stretching, Yvonne rose from the chair, "How are you feeling?'

"Fine, well actually very weak and tired."

"Has Tim been in yet?"

"Yes, he just left." She paused, "Yvonne, when did he get here?"

Yvonne thought for a second, "About four days ago. He came tearing in here like a man possessed. He loves you Jennifer; he was by your side the entire time you were unconscious. He wouldn't leave or take a break; he bathed you with cool towels and held your hand. Is there anything else you want to know?"

"No, thanks," Jennifer responded.

"Well, if that's all I'll be going downstairs to get something to eat." Yvonne left Jennifer alone. She lay quietly in the bed, thinking about what Tim said and what Yvonne said. Her thoughts were interrupted by Timothy who appeared with a breakfast tray. She smiled at him.

"Your breakfast, Jenny." He placed the small table over her lap.

She looked down at the massive breakfast. The plate was overflowing with eggs, ham, hot coffee and juice. "I can't possibly eat all of this." She looked up at him.

"You can and you will; you need this food to build up your energy."

"When I woke last night, I didn't recognize you; you've gotten so thin," Jennifer said as she picked up the fork.

Curious he asked, "What made you say my name?"

"Your eyes; they are a dead giveaway."

"Eat," he demanded. She smiled at him and began to eat as he watched her.

She stopped, putting down the fork, "I didn't think you were coming back."

His eyes widened, "You doubt me that much?"

"I didn't think you cared." She took a deep breath, "Before you left you seemed so cold, as if you didn't care."

"Care? I love you Jennifer. I've made my mistakes, which must be put right."

"Don't," replied Jennifer.

"It has to be said Jennifer. What I did to you on my ship was inexcusable. I lost all of my senses and I wanted to hurt you because you disobeyed orders. This may sound strange, but I thought you should know what could have happened to you if the mercenaries had captured you." He paused, thinking back. "Do you know what you do to me?" She shook her head. "Every time I see you, I'm driven wild with desire, I go completely out of my mind."

Jennifer smiled inwardly, perhaps he did love her after all, "How long will you be staying in London?"

"Until you are well and have made a decision," he said trying to keep his emotions in check because her words rang in his head, *how long will you be staying*...he feared she was going to not want him in her life.

Jennifer finished eating the last of her breakfast, "Would you open the window? It's stuffy in here."

He walked to the window, "For December, it's rather nice. Warm, sunny." He stopped in the middle of his sentence, staring out the window.

"What's wrong?" Jennifer asked.

He looked toward Jennifer's bed, "Nothing, I was just thinking. I'll take your tray downstairs." Lifting the tray from her bed he said, "Rest well." He left the room with the breakfast tray.

CHAPTER SEVENTEEN

The days that followed became colder, snow fell, lightly dusting the ground two days before Christmas. Timothy had busied himself with details for the holiday, wanting it to be perfect for Lion and Jennifer. Jennifer had become depressed over the loss of the baby. Her sadness increased when Yvonne left London to return to Spain for the holidays. Most of her time was spent in her bedroom, although Timothy sometimes carried her downstairs to the library or sitting room for a couple of hours. He had become the attentive husband, so much that he won Lizabeth over to his side. Lizabeth confessed to Jennifer that the Captain impressed her and that her original thoughts of him were wrong. Stefan spent much of his time working at the offices of his late Uncle, or collecting rents from the many houses and pieces of land owned by the Weatherly's. Lately, he had become secretive about his whereabouts; Jennifer and Timothy both agreed that he must have a lady friend. In actuality, Stefan was buying Christmas presents for the entire family, including his aunt at the Bryant Sanitarium.

Christmas Eve dinner was served in the main dining room. Timothy had carried Jennifer to the dining the room for dinner which consisted of several kinds of roast meats, vegetables and potatoes. Once dinner was done, Timothy helped Jennifer into the sitting room, which had been gaily decorated earlier in the day by him and Lizabeth. Jennifer smiling commented, "The room looks beautiful."

Lion who was beginning to look more and more like his father, was playing quietly on the floor. Timothy gave him a piece of hard candy, "I'm glad you like it. Lizabeth and I wanted it to be a surprise."

"It's very nice. Would you mind taking me upstairs. I'm a little tired."

"If that's what you want."

"Yes," she replied. She was a little disappointed that Timothy hadn't given her a Christmas present, but she really shouldn't expect anything from him, after the way she had been behaving. He picked her up and carried her to her bedroom.

She lay quietly for what seemed hours as she thought of Christmas. It was once a happy time, but this year with the death of her father and her child, it had become a sad time. A single tear trickled down her cheek, she brushed it away, closing her eyes.

The next morning Weatherly was ablaze with activities. Timothy was dressed in chocolate brown waistcoat and trousers with a cream-colored shirt. He went to Jennifer's bedroom with a small box in his hand, "Good morning."

"Good morning," she said forlornly.

"I think it's time for you to dress. You've been in bed three weeks and it's time to get up and get on with life."

He was right; she should be getting up and around by herself, "Tim, I want to wish you a Merry Christmas," she exclaimed. He extended his hand, revealing a small box, "What is this?" she queried.

"Take it and find out." His eyes twinkled with delight.

She took it from his hand and readjusted herself in the bed. Timothy sat on the edge of the bed as Jennifer opened the box. She gasped, as an emerald and diamond ring peered out at her. Her mind flooded with memories of the *Moonlight*. Her eyes filled with tears. She looked at him questioningly, "Why?"

He sighed, "I gave you that once before, this time I hope you keep it." A tear escaped her eyes, rolling down her cheek, Tim brushed it way with his thumb, "Do our memories upset you that much?" His eyes locked with hers.

She quickly composed herself, "I have no present for you."

"I don't want a present from you. At least not a present that is an object."

She stared at him for a moment, changing the subject, "What do you want me to wear today?"

He went to her closet, open the doors and began to search for an appropriate dress. Selecting an emerald green velvet, he turned to Jennifer, "I'd like you to wear this, it will look good with your coloring and the ring."

"You really didn't have to get me a present."

"I really didn't buy you this, it was mine, I think you remember it."

She blushed, "Yes, I remember."

"I'll get Lizabeth to help you with your bath and dressing." He turned to walk out of the room.

Jennifer put the open ring box on the bedside table, staring at the ring. Lizabeth came into Jennifer's room, "I'm glad the Captain convinced you to get out of bed."

"Yes, it'll be good to get out of bed and to try to resume a normal life once again."

Lizabeth spied the small box and its contents, "Miss Jennifer," she gasped, "What a beautiful ring! Did the Captain give it to you?" She asked looking at her.

"Yes," she blushed, "This morning."

"The more I know him, the better I like him; the man has excellent taste."

"He didn't buy the ring; it belonged to his mother," replied Jennifer.

"I see. Well, I'll draw your bath, and we'll fix you up very pretty for your husband."

Jennifer smiled thinking if Lizabeth had only known that they were not married, what would she say?

Timothy had taken Lion downstairs. The small boy played with the toys in the sitting room. Tim stoked the fire, staring into the flames as they flickered, casting shadows across his face. He thought of his past; Season, Jennifer, Amanda, and his son. Sighing, he realized that he hadn't written to Amanda to break-off with her. It would be a top priority for tomorrow. Jennifer entered the sitting room looking lovelier than he could remember. Sucking in his breath quickly, he said, "I made the right choice with that dress."

She smiled, "I came downstairs by myself."

"That's good," he answered never taking his eyes from her as he walked toward her. The room grew quiet for a few moments except for the sound of Lion playing.

Jennifer broke the silence, "I'm feeling very good. In fact, I should have been up days ago, I guess I needed the encouragement."

Timothy stared at her, it was as if they were strangers who were meeting for the first time, finding it hard to hold a conversation. "Have our differences become so great that we cannot hold a conversation other than the weather or your health?" She said nothing. "Jenny, I do care about you. What happened to the days when we could argue? When you were full of fire and spirit?" His golden eyes peered into her green ones questioningly.

"Those days are gone, Tim. I've lied for you. I've protected you, and I loved you. But I don't have the spirit that you seem to want in a woman."

"I think you do," he said softly.

Jennifer shook her head, "Not anymore."

"In a few days I'll want the answer to the question I asked you," he said tensely.

They were interrupted by Stefan who appeared with armload of presents for the entire family. "Good morning, Tim, Jenny and little Lion."

"Good morning, Stefan," answered Timothy. "Can I be of some assistance with those packages?"

"No, it's okay." Jennifer had moved to a chair near the fireplace, gazing into the flames. Stefan approached her, "This one is for you, Jenny. I hope you like it."

She looked at him, taking the box from his hands she placed it on her lap and began to untie the ribbons. She removed the cover, inside she found a beautiful hat, "It's lovely." She lifted it from the box, setting it on her head, "How does it look?" she faced Stefan and Timothy.

"Beautiful, and I have the perfect thing to go with it," answered Timothy. He stretched gracefully reaching for a large box, handing it to her, "Open it."

Stunned, she took the box from his hands. Opening it she drew in her breath, a gown made of the finest red velvet. Jennifer picked the gown up by the shoulders as she let the box slide to the floor. She smiled, "Thank you both." Standing, she leaned forward kissed her cousin on the cheek. Turning to Timothy, their eyes met, he was grinning from ear to ear.

"Don't I get a kiss?" he asked. She flushed. How dare he make her kiss him in front of her cousin. His topaz eyes were dancing in merriment, "Well?"

She walked towards him, "Thank you, Tim." Jennifer stood on tip toes, kissing him, just brushing her lips with his. His arms engulfed her, holding her to him, his lips forced hers to respond. Jennifer felt her knees weaken as she leaned against him. What had he done to her? He released her, his eyes twinkling with delight. He helped her back to her seat, noting that her cousin had discreetly left the room. She was furious, "How could you do that in front of my cousin?"

He smiled, "He must know that we've kissed before; besides, you enjoyed it!"

"You're incorrigible. Why did you buy me that dress?"

"It is part of your many Christmas gifts."

She was puzzled, "Many?"

He smirked, "Wait until you see the remainder."

Before Jennifer could reply, Lizabeth interrupted them. "Dinner is ready."

"We'll be along in a moment," answered Timothy. Turning to Jennifer, "I want an answer tomorrow. Come along Lion, we must wash your hands before we eat dinner." The small boy stood up and followed Timothy. Jennifer followed the two of them; they went into the kitchen, and Jennifer went into the dining room.

Several hours later, Jennifer sat in her bedroom reading. Her mind could not stay on the book, prompting her to put it aside. She rose from the bed and began pacing around the room, trying to sort out her feelings about Timothy. Months ago, when she first saw him, she thought he was a man who knew how to possess the soul of a woman. She was right. Timothy Lockwood certainly knew how to please a woman, how to protect her and how to hurt, she remembered bitterly. Through everything that had happened, she had found herself depending on him for support. He said he loved her, but was that just a ploy to get her back into his bed? She walked to the dressing table, picking up the gold handled brush and began to brush her long auburn hair vigorously. She brushed so hard, that the bristles of the brush were digging into her scalp. She stopped brushing, looked into the mirror, sighed, "What am I to do?" The answer was simple, but she felt that she must weigh her thoughts very carefully. She stood up and began pacing around the room again; he wanted an answer tomorrow. Tomorrow, the day after Christmas, she knew in her heart that she wanted to say yes, but her brain was telling her no. She argued with herself. On the one hand he had shown his devotion to her when she lost the baby; Yvonne told her so; she saw it for herself. He had dropped all of his business in Newport and came back to Weatherly, so he had to care. In the process, he had won Lizabeth over to his side. On the other hand, there was the rape and his cool treatment of her when they had returned. She lay down on her bed, closed her eyes and began thinking. Lizabeth went to Jennifer's room to find her asleep. She called the Captain, who helped with getting Jennifer under the covers.

Early the following morning, Jennifer woke with a start. Putting her dressing gown on, she went into the hall. It was dark; she made her way to Timothy's room. Trying the knob, she found it open. She walked in, spying Timothy asleep with a book laying on his chest, the fireplace flames cast dancing shadows on the wall. She moved toward the bed, taking one of his hands she went to take the book from his chest. Timothy moved quickly grasping her arm in the dark, startling Jennifer. His eyes flew open expecting to see a thief or an enemy, never expecting Jennifer standing over his bed, "Jenny."

"Let go of me, you brute." He released her; she rubbed her wrist.

"What the devil are you doing here?" He said trying to be quiet.

"I," she hesitated, "I thought perhaps you weren't asleep."

He sat up in bed, revealing his naked, lean body to the waist. Jennifer's eyes roamed over him, "Do you know that it must be at least three in the morning? Of course, I'd be asleep."

"I had to see you," Jennifer whispered.

"I noticed. You haven't taken your eyes from my chest. Is something the matter?"

"I've made a decision about us."

Timothy yawned, stretched and rubbed his eyes, "This couldn't wait?"

"No." she sat on the edge of the bed.

Timothy looked at her, "Well?"

"I want to stay with you. I'll go to Newport."

He grabbed her in his iron-like grip, pulling her down beside him; his body felt as if it was on fire. His lips touched hers, expecting to find her hesitant, but much to his surprise he found her mouth hungrily searching for his. Her tongue thrust itself inside of his mouth, searching, tasting him. His body rolled over so he was on top of her, his breathing had quickened as did hers. Her turquoise eyes glistened with tears; his gold eyes peered into hers, "I won't hurt you this time." His lips touched hers; their flames of passion burned. A clap of thunder, nature's fury, matched the lovers' embrace. Timothy began to untie the dressing gown, helping it from her body. The thin chemise came off next with one sweep of his hand. He stared at her body; the pregnancy had matured her once thin, lithe frame. Her breasts and hips had a new fullness, yet her stomach was as flat as his. He had waited for her to make this first move; now, their life together could be complete.

CHAPTER EIGHTEEN

Amanda Bowman sat in her study. Newport was becoming boring; Timothy had been gone for months with no word. She went to the desk to search for the paper she had written that woman's address on. Finally, finding it, she stared at it for several seconds. If she didn't hear from Timothy, and Robert didn't hear from him, then she would have to contact him. Timothy Lockwood was different from any man she had ever known; he was an expert lover and pleased her more than she thought was possible for a man to please a woman. Taking out the paper, she dipped the quill into the ink, *"My dearest Timothy, it has been months since you've left Newport. Quite frankly, I've grown bored; it has been lonely without you. When are you planning to return? Even Robert has begun to wonder about you."* She stopped writing; she had a much better idea. She had always wanted to tour London, perhaps she could convince Robert and his pitiful wife to join her. They could visit Timothy; hastily, she threw the papers into the desk and ordered her servant to have her carriage ready within the hour.

Robert and Molly Gray had risen late that morning. They were eating a quiet breakfast when Amanda came parading into the dining room. "Please don't get up on my account. I have a proposition that I wish to discuss with you."

Robert motioned for her to sit down. "What type of proposition, cousin?" A servant appeared with coffee and a sweet roll, placing it in front of Amanda.

"I've wanted to tour London for some time now and I thought that perhaps the two of you would like to join me."

"Amanda, that would be nice, but I do think it's out of the question right now. What with Timothy gone..."

Amanda interrupted him, "That's the whole point, we could see him in London and bring him back to Newport with us. I'm sure you could get someone to run the business."

"Well, I did receive a letter from Tim the other day while you were away." He added quickly, seeing the anger in her eyes, "He said he is not going to be returning for several weeks."

"See, what did I tell you! Turning to Molly, she said, "Molly, wouldn't you like to see London, go to the theatre, the opera, see the sights?"

Molly really didn't like Amanda, but this idea of hers was appealing. After all, Robert and she didn't spend too much time on a honeymoon. "Yes, I would." Looking across the table at Robert she said, "I'm sure Joshua Davenport could handle the shipping business. Please, Robert, a vacation would be nice. You could tell Tim in person about the progress on Lockwood and the business."

"You do have a point, Molly," said Robert.

Amanda put her coffee cup down, "Then that settles it, we'll all go to London!"

Robert rose from his seat, "I'll see about arranging passage on one of our ships. Amanda, I'll let you know the plans. Molly, I'll see you later." He bent to kiss her goodbye, leaving the two women to chatter about the upcoming trip.

Robert went to Gray and Lockwood Shipping Lanes to seek out Joshua Davenport. Joshua had worked for Robert several years and could be trusted with the business. Joshua came to Robert's office within the hour; he was a tall, lanky man with long black hair tied at the nape of his neck. "Robert, you were looking for me?" he said striding into the room, taking a seat in front of Robert's desk.

"Yes, I'm planning a trip to London to visit with Captain Lockwood. I was wondering if you'd take the responsibility of running the business while I'm gone."

"How long do you plan to be gone?"

"Month, month and a half," replied Robert.

"That is a great responsibility you wish me to have; I'm not sure I can do it." He tapped is fingers lightly on the arm of the chair.

"Joshua, I have the utmost confidence in you. It'll mean more money for you and your family. Say you'll take it."

More money! It was true that his family was feeling a financial pinch lately. The offer was tempting, He took a deep breath, "Okay, I'll do it."

"You won't be sorry, Joshua; I promise you."

"When are you leaving?"

"In two days on the *Nightbird.*"

"The *Nightbird?* You're going to take the *Nightbird* to London on its maiden run?"

"Yes, why?" asked Robert.

"I thought the *Nightbird* was built for Captain Lockwood's private use."

"It is Captain Lockwood's ship, but since I'm going to visit him, I thought I would surprise him."

"Who will be Captain?" Joshua asked out of curiosity.

"Gerald Johnson. He's one of our best."

Joshua stood up, shook hands with Robert and said, "Thank you for putting so much trust in me, sir, I won't fail you or Captain Lockwood."

Robert had also stood up, shaking Joshua's hand, "I'm sure you won't." Joshua left Robert's office humming to himself. Robert finished his paperwork, cleared his desk and set out to Amanda's house to tell her of the plans.

Robert rang the bell, waiting patiently for the door to open, Amanda herself opened the door, "Robert, you've come to tell me the plans, do come in." He entered the house following her into the library, "Can I get you something?"

"Brandy," answered Robert. Amanda went to the liquor cabinet, poured herself and Robert a drink, handing him his, "Thank you," said Robert.

Taking a sip of her brandy, "Well?" queried Amanda.

"We leave in two days on the *Nightbird.*"

"The *Nightbird?* I've never heard of it."

"I didn't think you had; it's Timothy's newest clipper. It has been designed for extremely fast travel."

"How fast?" asked Amanda.

"I'm not sure, but Timothy seemed to think that the *Nightbird* could reach London within ten days, where a normal clipper could take up to twenty-one days."

"Why does he want a ship so fast?"

Robert shook his head, "I don't know; he's been very vague about his plans for the ship."

"It's probably going to be used for trading," she paused, "Then in two days we leave. I've a million things to take care of. I'm glad you told me now."

"Yes, and now I must go home to tell Molly; if you'll excuse me," he placed his glass down on the table, "I'll be going."

Amanda rose from her seat opposite Robert, "Of course." The two of them walked to the door in silence. "Robert, should I come to your home with my luggage, or should I meet you at the docks?"

"My home," he kissed her lightly on the cheek, "Goodbye."

"Goodbye," she watched him climb into his landau and drive off. She went back inside; she wanted to look perfect for Timothy.

Two days later, Amanda appeared at Robert's with two large trunks. She walked briskly into the house, "Robert, Molly are you ready?"

Molly was coming down the staircase dressed in a lovely royal blue velvet gown, "Robert is in the stables, preparing the carriage."

"I see, then we are leaving for the docks when he returns with the carriage?"

"Yes." Molly reached the bottom of the stairs. "Do come into the sitting room, Amanda."

Amanda followed her into the sitting room, removing her cloak, "Have you seen this new ship?"

"No, I haven't, although Robert tells me it is very sleek."

Robert entered the sitting room, "Amanda, I'm glad you're here early. Let me get your trunks loaded and then we can leave." Once the trunks were loaded by Robert and the footman, Robert motioned for the women. Amanda put her cloak on hastily and Molly donned her hat, gloves, and cloak. Robert helped them up into the carriage before getting in himself.

The *Nightbird's* hull was much longer and narrower than any other clipper ship. Her bow was sharper and her floors flatter, so she could carry many more sails than the average clipper. Robert had been told by Timothy that once completed, the *Nightbird* should be able to attain speeds between twenty-three and twenty-seven knots, beating out the records set by the fast McKay clippers. Amanda was in awe of the ship; she had never seen a ship so narrow in the hull nor a bow sharper. The sails were massive, and she began to think of Timothy a fool for believing that such a ship could travel faster when it would be weighed down by such massive sails. The two women boarded the ship, each being shown to their respective cabins. Amanda glanced around hers, it was small, but what could she expect with such a narrow ship. A bunk lay against the left wall and a small desk sat on the opposite wall. She walked to the desk. Paper and quills had been left for her in case she wanted to write a letter. The stationary was marked *Nightbird;* she smiled; Timothy must have thought of such an idea. At the base of the bed, she found a chamber pot, a wash bowl, soap and linens. A small table with two chairs were against the wall opposite the door of the cabin. A small man appeared in the doorway, startling her, "Excuse me, Miss, your trunks are being brought in by two members of the crew. My name is Peter, and I've been assigned to you. If there is anything you need, please let me know." He bowed to her and waited.

"There is nothing right now, thank you."

"Once we have set sail, I'll show you around the ship." He bowed again and left.

The days on the *Nightbird,* passed quickly. Amanda had grown bored with ship life after the first day. The tour promised by Peter was boring and uneventful except when she turned the heads of certain members of the crew. She fantasized about Timothy and how happy he would be when she reached London. It was a matter of three or four days now and she would be going to the theatre, the opera and spending time with Tim seeing the city. Amanda was dying to meet his so-called wife and the mysterious woman, Jennifer, whoever she might be.

Molly Gray spent most of her shipboard time seasick, which, much to his dislike, left Robert in the constant company of his cousin. Gerald Johnson, the tall, thin, greying Captain for the voyage took an immediate liking to Amanda's beauty. Every chance he had, he would seek her out, take her for a walk or just sit and talk. Amanda thought he was charming and friendly but much too old for her. Whenever she could, she would ask crew members about Timothy, his background, what he did before he went to Newport and what his wife looked like. Much to her dismay, her questions were either ignored or answered indirectly. Many times, she felt that they were lying to her. Timothy was certainly a hard man about whom to get information.

The *Nightbird* reached London in a record time of eight days. Robert could hardly wait to see Timothy to tell him how right he was about the *Nightbird* and her speed. The two women packed their trunks and were prepared to leave within an hour. Robert rented a carriage and gave the driver the address. Amanda and Molly climbed in the carriage followed by Robert. The two women stared out the windows of the coach at the countryside. Weatherly loomed in front of them; Amanda instantly thought of the wealth that must surround a house like that, it must belong to Timothy, part of his wife's dowry. The carriage stopped in front of the large oak doors. Robert, Molly and Amanda got out of the carriage and the driver and footman began unloading the trunks into the snow. Robert pulled the door chime and waited. Harris opened the door, "Yes."

"My name is Robert Gray. I'm a friend and business partner of Captain Lockwood."

"Is he expecting you?" questioned Harris.

"No, I must admit that this is somewhat of a surprise." Amanda had been staring at the impeccably dressed man.

"Very well, this way please." Harris led them into the main parlor. "Please have a seat, I'll tell the Captain that you are here."

Jennifer was coming downstairs on her way to the library where she knew Timothy was working. In the main foyer she saw some large trunks. Seeing Harris, she stopped him, "Harris, where did those trunks come from?"

"Some friends of the Captain are here unexpectedly; I was on my way to tell him."

"I'll tell Timothy; it is obvious that they plan to stay. So why don't you find Lizabeth and Maggie and have them prepare the west wing for the visitors."

"Yes, Miss." Harris turned, walking in the opposite direction.

Jennifer continued on her way to the library. She opened the doors, startling Timothy. He rose, "Jenny, how are you feeling?"

She had risen with an upset stomach, "Fine; we have visitors."

"Visitors? I'm not expecting anyone."

"Harris said that they were friends of yours."

"Well, let's go see who they are." He moved from behind the desk, taking Jennifer by the arm and led her to the main parlor. He opened one of the doors letting Jennifer enter first and he followed. The first person he saw was Robert, "Robert, you devil, how are you doing?"

"Fine, Tim, we came to visit."

Tim realized that Robert wasn't alone, he turned, seeing Molly and Amanda. His face took on an ashen look, "Molly, Amanda, it is good to see you again."

"Tim, I've missed you," purred Amanda. Jennifer was standing quietly at the doors of the main parlor. She wanted to scratch out the woman's eyes; how dare she be so familiar with Tim. Jennifer glared at the dark-haired woman. Her stare icy.

Tim turned toward Jennifer, motioning for her to come by his side. "Robert, Molly, Amanda, this is Jennifer." Robert and Amanda recognized the name. Amanda looked Jennifer over quickly. Small, petite, green-eyed, and red-haired, her beauty was astonishing. "My wife." Amanda felt ill. He ran off to London to be with a wife that he said was in name only. "Jenny, I'd like you to meet my business partner Robert Gray and his wife Molly."

"It is a pleasure to meet the two of you."

Robert and Molly said simultaneously, "Same here."

Jennifer smiled; her attention now turned to Amanda. Tim said, "And this is Robert's cousin, Amanda Bowmen."

"How do you do, Amanda?" Jennifer smiled, straining against her instincts to lash out.

"It is a pleasure to meet you; Tim has told me much about you." Amanda smiled, she wanted this young girl to know that she had experienced her husband and would take him away.

Timothy was furious with Amanda; he could have strangled her. She was deliberately causing trouble; she wanted Jennifer to find out about her relationship with him. "Yes, Amanda and I became good friends while I was in Newport."

"So, I see," answered Jennifer curtly. Timothy recognized the tone of her voice; she was angry, and she'd be a spitfire when they were alone. "If you'll excuse me, I'll see to your rooms." Jennifer breezed out of the room, bumping into Stefan. "Sorry."

"Sure." He could tell she was upset. He entered the sitting room to find Tim and three people he did not know.

Timothy, who had been staring after Jennifer said, "Stefan, let me introduce you to some friends. Robert Gray, his wife, Molly, and his cousin, Amanda Bowmen. This is Jennifer's cousin, Stefan Weatherly."

"How do you do, Mr. Weatherly?" Robert said, shaking his hand.

The two women murmured together, "Pleased to meet you."

"It is a pleasure to meet all of you. I take it that you will be our house guests?" he said motioning to the trunks, "We haven't had guest for a long time."

"Yes, Jennifer said something about the west wing. She went to see to the rooms," answered Timothy; turning his attention to Robert he said, "Did you come on one of our ships?"

Amanda moved across the room, so she was standing beside Timothy, "Yes, we came on the *Nightbird*."

Timothy glared at Robert, "You took the *Nightbird* out of Newport?"

"Yes, I thought that you'd like to see it."

Timothy ran his hand through his hair, "I didn't want the *Nightbird* to leave Newport, let alone sail to London. I have plans for that ship."

"I'm sorry that you're angry."

"I'm not angry, it is just that I have private plans for the *Nightbird*."

"I know that."

Jennifer returned to the main parlor, "Your rooms are ready. If you'd like, I'll show them to you."

Stefan looked at her, "Jenny, I'll do it, you shouldn't be going up and down the stairs."

"Jenny, perhaps you better lay down for a while. You have been overdoing it the last few days," said Timothy.

The green eyes narrowed, "Really, Tim, I feel perfectly well. Stefan, I will show them to the rooms, it really isn't a problem."

Timothy could see that she was angry. Yet he couldn't understand why, "If you feel fine, then you feel fine. I'll come with you." Taking her by the arm he led her upstairs into the west wing with their guests following.

Amanda smiled inwardly. She knew that she could get to the young girl, but she was surprised at just how fast. She followed Timothy and Jennifer who led the way into the west wing. Amanda's room was first. Jennifer opened her door, "I hope you like the room, Miss Bowmen."

"It's Mrs., but you can call me Amanda. The room is very nice," She said looking around.

"Perhaps you'd like to take a bath and refresh yourself before dinner; I took the liberty of having Estelle draw the water for you. Estelle will be in charge of this wing. If there is anything you need, ask her."

"Thank you, Mrs. Lockwood." Amanda closed the door.

Jennifer turned to Robert and Molly, "Mr. and Mrs. Gray, please follow me." She led them down the corridor opening two large doors into a suite of rooms, "I hope you will enjoy your stay at Weatherly. If you need anything, ask Estelle. Baths have been drawn for the two of you, and your trunks will be brought up momentarily."

"Thank you," answered Molly. "A bath would be nice, and I would like to rest."

"Tim, I'm sorry about the *Nightbird*," said Robert.

"It's not important, Robert, we'll discuss it after dinner."

"Yes, after dinner." Robert shut the door.

Jennifer began to walk quickly down the corridor. Timothy grabbed her by the arm, "Jenny, what's wrong?"

"Nothing," she snapped. "Nothing at all."

They stood in the corridor, facing each other, "Don't tell me nothing is wrong, I can see it in your face, and I can hear it in the tone of your voice." He raised his voice."

She looked at him defiantly, "Lower your voice; someone will hear you."

His eyes shimmered dangerously, "What is wrong?"

"We will discuss it in the confines of our room, when no one can overhear us."

Taking her by the arm, Timothy led her down the corridor to their bedroom. Opening the door, he tossed her inside. Slamming the door behind him, she glared at him. "Well, Jennifer, we are now in the confines of our room."

"I seem to remember you tossing me inside another room."

"Let's not discuss it. I want to know what you're angry about."

"How well do you know Amanda Bowmen?" she said calmly.

"Not very." He lied.

"You're lying Tim, I'm no fool. The way that woman talked, I had the distinct feeling that she knew you very well."

He smiled, trying to diffuse what was coming, "You're jealous!"

"I'm not jealous. Did you sleep with her?" He remained silent, "Well?" her voice had become louder.

"You never cared before. What difference does it make?"

"When, Tim?" she asked holding back the tears. "When did you sleep with her?"

"A long time ago. I'm sorry."

She composed herself, "Today, you acted surprised to see them all, but you expected them, didn't you?"

"No, I had no idea they were coming. Believe me Jenny, I didn't want Amanda to come here."

Jennifer turned her back on him, walking to the window. Taking a deep breath, she said, "It was when you were in Newport, wasn't it?" He moved toward her, taking her by the shoulders, "Take your hands off me."

He turned her gently to him, so she was facing him, "I love you Jenny; Amanda was just a passing fancy. I came back to you when you were ill."

She shook her head, the tears filled her green eyes, but she wouldn't give him the satisfaction of crying in front of him. He had hurt her so many times in the past, but this time was the last straw. "I want an answer from you." She demanded angrily.

"Anything."

"Did you come back to me out of pity?" she asked, the tears brimming in her eyes now.

"No. I came back because I loved you. I still love you."

She lost control of herself; the tears streamed down her cheeks. Jennifer had never felt this angry or hurt in her life; she began to pound on Timothy's chest, "I'll tell you something. I'll never let you go." She continued punching him, yet he made no attempt to stop her, "I'll teach that whore who you belong to; how dare she seduce the man that I love? I hate her!"

Timothy was enjoying her actions, her admission of her love for him, but now those little fists of Jennifer's were beginning to hurt. He grabbed her wrists, stopping her from hitting him. "That's enough, Jenny, I think you've gotten it out of your system."

She stared at him for a couple of minutes; she could feel the tear stains on her face, "I mean it Tim; she'll have to fight me for you."

He released her wrists, "I'm attracted to you Jenny, not Amanda. I want to spend my life with you."

"So, you've said."

His eyes showed compassion, "I mean it. You should rest a while before dinner. Take a hot bath, you'll feel better."

She had calmed down and smiled slyly, "Why don't you take a hot bath with me?"

He began to laugh, "You are incorrigible, do you know that?"

"Yes, love me, Tim."

He bent to kiss her forehead; she closed her eyes. He kissed each eyelid, her nose and finally her mouth. He released her, "I'd really like that, my love, but I have to finish my work. Especially since the *Nightbird* is here."

Reaching for his hand, Jennifer looked into his eyes, "What is so special about the *Nightbird?*"

He kissed her softly, "I can't tell you, Jenny."

"Why?"

"It's a secret. Take your bath, I'll see you at dinner." He turned and walked out of the bedroom that they shared.

Jennifer stared after him. She wondered how the *Nightbird* was going to be used. It was a secret because it was something illegal, she was sure of it. Crossing the room to her closet, she looked for the perfect dress; she wanted to outshine Amanda Bowmen. She went through the dresses; the thought of that woman in Timothy's arms angered her. Amanda would pay. Jennifer vowed; Timothy will never be able to take his eyes off her when she came downstairs dressed in the deep burgundy satin gown with the plunging neckline.

CHAPTER NINETEEN

Amanda wanted to look her best tonight at dinner. She sat in the hot bath for an hour, plotting and planning as to how she would seduce Timothy, so his young wife might hear or better yet see. She smiled wryly as she thought that little Jennifer would be sorry that she ever met me. Opening her trunk, she looked for the perfect dress. The red velvet was Timothy's favorite. It would surely bring his attention solely to her.

Jennifer had just finished dressing when someone knocked on her door. Walking to the door she opened it. "Stefan."

Stefan was in awe of his cousin, she looked gorgeous from the burgundy gown to the ruby ring, to the flaming auburn hair and to her laughing smile. "Jennifer, are you and Tim going out?"

"No silly, why?"

He stammered, "It's just that you look," he paused, "You've never looked better. What is the occasion?"

"Nothing special. I just want to keep my husband's attention on me."

"Well, I don't know where else he would look."

"At Amanda Bowmen, who else?" She answered matter-of-factly.

"Amanda, our house guest? I don't think you have to worry about her; you're much more beautiful."

She laughed, "But you're prejudiced, because you are my cousin. Now, I'm sure you didn't stop by to discuss Amanda.

"No, I didn't. I came to tell you that I just received word from the Bryant Sanitarium."

"Did something happen to my mother?" she cried out frantically.

"No, calm down. The letter is from her doctors. They feel that it would be good for her if you were to visit."

"Visit? Has she improved at all?"

"Not really."

"Where is the letter?"

"Tim has it; he'd like to go with you if you decide to go to Bryant."

"Why did you give it to Tim? It's my mother, not his?"

"I wanted to ask his opinion as to whether you should see the letter or even know about it."

"Believe it or not, Stefan, I'm a strong person; just because I lost a child a month ago, does not mean that I, too, am a patron for Bryant." Amanda had been walking down the hall when she heard the argument from a bedroom; she couldn't recognize the voices at first but soon realized one of them was Jennifer's. She stopped to listen. "In fact, I don't understand at all why you should show the letter to Tim."

"He's your husband."

Jennifer wanted to yell out that he wasn't really her husband, but instead said, "But she is my mother! If the letter was addressed to me, then I should have received it."

"Jenny, the letter was addressed to me."

"You! Why?"

"Because I've taken over your father's affairs since his death."

"Stefan, in one month I'll be eighteen; you are only two years older than I; I think it's about time I, too, get involved in not only my father's affairs, but also my husband's. Now, I have to finish with my hair, and I'll be down to dinner. We will discuss these business dealings at a later date." Amanda had heard enough; she began to go downstairs to the sitting room.

Amanda was half-way down the long staircase as Stefan descended the stairs, "Miss Bowmen."

She stopped and turned, "Please, call me Amanda."

"Then you must call me Stefan." He said as he reached her. "May I escort you into the sitting room?"

"Yes, that would be nice. I'm afraid I took longer getting dressed and my cousin Robert and his wife, Molly, must have already come downstairs."

Reaching the foyer, they heard voices coming from the sitting room. Amanda heard Molly say, "I hope that we didn't put you and your lovely wife out by arriving unexpectedly."

"No, not at all, Molly. Jennifer needs the company; she recently lost a baby."

"I'm sorry, Tim. I had no idea that you were married. I must admit, as a business partner you are constantly surprising me," replied Robert.

Timothy smiled, "It keeps you on your toes, Robert."

Molly laughed, "The two of you remind me of my younger brothers, always egging each other on."

The two men laughed, but their laughter was interrupted by Amanda and Stefan. "Well, what is so funny?" Amanda purred.

Timothy's eyes met hers as he stopped laughing. "Just something that was said. It would take us much too long to explain."

Turning to Stefan she said, "It seems that you and I missed all the fun."

Timothy's eyes were glued to Amanda; the red velvet dress that he had bought her in Newport jarred his memory. His throat became dry. This was stupid, he thought. I'm lusting after this woman while my wife is upstairs. "Amanda, Stefan, can I get you some sherry or brandy before dinner?"

Stefan moved to the liquor table. Jennifer had been right. Amanda Bowmen was out to steal Timothy, and if Jennifer didn't get here soon, she just might succeed. "I'll get it, Tim. Amanda, what would you like?"

Never taking her eyes from Timothy, she said, "Brandy, please."

Jennifer came downstairs very confidently; if Stefan was in awe of the way she looked, Timothy would be speechless. When she entered the sitting room, Amanda was sitting so close to Timothy that she might as well be sitting in his lap. Her head was bent toward Timothy's in a provocative way, as they both were looking at a piece of paper. Timothy looked up, seeing Jennifer for the first time since she entered the room. He could tell by the expression on her face that she was upset; he started to rise from his seat, bringing Amanda's attention to Jennifer. "Jenny, I was wondering where you were."

She glared at him before speaking, "I was with Lion. He asked me where his father was; he hasn't seen you today."

"I've been busy; this is the first time I've really had to relax."

"Well, I had Maggie dress him for dinner; he'll be eating with us."

"Who is Lion?" questioned Amanda. Timothy had been staring at Jennifer. She outshined everyone in the room; she looked ravishing. Had no one been in the room, he would have taken her then and there. Jennifer was too jealous to notice the effect she had on him "Who is Lion?" repeated Amanda.

Timothy turned, "Lion is my son."

"How old is he?" inquired Amanda.

Jennifer answered, "Seven."

Robert was amazed; he learned more and more about his business partner every day. "I had no idea that you had a son."

Amanda sat in shock. This was his second wife! Tim was at a loss for words; how could he explain Lion. "I was married and my wife died when she gave birth to Lion."

"You've never mentioned him before," Amanda said, feeling defeated by a woman who gave Tim a son and later died.

"It was while I was amassing my wealth."

Jennifer smiled, only she and Timothy knew the truth. Not even Stefan had thought to ask about the child. "I think we should all go into the dining room."

Timothy took Jennifer by the arm. He bent close to her whispering, "I'm captivated by your beauty, my petite. I cannot wait until we are alone; if we didn't have guests, I think I might like to skip dinner." Jennifer smiled. So, he did notice, she thought.

Throughout dinner, Timothy never took his eyes from Jennifer. The dinner conversation was filled with chatter about various plans for theatre, opera, and sightseeing. Amanda sat to Timothy's left, constantly trying to monopolize the conversation to no avail. She was growing tired of everyone directing their attention to the young woman sitting at the end of the table. Jennifer Lockwood received most of the attention and no wonder, thought Amanda; the young girl was beautiful.

CHAPTER TWENTY

The days passed quickly into weeks; spring was just around the corner. Jennifer had grown tired of going to the theatre, the opera, and shopping with Amanda and Molly. Molly, she could tolerate, but Amanda was beginning to wear on her nerves. She hated being in the same room with the way she pawed over Timothy. Jennifer was ready to explode. One more incident between Amanda and her husband and she would literally have to tear the woman apart. Jennifer had Harris and Lizabeth prepare another guest room, for Yvonne would be arriving any day now. Hopefully, Yvonne could help her handle Amanda or at least tell her what to do and how to get rid of the woman. Timothy himself was weary of his visitors; so much had to be done concerning the building of clipper ships that would be exact replicas of the *Nightbird*. They would have to build the ships discreetly, of course, with their buyers remaining anonymous. Prior to meeting Jennifer, he had made arrangements with various pirates to supply them with sleek, fast ships, which would enable them to strike and be gone in a matter of minutes. The *Nightbird* was the first of those ships, and she had to be tested before manufacture. Once tested by himself with a crew of the potential buyers, the manufacturing could begin if the ship was approved. The next step would be to send messages to the respective buyers and have them come to Newport. It would be less dangerous for them to enter Newport than London. Many of them were too well known to enter a port in England; they would be arrested, tried, and convicted before stepping off their ships. No, it would have to be Newport. He could take Jennifer to Newport, show her around, settle her in and then take off with his pirate friends for the Barbary States. His main problem was his guests and his partner, Robert. Robert was already asking too many questions about the *Nightbird* and what the plans were for the ship. How could he tell Robert that he was a pirate? How could he tell him that he planned to make a huge profit by manufacturing several of these ships to be sold to pirates, some of the most dangerous and criminal men in the world. He couldn't tell Robert, but he would have to eventually tell Jennifer because she would want to know who all of the strange men were when they reached Newport. He began to make a mental list of the pirates that should be contacted.

Amanda had been plotting for weeks as to how to seduce Timothy. Tonight, the opportunity would present itself. Timothy and the little girl, Jennifer, were having a small dinner party with dancing afterwards. She would make a point to dance with Timothy, possibly leading him out of the main ballroom and into the sitting room where the seduction would begin.

Yvonne arrived later that day with all of her flamboyant glory. She shocked Harris at the door with a big kiss, causing him to blush. "Jennifer, Timothy. Yvonne is here!" She yelled at the top of her lungs.

Amanda went to the door of the sitting room to see who was causing the commotion. A tall blonde woman dressed in the most outrageous attire she had ever seen was making herself quite at home. Jennifer had been in Timothy's study when she heard Yvonne's bellow; flinging open the doors, she saw Yvonne dressed in a deep burgundy skirt with a red jacket, orange shirt and a hat with green and red plumes.

"Yvonne," the older woman whirled around to see Jennifer. "You haven't changed at all!"

Yvonne hugged her, "You look good. How are you feeling?"

Jennifer, for the first time noticed Amanda standing in the doorway of the sitting room. "Yvonne, I'd like you to meet one of our house guests, Mrs. Amanda Bowman."

Amanda was impeccably dressed. "How do you do, Mrs. Bowman? You can call me Yvonne."

"Hello, it is a pleasure to meet you, Yvonne."

Turning her attention back to Jennifer, she said, "You haven't answered my question; how are you feeling?"

"I'm fine, really. I'm sorry Timothy isn't here to greet you, but he had some business to take care of at Mr. Spencer's. Come, I'll take you upstairs where you can freshen up."

Yvonne followed Jennifer upstairs, leaving Amanda staring after them. Once inside the guest room, Yvonne turned to Jennifer, "Who is the fancy lady? A friend of yours?"

"No, she is, in fact, a former mistress of Timothy."

Yvonne was taken back by this revelation, "And she's staying here? Why that piece of swine; he brings his mistress into your house, right under your nose. Wait until I get a hold of him." Yvonne ranted, "How dare that whore even agree to come here?"

Jennifer smiled, "Then you'll help me?"

"Help you with what?"

"Keeping Tim."

"What do you propose to do?" questioned Yvonne.

"I want some tips on how to handle her. Tim really hasn't shown any interest in her, but she's been trying to seduce him ever since arrived." She paused, taking a deep breath. "I think he's having a hard time controlling himself. And to tell you the truth, I'm having a difficult time keeping myself from scratching her eyes out."

"You've got spunk kid! I think the best thing to do is to show her that you mean business. Keep an eye on her; try to catch her in the act of seducing Tim, then get her." Yvonne looked around the room, "Nice room, I like this one better than the last one."

"This is one of my most favorite rooms. I really enjoy the view." She walked to the window, pulling open the heavy green drapes, "Come and look."

Yvonne walked over to the window, seeing the Weatherly land and a lake in the distance. "Yes, it is very pretty."

"Well, I'll let you get settled in; we are having a dinner party tonight, just some friends and business associates, so I've got plenty of preparations to make. Please make yourself comfortable."

"Thanks; don't forget what I told you. Fight for what is rightfully yours."

"I won't forget," Jennifer replied as she glided across the room and out the door.

Timothy returned to Weatherly an hour after Yvonne arrived. He strode past Jennifer who was coming downstairs and went straight into the library, pouring himself a glass of rum. It went down smoothly as Jennifer stood in the doorway watching. "Is something wrong?" questioned Jenny, as Timothy poured himself another rum.

He turned to face her, "Come in, and shut the door." She obeyed him and took a chair near the desk. Timothy sat down across from her, "How would you like to go to Newport?"

"When?"

"Within two weeks. I have a great deal of work to do, and I want to test run the *Nightbird* myself."

She looked at him questioningly, "What is the *Nightbird* going to be used for Tim?"

"I can't tell you at the moment; my plans for it and others like it are still up in the air."

The golden eyes had grown dark, warning her not to push him for more answers, yet Jennifer chose to ignore what they were telling her. "The *Nightbird* has something to do with your double life. Trust me, Tim. I know that Robert doesn't know anything about the ships, and I know he doesn't know who you really are either."

His eyes flickered dangerously, "I told you, Jennifer, I do not wish to discuss it. Now answer my question; can you be ready to leave for Newport within two weeks?"

"Yes, but I want to know what is going on. I don't like the secrecy of all of this; I want to be prepared for whatever may come."

"I will tell you this, Jenny, work on your skills with a rapier."

"What you're involved in is dangerous, isn't it?"

The topaz eyes were smoldering, "It can become very dangerous. More dangerous for me than you can imagine."

Jennifer rose from her chair, "This does have something to do with your double life! What happens if you get caught?"

He took her arm, "Jenny, just be ready to leave. I promise you that before this project is ready, you will know all of the details."

She was angry with him; sometimes he treated her like a child! Why couldn't he tell her now? "Everything for the dinner party tonight has been arranged. I'm going to get dressed, and I would suggest that you do the same; our guests will be arriving within an hour."

"I'll be up in a little while," he said looking at the papers on his desk.

"Don't embarrass me Tim, I want you to be ready in time."

Timothy looked up from his papers to see her green eyes blazing with anger; he smiled, "I won't embarrass you, Jennifer. I'll be on my best behavior."

Her eyes softened, she smiled and said, "You had better," she retorted. Turning abruptly, she left the room.

CHAPTER TWENTY-ONE

Timothy was running late as he left the library seconds before the first guest arrived. He could not help but notice Jennifer's glare. She was angry, and she had every right to be; he had promised her that he would be by her side when the guests arrived. He smiled to himself as he took the stairs two at a time. Tonight, Jennifer and he would argue; she would call him a variety of names, hit him, then he would pick her up and carry her to their bed. She would fight him at first, but then her body would betray her, and she would succumb to his lovemaking with such fury and intensity that it would drive him to the brink of insanity. Yes, tonight would be a good evening, Jenny and he were always good together during sex.

Jennifer greeted the guests as they came, smiling and engaging in polite chatter. Inside, she was furious at Tim; half of these people she had never met before, and they were a strange lot. Many of their accents she could not place; some were Dutch, others Spanish, but some were accents she had never before heard. Tim came downstairs within a half-hour; he smiled at Jennifer, who smiled coolly at him. Her emerald eyes were icy, and Tim could tell she was furious.

Amanda, who had been watching from across the foyer, gloated inside. Already the evening was tense between her two hosts. She smiled; by the end of the evening, Tim should fall right into her hands. She slipped quietly into the ballroom to mingle with the other guests as Timothy guided Jennifer to the room.

Robert asked Jennifer to dance first. Other men asked her to dance, telling her she was beautiful, charming and that the Captain must be very proud to have a lady like her at his side. Jennifer smiled as the dance ended. Timothy walked quickly across the room and grabbed her by the wrist, his grip ironlike as he dragged her back onto the dance floor. He held her wrist tightly. "What the hell do you think you're doing, Jennifer?"

She glared at him, "Dancing. Let go of my wrist, Tim, you're hurting me."

"Some of those men might misread your intentions."

"What do you mean? They have all been perfect gentlemen."

Everyone's attention was on the couple in the center of the dance floor. It was obvious that they were involved in a heated discussion. The tall Captain was holding the auburn-haired woman so close that it was on the verge of obscenity. Amanda could not take her eyes from them as they whirled around the floor. Many of the women blushed, and the men whispered to each other. "They are all dangerous men, Jenny. They would no sooner cut my throat in order to ravage you."

She stared at him in disbelief, "They are pirates!" Tim said nothing. "Answer me, Tim, are they pirates? This whole ball was not arranged for our house guests; this was so you could bring pirates here. This whole thing is because of the *Nightbird!*"

It was true. The prospective members of the stronghold had decided to meet in London instead of Newport. He pressed her closer and whispered into her ear, "Keep your voice down, Jennifer, if you know what is good for you, me and our guests, you will keep your voice down and drop the subject."

She began to pull away from him, but he gripped her tightly, "I will not drop it, Tim; I want some answers," she demanded.

"I told you before, you'll get answers when I'm ready to tell you. For now, keep your pretty mouth shut." His grip on her tightened, "Play the part of a good hostess, Jennifer, but don't let these men think they can touch you. The last thing I want tonight is to duel over my wife." He released her.

The emerald eyes hardened, "I'm not your wife yet, Captain. And I don't think you ever plan to make me your wife. So, I can do what I please." She pulled away from him and headed off the dance floor.

Timothy followed her, catching her by the arm, turning her around to face him, "We will discuss our problems later. Don't do anything you may regret."

Amanda, who had been watching Timothy and Jennifer since they began their dance and argument, sauntered over to the couple who were oblivious to the other people in the room, "Tim, I believe you promised this dance to me."

Jennifer shot her an icy stare. "Please don't let me stand in your way, Amanda, do dance with Tim."

Tim took Amanda by the hand and led her out on the dance floor. Jennifer watched the two of them become closer, tears brimmed in her eyes. Captain Cliff McArnold asked her to dance, and she accepted. Instantly, Tim tensed and instinctively drew Amanda closer to him as he watched Jennifer dancing with McArnold, a handsome, first rate privateer. "Tim," purred Amanda, "You are holding me so tightly, I can hardly breathe." His arms loosened, "No, it's alright; it reminds me of the days we spent in Newport."

The scent of her close to him after all these months excited him; it was good with Amanda. He looked over at Jennifer who seemed to be enjoying herself immensely. He and Amanda moved steadily toward the doorway of the ballroom as the dance ended. Timothy's eyes searched the room; Jennifer already had another dancing partner, Captain Mark Gregory. Tim turned and walked angrily out of the ballroom, heading for the library. Amanda stared after him, not understanding why he strode out of the room. Molly came over to her and whispered, "Isn't this a lovely ball?" Amanda seemed not hear, "Amanda?"

She turned, facing Molly, "Yes."

"I said, isn't this a lovely ball?"

"Yes, it is," replied Amanda.

Molly tilted her head towards Amanda, "You don't seem like you've been enjoying yourself."

Amanda smiled, "I'm having a wonderful time, but it appears that there is trouble in paradise.'

"What are you talking about?"

"Our hosts of course! Didn't you see them arguing?" questioned Amanda.

Molly shook her head, "No. I hadn't noticed."

"I thought everyone noticed," Amanda said, almost gleefully.

"Well, Jennifer seems like she's having a good time, but I don't see Tim anywhere around."

"Perhaps he has business." Amanda replied, as Robert walked towards them.

"Have either one of you seen Tim?" questioned Robert.

"No," Amanda lied, "Perhaps he's having a private discussion with a business associate."

"The other guests are from all over the world. I never knew Tim had so many worldly friends. Molly, would you like to dance?" He asked extending his arm.

Taking his arm, she replied, "I never thought you'd ask."

Amanda watched the two of them walk toward the dance floor. She slid over to the doors to make her way to find Timothy. Timothy sat alone in the dark library, drinking rum. He was angry at Jennifer for causing such a scene; he would have strangled the life out of her if he didn't love her so damn much. He heard the door open and close; a shadow appeared on the wall. "Jenny?"

"No, it's Amanda," she replied as she walked closer to the desk, so Timothy could see her.

"Why did you follow me?" Tim asked from the darkness.

"I wanted to talk to you privately. You haven't had that much time on your hands, and I thought we should talk."

"Amanda, we have nothing to talk about. You and I are finished. You can keep the house, the clothes, the jewels and whatever money you have left. I know that you can manage."

"I need you, Tim, and I think you need me too."

He was getting angry, "I don't need you."

"But you want me, don't try to deny it."

He moved from behind the desk to light a small lamp. He was standing very close to her now, "I don't need you, and everything I want and need is here in this house."

She put her hand on his chest, "You are attracted to me, Timothy Lockwood, I can feel the heat from your body." Her hand slid down his chest to his hips and then to his loins. She pushed herself closer to him, kissing him. He didn't return her kiss; she rubbed herself against him, feeling him start to harden with desire. She looked up at him, smiled, "See, you do want me."

He made no attempt to move as he said, "Any good whore could do that to a man."

She moved away from him and snapped, "Can your precious little wife do the same?"

He smiled, "That is none of your business."

"Don't tell me that she is as good in bed as me. She couldn't possibly have had enough experience."

"And you've had too much. Why don't you see who you can seduce at the party?"

In the heat of their argument, another person had entered the library and stood hidden in the shadows, listening. Jennifer stood quietly watching the interchange between her husband and their guest.

Amanda purred, "It's so good between us."

"It was Amanda, I'll admit that, but you must understand that you were a toy. I am a man, and I cannot lead a sexless life. I am not as strong as you think. I need a woman beside me at all times." Timothy was trying to be gentle, and Amanda was on the verge of hysterics.

Jennifer decided to make her presence known; she stepped out of the shadows and said, "I am that woman he needs."

Timothy was amazed. How long had she been standing there? How much did she overhear, and how much has she seen? Amanda whirled around to face the small, petite Jennifer. Tears filled her eyes, "An eighteen-year-old girl has won the only man I have ever loved." She turned and left the library, leaving Timothy and Jennifer alone.

"I love you Jennifer Weatherly."

"If you love me so much, when do you plan to make me your wife?" she questioned coolly.

Tim was serious, "Would you be happy if I said tomorrow?"

"Tomorrow?" She was a little shocked. She had expected him to put her off.

"Yes, tomorrow. It can't be anything elaborate. We can have Stefan and Yvonne as our witnesses."

"Do you honestly mean it?"

"Can you doubt me?" he questioned. She said nothing, she didn't want to doubt him, yet from past experiences she couldn't be sure. "Well?"

She shook her head, "No, I don't doubt you, Tim; considering our past experience with each other, I should."

"Things will change, Jennifer, just wait. In the next couple of months, things will change."

"I think we should return to the party. After all, we are the hosts."

He took her arm and led her to the ballroom where the guests had hardly noticed they were missing. Jennifer's eyes scanned the room; Amanda sat on the divan staring at Timothy who was now talking to Robert. The guests were gradually leaving, and only a few remained. Jennifer sought out Yvonne who was talking to Captain Mark Gregory. She approached the two of them as Gregory stared at her. "Ah, Jennifer, you are a marvelous hostess. Timothy must be very proud of you."

She blushed, "Thank you, Captain Gregory.'

Timothy joined them. "Tim, I was telling Jennifer that she was an excellent hostess this evening. You must be proud of her."

Timothy smiled broadly, "More than you can ever imagine, Mark. If you're through with the ladies, I would like to speak with you."

"Surely" he said to Timothy; turning, he said, "Ladies, please excuse me."

Jennifer and Yvonne smiled as the two men walked away, "Yvonne, Tim and I are going to be married tomorrow and we would like to have you as one of our witnesses."

"Tomorrow! How did you ever manage it?"

Jennifer replied, "He suggested it."

"That's a switch. I know that the man loves you, but the way he postponed that wedding in the past, I was beginning to wonder," mused Yvonne.

"Yvonne, would you be one of our witnesses?"

Yvonne began to laugh, "Of course; I wouldn't miss this for the world."

Jennifer hugged the older woman, "Thank you. You've been more than a friend to me."

Yvonne's eyes grew watery as she pulled away from Jennifer. She wiped her eyes. "I don't know why I'm crying, except that I haven't had a friend like you since Season. The funny thing is, you're involved with the same man."

"I'm sure Season loved Tim as much as I do. Sometimes I wonder why I'm so attracted to a man who can be so ruthless."

Yvonne smiled, "You love him, Jennifer, because he represents something that society rebels against, because he can be ruthless, exciting and sensual. Never mind the fact that he's so damn handsome."

Jennifer laughed, "He certainly is all of those things. We should get to bed. Tomorrow is going to be a big day."

"What are you going to wear?"

"I'm not exactly sure. I think maybe the gold brocade gown or the deep green velvet."

"Whatever you decide, I'm sure you'll be gorgeous in it."

The two women left the room, pausing outside the library and then making their way upstairs. Yvonne left Jennifer at her door and walked to her room. Her thoughts were on what was happening between Gregory and Tim. What was Tim up to? He had taken a chance by inviting some of the most celebrated pirates and privateers into Jennifer's home along with some respectable people. She didn't like it nor did she like the fact that he decided to marry Jennifer tomorrow. Why tomorrow? After postponing the wedding several times, he decided that to-morrow was to be the day. Timothy Lockwood, 'Captain Bloodthirsty', had something up his sleeve, and she was sure that eventually, she, too, would be included in his plans. She reached her room and retired for the night.

Jennifer lay awake, wondering what Tim urgently needed to talk with Mr. Gregory for tonight. Why couldn't it wait? Gradually, she fell asleep.

Tim and Mark Gregory sat facing each other in the library. Each had a glass of rum in his hand, "Tell me, Timothy, how does leading a double life work out?" questioned Mark.

"Fine, no one suspects who I really am; my business partner has no idea whatsoever of my past."

"What about the girl, Jennifer?"

Timothy looked away for a second, turning back to Gregory he said, "Jennifer knows who I am."

"That can be dangerous. You should never let a woman know about your personal life."

Timothy sighed, "It couldn't be helped. When I met her, I was Captain Lockwood; we were both betrothed to someone else. However, circumstances forced me to rescue her from the Barbary Coast and that feat took Captain Bloodthirsty."

"You're not married to her?"

"No."

"What does her family think of that? He smiled wryly; "Why, you're sharing her bed, they must have said something."

"The only people that know we're not married are her cousin Stefan and Yvonne. Of course, my men know it, but they know enough to keep their mouths shut. But," he paused, his topaz eyes twinkling, "tomorrow we will be married."

Gregory stood up, "You damn fool, don't marry the woman be-fore you embark on what could be the most dangerous expedition of your career."

"Why, Mark?"

"It's much harder losing a husband than a lover."

"Suppose something happens, and I get killed or captured? Jen-nifer and my son, Lion, will be left with nothing. Because of her affiliation with me, she'll be an outcast. I can't have that; if anything happened, I would want her to be well taken care of for the rest of her life."

Mark said, "If, something happens to you, the rest of us will see that she's well provided for as well as your son. She comes from a wealthy family. I'm sure her cousin would take her in if you were killed."

Tim shook his head, "No. Mark, I want to spend the next few months with her as her husband. I'm going to have everything I own transferred to her name and Lion's. If anything happens, at least they'll have Lockwood and the business."

"I guess I can't talk you out of it then," he said, sitting down once again.

"No, you've been like a father to me, but I can't take your advice this time. Besides, if I change my mind, she'll definitely know that something is wrong."

"You really love the girl?"

Timothy smiled, "Yes. It took me a long time to realize it, but I do love her."

Mark smiled, "To find love is a blessing, to give love takes a little extra. Well, let me leave you until tomorrow. I'll be in touch."

Both men stood and shook hands. Timothy showed Mark to the door then bolted it and went back into the study to snuff out the lamps before going to bed.

The next morning, Tim woke to find Jennifer staring out the bedroom window. "Jenny, is something wrong?"

"No, I was just thinking," she said her back still toward him.

"Come back to bed."

She turned away from the window and smiled, "Today is the most important day of my life. Tim, I'm scared. I don't know if I'll make a good wife for you."

"Of course, you will," he patted the bed; "It's early; come back to bed."

Jennifer sat on the edge of the bed facing him, "Why was it so important that we marry today? I thought you wanted to wait until we reached Newport."

He smiled, "I did, but I've changed my mind. Stefan is here and Yvonne, and the present is much better for a wedding than the future. Besides all of which, I promised your cousin that I would marry you."

"I believe that you will, and I'm sure Stefan does too."

He cut her off, "No. I want Stefan to stand up for us. It's important that he sees that I'm indeed an honorable man." He sat up, gently reaching for one of her auburn curls.

She stared at him, the green eyes probing for answers, but getting none from the man who sat before her. "I need you Tim." She leaned forward to kiss him, she waited for his answer, yet he never said what she wanted to hear. Tim responded hungrily to her kiss, but she pulled away, "No."

"What's wrong Jennifer? You tell me that you need me and then you pull away from me. I'm not the kind of man that you can tease."

"I'm sorry, I have a lot to do. I have to pick out a dress for the wedding, take a bath and have Yvonne help me with my hair."

"It's early, you have plenty of time," the topaz eyes pleading with her.

"Not really, Tim; besides, we'll have other times to make love."

He was disappointed, but she was right; he moved from the bed. "Well, I might as well tell Stefan that we're getting married." Jennifer smiled at him as he went into her washroom, leaving her to stare out the window.

Her eyes scanned the Weatherly estate; in less than two weeks she would be on her way to Newport, Rhode Island. Mistress of Lockwood. Deep down she was afraid of leaving because she felt if Tim and she left, they would never return to Weatherly again. It was foolish; she scolded herself for thinking such thoughts. She left the window to look in her closet. The white satin dress with delicate lavender flowers stared her in the face. It would make a beautiful wedding gown, yet, it might be too obvious if Lizabeth saw her in it. No, the white gown would never do. It would have to be the dark green velvet.

Tim came back into the bedroom freshly shaven, smelling of spice and proceeded to dress. Jennifer watched him quietly, wondering what Newport would be like. "What are you thinking?" he asked, his golden eyes puzzled by her stare, "Is there a spot on my shirt?" He glanced down at the front of his beige shirt.

"No, I'm sorry. I didn't mean to stare. I was thinking about my new life as Mrs. Timothy Lockwood."

"Well, in about two hours, you will be Mrs. Lockwood."

"I know," her green eyes danced.

"I've got to talk to Stefan and then I have some business to take care of, but be ready for when I return and we'll get married." She nodded her head, kissed him goodbye and watched him leave the room.

Two hours later Stefan, Yvonne and Jennifer sat in the sitting room waiting for Tim. Amanda appeared shortly before Tim arrived, "Where is everyone off to at ten in the morning?"

Jennifer stared at the woman coolly. "We have business to take care of before I depart for Newport."

Amanda held her breath for a second before speaking, "I see, so we are to be neighbors?"

Jennifer glared at Amanda, "I certainly hope not." Yvonne had to keep herself from busting out in laughter at Jennifer's words.

"So do I; in fact, I just may move back to Providence. Newport bores me."

Jennifer retorted, "Perhaps you should start packing your bags, Amanda."

Tim entered the room before Amanda could reply, "Good morning, Amanda, it's about time you've risen at a decent hour, compared to your normal noon rising." She glowered at him; there were many mornings in Newport that he stayed in bed with her until twelve. Turning his attention to the others he said, "Are you ready?"

Stefan rose, "Yes, we've been waiting. Ladies, let's go, we don't have all day." The four of them left Amanda in the sitting room wondering why everyone was so dressed up and where they were going at this godforsaken hour.

The ride to the minister's house took approximately two hours. Timothy had found a minister on the furthest outskirts of London, making sure that they were not followed; to ensure secrecy from the minister, he made a sizeable donation to the church. The ceremony was quick and to the point. It wasn't the type of ceremony that Jennifer had always wished for as a child, but at least she was married to the man she loved. Everyone was happy, especially Stefan.

Once inside the carriage, Stefan said, "Jenny, your father would have never approved of such a wedding or romance, but I do. Timothy Lockwood is a very fine man, and I'm proud to have him in the family."

Tears rose in Jennifer's eyes; she leaned across the carriage and hugged him. "Thank you; you've been like a brother to me and to have your approval on my marriage means a great deal."

Timothy watched the interchange between Jenny and Stefan; they loved each other as brother and sister. Jennifer released Stefan, and Timothy extend his hand, "It is a pleasure for me to be included in such a fine family. Stefan, believe me, I will take good care of her."

"I believe you, Tim."

Yvonne couldn't stand it any longer, "This calls for a celebration. I think the four of us should have a special dinner. Let's splurge."

Jennifer looked at Tim, "Can we?"

Yvonne spoke before he could answer, "I'll pay for the dinner and champagne."

Tim laughed, "Very well, Yvonne. I do think a celebration is in order."

"Good, tell the driver to take us to the best damn restaurant London has to offer," she exclaimed; her delft blue eyes shimmering with excitement of a party.

Tim opened the small window, calling up to the driver, "Take us to the best restaurant London has to offer."

"Yes sir," replied the driver. Tim closed the window.

"Since Yvonne is paying for our dinners, I will give the driver some money to buy himself a dinner and to return for us in two hours." He put his arm around Jennifer's shoulders. "Then, when we reach Weatherly later this evening, Jennifer and I can have some time alone." His eyes twinkling as he spoke. Jennifer could feel the heat raise in her face, flushing her a brilliant red. After all she had been through, she was surprised that she would still blush. She nudged Timothy with her elbow, which seemed to egg him on, "I plan to assert myself as her husband; she wouldn't let me take liberties with her this morning, but I fully intend to take them tonight."

"Tim, please stop, you're embarrassing me."

He laughed, "I'm joking, in actuality Jennifer, I cannot be with you this evening."

"Why?" she demanded.

"I have business on my ship which will probably take all evening, which is why I agreed to this dinner."

"Why tonight, Tim?"

"Because our departure from London will probably be within the next three days, and I must clear up some business with my crew if they are taking Robert, Molly and Amanda back with them. Of course, we will be traveling on the *Nightbird*."

She stared at him in disbelief; how could he do this? He said that they were leaving in two weeks; now it's three days. The green eyes glared at him, but before she could scream at him, Stefan said, "Jennifer, calm down. Tim must take care of his business before the two of you leave."

Jennifer looked her cousin squarely in his eyes, "You knew?"

"Yes, I've known since earlier this morning when Tim asked me to be a witness."

"I see," she was angry now as she turned to Yvonne, "Did you know, too?"

"No, I had no idea that he was planning to leave so soon. I guess that means that I'll have to organize my crew and leave sooner than I expected." She turned her attention to Tim, "I thought you weren't going for another two weeks?"

Tim looked at Yvonne, "There has been a change of plans. I must leave within the next three days."

Jennifer snapped, "What caused this change in plans?"

Timothy's topaz eyes flickered with seething anger, "It is something I can't discuss at the moment. I'm sorry," he said, coolly.

"Don't be; it is just that I'm not used to being left in the dark on business matters," Jennifer said, sarcastically.

"My dear, these business matters are not to worry your pretty little redhead." Yvonne and Stefan were obviously ill at ease; Tim turned to Yvonne, "Where will your travels take you?"

"I'm not exactly sure. I've been wanting to return to Java, but with the conditions being the way they were when we left them months ago, I won't be returning there for a while."

"Why don't you come to Newport with us for a little while. I would really like you to come with us."

She hesitated before answering; he was up to something, and now she was going to be included in the game. "I guess the *Sea Witch* could follow you to the Americas."

"No, I want you to come on the *Nightbird* and see how fast she travels. You would be company for Jenny, and the *Sea Witch* could come later."

"I don't know, Tim. I've never let the *Sea Witch* travel without me."

"She wouldn't be traveling without you; she would be right behind us. Besides, I think it would be advantageous for you to be on the *Nightbird*." What was it with this ship? She had seen it in the harbor; it was a clipper ship, yet it was built slightly different than most clippers. Her hull was much longer and narrower than most, and her bow was sharper. She also carried many more sails than a clipper. "Yvonne, what do you say? Will you travel on the *Nightbird?*"

Yvonne's curiosity was peaked, "Yes, all right." The remainder of the ride was quiet. Yvonne was deep in thought over the *Nightbird*. Timothy Lockwood was up to something, probably illegal and most definitely dangerous. Only time would tell what it was with this ship, the *Nightbird* and Timothy.

Part II: The *Nightbird* and Newport

(1849-1850)

CHAPTER TWENTY-TWO

Yvonne sat in her cabin for the last time. Eight days aboard the *Nightbird* had proved to be very educational as well as interesting. After her first day on board this newly designed clipper, she discovered that she was not the only passenger. The other passengers were men who Timothy passed-off to Jennifer as prospective buyers for clippers similar to the *Nightbird*. However, she knew differently; the *Nightbird* had a passenger list that read like a who's who of the Barbary Coast pirates, and the Caribbean pirates as well as privateers from various countries. Her presence on this ship was no accident. She had kept her eyes and ears open enough to know that Timothy was planning on selling ships to each of the people aboard, herself included, as she was informed the evening before by Timothy. He was involved in something that was much more dangerous than she had anticipated. Timothy Lockwood was planning on starting a pirate fleet. A fleet of twelve clipper ships like the *Nightbird* to travel in twos. The selected group of pirates and privateers would have total control and reign over the Barbary States and the Caribbean. Timothy stipulated that before they could purchase one of the fast clippers, all interested had to sign a document saying they would carry material goods only, no live goods, meaning slaves. They were to overtake any other pirate vessels that were not with the stronghold, particularly those carrying slaves to either the Barbary States or the Caribbean. Once taken, all booty would be placed in a neutral port.

Yvonne had to laugh when Timothy told her his plan to unite all of these people into one unit, but he was determined to go through with his plans. He had told her that all booty confiscated would be taken to

Lockwood, which was built with an underground docking system. Ships would enter a cave under the cliffs and unload all merchandise; all goods were to be catalogued by members of the crew and taken to the lower cellar in Lockwood where arrangements would be made to sell them to make a substantial profit. She was impressed, but still thought him a fool to think he could pull something like this off, but if he did, he could become a very wealthy man and those involved in this scheme would also be very well off. As much as she thought it wouldn't work, she agreed to become a part of this select stronghold. It wasn't that she felt the others would keep their promise, but she felt that the danger involved in something like this could be disastrous for all involved. Yvonne, was sure the others were thinking the same; the danger of being caught was more than double. First of all, the ships could be traced back to the Gray and Lockwood firm. What then? The names of all those who purchased slips could be taken by the authorities and they could search the ships. Secondly, ships coming into Newport and disappearing when they passed Lockwood would certainly cause some curiosity among the people of Newport. Most importantly, where would the goods be sold? How could Timothy explain such an abundance of goods and their origin. These were questions that she had to ask Timothy at the meeting this evening, before the *Nightbird* docked in Newport. She finished packing the last few things in her trunk before going to look for Jennifer.

The last few days Jennifer had felt strange on this ship. It was as if something was brewing among the passengers, something deadly. When she questioned Tim about it, he just ignored her or changed the subject. Tonight, he promised that he would tell her everything. Hearing a knock on her cabin door she asked, "Who's there?"

"Yvonne."

"Come in." Jennifer was sitting on the bed when Yvonne entered the cabin, "Yvonne."

"I thought that maybe you would like to come out on deck for a walk. We are traveling down the eastern coastline, and it's quite breathtaking."

Jennifer stood up, "Let me get my cloak, and we can go." She got her cloak from the closet, put it on and turned to face Yvonne, "Let's go." They left the cabin for the deck.

Timothy came down the stairs toward them, "I was just coming to get the two of you."

"Why?" Yvonne asked.

"I want you to see the coastline; it's beautiful." Taking Jenny by the arm, he led her up the stairs with Yvonne following close behind.

The three of them strolled along the deck until they were approached by Cliff McArnold. McArnold was a tall man, although not nearly as tall as Tim. He had deep green eyes and sandy blonde hair. His shoulders were broad, and he had a very thin waist. "Well, Mr. McArnold, we are almost in Newport. Have you enjoyed the voyage aboard the *Nightbird*?"

"I certainly have, Captain."

"I'm glad." Jennifer and Yvonne were watching the coastline, occasionally seeing a fishing village.

"I was wondering if Yvonne would like to take a stroll around the deck with me," asked McArnold.

Yvonne, hearing her name, turned to face McArnold, "That would be lovely, Mr. McArnold."

"Please, call me Cliff." He said as he extended his arm to her. She placed her arm through his and walked beside him.

"Tell me, Cliff, are you going to become involved in Timothy's plans for a pirate stronghold in the Barbary and Caribbean waters?"

He was surprised that she would know about the plans, but perhaps the Captain's lovely wife had told Yvonne, "I had no idea that you knew of his plans."

She smiled, "Of course I know about them, I'm involved."

"Involved? How could you possibly be involved?" he asked in disbelief.

"I own and operate a ship called the *Sea Witch*; I'm a pirate."

It was obvious to Yvonne that he was astounded by her statement. "I've heard of you and the *Sea Witch*. I thought you had a partner; I believe her name was Season." Yvonne's blue eyes began to water, "I'm sorry. I've upset you."

"No, it's alright. That was a long time ago, Cliff. Season is dead."

"I'm sorry." He looked out into the ocean where they had stopped walking.

"She didn't die because of a fight with another ship; she died in childbirth."

"Oh."

"Tell me, Cliff, what are your plans? Will you be buying into this pirate's line?"

"To tell you the truth, I'm undecided. I don't even know why I'm here at all."

Yvonne stopped walking and stared at him, "What do you mean?"

"I am the only person on this ship that is a privateer, I'm not a pirate," responded Cliff.

Yvonne smirked, "Technically you are, Cliff; you are a licensed pirate for England."

"I realize that, but my cause is for the protection of my country. What is a pirate's cause? I only see them taking slaves and goods that belong to other individuals. Innocent individuals."

"Yvonne was angered by his statement, "How dare you assume that pirates are in the business of piracy for ourselves."

He looked at her in awe, "Well, aren't you? You made the choice to become a pirate."

"Is that what you think?" Yvonne's face was beginning to redden with anger.

"Well, isn't it?"

"No," she yelled, then lowered her voice in fear of being heard. "Do you honestly think I became a pirate by choice? Do you think Timothy Lockwood became a pirate by choice? Think again if you must. Most of the pirates on this little cruise to show off this sleek new clipper were forced into piracy one way or another, Timothy Lockwood and myself included."

"I'm sorry I upset you," said Cliff.

"Upset me? Listen to me and listen well; more than half of the pirates on this ship have nobility in their blood but cannot claim their inheritances because they were exiled from their families or were kidnapped when they were young and raised on pirate ships. Timothy was seventeen or eighteen when the ship he was on was taken by Mark Gregory, and he was forced into a life of piracy. I was a scullery maid when I was kidnapped. So, don't say we made the choice to become pirates. We did it for survival. For me, it's the only thing I know. For Tim, it's the adventure and even more."

"You are a strong lady, Yvonne. If I do decide to join in, I would be honored if you would be my partner."

"If you do decide to become one of us, you're going to have to change. You're going to have to work for our cause and not England. If you would excuse me, I must go back to my cabin." She turned and strode away, leaving Cliff McArnold at the rail of the ship. Cliff watched Yvonne stride away towards her cabin. Thinking, he looked out into the sea.

Timothy had asked Jennifer to sit at the table while he gathered his thoughts as to how to tell her about his plans. He turned to face her, "Jenny, I know you have questioned me a thousand times as to what the

Nightbird is going to be used for," he paused, "You have asked me several times if it was going to be used illegally."

"Is it Tim?" she questioned.

He sat down, "Yes and no."

Jennifer's eyebrows raised, "Yes and no! What kind of answer is that?"

The golden eyes were expressionless as he answered, "An honest one."

She stared at him in disbelief, "An honest one,"

He looked at her, "Yes, if anything, it's an honest answer. The *Nightbird* and several ships like her are going to be used to gain control in the Caribbean and Barbary Coast."

Jenny rose from her seat, "Are you out of your mind? You could be killed."

"I won't be killed." He said flatly.

"What if you are? Tell me, Tim, what happens to me if you are?" Her eyes were welling with tears as she spoke. How could he do this to her, especially in a foreign country?

"You will be well provided for if anything happens to me. So will Lion. Even if I'm captured, you will be taken care of financially."

She was crying openly now, "But you promised me. Please, please don't do this."

"Jennifer, trust me. You are a strong woman; pull yourself together and listen to me." He rose and pulled her to her feet, holding her to his chest, whispering into her hair, "I love you, Jenny."

She pulled away to look at him, angry and hurt, "How can you say you love me? How? When you are going to do something like this?"

His brows moved together in a frown, as he spoke softly, "If I didn't love you, I wouldn't have married you. I would have just taken you here as my mistress."

"Wouldn't that be better?" she snapped.

"No, you are a fine woman, and you deserve respect in the community. If anything happens to me, you will be the richest woman in Newport, possibly in all of Europe as well."

Slowly she pulled her wits together, "Tell me the plan you have; I'll listen."

"Please sit down," he paused, "When I was younger and lived on the Barbary Coast, more specifically, Morocco, I worked hard, very hard, to abolish slavery in the States and piracy slavery as well. I want to stop it completely." He rose from his seat aside of her and went to the table to pour himself a glass of rum. "I want control; I will stop slavery in the Barbary States and the Caribbean. Every person aboard this ship has virtually agreed to become part of a pirate stronghold. They are going to buy ships like the *Nightbird* and work together in twos. They will overtake any pirate ship carrying slaves. All slaves will be put in a neutral port, and any booty aboard the ships will be confiscated and brought back to Newport."

Her sea green eyes opened wide, "You're not serious? Do you know how dangerous that can be? How are you going to unload stolen goods and sell them?"

He grinned, "It's easy. Lockwood is built on a high cliff. There is an opening, a cave, at the base of the cliff that a ship can fit into."

"Are you telling me that any ship can fit into this," she paused, "this cave?"

"Yes, but this is not an ordinary cave, and no ordinary Captain can get his ship into the cave."

"What do you mean?" Jennifer was intrigued.

"The cave, which should be finished by now, is attached to the lower cellar at Lockwood, which will be used for storage of the stolen goods. And before a ship can get into the cave, the Captain must navigate an area filled with rocks and coral, which is why I picked the twelve best Captains in the world."

"Yvonne's included in this?"

"She hasn't given me an answer yet, but I'm sure she'll agree to this because anyone who joins with me will become very wealthy."

Jennifer thought for a moment, "What about Robert?"

"Robert doesn't know the background of any of these people, and he won't because no one will tell him."

"Am I to have a part in this scheme of yours?"

"Yes. You may just have the most important part of all," He poured himself another glass of rum.

"What am I to do?" questioned Jennifer.

"You will be in charge of the cataloguing of the merchandise, keeping up appearances and covering for my absences from Lockwood.

"Will you be absent from Lockwood a great deal?"

Timothy drew in his breath, "Only in the beginning; then it will be periodic."

"I see," Jennifer paused, "On the cataloguing of the goods, will I have an assistant?"

"Yes, but I haven't decided who it will be yet. Maggie will be in charge of taking care of Lion while you work. I think she can be trusted with the knowledge of what is going on so that she can cover for you."

"Do you really trust her?"

The golden eyes simmered, "Yes, I took her from the Harrington's and put her into a better place to work. I saved her from Laura Harrington," he smiled ruefully, "and anything I request from her, she will do."

Jennifer was worried; what if the others rebelled? "Tim, what happens if the others go against you?"

"They won't," he said firmly.

"What makes you so sure?"

I have Yvonne and Mark Gregory on my side. Mark and I go back a long way, and I have enough strength and respect as a pirate to keep the others in line."

"What if they don't agree to your plans?" Her mind was racing now, "What if only four of you plan to continue?"

"It's very simple. If it comes down to only four of us, we will concentrate on the Barbary Coast. The others wouldn't bother us; besides, we would be too fast for them."

"This is a well-calculated plan, but I'm still scared," said Jennifer.

"There is nothing to be afraid of; I know what I am doing," replied Timothy.

"What if your identity is revealed? What if they search the house?" questioned Jennifer.

Timothy smirked, very proud of his plans, "If they search the house, they will find nothing because they will never be able to find the secret passageway which leads to the second cellar."

"We have to have some sort of plan if you get caught; they'll come after the rest of us," worried Jennifer.

Timothy was quiet, "If I am caught, one of the other ships will get to Newport before any authorities can be reached. You, Lion and Maggie will get on the ship and you will be taken back to London" he paused, "No wait, you can't be taken to London. If they don't find you in Newport, they will look for you at your family's home first." He shook his head, "No that won't do."

She thought, "What about that island that Yvonne lives on?"

"You mean Ibiza?"

"Yes, I can go there if you're caught; at least I can be with Yvonne."

"Very true, but I won't be caught. The *Nightbird* is too fast of a ship," he answered determinedly, "Let's get ready for dinner. Tonight, we will find out just how many of these pirates are interested in this scheme."

CHAPTER TWENTY-THREE

Jennifer looked exceptionally beautiful this evening in her gold brocade gown. While she was dressing, Timothy had presented her with a topaz necklace and matching earrings. He was dressed in black trousers, white shirt open at the neck, burgundy waistcoat and black jacket. He and Jennifer walked into the dining room of the ship. Timothy helped Jenny into her chair, which was to his right at the head of the table. Jennifer sat across the table from Yvonne, who was at the far end of the table and was dressed in a dark blue gown. Cliff McArnold, Captain Jack Webster, Joseph Brentwood, Dante D'Mattea, and Michael Brentwood sat to Yvonne's left. Mark Gregory, Rick Jordan, Cutthroat John, Devlin Jones and Jacques LaRoche sat to Yvonne's right.

Timothy told Jennifer about every individual before dinner. Her eyes scanned the quiet table while dinner was served. The Brentwood brothers were once England's most prized privateers until they realized that more money could be made in piracy. Both men were blonde with deep blue eyes and light complexions marked with pits and holes, most likely from the pox.

Captain Jack Webster was a small man who had retired from piracy. He had settled down in the Caribbean in New Providence. Jack Webster was actively involved in releasing slaves brought into the area. He was like Timothy; each had a passion for freeing men or women. He was willing to come out of retirement in order to try to stop the slave trade in the Caribbean.

Rick Jordan was an Englishman, who, like Timothy, had been on a ship when it was captured by pirates. Jordan, however, was six years old when the ship was taken. His father was brutally murdered and his mother auctioned-off as a slave; he was used as a cabin boy until he was fifteen when he became a regular member of the crew. At seventeen, he left the ship with several crew members who were displeased with their cut in the booties. They formed their own crew, bought a ship and dealt heavily in the far east and Dutch waters for a couple of years before returning to the Barbary Coast. Jordan's life as a pirate was a celebrated one. Although he was wanted for piracy in several countries, including the Americas, it never stopped him from socializing in the courts of kings. He was a man who prided himself on his extreme good looks; he had large brown eyes, an aristocratic nose and a full, sensuous pouting mouth. He was a couple of inches shorter than Timothy and had pale brown curls that framed his face. His build was medium. He could not be thought of as a weak man. Jordan never failed to have a woman at his side, whether she be a friend, consort or a most recent acquisition, his taste in women was most unique. All of his women were large boned, tall, slightly overweight blondes, who were extremely beautiful. Some people who knew him well said they represented a mother image to him.

Cutthroat John was a short, slightly bald fat man. He received his nickname from the Captain of the first pirate ship he worked on because he enjoyed killing his enemy by slicing their throats and watching the blood ooze from the wound. He was somewhere around fifty years old and had spent most of his piracy days in the Caribbean.

Dante D'Mattea, the Italian prince turned pirate, was a close friend of Rick Jordan. The two men met at a lavish party in honor of D'Mattea. The Prince was intrigued with Jordan's life and served his apprenticeship aboard ship with him for two years before joining forces with him. The two men worked as a team, each with his own ship. One would attack from the side and the other from the rear. The Prince was slightly under six feet tall, broad shouldered and thin waisted. He cut a dashing figure with his black hair, dark foreboding brown eyes and olive skin. He too, was never at a loss with women. While Jordan had one woman on his arm at parties, the Prince juggled at least four, and none of them seemed to mind. He lavished all of his women with jewels and gowns. His favorites had their own homes, which he visited frequently.

Devlin Jones had bright red hair that made him stand out in any room. Jones was from Massachusetts, where he owned and operated a small trading store. He was once a well-known pirate in the Caribbean, but he met a woman, married her and settled in Massachusetts. No one knew of his past except his wife who had died the year before. With no one to hold him back, he began to travel again and ran into his old friend, Jack Webster. Webster told him of Lockwood's plan, and he asked if he could be included.

Jacques LaRoche, the Frenchman, was notorious in the Barbary States for destroying the control of the Deys. He was well hated in Algeria, where he singlehandedly stole the Pasha's newest and most beautiful concubine who turned out to be a missing Russian Princess for whom he was greatly rewarded.

Jennifer looked around the table at the well-dressed men; smiling as she thought to herself that no one would ever think they were pirates. Ruthless, deadly men, who were like volcanoes ready to explode at any given time.

Gideon appeared, collected the last of the dishes and then returned to fill the mugs with a hot rum toddy. Timothy dismissed him and addressed the men and women seated at his table, "Ladies and Gentlemen, I need to know your answers. Are you with me? You've seen how fast the *Nightbird* can travel; those of you who are with me, say aye."

Yvonne interjected, "Before I can give an answer, I need to ask some questions."

Timothy looked in her direction, "Yes?"

"Can the ships that we purchase from your firm be traced to us?"

"No," he paused, "All of the ships will be bought anonymously under assumed names."

Yvonne narrowed her eyes, "I see."

Timothy asked, "Is that all?"

"No, there are two other things. First, aren't the townspeople going to be curious about disappearing ships when they pass your land, and secondly, how do you plan to explain the amount of goods that will be coming in at such a rapid speed?" quizzed Yvonne.

Timothy smiled, "Both are good questions. Let me answer the first," he paused to collect his thoughts. "Lockwood is built on a high cliff overlooking the Atlantic Ocean, and it is far removed from the city of Newport. The mile of land on both sides belongs to me." Jennifer was amazed, he must have been planning something like this for years. Timothy continued, "The goods will be catalogued by a select group of people and then re-catalogued by Jennifer. Only a certain amount of goods will surface each month."

Prince D'Mattea, who sat quietly asked, "What will be our share of the profits?"

Timothy looked down the table at him, "Everyone will get an equal share because everyone is involved equally."

Devlin Jones spoke in a low, scratchy voice, "I have some men, who work in my store," he hesitated before continuing, "If you're interested, some of the goods can be sold in my store."

Jordan said, "Do you trust these men?"

"Yes," replied Devlin, "They were members of my crew."

Timothy looked around the table, "Yvonne, are you with me?"

Yvonne bit her lip before speaking, "Yes, against my better judgement, I'm in."

Timothy turned to Mark, "Mark?"

"Yes," he replied.

"Cutthroat John?" asked Timothy.

Cutthroat John smiled broadly, "Yes, I'm in. This is probably going to be the most excitement I've had in years."

Timothy grinned, "How about the two Brentwood brothers?"

Michael looked at Joseph before answering, "I can only answer for myself and I say yes. England hasn't done anything to stop the capture of innocent people, so I say we do."

Joseph said quickly, "I agree!"

Timothy looked at Jones, "Devlin, from what you said earlier, am I to assume that you're in?" Devlin Jones nodded his head. Timothy looked at Rick Jordan, "Good; Jordan what do you say?"

Jordan responded, "You know I'm in, Lockwood."

Timothy asked, "Prince D'Mattea?"

The dark-haired man hesitated, "Yes, I'm looking forward to this comradeship."

"Jacques?" questioned Timothy.

"I'm in."

"Webster?" questioned Timothy.

"Count me in; this retirement thing has gotten boring."

Timothy looked at McArnold, he knew of them all that Cliff might be the most difficult to convince, "McArnold, are you still undecided?"

Yvonne stared at him; her eyes pleaded with him to say yes. "No, I've made a decision, I'll join the stronghold. The last few days I've done a lot of thinking and with hearing a lecture from Yvonne on how most of you were forced into your lives as pirates, I decided that I could help do something about slavery."

Jennifer rose her glass, speaking for the first time, "I would like to propose a toast." Everyone turned to stare at her. Timothy flashed a brilliant smile, marrying Jennifer was the best thing he had done in his life. "To my husband, Timothy, and his invention of a ship called the

Nightbird and to all of you. I hope that your successes in the Barbary States and the Caribbean prove to be prosperous." They raised their glasses in the air and drank to Jennifer's toast.

Jennifer excused herself, leaving the men to sit and drink. She walked along the deck, observing the full moon so bright almost as if it was daylight. She wondered if she did the right thing back there at the meeting. Should she have made the toast? She worried about Timothy; if he got caught or worse, got killed, how would she deal with the loss? She stood at the rail of the ship staring out into the darkness. She was strong-willed, and she was emotionally strong; she could deal with anything that may happen. If forced to, she would control the others if anything happened to Timothy. She was in such deep thought that she didn't hear the footsteps behind her. Suddenly, a hand grasped her shoulder, spinning her around. She gasped as she heard her husband say, "Did I scare you, Jenny?"

"Yes," she whispered.

The golden eyes flickered in the darkness, "I am so damn proud of you." He leaned forward kissing her full mouth. She melted in his arms; he said softly, "Let's go to our cabin."

Jennifer sighed. She leaned against Timothy, who put his arm around her as they walked to their cabin. Upon entering the cabin, Jennifer removed her heavy cloak, draping it over a chair. Timothy stood behind her, nuzzling her neck. She leaned back against him closing her eyes, sighing happily. Slowly, he turned her, the amber eyes smoldering with passion; he leaned toward her, kissing her as his fingers worked the buttons on the back of her dress. He moved from her mouth to her nose, cheeks, chin, neck and back to her mouth. Jennifer could feel the passion and lust blazing inside of her. Her legs felt as if they were turning to rubber. Her hands began to unbutton his vest, as he began easing the gown from her shoulders. The heavy gold brocade gown fell to her feet shimmering in the candlelight. She stood before him in chemise and numerous petticoats. Timothy began to remove the rest of his clothes, slowly, methodically, starring at Jennifer. She could feel the searing heat of his eyes as she seductively began to remove her petticoats and chemise. Once she was completely undressed, she walked toward the bunk, swaying her hips, calling him to her without words.

Timothy blew out the candle, getting in bed with her, whispering softly in her ear, he said, "You're a temptress, Jennifer. No man will ever be able to look at you without wanting you. I've noticed several on this ship doing so, but they know not to touch."

She kissed him feverishly, "No man will ever have me as long as I have you, Timothy Lockwood. You are my life." Slowly, she began to make love to him; she kissed him hard yet softly, the rose-colored lips tracing his neck, his chest. Timothy felt his desire mounting in an urgent fury. Jennifer, a mere girl, was bringing him to the height of insanity. His lips urgently found hers, kissing her much more passionately than he thought he had ever kissed anyone. She responded with ardent pleasure, pressing closer to him. He entered her quickly, causing her to gasp. She met his powerful strokes, matched his intensity, and for the moment, nothing mattered to either of them. The past, the future didn't exist, the *Nightbird* and the others faded into the background of their minds. The only important thing was the present and the pleasure each wanted to give and return to the other. The love they had for each other became stronger and more intense. They made love two more times that evening. Spent, and bathed in the musky smell of lust, they fell asleep entwined in each other's arms.

Timothy rose early, dressing in grey flannel trousers and heavy white cotton shirt. He left the cabin for the galley. Half-way there, he saw Gideon, who he sent to get breakfast for him and Jennifer. Timothy then went topside; he could see Newport in the distance; another hour or so, they would be home. He went back to his cabin; Jennifer was still asleep, her reddish-brown hair was a mass of tangles, spread out over the pillow. He gazed at her longingly; he wanted her, yet he knew couldn't have her this morning. He sat down on the edge of the bunk, leaned forward and kissed her softly on the lips. Her eye lids fluttered open, "Good morning," she said yawning.

"Good morning. Gideon is getting us breakfast."

"Are we almost in Newport?" She asked rubbing her eyes.

"Yes," replied Timothy, "about another hour."

Jennifer threw back the covers exposing her nude body to the cold morning air. She shivered as she reached for the heavy red velvet robe that had been designed especially for her. She pushed the auburn hair from her face, trying it back with a ribbon. Going to the wash bowl, she washed her face with cool water. Turning to Timothy, she smiled, "I'm exhausted. I think I am getting sick."

"You do look pale; perhaps you've caught a cold."

Gideon knocked twice and entered the room with a tray full of steaming food. Placing the tray on the table he said, "We'll be arriving in port soon, is there anything I can get for you?"

"No, thank you," replied Jennifer.

Timothy turned to Gideon, "That will be all Gideon; when we reach port, get your belongings together and come to Lockwood."

"Yes, sir." Gideon left the cabin.

Jennifer looked at the food; the oatmeal was piping hot as were the eggs, ham and potatoes. She poured coffee into the cups while Timothy searched his desk, "What are you looking for?" questioned Jennifer.

"I found it." He walked back to the table holding a long box. "This is a gift for you."

She took the box from him, "Why are you giving me these gifts?"

"This is a special one, open it." The topaz eyes twinkled as she opened the box to reveal a leather-bound ledger; she started to giggle, "It's for your cataloguing,"

"I know." The green eyes danced in merriment, "Do you know that you're crazy?"

He smiled, "Yes, now eat before it gets cold."

Jennifer took a quick bath after breakfast. She dressed in her heavy burgundy velvet gown with matching cloak trimmed in fox. On her way topside to look for Timothy, she met the Prince who was leaving his cabin, "Good morning, Prince D'Mattea."

"Good morning, Mrs. Lockwood."

"Please call me Jennifer."

"Only if you stop calling me Prince and refer to me as Dante."

"I am well trained," she laughed, "I was sent away to school."

"Oh, I see," replied D'Mattea. "If I may, I'd like to ask where you got your cape?"

"Tim bought me a burgundy gown, and decided I needed the matching cape. I believe he bought in in LeHarve but I can't be sure."

"I must ask him. I have a lady friend who would look most stunning in such an outfit." His dark eyes sparkled, "Of course, she isn't as beautiful as you."

Jennifer blushed, the man was, indeed, charming, "Tell me, how do you ever entertain four women at once?"

He laughed, "You've heard about that. Your husband keeps you well informed."

"Yes, I've heard about it. What I want to know is how you do it? Women like to be the center of a man's life and know that she's the only one."

Dante half smiled, one side of his lips turned up, "I choose my women friends very selectively. They must be of the highest intelligence, people that I trust implicitly, and they all must understand that I don't have time for a serious romance."

"I see," replied Jennifer, "but I don't think I could tolerate Timothy having several other women around, whether they be friends or acquaintances."

Dante smiled broadly, "I don't think you have to worry about that, Mrs. Lockwood; your husband seems to be smitten with you. Besides you are a special kind of woman that needs a special kind of man. If only I had met you before your husband did, I think you might have," he paused, "what do you say, swept me off my feet."

"I am indeed, flattered." Jennifer and Dante had reached the deck, and Timothy was walking toward them.

"Good morning, Prince D'Mattea," said Timothy.

"Please, I was just telling your lovely wife that you must call me Dante."

Timothy grinned, thinking to himself that the good Prince better keep his hands off his wife, "Did you enjoy your trip, Dante?"

"Yes, I did. If you would excuse me, I must find Jordan. Have you seen him this morning?" Dante asked. Timothy Lockwood was quite the man, and he made him nervous.

"No, I haven't. Why don't you try the galley," replied Timothy with a small smirk knowing full well that he made the Prince nervous.

"Thank you." The Prince walked away, leaving Jennifer and Tim together.

Jennifer looked out into the harbor. Timothy joined her at the rail, "Can you see Lockwood from here?"

"No, but I think you'll love it."

She gazed up at him, "I'm sure I will."

"You seem to have made friends with Dante, the Prince," said Timothy sarcastically.

She smiled, "Yes, he's a very nice man. He wanted to know where I got my outfit."

"Really?" he was amused.

Jennifer looked at Timothy, "Yes, he said he would like to give a similar outfit to a lady friend of his," Timothy raised his eyebrows, "Wait, are you jealous?"

Tim grinned, wondering if the Prince would buy several outfits to distribute to his lady friends. "Hardly. I've hired a carriage to take you to the house. Our guests will be arriving later."

"Aren't you coming with me to the house?"

"No, Gideon will be escorting you. I'll be there in a little while. I have to stop at the shipping offices and put in an order for eleven more ships like the *Nightbird*."

"Are any servants at the house?"

"No, Gideon will serve as our cook. Which reminds me, I must give him some money, so he can prepare dinner for all of us."

"I can help him. Is there a marketplace around here?"

"Yes, Brick Market; it is an open marketplace; pay attention to the cobblestones, as they can be somewhat dangerous when walking on them."

Jennifer said, "I've walked on cobblestone before. I will be careful. Give me the money, and Gideon and I will stop for the food. Can we get fresh vegetables and meat?"

"Most of the time you can get all kinds of things in the market square," replied Timothy.

"Fine, give me the money, and would you like me to pick up some wine?"

"No, there is a wine cellar." Timothy reached into his pocket for the money. "Be careful."

Jennifer's green eyes met his golden ones, "Don't worry about me."

"I do worry. You don't know Newport, and you're carrying a great deal of money."

"Nothing will happen; I have Gideon with me, and I can take care of myself." She pulled a knife out of her cloak pocket.

Timothy laughed, "I see you've learned a few things due to your association with pirates."

Jennifer smiled, "I certainly have; now, if you'll call for Gideon, we can be on our way."

Timothy waved to Gideon, who was strolling towards them. "Gideon, you and Jennifer will go to the marketplace to purchase food for this evening. Please stay by her side."

"Yes, sir. I won't let Mrs. Lockwood out of my sight." Gideon extended his arm to Jennifer, leading her down the gangplank and into the waiting carriage.

Jennifer marveled at the sight of the city. Some of the buildings were made of marble, and people filled the streets. Brick Market was a large marketplace selling goods both inside and outside. Jennifer found herself buying some dried beef and fresh chickens. She bought several crates of fresh vegetables and fruit. Many of the people in the marketplace stared and pointed at her. Gideon stood close to her as she bought some fresh fish.

"Mrs. Lockwood, don't be alarmed at the people staring. It's just that people as finely dressed as you don't go to the market. They send their servants."

"I'm not alarmed; they can stare all they want." Jennifer looked over her shoulder at Gideon, who had grown in the year she had known him. "Don't worry, I can take care of myself." She looked into the crowd of people and drew in her breath quickly. She couldn't believe her eyes; Geoffrey Lyndon was standing not too far away. She suddenly felt faint as she raised her hand to her forehead.

"Mrs. Lockwood," said Gideon grabbing her arm to keep her from falling, "Is something wrong?"

She had become pale, trying not to draw attention to herself she said, "Please, Gideon, let's go. I'm not feeling very well." She pulled her hood closer to her face and let Gideon put her into the carriage. She stared out the window at Lyndon who was talking to another man. Her mind raced while she was waiting for Gideon to load the carriage with the goods they had bought. Geoffrey Lyndon was dead; Timothy said he was; why would he lie? She felt herself shaking with nerves. When Gideon opened the carriage door, Jennifer jumped. She smiled weakly, "You startled me."

"I'm sorry." Gideon sat quietly across from her.

When they reached Lockwood, Jennifer stared at the massive house. Once inside, she was surprised to find it was completely furnished with some of the most exotic furniture she'd ever seen. She walked from one room to another touching the furniture and looking out the windows. She removed her cloak and rested it over the sofa in the main drawing room. Even though she was wearing the heavy velvet, the house was freezing. The first thing she must get Gideon to do is start lighting the fireplaces. Gideon was unloading the crates in the kitchen when Jennifer found him. "Gideon, I'll do that. Would you light the fireplaces? It's terribly cold in here."

"Yes, Mrs. Lockwood."

"And please, Gideon, would you call me Jennifer? Stop being so formal."

"Yes, Mrs., I mean Jennifer."

She smiled as she watched him hurry off to light the fireplaces. She unbuttoned her sleeves and rolled them up as she began to unload the boxes. When she finished, she started the kitchen fire and put some water on for tea. She couldn't get her mind off seeing Geoffrey Lyndon.

Gideon returned to find her staring intensely at the fireplace. "Jennifer, have you thought of what you would like for dinner?"

"Yes, I bought five fresh chickens that I would like roasted with some potatoes and carrots."

"Would you like a soup of some kind before the chicken."

"Yes, that would be nice and a pie for dessert," responded Jennifer.

Gideon was concerned because she seemed somewhat out of sorts, still pale looking, "Jennifer, why don't you lay down while I prepare dinner."

"No, I'll help you with the vegetables for the soup, and I'll help you prepare the pie. I've plenty of time to rest."

"You really do not need to help me," replied Gideon.

"I insist."

Gideon looked at her, "Then I would suggest that you change your dress. They delivered your trunk before I came back into the kitchen." He paused, "I took the liberty of placing it into the master bedroom, which is located at the top of the first set of stairs."

"Thank you." Jennifer left the kitchen and went to the master bedroom. The room was massive, and her trunks lay in the middle of the floor. She looked around the pale-yellow room with its dark brocade curtains. Going to the window, she gasped at the breathtaking view. She stood there silently looking out the window at the bay. Timothy had returned early and went straight to the bedroom. When he entered the room, he saw Jennifer standing at the window gazing at the scenery. She was beautiful standing there in the sunlight, which was causing her auburn hair to look redder than it actually was; he touched her and she let out a bloodcurdling scream fainting into his arms. Yvonne, whose room was next door, heard the scream and raced into the master bedroom with her sword in her hand to find Timothy sitting on the edge of the bed, fanning Jennifer.

Yvonne put her sword down, "What happened?"

Timothy looked bewildered, "I'm not sure. I think I scared her." Jennifer's eyes fluttered open. Seeing Timothy on the edge of the bed, she bolted up and threw her arms around him sobbing. "Shush, shush, Jenny calm down, what's wrong?"

"I saw him; he's alive." She answered in a hysterical voice.

Timothy held her close to him, "Who did you see? Tell me."

Jennifer cried out, "Geoffrey Lyndon."

"Jennifer, calm down; you couldn't possibly have seen him; he's dead."

"Please believe me," the tears rolling down her cheeks, "I saw him in the marketplace."

She had pulled away from him, and he began brushing the tears from her face, "Maybe it was someone who just looked like him." Yvonne had backed out of the room, shutting the door behind her; it was best that they had this time alone together.

Jennifer shook her head, "No, it was him."

Timothy was trying to be soothing but now his patience was wearing thin, "Jenny, you couldn't possibly have seen him; he's dead. I killed him."

"Are you sure he was dead?" Her eyes searched his face.

"Yes." The truth of the matter was he wasn't sure, but Jenny need not know that. If Lyndon was alive, he wouldn't be for long. If he was in Newport, he would meet with a most untimely end. He reached for Jennifer and held her close to him whispering, "Everything's going to be alright. You probably saw someone who looked like him," he said again. trying not to show that he was concerned.

Jennifer pulled away from him; brushing a tear away, she said, "I feel like a fool. Everyone probably thinks you killed me with the way I screamed and fainted."

Tim flashed a smile, "No, I'm sure Yvonne just told them I frightened you."

"I've got to calm down because I promised Gideon I'd help him with dinner."

"It's fine. I'm sure Gideon will understand if you don't help him. He told me you weren't feeling well. Why don't you lie down?"

"What about Gideon?"

"Don't worry about Gideon. He is used to preparing dinner for a much larger group of people in a much shorter period of time."

Jennifer sighed, "I guess I'm just tired. Maybe I'm getting sick, I've been feeling awfully tired the past few days."

Timothy squeezed her hand, "Well, a lot has happened. Why don't you take a nap? I'll tell Gideon to prepare dinner."

"Okay," she said meekly.

He kissed her forehead, "Rest, Jennifer. Don't worry about the trunks," he turned and left the bedroom.

Shutting the door behind him, Timothy thought about what Jennifer had said. The possibility of Lyndon being alive was greater than he realized. What if he just passed out? After all, he didn't hear Lyndon's neck snap. If Jennifer did see Lyndon, he wondered if Lyndon saw her.

He would have to make sure that she was well protected and watched every second of every day and night.

CHAPTER TWENTY-FOUR

Several months later, after much inquiry, Timothy could relax. Geoffrey Lyndon did not live in Newport nor the surrounding areas. Jennifer, who was now about six months pregnant and bedridden due to the difficult time she had in London when she lost the last baby, must have seen someone who bared a resemblance to Lyndon. At this stage in her pregnancy, Jennifer was extremely upset that she would have to stay in bed. In the early months, she helped Timothy and the others with the storage room. Every person involved in Tim's scheme was familiarized with the secret passageways in case of an emergency. Jennifer and Timothy had set up a perfect cataloguing system with shelves, files and a desk. Now that the doctor told her she must stay in bed for the next three months, she felt helpless. Timothy and Mark Gregory already went out on one expedition as did everyone else except Cliff McArnold and his partner, Yvonne, whose ship was not yet completed. Yvonne and Cliff, for the time being, worked in the storage cellar. When Yvonne's ship, *Season's Fury,* was completed sometime next week, Maggie would take their place. Maggie would have her hands full with cataloguing and taking care of Lion, who was growing by leaps and bounds, looking more like Timothy each day. Gideon would be helping Maggie as he was now permanently on the household staff.

Timothy divided his time between his business and the activities at his home base when he was in Newport, which wasn't too often these days. He had renamed the *Nightbird,* to *Crimson Lady* for Jenny. When he was in Newport, he would spend a couple of hours a day with Jennifer, just talking to her and making her feel wanted and missed. She wasn't lonesome for company; when his ship was in port, Prince D'Mattea would stop by daily. She had literally charmed the pants off the Prince, who periodically gave her gifts to honor his friendship with her and her husband.

Since their arrival in March, the weather had steadily gotten warmer. Now, the end of July, it was terribly hot, yet the house remained relatively cool because of the sea breeze. Robert and Molly stopped in occasionally to see Jennifer; and when they did, Robert would drill her about Timothy's whereabouts, especially since he noticed that the *Moonlight* had been moored since they came to Newport. Jennifer said Timothy had business matters in London where he sought trading deals. She made a mental note to tell Tim about the questions Robert asked.

Yvonne's ship, *Season's Fury*, was finally finished, and she and Cliff set sail for the Barbary States. The day they left was difficult for Jennifer; Timothy and the others had been gone almost a month and she was feeling lonesome. Yvonne and Cliff had become best friends but there wasn't any romance. Yet, Jennifer noticed the sparkle in Yvonne's eyes and the gleam in Cliff's; she was positive that they were in love with each other but neither realized it.

Several weeks had passed since Yvonne and Cliff had left; it was now early September, and Jennifer's due date was two months away. Several of the men working the Caribbean waters had returned to unload their full holds. Devlin Jones brought with him a sixteen-year-old girl that he and his men rescued from an auction block. The day he took the girl to Jennifer's room, he said, "Excuse me, Mrs. Lockwood, but I've brought you a new friend."

Jennifer stared at the girl, "Hello, what's your name?"

"Daphne," she answered timidly.

Devlin said, "She's lost both her parents, the bloody pirates," he paused thinking to himself that they were also pirates, "killed both of them and were about to auction her off as a slave when we took them by surprise."

Jennifer made eye contact with Devlin, "I see, but why did you bring her here?"

"Well now, the lass says she doesn't have any family, and we couldn't leave her on that bloody island with those savages. So, I figured, that maybe you needed somebody to talk to, a companion."

Jennifer's eyes had a touch of merriment in them as she thought about Devlin mentioning the 'bloody pirates' when he himself was a pirate, "Actually Devlin, it is pretty boring here."

"Well, she's got an education, and I figured, with her being around your age, she would make a nice friend for you."

Jennifer looked at the girl, she needed a bath and some new clothes, "Is it true that you have some education?"

"Yes, Miss." She answered softly.

"Where did you go to school?"

"In France, Miss Lillian's School," replied Daphne.

Jennifer squealed with delight, "I went to school there! How is dear Miss Lillian?"

"Fine, Miss," replied Daphne.

"Please," she paused, "please call me Jenny." Devlin slipped quietly out of the door. "I think you and I will become fast friends."

"I'll," she hesitated, "I'll work for you?"

"No, you must be my friend." She threw back the covers and started to get out of bed.

"Don't get out of bed. Mr. Jones said that you had to stay in bed because you have difficulty carrying a child."

Jennifer smiled, "Mr. Jones must have told you a lot about me."

Daphne blushed, "He said that you were very beautiful and very smart, and he was right. You look just like he described you."

Jennifer was curious now, "What else did he tell you?"

"He said that you were close to my age, either eighteen or nineteen and that you were envied by many women because your husband is a very rich, powerful and handsome man."

Jennifer smiled a sad smile, "Yes, Timothy is all of those and more." A knock on her door brought her back to the present, "Yes?"

Maggie entered the bedroom, "Excuse me, Mrs. Lockwood, but Rick Jordan's ship just came in and he said Prince D'Mattea, Mr. Lockwood and Mr. Gregory would be here in a couple of days."

"Maggie, this is Daphne, would you please give her the room next to Yvonne's and draw a bath for her."

"Yes, Mrs. Lockwood."

Jennifer turned her attention to Daphne, "Daphne, you may choose any dress you like out of my closet to wear until my husband returns and can take you to buy some clothes."

"Really?"

"Yes," Jennifer pointed to the closet. Daphne walked to the closet, opening the door timidly. She was amazed that anyone could possess so many gowns of so many different colors. She didn't know which one to pick; what if she picked Jennifer's favorite? "Daphne, just don't stand there, choose one."

"I," Daphne paused, "I don't know which one; they are all so beautiful." She touched the pale grey gossamer silk dress as she spoke.

"Do you like the grey silk?"

"Yes, it is very beautiful," replied Daphne.

"Take that one if you like."

Daphne turned to face Jennifer, "Are you sure? If this is a favorite of yours, I'll take another one."

Jennifer shook her head, "No, it's not a favorite, and actually, I've never worn it."

"Then I won't take a dress that you've never worn."

"No, take it. Tim likes to see me in bright colors. Reds, burgundies and greens, so take the dress."

"Thank you."

Maggie, who had returned to the room, said, "Miss, if you would follow me, your bath is ready."

Daphne began to follow Maggie out as a tall, handsome man with long curly hair entered the bedroom. "Maggie," he nodded. "Jennifer, how are you feeling?"

"Fine, Rick. Maggie tells me that Prince D'Mattea, Tim and Mark are going to return shortly."

"Yes; who is the young girl?" he asked after Maggie and Daphne left.

"Devlin brought her back from the islands. She has no family, and he thought I could use a companion."

"Thoughtful of him." Rick moved to close the door. "We were very successful this trip. More than we have ever been."

"Tell me, did we get a lot of goods?"

"We got a great deal of goods. Goods that can be sold openly and at a good price."

"Excellent!" exclaimed Jennifer.

His eyes widened with excitement, "But, the best part of all is we saved one hundred and fifty women. D'Mattea, Tim and Mark are taking them to Italy and giving them money to return to their homes."

"This is amazing news!" Jennifer paused, "Rick, by any chance, did you bring back any silk?"

"No, not this trip. We hit a ship that was carrying porcelain, of all things. But we do have some silk that is catalogued, but why do you ask?"

"For Daphne."

"Who in the devil is Daphne?"

"The girl you asked me about."

"Oh," he thought for a second. "Why don't I get cleaned up and I'll take her to buy some new clothes. Anything she wants."

Jenny smiled, "And what do you want in return?"

"Nothing," Rick said.

"I know you, Rick Jordan, and remember, she's only sixteen years old. The poor thing's frightened out of her wits, and she doesn't need to be frightened of men."

"I wouldn't touch her; I promise you," replied Rick.

"I have your word?" questioned Jennifer.

"You have my word," responded Rick, seriously.

Jennifer smiled, "Thank you."

"I'll see you later." Rick walked out of the room leaving Jenny alone to think.

Several hours later, Daphne came running into Jennifer's bedroom. The grey gossamer silk was slightly large in the bust, but fit her well in other areas. "Jennifer, Mr. Jordan took me into town and bought me five dresses, petticoats, shoes and two cloaks."

"You must show me what he bought you. I hope he bought you some warm clothes."

"I'll go get them." Jennifer was pleased that Daphne was so happy. Daphne returned with the boxes, "Of course they're not as beautiful as yours, but they are just fine for me." Daphne took the first dress out of the box; it was a navy-blue velvet with a paler blue lace trim. The second dress was a dark green brocade satin with a high neckline and long sleeves. The third dress was a deep burgundy with a round neckline. The fourth, a deep brown muslin dress and the fifth, a red velvet with white trim. The cloaks were made of a heavy wool, one in deep blue and the other in dark green to match the green brocade gown.

"They are all very beautiful, Daphne, and I'm sure you look very pretty in them."

"I'll put these back in my room, and then I'll come to talk with you."

"Fine, take your time." She watched the dark-haired girl with the big violet eyes leave the room.

Moments later, Daphne appeared with a tray of hot tea and homemade cakes. "I met Maggie in the hall, and she was bringing us this, so I took it from her." She set the tray on the table and helped Jennifer to the wicker lounge near the window.

"Daphne, please; I'm not as fragile as everyone thinks."

"It's alright; I don't mind." Daphne served the tea and cakes.

"How did you happen to go to school in France?"

"I was an only child, and my mother was very well educated, and she wanted me to have the same opportunity. My parents, from the day I was born, put aside some money each week for my education."

"I see."

"My mother married someone that her family felt was beneath her, so they disinherited her."

Jennifer replied, "I'm sorry."

"You needn't be. My father was a good man and a good provider." Jennifer sipped her tea, "Tell me how you met your husband. Was it romantic?"

Jennifer wet her lips, "Not exactly."

"Please tell me, Jennifer, was your marriage arranged? Mr. Jones told me you were an heiress, so I'm sure your marriage was pre-arranged."

Jennifer took a deep breath, "Well, I was supposed to marry someone else, but I didn't love him."

"Were your parents angry?"

"My father died before I married Tim."

"If this was not pre-arranged, how did you meet him."

"Well, this may sound stupid, but the day I returned home from France, I saw him on the ship moored aside of mine. I found him very attractive, and he watched me disembark." Jennifer's mind drifted back in time as Daphne sat listening intently. "I met him on his ship when I went to ask for an outfit to wear to a costume party."

"A costume party sounds exciting!" exclaimed Daphne, "What kind of a costume did you get from a ship."

"Well, Gideon," Jennifer paused, "Have you met him yet?"

"No."

"Gideon was Timothy's cabin boy, and he was about my size, so I borrowed some of his clothes to go to the party as a lady pirate."

"A lady pirate, that must have a sight! How old were you? What did your father say?"

"I was seventeen, and my father didn't know what I was planning." She paused, remembering the expressions on the faces of the people at the party. "When I arrived at the party, I found out that my plan to shock the guests had already been tried by one Timothy Lockwood."

Daphne looked bewildered, "I don't understand."

"He went dressed as a pirate and caused quite a commotion."

"Oh." She giggled, "Do you think he did it purposely?"

Jennifer cocked her head to one side, "I've never thought about it. He just might have done it deliberately."

Daphne clasped her hands together, "Tell me what happened at the party? Did the two of you dance?"

"No, we went outside, and he agreed to take me to Spain to escape marriage to a man I hated but," Jennifer paused, "I was kidnapped from the party."

"Kidnapped! By who?" Daphne was shocked.

"By the man I was supposed to marry."

"He must have loved you."

"No, he didn't," replied Jennifer, "he hated me; he kept me hidden for a good part of the night, and then he sold me to this big fat man with few teeth."

"Sold you?"

"Yes, I was put on a ship and brought to the Barbary Coast, put on an auction block and sold to Captain Bloodthirsty."

Daphne's eyes opened wide, "Captain Bloodthirsty! I've heard of him, he's a pirate and a dangerous one, isn't he?"

"He is a pirate, and I guess other people consider him dangerous, but he never was mean to me." There was no need to go into details of what transpired on the ship with Daphne. "Captain Bloodthirsty turned out to be Timothy Lockwood."

Daphne was taken aback, why would Jennifer tell such an outrageous story, "You're kidding."

Jennifer shook her head, "You must swear to me that you'll never speak of this as long as you live." She wasn't sure why she trusted Daphne so much, perhaps because they attended Miss Lillian's or maybe because Daphne unwittingly had no idea that she was saved from a life of slavery by pirates herself.

"I promise."

"It's important that you not mention it to anyone. Timothy is fighting against slavery, and it's because of him that you are here."

Daphne gazed at the auburn-haired woman who seemed much older than she was; in certain ways, Jennifer Lockwood's was well beyond her age. "I promise you I won't say anything to anyone. But I don't understand; Mr. Jones took me here."

"Mr. Jones, Mr. Jordan and others all work for my husband. Tim is trying to abolish white slavery in the Caribbean and the Barbary States. So he is a good man." Jennifer paused, "I think he'll like you, and we do need other people on our side."

"You must tell me more about Mr. Jordan."

Jenny smiled, "You find Mr. Jordan attractive? Hmm."

Daphne blushed, "Yes."

"I'll be truthful with you. Rick Jordan is a womanizer. He takes without asking and never lacks for female companionship. I've heard that he makes women fall in love with him and then he leaves them."

Daphne was disappointed, "But he was so nice. I can't believe he would do such a thing."

"I'm sorry I told you the way I did, but I felt that it was important that you knew about his wild ways." Jennifer paused, "There are other men in the sea, and you're young enough and pretty enough to catch one."

"Do you really think I'm pretty?"

"Yes. There is one other man I must warn you against."

"Who?"

"Prince D'Mattea. He'll be here in a few days."

"A Prince?"

"Yes," replied Jennifer. "He's very handsome and charming. But he has a flaw."

"Which is?" inquired Daphne.

"He has a habit of becoming," she paused, "I was going to say involved with several women at the same time. Well, I guess that would be true, but he keeps himself from getting romantically involved on a serious level."

"How does he keep his emotions so controlled?"

"I'm not exactly sure. The funny thing is the women don't seem to care. He provides for all of them equally."

"Are you telling me that the man doesn't care anything at all for any woman?"

Jennifer thought for a second, "Timothy told me that the Prince has a very close female friend who has protected him from the authorities several times. When something goes wrong in his life, he goes to the Countess, and she takes him into her home."

"Do you think they are romantically involved?"

"No, the Countess is married to the Comte de Lucerne, and she and Prince D'Mattea have known each other for years; they are merely friends. On the other hand, she has risked her life and her title several times in order to protect him."

"Amazing!" Daphne said, "Then you think he cares for her?"

"I would think so. They've been seen in each other's company many times; plus, during a recent riding accident, the Prince rushed to her side and stood with her throughout her six-week recovery.

"What did her husband say?" inquired Daphne.

"Nothing. He was busy in Paris at the time with another woman. But of course, much of this is gossip."

Daphne marveled at Jennifer; she was what Daphne herself wanted to be like. "I'll take the tea dishes downstairs." Daphne collected the cups and the remainder of the small cakes, placing them on the silver tray. Picking up the tray, she walked to the door, balancing the tray on one hand and opened it. A man was standing in the doorway.

Jennifer looked toward the door, "Stefan! What are you doing here?"

Stefan raced across the room to hug his cousin, "When we heard you were with child we had to come."

"We?" Jenny raised her eyebrows.

Stefan smiled, "Yes, Lizabeth and Harris are here too."

"Daphne, I'm sorry. Please come here." Daphne rested the tray on a table near the bedroom door, "Daphne, this is my cousin, Stefan Weatherly."

"How do you do, Mr. Weatherly?"

"Fine, Miss…"

Daphne interjected, "Charbonneau."

Jenny interrupted, "Daphne is a friend of Mr. Jones' family."

"Mr. Jones?" He thought confused, "Oh, Mr. Jones, that Captain friend of Timothy's."

"Yes." Daphne wondered why Jennifer would lie to her cousin, but said nothing. "If you would excuse me, I'll bring this downstairs and help Maggie with dinner."

"No, why don't you rest and then when you've finished dressing for dinner, come back here for a few minutes."

Daphne smiled, leaving Jennifer and Stefan alone to talk. Stefan turned toward Jennifer, "How are you feeling, Jenny?"

"I feel fine; the doctor just doesn't want me to take any chances."

"I'm sure he knows best." Stefan looked her over, "Are you sure you feel fine?"

"Other than being lonely, I assure you I'm in perfect health."

"Lonely," His mind questioned, "but what about Miss Charbonneau?"

"She's just arrived, as did you." She paused, "What's happening in London?"

"Really nothing. Weatherly is virtually the same, although it has been very quiet since you've left."

"Stefan, what you need is a wife," Jenny answered, her eyes twinkling mischievously.

"What are you thinking?"

She smiled, "How long will you be in Newport?"

"Until after you have the baby and are back on your feet, why?"

Jennifer looked at Stefan, "Just wondering." The fact that they were staying that long presented a problem, but Jennifer kept smiling.

"Why?"

She shook her head, "No particular reason."

"Where's Timothy?"

"He should be home any day now; he's away on business."

"I see." Stefan was suspicious of Timothy and his random disappearances.

"Stefan, I'm terribly tired. Would you help me to my bed and then leave so I can rest for a little bit?" she asked.

"Sure." He helped her from the wicker lounge to her bed.

"Thank you."

"I'll see you later."

"Would you tell the others that I'm sleeping and do not wish to be disturbed."

"Of course." Stefan left the room, shutting the door behind him.

Jennifer waited a couple of minutes to make sure he had gone. She got out of her bed, locked the door and put on her heavy robe and slippers. Going to the table, she lit a candle and placed it on the table near her closet. Raising her hand towards the top of the closet door she hit the mechanism that opened the secret passageway that led to the storage area. The stairway was dark and damp, she was afraid she would lose her footing, but she had to go down to the storage area. Stefan would have to come unexpectedly while Timothy was away. She had to warn whoever was in the storage area. As she reached the bottom of the stairs, something furry scurried by her. She drew in her breath so not to scream and continued along the narrow passageway. In the distance, she could see a light. When she reached the storage area, it was deserted. She thought to herself that they must be unloading Rick Jordan's ship. She began going down another flight of stairs to the hidden wharf. She had seen it once, and the area was large enough to dock six of the twelve ships. She heard Rick's voice in the distance. It was getting colder in the cave as she neared the docks.

Rick had turned and was heading to the passageway that would lead him to the storage area when he saw Jennifer, "What the devil are you doing down here?" He walked over to her. "If Timothy finds out, he'll kill me and possibly you."

Jennifer looked at Rick, "We've got a problem."

"What kind of problem?"

"Big ones."

"Well let's not stand here. Can you make it back up the stairs?"

"I think so," replied Jennifer. In truth she was uncertain because they were very steep.

"Come on. I'll help you." He led her up the stairs, "What kind of problem?" he asked as they reached the storage area.

"My cousin, Stefan, came from England unexpectedly along with two servants."

The information didn't appear to be a problem to Rick, "So?"

"He doesn't know about the operations here. He doesn't know about Tim; he doesn't know that we're smuggling goods," her voice became shaky because she feared what could happen.

"Calm down," Rick said as he questioned, "He doesn't know anything at all?"

"No, he doesn't. I came down here to tell you not to use the kitchen entry way and now with Harris…"

Rick interrupted her, "Who's Harris?"

Jennifer said, "He was the butler at Weatherly, and I'm sure he'll assume the same duties here."

"Which means that we have to enter the house from the front door."

"Right," replied Jennifer.

"We really do have problems." He thought quietly, "I have to figure out a way to get to the front door."

"What if you came into the house through a passageway and then leave through the rear door."

"What about the other servant?"

"Gideon could take care of her, I'm sure. Besides, she was like a personal maid, and I'm sure that she will be doing the same thing."

A tall, thin man approached them, "Excuse me, Captain Jordan, the *Rogue* just pulled in, and she's carrying some wounded."

"Wounded? What the devil? They were fine when I left them."

Looking at Jennifer and then back to Rick Jordan he said, "There was a battle at sea and the *Crimson Lady* came to the *Rogue's* aid; the *Crimson Lady's* about an hour behind.

Jennifer began to worry; what if Timothy had been injured? "What about the *Crimson Lady*? Were there any injuries?"

"I don't know, Mrs. Lockwood." The truth of the matter was Timothy Lockwood was aboard the *Rogue* and seriously injured. The *Crimson Lady* was being Captained by George.

Rick Jordan took control, "I'm going to bring Mrs. Lockwood back upstairs. Handle the situation."

"Yes, sir."

"Jennifer, come let me take you to your room."

"Will you promise me that as soon as Tim gets here, you'll send him up?"

"I promise." He led her back up the hidden passageway and into her bedroom. "Stay put." Rick left the room through the passageway and hurried back to the wharf; the *Rogue* had injuries and if she did, so did the *Crimson Lady*. He was met by Mark Gregory at the wharf, "How many injured Mark?"

Mark Gregory looked at Rick gravely, "We have several minor injuries, but we also have one major injury." Rick felt sick to his stomach, preparing himself for what he instinctively knew he would hear, "Timothy," responded Mark.

"Timothy," he knew it; he could tell by the look in Mark's eyes, "What the hell was he doing aboard the *Rogue?*"

"He wasn't on the *Rogue*. I don't have time to tell you the details. We've got to get him into the house and then get a doctor."

"What kind of injury?" Rick asked as they ran to the ship.

"Sword. Right through him. It entered from the back and exited out the front."

"Damn," replied Rick.

Mark continued, "He's lost a lot of blood, and he's developed an infection. I'm surprised we haven't lost him."

"Where?" Rick asked as the two men ran up the gangplank.

"Outside of LeHarve; the damn French took us by surprise. Privateers." They entered the cabin where Timothy lay immobilized in the bed. Sweat pouring off of him, his hair was soaked as were the bedsheets. A large bandage with blood stains was wrapped tightly around his midsection. "The men are rigging up a stretcher. We've got to get him into the house."

Rick took a deep breath, "We've got a problem about that."

Mark turned to face him, "What?"

"Jennifer's cousin came to visit and brought two servants. We'll have to wait until later when everyone's asleep."

Mark's stare was deadly, "We can't. He'll die."

Rick looked at Timothy and then at Gregory, "We'll have to take him up to the kitchen and out the door and then back into the front."

A couple of men came into the room with a makeshift stretcher. The four of them placed blankets on the stretcher and then lifted Timothy onto it, covering him with blankets. The trip up the narrow staircase was difficult and dangerous; several times, the stretcher slipped out of the carrier's hands, and Timothy groaned in pain. When they reached the top, Rick listened against the door, opening it slightly he saw that Gideon was the only one in the kitchen, "Gideon."

Gideon turned around seeing Rick Jordan; Rick moved into the kitchen, clearing the way for the stretcher. Gideon stared past Rick at the stretcher, seeing Timothy unconscious, the color draining from his young face, "What happened?"

"We've got to get him upstairs," responded Rick.

Gideon looked at his Captain, "Is he going to be alright?"

"We don't know. Someone is going to have to go for a doctor." The men walked by Rick as he continued speaking, "We've got to get Tim upstairs; first, can you distract our guests?" Gidden nodded his head, "Good."

Rick went out after the others, and Gideon set out to make sure no one saw them enter the house. Rick Jordan wondered how he was going to tell Jennifer. She had to be told because of the seriousness of his injury.

Mark Gregory took one of the horses from the stables and went to get a doctor, while the others carried Timothy upstairs to a private bedroom. Rick Jordan went to Jennifer's room; he knocked, "Come in," replied Jennifer. He entered her room closing the door behind him.

"Excuse me, Mrs. Lockwood." His eyes scanned the room seeing Lizabeth, Stefan and Harris visiting. "I need to talk with you privately."

Jennifer noticed a strange look in Rick's eyes and an urgency in his voice, "What's wrong? Something happened to Tim, I know it."

"Jennifer, I mean Mrs. Lockwood, I think we need to talk alone," replied Rick. Stefan didn't like the familiarity the man had with his cousin.

Blinking back tears, she said to her guests, "I have business matters to discuss with Mr. Jordan, why don't you take a walk around the grounds; look at the beautiful view of the ocean."

"Jennifer, do you really think you should discuss business?" questioned Stefan.

"Stefan, I'm perfectly fine." She threw a quick glance at Rick; there was such a strange urgency in his eyes, "Really, please I must take care of this matter." Jennifer watched her cousin leave reluctantly with both Harris and Lizabeth in tow. She glanced back at Rick, motioning to him to check the hall.

Rick turned around towards Jennifer, "He's gone," he said as he closed and locked the door, so they would not be interrupted.

"Good, what happened? I know that something is wrong."

"I'm sorry, Jennifer, there is no easy way to say this but Tim's been injured." He said it bluntly, the only way to tell a woman like Jennifer bad news.

She blinked back her tears, trying to be strong, "How bad is he?" Rick's eyes drifted away from hers, "Look at me, Rick Jordan." Rick stared at her, trying not show any emotion, "He's bad, isn't he?"

"Yes, Jennifer, he's very bad." She began to get out of bed, "You shouldn't be out of bed."

"Don't tell me what to do." She snapped.

"But the doctor said..."

Jennifer interrupted him, "Damn the doctor. I know how I feel. Where is Timothy?"

"They've taken him to one of the bedrooms."

"Bring me to him." By this time, she had gotten out of bed and had put on her robe.

"Mark went to get a doctor." He took Jennifer by the arm and led her down the hallway.

"Where did this happen?" questioned Jennifer.

Rick replied, "Outside of LeHarve."

"LeHarve? What were pirates doing attacking us outside of a French port?"

Rick looked at her, "It wasn't pirates, Jennifer, it was the damn French privateers thinking they were going to capture American ships." They had stopped in front of one of the bedrooms. "Before you go in, I have to tell you that the sword entered his back and came out the front."

"My God!" Tears welled in her sea green eyes.

Rick continued, "It's very serious because an infection has set in."

Jennifer seemed as if she was in a daze, "Infection? But why didn't they get help in London?"

Rick shook his head, "I don't know." He opened the door and let Jennifer walk into the room, following closely.

Jennifer looked at Timothy, he seemed so peaceful, almost serene, as if he was asleep. The bedsheets were pulled up to his waist, exposing the massive chest which was bound by white linen stained with crusty blood. She put her hand up to her mouth feeling as if she would swoon. Rick steadied her as she sat on the edge of the bed. Staring at his face, sweat pouring from it, Jennifer touched his cheek, he was burning with fever. A tear trickled down her cheek, she wiped it away angrily. She couldn't cry, not now; she had to be strong, especially now, "Rick, get some cold water."

Rick left the room to get the water. Jennifer wondered how a swordsman like Timothy could have been caught so off guard. He moaned, bringing her back to the present, "Season, Season," He mumbled, "I'll kill you Rafael." Jennifer wondered who Rafael was and why Timothy said he would kill him. Rick returned with the cold water and a piece of cloth. Jennifer took the bowl of water from him, dipping the cloth in the water, she began to bathe Timothy's face. He continued to mumble, sometimes coherently and other times incoherently.

Mark returned with the doctor, who looked disapprovingly at Jennifer. He examined Timothy for a half an hour, prescribing opium for the pain and infection. He then turned toward Jennifer, "Mrs. Lockwood, what are you doing out of bed?"

"I feel perfectly fine, Dr. Goldman."

He frowned at her, "You should be taking care of yourself."

"I will, but I'm not going to leave my husband, with him being so ill."

"I'm sure that there are plenty of people in this house that can take care of him," replied Dr. Goldman, thinking to himself that this was a strange lot of people, but Lockwood paid him handsomely to keep his mouth shut when such medical occurrences such as this one erupted.

"How serious is he?" pressed Jennifer.

"Mrs. Lockwood, that's hard to tell."

"Listen, Dr. Goldman, I want to know exactly. Don't tell me that you don't know because I know that you do."

"Very well, Mrs. Lockwood, your husband is seriously ill. Most people do not survive wounds in the area in which it is located."

Jennifer fought back the tears, "Are you telling me that he's going to die?"

"I don't usually prescribe opium for patients," replied Dr. Goldman, ignoring Jennifer's question.

"Answer my question, Doctor, is my husband going to die?" Jennifer demanded.

Dr. Goldman looked her in the eyes, "I honestly can't say, but his chance to live is much smaller than his chance to die."

Jennifer swallowed hard, her throat dry, and a lump was forming in her throat. Her words were barely audible, "I see."

"It is important that you administer the correct dosage of the opium. The drug will let him rest more comfortably and ease the pain. His fever must be arrested, and he must be watched twenty-four hours a day. And Mrs. Lockwood, you are not to administer the opium due to your condition."

Jennifer shook her head, "I understand," she replied fighting back the tears.

"Mrs. Lockwood, you must also get your rest."

"Yes, I have servants that can help with Timothy."

"If he does survive, he'll have to be weaned off the opium because it is very addictive."

Jennifer turned from staring at her pale, dying husband and looked the doctor in the eyes, "Thank you, Doctor."

"I will be stopping in daily to check on the both of you."

"Thank you." She said in a small voice.

Rick Jordan escorted the doctor downstairs, "Dr. Goldman, what are his chances? Really, what do you think?"

The middle-aged man looked at Jordan, "He has one chance out of a one hundred to live." Jordan's facial muscles tightened, "Mr. Jordan, I've treated ten cases of his kind and my treatment began before infection had set in and none of them lived," responded the doctor solemnly.

Trying to maintain his own composure, Rick nodded and said, "I see."

"I give Mr. Lockwood a week, maybe two." Rick opened the door, thanking the doctor and watched him leave. Timothy Lockwood's life appeared to be fading in the midst of the fall afternoon. Rick wanted to believe that the doctor was wrong, and Timothy would pull through this ordeal; however, he also knew first hand that individuals with these kinds of wounds did not make it. What would happen to the stronghold if Timothy died? Who would take it over? Jennifer? Yvonne? Mark Gregory? Lost in his thoughts, he went to Timothy's study and poured himself a glass of rum.

CHAPTER TWENTY-FIVE

Prince D'Mattea's ship, the *Italian Princess,* docked with a full hold. The Prince was shocked to hear of Timothy's injuries and went to visit Jennifer, who was resting in her bedroom. When he reached her bedroom, the door was opened by a lovely young woman with violet eyes, who informed him Mrs. Lockwood was sleeping. The Prince went to find Jordan to discuss what the plan, for going back out to sea.

Jennifer woke, and Daphne helped her get dressed, so she could go to Timothy's room to tend to him. When Jennifer reached the room, she relieved Mark Gregory who was not taking Timothy's injury well. Jennifer sat on the edge of the bed, bathing Timothy with the cool water. The opium had to be administered every three hours, and Rick promised her that he would take care of the medicine. The next days were long ones with Jordan, Jennifer, Daphne, the Prince and Mark Gregory all taking turns to care for Timothy whose fever raged. The opium was administered with great difficulty, and Jennifer was happy that the men took care of this. Timothy never regained consciousness for the next week. His pain appeared to increase, and the doctor increased the dosage of the opium. Jennifer began to worry more and sleep less. She spent most of her day at Timothy's bedside praying for his health and bathing him in an attempt to get his fever down. Two weeks had passed, and Dr. Goldman was amazed that the man was still hanging on to life. Jennifer had just about two weeks for her time to birth the baby as November neared. Given that her husband was very near death, Dr. Goldman knew it was futile to demand that she stay in bed for the remainder of her pregnancy.

Timothy, in his delirium, called out for Season, Lion and Jennifer. He spoke of killing two men, Justin Raphael and Geoffrey Lyndon. One afternoon, three weeks after Timothy had been brought home to Lockwood, he called out for Jennifer. Prince D'Mattea, who was on watch, called down the hall for Maggie.

Maggie ran to the room, "Yes, Prince D'Mattea?"

"Get Mrs. Lockwood, hurry."

Maggie ran down the hall to get Jennifer, when she reached the bedroom, she found Jennifer asleep, shaking her gently she said, "Mrs. Lockwood, wake up."

Jennifer's eyes fluttered open, seeing Maggie standing above her, frightened her, "What's wrong?"

"Prince D'Mattea said you are to come quick." Maggie, had already began removing the covers from Jennifer. Helping her up from her bed, she helped her mistress into her robe and led her down the corridor.

When Jennifer reached the room, she looked at Dante, "What's wrong?"

"He called out for you; his eyelids moved." The Prince looked at her sympathetically, admiring her radiant beauty and the disheveled look of someone who had just woken. "Talk to him, Jennifer, I think he might come awake."

"Dante, do you really think so?"

"Yes, I'll be outside if you need me."

"No, stay. I don't mind."

"Are you sure?" questioned Dante.

"Yes." Jennifer crossed the room and sat on the edge of the bed. She brushed his hair from his forehead, "Tim," she paused, "Tim, it's me, Jenny." He moaned, "Tim, I'm here, wake up darling, please." She pleaded. He moaned again, this time it was more like a whimper. What should she say? Was he still delirious? "Do you remember the first time we met on the *Moonlight*? I remember it like it was yesterday." Dante sat staring at her. She rattled on about her life with Timothy; he learned about the two of them. "Remember the night in Java, when you raped me? I deserved it because I can't follow orders...." The tears began to stream down her face as she continued, her voice breaking several times in half sobs, "I loved you from the first time I saw you on the docks, and I made you, my goal. I was seventeen and knew nothing about love or what it meant to be committed to another person." Jennifer began to break down sobbing. Dante wanted to comfort her. He thought to himself that Timothy had put her through living hell. Jennifer spoke again, interrupting the Prince's thoughts, "Please Tim, you've got to get better. You've got to wake up. I need you; Lion needs you, and our child needs you. You taught me the meaning of love, what it was like to be truly loved by a man." She paused, picking up his hand; she lifted it and kissed it. "I'm sorry I shut you out because I thought you didn't love me. You did love me; I know that now. I knew it when I woke after losing the baby and I saw your face." She kissed his hand again rubbing it against her face, "Don't leave me Tim, I need..." A sharp spasm wracked through her body causing her to yell out and drop Tim's hand.

Dante jumped to his feet, "What's wrong?"

She blinked back tears as another spasm passed through her body, "Dante, I've got so much pain."

"Calm down, I'll help you back to your room."

She was on the verge of hysteria, "I can't lose this baby, Dante, I can't."

Trying to be strong for her, Dante said calmly, "You won't. Let me help you, Jenny."

Dante helped her to her feet; her voice cracked, "I feel wet." Her water had broken.

He yelled for Maggie and lifted Jennifer in his arms, carrying her to her bedroom. Jennifer screamed as they reached her bedroom, the pain was unbearable. Dante placed her on the bed, while Maggie ran to get Lizabeth. Lizabeth, having heard Jennifer's screams, was already on her way to Jennifer's bedroom, as were Stefan, Jordan and Gregory.

Mark Gregory was the first one in Jennifer's bedroom, "What's wrong?"

"I think she's going to have the baby," answered Maggie.

Jennifer screamed again, grasping Dante's hand tightly. Mark said, "I'll get a doctor." He raced out of the room and down the stairs.

Dante held Jennifer's hand while she screamed again and again. Lizabeth, Maggie and Daphne brought water, and fresh linens to the bedroom. Lizabeth took charge, "Sir, would you please leave? This is woman's work."

He looked at Jennifer, whose eyes had taken on a wild look, one filled with fear. He patted her hand and left the room. When the doctor arrived, she had been in labor an hour. It appeared that the birth would be a long, difficult one.

Prince D'Mattea had gone back to Timothy's bedside, fearing for both of his hosts' lives. He stared at Timothy, willing him to wake up and said, "Come on Tim, wake up. You've got to live. Your wife needs you." Mark Gregory came in as the Prince was speaking. D'Mattea looked at Gregory and knew he was there to relieve him. The Prince left exhausted from watching Timothy for hours.

Six hours had gone by since the doctor arrived. Jennifer had lost consciousness several times, and it appeared that she would hang on for several more hours before giving birth. Timothy had moaned a couple of times, calling out for Jennifer. He wasn't sweating with fever as much as he had earlier. Twelve hours had passed when Jennifer screamed a blood curdling scream. Dante, Jordan and Stefan raced down the hall to Jennifer's bedroom. They heard a baby crying. Maggie came out of the room, "It's a girl!"

The three men grinned, but their smiles faded when Jennifer screamed for a second time. Maggie raced back into the bedroom. The doctor was delivering another baby, this time a boy. Twins! Maggie ran back outside, "She's had another, a boy!"

"Twins, I'll be damned," said Stefan.

Jennifer lay still in the bed looking at her twins. She wished Timothy could be by her side at this moment to have seen the birth of their children. The doctor motioned for Lizabeth to follow him outside, "Mrs. Lockwood, had a difficult birth. The possibility of her hemorrhaging is great. She must be kept quiet and still, and she cannot have other children."

Mark Gregory, who was standing silently by said, "Will you tell her that?"

"Not now. Tell me sir, how is her husband fairing?"

Gregory replied, "His fever has appeared to go down, and he's murmuring more than he was, only this time more coherently."

"Amazing. I'm surprised that he's lasted this long."

"Tim Lockwood is a strong man, he'll pull through," replied Mark, determinedly.

"Maybe, well, I have to go. Keep Mrs. Lockwood still; she cannot get out of bed for at least one week."

"We understand," Dante answered.

Daphne had come out of the room, "Jennifer's sleeping, and I think that is what the rest of us should do."

The Prince's dark eyes flickered, "I don't believe we've been introduced."

"My name is Daphne Charbonneau."

Dante lifted her hand to his lips and gently placed a kiss on her hand, "Prince D'Mattea, but please, call me Dante."

"I've heard about you."

"All good I hope!" Daphne smiled as he continued, "Perhaps we can have dinner together."

Daphne shook her head, "No, I don't think so."

Rick Jordan stepped in, "Daphne, why don't you go and get some rest; I have to talk to the Prince." Daphne left the two men standing in the hall as she went to her room. Rick turned to Dante, "Dante, don't you think you have enough women?"

Dante looked Jordan in the eyes, "I have none here."

"And you won't," said Jordan, sternly, "she's only sixteen years old."

Dante smiled, "I'm just ten years older than her."

"Too much older than her; pick a woman with more experience; she's just a child."

"What did you think I was going to do, Jordan? Seduce her?" The Prince looked at his friend in disbelief.

Jordan laughed, "I wouldn't put it past you, but no, I didn't think that at all. Jennifer asked that the young girl be watched over. The kid has had a hard time of it."

"I was just trying to be friendly," replied Dante.

Jordan chuckled, "Isn't that a trait of yours? Friends with women, intimate friends? What if she fell in love with you, Dante?"

"What if she did?" he questioned wryly.

"You and I both know that you're incapable of loving anyone but that damn Countess."

"I do love the Countess, but as a friend."

"Wake up, Dante, you've been in love with her for years. Your problem is that you can't admit it to yourself."

"She's just a friend," insisted Dante.

Rick smiled, "She must be one hell of a friend if you've run to her side at the snap of her fingers. You're like a puppy dog. Let me tell you something else; the Countess is in love with you, too; otherwise, she wouldn't risk her life or her title to help you out when you get into scraps."

"She loves her husband," said Dante, flatly.

"It's too bad that her husband doesn't love her. And you, you're just waiting for the two of them to separate, so you can make your move."

Dante was becoming angry; Rick Jordan knew him too well, "Let's drop this discussion; I'm tired. I'm going to bed." He turned and walked away, thinking about what Jordan had said.

Rick watched D'Mattea saunter down the hallway; he was right about him and the Countess; he saw it in his eyes. If only Dante could admit it to himself, he'd be a much happier man. Of course, the Countess would hang on to her precious husband for as long as she could; she thrived on his power. But once she saw the Comte de Lucerne as the man he really was, she would drop him, finding herself headed for the open arms of the Prince. Rick sighed; so much had to be done. Jennifer had to put someone in charge of operations while Timothy was ill. His thoughts were interrupted by Stefan, "Excuse me, Captain Jordan, but I would like some answers to a few questions."

Rick looked at Stefan, "Yes?"

"What really happened to Timothy?"

"He's ill," replied Rick flatly.

"That's what I've been told by several people, including Jennifer. I want to know what kind of illness he has, as I can't get into his room to check on him."

"He doesn't have an illness." Rick thought for a moment before continuing, "He was wounded outside of LeHarve when privateers tried to take his ship."

"I take it that he was badly wounded?" questioned Stefan.

Rick didn't blink, "Yes," he paused, "sword right through him."

Stefan's eyes widened, "He's seriously wounded then."

"Very," replied Rick.

"Will he recover?"

Rick shook his head, "That, sir, I don't know. Dr. Goldman has had similar cases and none have survived. But none of those men were Timothy Lockwood."

Stefan was silent for a moment, "Thank you, Captain Jordan, you have been the only person to answer my questions in the three weeks he's been ill."

"You're very welcome Mr. Weatherly, if you would excuse me, I must relieve Mark Gregory." Rick walked off in the direction of Timothy's room, leaving Stefan standing in the hallway.

Dawn came quickly this November morning; Prince D'Mattea stood at this bedroom window after being awake all night. He thought of the Countess, his friend, his confidant. Who knew him better than her? The answer was no one, except maybe Jordan. Who knew her better than him? Not even her husband knew her that well. Could Rick Jordan, his friend for the past seven years, be right? Could she possibly love him as much as he loved her? No! She had her husband; she didn't want him.

He rubbed his eyes; he was tired, but he had to relieve Rick from watching Timothy.

Rick sat on the edge of Timothy's bed all evening; the time giving him a chance to put his thoughts in order. Every once in a while, he would look toward Timothy who seemed to be resting much easier. Rick thought of what Timothy and Jennifer had together. They were partners, not because they were married but because they were friends; he idolized her and she him. He could not understand how any man could be totally possessed by the love of one woman. Rick guessed that if he had met a woman like Jennifer, he might also fall under her spell. Yet, the love they had for each other was dangerous, very dangerous, because without the other, each would fall apart. That was sad, because each had so much to give with or without each other.

Prince D'Mattea entered the room, "Good morning."

Rick looked up at him, "You look like hell."

Dante smiled weakly, "I feel that way, too."

"You're here early."

"I know, but I haven't been able to sleep. What were you thinking about?"

"What makes you ask?" questioned Rick.

"When I came in, you were very far away."

"I was thinking about Timothy and Jennifer," he paused, "About the deep devotion and love they have for each other."

Dante sat in a chair opposite Rick, "They are devoted to each other. Just think of it, what woman would stand by a man who is a confessed pirate?"

Rick smiled slyly, "One that loved that man, like the Countess."

"Please don't start that again; what you said kept me awake all night."

"Fine, I'll just think it. Someday, Dante, you'll realize that I'm right."

"Has anyone heard from Yvonne and Cliff?" questioned Dante, deciding it best to change the subject.

"No, not that I know of; perhaps Gregory knows?"

"They've been gone for a couple of months; I hope nothing has happened to them."

"I doubt it; Yvonne's one hell of a fighter," replied Jordan.

"Yes, she is, but, McArnold, I don't know if he's cut out for piracy."

Jordan smirked, "He better be if he wants to impress Yvonne."

"Impress her?" questioned Dante.

"Have you seen the way he looks at her?"

"Can't say that I noticed," responded Dante.

Rick laughed, "You, of all people, I thought would notice."

"What is that supposed to mean?"

"You look at women in that way all the time," replied Rick.

The Prince drew in his breath and pulled himself up straight in his chair, "Well if I do, so do you, Jordan. Hell, you've had just as many women as me."

"Not true," replied Rick. He loved to rile his friend.

"It is true! Count them. There was that fat blonde in Paris…"

"She wasn't fat," interrupted Rick, "She was pleasingly plump."

"What about that big, tall blonde in LeHarve?"

"She doesn't count," responded Rick.

"Why?" questioned Dante.

"She was a trollop."

"Aren't the others?"

"No," replied Jordan, getting a little angry with his friend.

"Okay, what do you want to call them? How about the 'pleasingly plump' redhead in London, or that dark-haired beauty in Venice?" questioned Dante.

"Well, what about you? You must have women in every port," shot back Rick.

"Not true."

"It is true," Rick's eyes twinkled.

"It isn't."

Timothy had opened his eyes to find two of his most skilled pirates arguing about women, "Shut up. The two of you sound like goddamn little boys."

Both men turned to the bed, "I'll be damned, Tim, you're awake," said D'Mattea.

"Of course, I'm awake, who could sleep with two grown men sounding like two cackling hens."

"How do you feel?" questioned Dante.

"Hungry, where the hell am I?" questioned Timothy.

"At Lockwood," answered Rick.

"Lockwood? The last thing I remember was being attacked at sea outside of LeHarve."

D'Mattea said, "That's true, you were."

"Where's Jenny?"

"Asleep," answered Rick, "Last night she gave birth to twins."

"Twins," Timothy grinned, "What were they?"

"One of each," answered D'Mattea.

Tim started to move, "I've got to see her."

"No, you can't get out of bed, you'll open the wound." Rick said as he moved closer to the bed.

"How did I get wounded?" questioned Timothy.

"Sword. It entered your back and exited out the front." Replied D'Mattea and Jordan in unison.

Timothy vaguely remembered feeling the sword enter his back, "Does Jenny know?"

"Of course, you've been here for over three weeks," responded Rick.

Dante said, "I'll go get you something to eat, and I'll send Mark Gregory up." The Prince left the room.

"How is Jennifer, Rick?"

Rick lowered his gaze when he said, "She's doing fine, the babies are healthy."

Tim was alarmed, "There is something you are not telling me."

"I'm telling you everything."

"No, you're not. You said the babies are healthy, but you didn't say that about Jenny. What's wrong with her?" He asked becoming more alarmed by the moment. She was the only thing in his world that meant anything. He would give up everything just to be with her.

"Tim, I'm sorry to have to tell you this, but it was a difficult birth. Dr. Goldman said that she has to be kept perfectly still for at least one week, so she doesn't hemorrhage."

The topaz eyes became glazed, fighting back tears, Tim said, "Damn."

Rick continued, "Also, she can't have any more children because her body wouldn't be able to take the pressure, and it would kill her."

"It doesn't matter. I didn't want her to be a broodmare, I just want her to be my wife."

Dante returned with the food and Mark Gregory. Mark crossed the room, "Tim, you don't know how happy I am to see you awake. You scared the hell out of me, I thought you were going to leave us."

Tim grinned, "Not a chance."

Mark said, "We've got some problems."

"What kind of problems?" questioned Timothy, "No one has deserted because of me?"

"No, your wife's cousin came to visit on the very day of our return, along with a maid and a butler."

"I don't see that as a problem. We can still operate; you all have secret passageways in your rooms; use them." Dante had placed the tray of food in Tim's lap. He managed to sit up grimacing, yet he didn't have the strength to lift any of the utensils, "Someone is going to have to feed me."

The three men looked at each other, Dante walked to the door, "I'll get Daphne, I'm not going to feed him. We'll let her do it."

"Who the hell is Daphne?" questioned Tim.

Rick Jordan looked at him, "She's a young girl that Devlin saved from the auction block. Her family had been killed, so he brought her back here for Jennifer."

Daphne entered Tim's room in a robe; Tim looked her over; she was awfully skinny, but she was pretty with long black hair and violet eyes. She rubbed the sleep from her eyes as Rick Jordan introduced them, "Daphne Charbonneau, this is Captain Timothy Lockwood. Tim, Ms. Charbonneau."

"How do you do, Captain?"

"Fine, but very hungry, could you please feed me because I don't have the strength to do it myself," replied Timothy.

"Certainly." She said as she crossed the room and sat on the chair that had been placed close to the bed. Mark, Rick and Dante left the room to get some much-needed sleep.

Tim wondered how much Daphne knew, "How old are you?'

"Sixteen," she answered shyly as she fed him. "I have to give you your medication."

"Medication?"

"Yes, the doctor prescribed opium for your pain and the infection, but he may want to change the dosage now that you've woken."

"You sound well educated," replied Timothy.

Daphne smiled, "I went to the same school as your wife."

"I see."

"Jennifer will be pleased that you are awake," she said as she continued to feed him.

When she finished with the last drop of his breakfast he said, "Has she named the babies yet?"

"Not that I know. Are there any particular names you would like me to tell her?"

"Not now; I have to think about it," replied Timothy smiling.

"When you do, let me know. I'll send someone for the doctor, so he can examine you. If you would excuse me, I must get dressed." Timothy nodded and watched her leave the room. He was bored and tired, yet he had just woken up. Timothy was worried about Jennifer; his mind began to think of all the memories he had of her.

Jennifer woke to find Daphne changing the babies, "Good morning."

"It is indeed!" exclaimed Daphne.

"My, aren't we cheerful this morning?"

Daphne smiled, "I think you will be, too."

"Why?" Jennifer asked as she rose to a sitting position.

"Your husband is over his crisis. I just fed him as he was too weak to do so himself."

"He's awake?" Tears spilled from her eyes; she wiped them quickly with the back of her hand, "I want to see him."

"You can't because you must stay in bed for a week. Have you named the babies?"

"No," replied Jennifer, "I really haven't thought of any names. Why do you ask?"

"Your husband asked; he said he would think of something."

"Oh!" Jennifer smiled. If Tim picked the names for the twins, she would be sure that they would be strange ones.

Timothy sat quietly, thinking what to name his children. After much thought, he decided to name his daughter Arianna. Arianna Lockwood. His son's name was more difficult, with one son named Lion, he would have to think of something as strong to name his newest son. He liked the name Jared, yet he also liked Lucas. He must write Jennifer a note and let her decide. Mark Gregory came into Tim's room, the doctor close on his heels.

"Good morning, Mr. Lockwood."

"Morning, Dr. Goldman," replied Tim.

"How do you feel?"

"Basically, I feel fine except for being weak and drowsy," replied Timothy.

"That's understandable." The doctor began unbandaging the wound to take a look at it. Timothy held his breath; the wound smelled like rotted flesh making him want to gag, "Hmm, you are healing from the inside out; that's good."

"The odor is horrible," remarked Timothy.

"There is nothing you can do about it except keep it clean and put fresh bandages on it daily," replied Dr. Goldman.

"When can I get out of bed?" questioned Timothy.

The doctor laughed, "You can't be serious."

Timothy's topaz eyes bore into him, "I am; I want to see my wife."

The doctor ran his hand over his chin, thinking, "I guess you could visit with her for an hour a day if someone helps you go back and forth to her room."

Timothy looked at Mark, "Mark, you'll help, won't you?"

Mark replied, "Of course."

Turning his attention back to Dr. Goldman, he said, "When can I leave the bed permanently?"

Dr. Goldman replied, "In about five to six weeks, maybe sooner. It all depends how long it takes your injury to heal."

"I see. Thank you, doctor."

Mark stopped the doctor before he left the room, "What about the opium, do we change the dosage?"

"Yes, at each dose, give him a quarter less than the normal dose for several days. When I come back to check on him in a few days, if the new dose has been successful, we will decrease it again. It is very important for him to be weaned off the opium," replied Dr. Goldman.

The doctor left the room, Timothy grinned, "Mark, you've got to help me."

Mark went to Timothy, "Sure."

"First, get a razor and help me shave. When I see my wife, I want to be clean shaven."

Dr. Goldman made his way down the hall to Jennifer's bedroom. After his examination of her he said, "Mrs. Lockwood, I'm sorry to have to tell you this but you can no longer conceive."

"What?" She was shocked.

"You had a difficult birth last night. At first, I thought that you would not be able to have other children because your body wouldn't be able to take the pressure. Now after this examination, I realize that you can no longer conceive, I'm sorry." Jenny held back her tears; at nineteen she had lost the ability to conceive. What would Tim say? Her face was expressionless, no emotion showed. Dr. Goldman said, "Mrs. Lockwood, are you alright?"

"Yes, just fine." She answered weakly.

"Good. I've given your husband permission to visit with you."

Her eyes brightened for a moment and then saddened, "Is he going to be alright?"

"I don't see why not."

Mark Gregory had helped Timothy shave and dress in a heavy robe. When they reached Jenny's door, Mark knocked. The door was opened by Dr. Goldman, "Come in; if you would excuse me, I must be going."

Timothy looked across the room; Jenny looked beautiful. The dark auburn hair was spilling around her shoulders. He smiled; Mark helped him to Jennifer's side.

"Tim, how are you feeling?" Jennifer's eyes searched his face.

"Fine," he replied trying to not show the pain he was in, "what about you?"

Jennifer replied, "I'm fine, did you see the babies?"

"No," responded Tim.

Jennifer smiled, "They have the strangest color eyes I've ever seen."

Timothy smirked, "Really?"

"They're greenish-gold," she responded, "Daphne told me that you were thinking of names."

"Yes, I picked one out for the girl; I want to name her Arianna."

"Arianna Lockwood, it's very pretty." Mark Gregory left the room, so the two of them could be alone, "What about our son?"

"That one's a little more difficult, I can't decide whether he should be called Jared or Lucas."

Jennifer smiled, "How about Timothy Lockwood, after his father?"

"I'm flattered." She couldn't hold back her tears any longer, "What's wrong?" He wanted to hold her, but with his wound it was too risky.

"I can't," she took a deep breath trying to pull herself together, "I can't conceive anymore."

Timothy took her hand and squeezed it, "It doesn't matter. I fell in love with you, not with how many children you could give me. I love you, Jenny."

Green eyes met gold ones, "Honestly?"

Tim kissed her hand, "Honestly. If having another child will kill you, I don't want another child."

"No, Tim, that is what Dr. Goldman thought, but this morning he found that I could no longer conceive."

"All the better; we won't have to be careful of getting you pregnant. It doesn't matter; I love you, and I want you. That will never change."

"When did you become conscious?" questioned Jennifer.

"Early this morning when I heard D'Mattea and Jordan arguing over women."

Jennifer giggled, "What were they saying?"

"D'Mattea was saying something about a fat woman with red hair and then Jordan accused D'Mattea of having a woman in every port."

"It sounds funny."

Timothy laughed, "It was, but not to them."

"Did you eat anything," questioned Jennifer.

"Yes, Daphne fed me."

Jennifer was excited, "You met her! I told her about you."

"How much did you tell her?" questioned Timothy.

"I told her about our operations in the lower part of the house, and she's grateful to us for saving her from a life of slavery, so there is no need to worry about her."

"If you trust her, that's all that matters," replied Timothy.

"I do."

Mark entered the room, "I'm sorry to break this reunion up, but it's time you got back to your room." He helped Timothy to his feet, turned to Jennifer and said, "Hope you are doing well." Jennifer nodded yes.

Timothy said, "I'll see you tomorrow. Rest well, my love."

"Promise me you won't overdo it, Timothy Lockwood," she said, trying to make sure he knew her expectations of him healing.

"I promise," the golden eyes twinkled.

Jennifer watched Mark help Tim, and she noticed exactly how weak her husband was and that he must have been in great pain sitting with her. Although he promised not to overdo it, she had a feeling that it wouldn't stop him from trying. She knew that by the end of the week, he would have Dr. Goldman wrapped around his finger and just about everyone else in the house. She sighed. Soon it would be feeding time for the twins; she must think about hiring a wet nurse in the near future.

CHAPTER TWENTY-SIX

Geoffrey Lyndon had established himself in Newport under the assumed name of Steven Marshall. He had built a reputation as a gambler of high class. Many people in the city found him extremely interesting, especially when he told tales of his days in London. Several months prior in the marketplace, he thought he saw Jennifer Weatherly, but that was impossible. She was now a slave for some Algerian pasha or maybe the mistress for a pirate.

He had recently returned to Newport after a two-month absence, when he overheard some men in the *White Horse Tavern* discussing one Timothy Lockwood. Lyndon's ears perked up; he had been looking for Lockwood; now it appeared that the man had been injured in some sort of sea battle and was laying at death's door on his estate. Geoffrey left the *White Horse Tavern* to go look for Lockwood. When he found the massive estate, it reminded him of a fortress, one that was impenetrable. Timothy Lockwood must pay in some way for all the pain and loss he had caused Geoffrey. He needed a fool-proof plan, one that would totally stun Lockwood, taking him by surprise. The first thing he must try to do is find out who else was living in the house. Perhaps Lockwood had married; he must ask questions about him around Newport. He quickly rode back to the tavern, as he felt that was the best place to begin, where he had first overheard some men discussing Lockwood's illness. When he reached the tavern, he dismounted and strolled towards the bar. He ordered a drink of bourbon and listened to the conversations around him. One large man, chewing on tobacco said, "I heard that Mrs. Lockwood had twins." Geoffrey's ears perked up.

"Aye, I heard the doc telling someone the other day," said another man that Geoffrey did not know.

"What's her name? She's a pretty little thing with those green eyes and that brownish-red hair."

"I don't know."

Geoffrey decided that this was a good time to join in the conversation, "Are you gentlemen discussing the owner of that large estate?"

"What's it to you?" asked the larger of the two men.

Geoffrey drew in his breath, sipped his drink and said, "Nothing really. It's just that when you described his wife, I thought I might have known her. What did you say her name was?"

"We're not sure," answered the smaller man.

"How would you possibly know her, she's from London," replied the bigger man.

Geoffrey smiled, "I'm from London, too. I just recently moved here."

"Hey, ain't you that big shot gambler?" questioned the smaller man.

"Yes," replied Geoffrey.

"Want to play poker? We got a game going a couple of nights a week," said the heavier man.

Geoffrey took out a cigar and lit it, "That might be interesting."

"What's your name?" questioned the smaller man.

"Steven Marshall, and you gentleman are?"

The bigger of the two men said, "I'm Sam Connors."

"And I'm Henry Lewis."

"It is a pleasure to meet the two of you. Are you sure you can't remember Mrs. Lockwood's first name?" questioned Geoffrey.

"No, but I bet you that Mattie will know," said Henry.

"Who is Mattie?" questioned Geoffrey.

Sam answered, "The barmaid. She knows just about everything."

"Well then, call her over, so I can buy you two gentlemen a drink," responded Geoffrey.

"Hey, Mattie, come over here."

She walked casually to the table, "What can I do for you gentlemen?"

"Let me introduce myself; my name is Steven Marshall; I'm new in town, and I overheard these gentlemen discussing something that I hope you can provide me with the answer. But first, let us have another round of drinks."

Mattie sauntered off in the direction of the bar, returning several minutes later with their drinks, "Okay, Mr. Marshall, what do you want to know?"

"What is Mrs. Lockwood's first name?"

"Why?" Mattie was suspicious.

"It's possible she might be an old friend of mine."

Mattie thought it over, "An old friend you say? She's kind of young to have been friends with you. Although I dare say her husband's a good ten, maybe twelve years older than her."

Geoffrey was getting impatient, "Do you know her name?"

"Well, Mr. Marshall I just happen to know her name; it is Jennifer." His eyes lit up, "You know her then?"

"Do you happen to know her maiden name?"

"Hmm, That's a tough one. I think it has something to do with the weather."

Geoffrey was excited now, "By any chance does Weatherly ring a bell?"

"That's it, Weatherly, Jennifer Weatherly!" exclaimed Mattie.

"I knew her in London, a fine young woman." His eyes flickered in remembrance of her biting him and slapping him across the face. "Does her husband treat her well?"

Mattie pushed her hair out of her eyes, "He buys her a lot of gifts, if you know what I mean. Why you should have seen all those things sent up there for those babies."

"Really, so he treats her good."

"He more than treats her good. I hear people talk and they say he worships the ground that she walks on and that he's very protective." She paused, "Although I've heard she's a wild one."

Geoffrey was intrigued, "Wild? What do you mean?"

"Well, I have heard some stories, I don't know how true they are, but they say that she doesn't take orders very well and that she had some sort of escapade in the Barbary States, of all places," said Mattie.

"Amazing!" He thought to himself, Jennifer managed to escape the Barbary States. He wondered if Lockwood had anything to do with her escape.

Mattie said, "Yes, but like I say, I don't think it is true, mostly rumor."

Geoffrey took some gold coins out of his pocket and handed them to her, "Mattie, this is for your trouble."

She bit the coins and then deposited them in the pocket of her dress, "Thanks."

"No, thank you!" He watched Mattie walk away, then looked at Sam and Henry, "So where is this poker game?"

Sam grinned, "It'll be here at seven o'clock tonight."

"Meet us here by quarter to seven; we play in the back room," said Henry.

"Fine," Geoffrey stood up, shook their hands and said, "I'll be looking forward to this evening." He tossed some money on the table. "Have another drink on me."

"Thanks," They said simultaneously.

Geoffrey left the *White Horse Tavern* walking aimlessly along the street. He thought quietly to himself, so Timothy Lockwood had married Jennifer Weatherly, and he worshipped her. This fit into his plan perfectly; Jennifer would once again become his target for revenge.

It had been two weeks since Jennifer had given birth to Arianna and Timothy. She was back on her feet and never felt better. She devoted much of her time between the twins and Timothy, who was still recovering. Rick Jordan and Mark Gregory went back to the Barbary States as a team. Gregory's ship, *The Rogue*, had been repaired and Jordan's ship, *Passion's Pride* was stocked with goods for Jordan to sell in London before continuing on to the Barbary States. The reason Rick wasn't sailing with Prince D'Mattea on this trip was because the *Italian Princess* was sailing to Lucerne. The Prince was making an overdue visit to the Countess and then he would return to Italy for personal matters with his family.

Cutthroat John's ship, the *Virgin Mistress* went down off the coast of New Providence when it was attacked by Caribbean pirates. His partner, Jacques LaRoche, returned to Lockwood to deliver the bad news to Timothy about Cutthroat John's untimely death and the destruction of the *Virgin Mistress*. Timothy demanded to know why the *Fleur de Lis* did not come to the aid of the *Virgin Mistress*. Jacques LaRoche said they set the *Virgin Mistress* on fire during the middle of the night. They tried to attack the *Fleur de Lis* after burning Cutthroat John's ship, but the *Fleur de Lis* outran the attacking ship and headed back to Lockwood. Timothy suggested that since LaRoche was well known in the Barbary States, that perhaps he should wait until Yvonne and Cliff returned and then he could sail with them. LaRoche decided to stay on and wait. Working in the Barbary States would prove to be a challenge. Timothy's recovery was slow because of the seriousness of the wound he had sustained, and he was becoming restless. Every day the dosage of opium was decreased, and he felt a bit better.

The *Seabird* and the *Caribbean Lady*, the two ships belonging to the Brentwood brothers, came into port, carrying a great deal of goods. They reported that the area of the Caribbean where they were working had relatively little slave trade but the amounts of goods they could confiscate were grand. They also reported that they had heard about Cutthroat John's death and the sinking of the *Virgin Mistress*. Additionally, they told Timothy that New Providence was ablaze with talk of pirates that were attacking other pirates in order to stop white slavery. Most of the people felt it was something that was being done by more than one person, perhaps a group of people. Timothy was happy; his plans to put a hold on white slavery was working. People were beginning to talk about it and approve of it. White slavery may never be abolished completely, but at least some innocent people would be saved.

The Prince's return to Lucerne was met by the Comte de Lucerne, who informed him that the Countess was not in Lucerne, but on her way to Italy for a holiday. Since he was on his way to Italy for family matters, he would leave earlier, take care of his business and then try to find the Countess. The *Italian Princess* left for Venice immediately. Prince D'Mattea was excited about returning home for the first time in over a year. His return was marked by tragedy; his cousin, Roberto, had been killed in a sword fight over a woman. All of Roberto's family holdings were being divided among the other members of the family. The Prince attended the funeral in Venice and dealt with his family over various business and legal matters. Once again, his father tried to convince him to return permanently to Venice and give up his life as a pirate. And for the second time in his life, Prince Dante D'Mattea stormed out of the palace and back to his ship. He decided that he would devote all of his time searching Italy for the Countess. His search did not last long because the Countess came to him. Prince D'Mattea had been in Venice a little over a month with no sign of the Countess when she suddenly appeared on the *Italian Princess* while he was in St. Mark's Square meeting with some friends.

Countess Sirena was a beautifully formed woman. Her face was that of aristocracy, a slim slightly turned up nose, full, sensuous lips and deep brown eyes and high cheekbones all surrounded by a mass of long, full, dark-brown hair which she preferred to wear loose and wild but usually wore it neatly in a chignon. She had a full bustline, tiny waist and full hips. She was, indeed, a stunning woman. She waited over an hour for the Prince. When he finally returned, he found her sitting at the desk sifting through his papers. "Sirena."

She jumped, turning around, "You scared me." She ran to him, hugging him when she reached him, "My dear friend, I have missed you."

He released her, "I've been looking for you."

"I didn't come directly to Italy. I went to Salzburg to visit Ginger Ashworth, only to find out that she is missing and has been missing for several months."

"Who is Ginger Ashworth?" asked D'Mattea.

Sirena looked him in his dark brown eyes, "My husband's mistress."

"Do you always visit your husband's mistress?"

Sirena smiled a sad smile, "Not usually. But this one is different."

"How is she different?"

"She's a whore, and I wanted to see what made her so very special that caused my husband to spend several weeks with her in France, providing her with all kinds of jewels."

Dante stared at her in disbelief, "Why do you torture yourself, Sirena?"

"I can't help it, Dante. Do you realize I have actually come to hate the only man I thought I could ever love?"

"I'm sorry," Dante said.

"Why?"

"You can change the subject without batting an eyelash and ask about me." Sirena smiled as Dante continued, "There are no new romances except my romance with the sea."

She took him by the hand and led him to the big bed; the two of them sat crossed legged facing each other, "Your romance with the sea is an old one, Dante. What about women?"

He laughed, shaking his head, "I always have romances, but none of them mean anything."

"Why?"

"I don't know, Sirena. I think it is because I can't find the woman for me."

"Either that or you've let her slip through your fingers," she said as she held his hand.

His eyes met hers, "Maybe I have."

"What about this new life of yours? Do you like it?" questioned Sirena.

"I like it, and I like the people I'm working with; I think you would like them, too," he responded smiling.

Sirena stared at him intently, "Dante, I must ask you a special favor."

"You know there isn't anything I wouldn't do for you."

"I need your help."

Dante replied, "What do you want me to do for you?"

Very calmly, she looked deeply into his eyes and said, "I want you to kill my husband."

Dante ran his hand through his dark hair, "Kill your husband? The Count? Sirena have you gone mad?"

"Don't question my sanity, Dante. Please, I'm begging you to do it."

Dante shook his head, "I can't kill another human being, Sirena."

"Of course, you can. I'm sure you've killed for piracy."

"That was different, Sirena. I had to kill in order to save myself."

"Don't refuse me, Dante. I've never refused any of your requests," she said sadly.

He hated to see Sirena plead with him, but he couldn't kill her husband, "I'm sorry Sirena, but I can't do it."

She rose from her sitting position on the bed, furious, "You can't do it? Why?"

Dante rose from his seat on the bed, "Sirena, your husband has never done anything to me that would make me angry enough to kill him."

"What about me? Don't you care about me? Look what he's done to me!" Her voice was on the verge of hysteria, "I've been made the laughingstock of Lucerne because of his infidelities." The brown eyes were filling with tears.

"Sirena, why don't you leave him, divorce him?" Dante questioned as he poured himself a glass of rum.

"Divorce him? I can't."

"Why not?" asked Dante calmly.

She had a strange look in her eyes, a mixture of fear and anxiety, "If I leave him, I won't get anything. No money, no home, nothing."

He stared at her in disbelief, "Is that all that matters to you?"

She put her head down as she couldn't face, him trying to avoid his eyes, she said quietly, "Yes."

Taking her chin in his hand, he turned her face towards him, "You've changed, Sirena; what happened to the woman that I used to know?"

"I'm sorry, Dante, but when a man shows a woman no love, when he mistreats her in front of guests, when he uses her for his own sexual satisfaction at any damn time and the only thing she gets out of the relationship are money and nice clothes," she took a deep breath, "that woman becomes ruthless, bitter and money hungry."

A tear rolled down her cheek; Dante brushed it away, not really understanding his friend's torment. "What do you mean when you say he's mistreated and used you for his own means?"

She was crying openly now. "You've been away for such a long time. After the last time I saw you, he's taken to beating me. I've had to prostitute myself for him. What he makes me do is degrading. He makes me," she paused, "he makes me…"

"Don't finish. I know what he makes you do. The bastard! You're a lady and you'll always be one in my eyes." He paused, taking a deep breath, "Stay with me Sirena; I'll take care of you. I'll give you all the money you need, all the clothes you want and I ask for nothing in return, because you've already given me so much."

"I wish I could stay with you, Dante, but if I stay, I'll lose my title."

"Damn the title, damn him," Dante was so angry he blurted out, "I love you; I want you; I've wanted you for years. There, I've admitted it. That bastard, I'll kill him for making you feel less than a woman."

She was stunned by what he had just revealed to her; he loved her, "What did you say?"

He swallowed his rum, "I'm going to kill the bastard!"

She shook her head, "No, before that."

He moved closer to her, "I love you Sirena; I always have; that's why no other woman will satisfy me. They can't hold a candle to you."

Her eyes seemed to be penetrating his as their stares locked, "Kiss me." She said softly.

Taking her gently by the shoulders, he drew her close to him, kissing her softly, yet firmly. He put his arms around her, holding her close to his chest. "I love you, Sirena."

"I," she paused, "I love you. I never thought you loved me."

He led her to the bed, sitting her down and then sat facing her, "I've always loved you. Why didn't you think that I did?"

She sighed, "I always knew that you loved me as your friend and confident, but there were so many other women in your life that I thought I was unappealing, too plain, and too poor for you." She paused before continuing, "Do you know what it was like for me to see you with so many women?"

"Probably the same way I felt when you met and married the Count. I hurt that day more than I could possibly tell you." His eyes had become darker.

"Why didn't you stop me?"

"Would you have listened?"

"I think so."

"Then I wish I had stopped you. I could have saved you from the agony he's put you through all these years."

She leaned forward, kissing him, "Make love to me Dante. Show me what it's like for a man to love a woman."

He kissed her, harder than the first time and longer, his breath quickened, "I want you, Sirena."

"Take me; I'm yours," she replied, breathless.

He kissed her again and again, wanting desperately to take away the pain and hurt that she was feeling. "I'll be gentle with you, Sirena; I won't hurt you. I promise you."

Dante didn't have to tell her because she knew he would be gentle. His fingers moved along the buttons at the back of her dress. The thick velvet came away from her body; she loosened her hair, letting it fall in dark waves around her shoulders. Her chemise barely covered her breasts and the rose tipped nipples protruded through the light material. Dante couldn't take his eyes off of Sirena; to him, she was beautiful; she always had been, and she would always be the only woman he would ever love. She could feel the heat of his eyes on her body and her own heat. Dante waited for this moment for eternity, and now that it was here, he was nervous. He wanted to please her, but he felt as if it was his first time all over again and just maybe it was his first time because he never felt this way for a woman. He had snuffed out the lamp and locked his cabin door. Returning to Sirena, he kissed her harder than he had previously. He moved from her mouth to her neck, to her breasts, pulling, sucking gently. Sirena moaned, pulling his head back to her; she kissed his lips fully, sensuously, seductively, her fingers entwined in his hair, she could feel his manhood pressing against her body. He moved over her in one smooth motion, entering her slowly. His body lay on top of hers for a few seconds; tears of joy rolled down her cheeks; slowly, he began to move inside of her. Sirena matched his every thrust, which began exquisitely slow and deep, so she could feel every inch of his member. Neither Sirena nor Dante could hold back much longer; she pushed wildly against him, and he knew she was close as was he, and he began to quicken his pace with powerful thrusts, bringing both of them to a stunning climax.

Dante's breathing slowly returned to normal, and he whispered in her ear, "I love you, Sirena. Come to Newport with me."

"I love you, too," she hesitated, "But I can't come to Newport."

He rose up on one elbow, "Why not?"

She stared at him, "My husband would stop me."

"Not if you never returned to Lucerne."

She smiled, "But mostly everything I own is in Lucerne."

"I can give you anything you want. Please let me take you back with me," replied Dante.

She smiled, raising her hand to stroke his cheek, "I'll come with you, my darling."

He kissed her, "You'll love it there. Wait until you meet Timothy and Jennifer, I know you'll like them."

"I'm sure I will." She moved closer to him and without words made him understand that she wanted him. Their lovemaking lasted over an hour, until each was spent. They fell asleep, entwined in each other's arms.

The *Rogue* and *Passion's Pride* docked in the Barbary States. Rick and Mark went to the *Timbtu Inn* where they bumped into Yvonne and Cliff, who were having dinner. Rick Jordan sauntered up to the table, "I'll be damned. Look at the two of you."

Cliff stood up, shaking Rick's hand, "Where's D'Mattea?"

"He's somewhere in Italy, probably entertaining a delightful young woman."

Yvonne smiled, "Ah, so you're here alone?"

"No, Mark Gregory's my partner for this trip."

"Where's Timothy?" questioned Cliff.

"Injured," replied Rick as Mark walked over to the table.

Yvonne stared at Rick, "Please sit down and tell us what happened."

Rick and Mark took seats at the table; Mark Gregory began, "I guess I should tell the story since I was there when it happened."

"Go ahead," said Cliff.

"Well, we were on our way home to Lockwood, and we were outside of LeHarve when French privateers attacked the *Rogue*." He paused, collecting his thoughts, "We didn't have all our sails up, so we were moving at a leisurely pace when they attacked."

"What was Timothy doing on board of the *Rogue*?" questioned Yvonne.

"He wasn't on the *Rogue*; he was on the *Crimson Lady*. His ship came to our aid. He and some of his men attacked and boarded the

French privateer. Timothy was fighting two of the privateers when a third pierced him from the back."

"It wasn't serious was it?" asked McArnold.

Rick Jordan stared at him; he had his reservations about McArnold and his question confirmed it to Rick, "Hell yes, it was serious. The sword entered his back and exited out the front of him."

The barmaid brought them a round of rum. Yvonne said, "Is Timothy alright?"

Mark answered her, "Let me finish the story. One of Tim's men put him on the *Rogue* after we destroyed the privateer. George took command of the *Crimson Lady*. Timothy was at death's door for over three weeks, and he finally awoke from his coma. The doctor said he should be as good as new in about six weeks."

Rick Jordan added, "Jennifer gave birth to twins the night before Timothy awoke."

Yvonne exclaimed, "Oh, I wish I could have been there, but we caught wind of a big shipment of slaves coming into Algeria."

Cliff interrupted her, "We helped to free three hundred women in the last three days. We're planning on leaving for Lockwood tomorrow morning with the tide."

Yvonne continued, "Our holds are filled to the brim."

Mark Gregory said, "When you're passing through French waters, be careful and be alert. The damn French have privateers all over the place."

They finished the rum and left the *Timbtu Inn*. Yvonne was anxious to return to Lockwood to see Jennifer, Timothy and the new arrivals.

The poker games at the *White Horse Tavern* were twice a week every Monday and Thursday. Geoffrey had been playing in them for weeks now, sometimes winning and sometimes losing. His sole purpose of playing was to gain information about Lockwood, Jennifer and whoever else might be living in the house. He couldn't make himself visible around town in case he was seen by someone who knew him in London. One piece of information he obtained was that Stefan Weatherly had come to visit several weeks earlier. Stefan had planned on staying only a couple of weeks after his beloved cousin Jennifer delivered. However, since that time, he had become smitten with a young woman named Daphne Charbonneau, a house guest and companion of Jennifer's. Lately, the two of them were frequently in the city, either attending plays or going out to dinner. Geoffrey was beginning to worry, if Stefan Weatherly continued to be smitten with the young woman, he would

undoubtedly hang around Newport for a longer time than he had originally planned. He would have to be extremely careful not to be seen by
Weatherly. His entire plan to take his revenge against Jennifer would be
destroyed if Weatherly saw him in the city. He knew that Weatherly
would tell Captain Lockwood of his presence in Newport, and his life
would be in jeopardy.

CHAPTER TWENTY-SEVEN

It was close to Christmas; most of the members of the stronghold had returned to Lockwood for a Christmas holiday. Timothy's injury was barely noticeable, and he had grown irritable because of his boredom. Several days earlier, he convinced Dr. Goldman that he was well enough to go out to sea after the new year. Prince D'Mattea was the last member of the stronghold to return to Lockwood. His arrival came two days before Christmas. Rick Jordan saw the ship enter Newport Harbor through his spy glass. His friend and partner had returned.

Dante D'Mattea docked his empty ship in Newport Harbor, and he and Sirena rode to Lockwood in a rented carriage. They were met by Harris at the door of the mansion. Jennifer was just coming out of the study when she saw the Prince, "Dante, I didn't think you'd make it back before the festivities began." She stared at the beautiful woman standing aside of him.

"Let me introduce you to my friend and confident, Countess Sirena of Lucerne."

"It is a pleasure to meet you Countess. I am Jennifer Lockwood."

The Countess smiled, such a young woman, "Please, you must call me Sirena."

"Sirena and Dante, let's not stand in the hall. Tim is in the sitting room with Rick, Mark, Yvonne and Cliff. Jack and Devlin are unloading their ships and the Brentwood Brothers went home for Christmas, as did Jacques LaRoche." They followed her into the sitting room.

Rick Jordan's mouth fell open in surprise, but he quickly composed himself. Dante had brought the Countess with him and for Christmas, "Dante, old buddy, you've returned to our humble establishment."

Dante smiled, "I've brought with me my friend, the Countess of Lucerne, Sirena Dandeneau."

Timothy rose from his seat, bowed before the Countess, took her hand and kissed it. "It is a pleasure to make your acquaintance, Countess."

"It is a pleasure to meet you, Captain. I've heard a great deal about you." Dante helped her remove the dark blue velvet cloak which revealed a stunning royal blue silk brocade gown.

Jennifer offered the Countess a small glass of sherry. "I'll tell Maggie to prepare a room for the Countess.

She started to leave the room when Dante said, "Jennifer, that won't be necessary."

"Why? Isn't she staying for Christmas?" questioned Jennifer.

Timothy began to laugh loudly, "No, dear, I think what the Prince is saying is that the Countess will be sharing his room."

Jennifer flushed a brilliant red, "I'm so sorry."

Dante looked at her, "No need; the Countess has left her husband."

Rick Jordan was amazed; his friend had gone and taken his advice. "Mrs. Dandeneau, I'm terribly sorry to hear about your misfortune."

"No need, Rick," answered the Prince. "It comes as no surprise to those in Europe where the Comte had become known as a womanizer."

Jennifer tactfully tried to change the subject, "Yvonne, do you have a favorite past Christmas?"

"No, what about you, Jenny?" Yvonne had decided that it was best she played along.

"Well, I think this year will be most favorite."

"Why?" questioned Timothy.

"Because all of my friends are here, my husband, children, and most importantly, it's going to be a much better Christmas than last year." Everyone who had been around at Christmas time the year before knew that Jennifer was referring to her miscarriage.

After an early dinner, the men went into the library and the women remained in the sitting room. Rick took Dante by the arm, pulling him aside, "Did she really leave her husband?"

"She's here, isn't she?" responded Dante sarcastically.

"Don't get that way with me, Dante," replied Jordan.

"I'm sorry; my mind is on something else," said Dante.

Timothy approached the two of them; speaking quietly, he said, "Later this evening I want the two of you to meet me in the storage area."

"What time?" asked Dante.

"About eleven thirty, I have to make sure that everyone is asleep."

"Do we have a problem?" questioned Rick.

Timothy shook his head, "No, I want to tell you the plans for January."

Dante said, "Fine."

Later that evening, Jennifer had gone to feed the twins and Timothy read Lion a bedtime story. When Lion was asleep, Timothy went to Jennifer's bedroom. Jennifer was at her dressing table, brushing her long hair. Their eyes met through the mirror. Timothy sucked in his breath; she was beautiful, sitting there in the red silk nightgown and matching dressing gown. She turned to face him, smiling. He crossed the room in three strides, pulling her to her feet, kissing her, "It's been such a long time."

She kissed his neck, her fingers tugging at his hair, pulling him closer to her, kissing him fully, "I know."

He released her, "I can't stay. I'm having a meeting with the others at eleven thirty. But," he noticed the disappointment in her eyes, "When I return," his eyes twinkled, "I'll expect you to be waiting for me." Timothy left for his meeting with the others. Jennifer decided to use the time to catch up on her reading. She removed her dressing gown, climbed into bed with her book and began to read. Within the hour, she had fallen asleep, the book resting on her stomach.

Tim returned at two in the morning. When he entered the dimly lit room, he could see Jennifer asleep. He moved quietly toward the bed, gently he took the book from her hands. She was beautiful, even in her sleep. He undressed methodically, hanging his clothes in the closet. Jennifer woke, rubbing her eyes; she stared at her husband's naked backside hesitating on the scar and then moving down with her gaze along the strong muscular legs. She sighed, causing him to turn, their eyes locked. Jenny sat up, the covers falling to her waist. His eyes went directly to the thin material covering her breasts; he could feel the searing heat of his desire as neither spoke. Jennifer's eyes began to move downward, pausing on the barely noticeable stomach scar hidden by the hair on his chest. He was the perfect specimen of a man. Her eyes continued to the thick patch of dark hair above his manhood, which was already beginning to swell with desire. Her eyes met his once again as Timothy moved slowly to the bed. Jennifer's eyes never moved from his. He climbed into the bed and surrounded her with his ironlike grip. Their lips found each other, his tongue pushing for entrance. Jennifer moaned; her own passions, which had been lying dormant for such a long time, were being stirred. Her fingertips ran down the length of his back and up again to his hair. His lips moved to her neck, while his fingers worked quickly at the ties of her nightgown. His large hands covered her breasts, his thumbs exciting her nipples. He bent his head toward one breast, his tongue flicked one nipple and then the other one; Jennifer whimpered and wriggled under him. Timothy was taking his damn sweet time bringing her to a high-pitched fever; she wanted him and wanted him now. She couldn't stand it any longer. His member was pressing against her thigh; it had swelled but not to what he was capable of; he wasn't ready; he was holding back. Her hands slipped between the two of them as Tim moved back to her lips. She took him in her hands, stroking him, feeling him harden faster. His breathing, like hers, had become irregular; she wrapped her legs around him as she guided him into her. She matched him thrust for thrust; they were like two wild animals, tearing at each other; her nails dug into his back as she arched towards him. Timothy's hair was damp with perspiration; he thrust into her again and again, each time quicker and harder. His body shuddered, and in one final thrust, he and Jennifer climaxed with such intensity that both screamed silently. He rolled off her body, cradling her in his arms. Both were breathing rather heavily; he could smell the scent of her hair as his breathing returned to normal. "I love you, Jenny."

She turned so she was facing him and kissed him, searchingly, "I love you, too."

"It's been a long time. I think I'm going to be sore tomorrow," replied Timothy.

Jennifer's hand rested on his chest; she wanted him again; she rolled over, kissing him, she moved from his lips to his neck. He responded by kissing her hair which had become a mass of tangles, reminding him of a lioness. He pulled her to him, but she pulled away; the green eyes were darker than he had ever seen them, "No, let me make love to you."

He grinned, normally he was in charge of their lovemaking, and occasionally Jennifer would take charge. She was doing this for him, not because she liked it, but because he did, and she wanted to please him.

He laid back against the pillows, Jennifer's lips and tongue moved from his neck to each of his nipples, which he guessed that he liked as much as she. Carefully, without hurting him, she took playful little bites of his nipples causing him to moan. She moved on, not wanting him to become too excited yet. Her tongue flicked his navel and she kissed it, drawing small circles around it with her tongue. Her hand found his penis, which had already begun to come back to life with what little she did to him. She ran her fingers lightly over the shaft and head of his ever-growing organ. Her lips moved from nis navel as her fingers worked on his member. She continued kissing him, and his breathing had become labored. His body twitched, and she could feel the pulsating need of his organ. Her tongue touched its tip, which had become massive in size. It always amazed her, that the size of his organ always seemed bigger when she made love to him. Her tongue moved back and forth across the tip, sending spasms shooting through his body. Tim closed his eyes moaning; she was making this unbearable. She ran her tongue over the shaft of his penis; Tim's hands reached for her head; he couldn't stand the pressure any longer. "Now, Jennifer," he gasped as another spasm raced through his body, "Now." She moved quickly taking him in her mouth just seconds before he ejaculated, filling her mouth with his seed. When he finished, she licked him like a greedy kitten, exciting him again. He sat up, pulling her on top of him and rolling over onto her, "Not this time, my little vixen. If you do that to me again, you'll kill me."

Jennifer smiled, the green eyes taunting him, "I wouldn't want to do that." She playfully bit the tips of his fingers. "Tim, if we're not going to make love, would you get off of me, you're rather heavy." He rolled off of her, "What was your meeting about?"

Timothy leaned back, "We have decided that on January 2nd, all ships would pull out. Each ship will be gone for a minimum of three months and the maximum of five. The sole purpose of this voyage is for us to free as many slaves as we possibly can. When we return to Lockwood, all of the goods which we have accumulated will be sold before we set out on another voyage."

Her eyes pleaded with him, "Tim are you going with them?"
"Yes."

She moved away from him, climbing out of the large bed. He watched her lithe figure in the moonlight as she reached for her dressing gown. She stared out the window, not looking at him. Why did he do this to her? He was always leaving; he'd stay for a month and then leave. Timothy got out of the bed and stood behind her; she could see his reflection in the window. He grasped her by one shoulder spinning her around, "What's wrong, Jenny?"

Jennifer looked up at him, "You're always leaving me."

"I'm not leaving you."

"But you just said you were going; you never stay more than a couple of weeks."

He sighed, "I've been here for several weeks, so many in fact that I'm about to go out of my mind."

Promise me you'll be careful."

"I promise."

She hugged him, "I need you in my life, Tim."

He held her tightly against his chest, "I need you in my life, always." He kissed the top of her head, "Come on, let's go back to bed."

The Christmas festivities were fairly boring until Robert and Molly came over to visit with Amanda. Jennifer tried to be courteous to the woman but found it extremely difficult. Amanda, it appeared, took a liking to Prince D'Mattea. Dante tried several times to get out of her grasp, but the woman just chattered on about herself and continued flirting with the Prince. Sirena was becoming angry, very angry, and Jennifer could feel the tension mounting in the room when Maggie suddenly and fortunately appeared to announce that dinner was being served. Amanda sat in the seat intended for Sirena, so Sirena had to sit next to Rick Jordan on the opposite end of the table. Sirena's dark eyes were glittering dangerously throughout Christmas dinner. She did not like being made a fool of, and this woman, this lecherous woman, Amanda, would pay for the inconvenience. After dinner, the guests returned to the sitting room where the men had brandy and the women, tea. All of the pirates were guarded in what they said because of Robert and Stefan. Jennifer watched her cousin and the attention he was showing Daphne Charbonneau; she was sure she'd see her friend Daphne leave Newport as Stefan's bride. The two had become inseparable since they met.

Jennifer's attention was brought to Amanda, who was directing her attention to the Countess, "So, you're a Countess. Where did you say you came from?"

Her velvety brown eyes showed no expression as she said, "I didn't."

Amanda wasn't about to give up with the curt answer, "Where do you come from Countess, and how did you manage to end up in Newport at Timothy Lockwood's home?"

"I'm from Lucerne, and in answer to your second question, it is none of your damn business."

Amanda smiled slyly, "My, my we don't have to get testy about it. You might think you were Timothy Lockwood's mistress. I was once."

"How dare you insult Mrs. Lockwood," the Countess began.

Jennifer stared at the blonde woman with icy green eyes, "Amanda, enough."

Amanda persisted, "He is marvelous in bed, strong as an ox."

Jennifer, who was sitting aside of Amanda, stood up, drew back her hand and slapped the woman across the face as hard as she could, screaming at the top of her lungs, "Get out of my house."

The men were all staring, and Timothy began to cross the room. He knew that Amanda must have said something to upset Jenny.

Amanda was furious, "How dare you slap me in front of all these people. Why, if I were a man, I would challenge you to a duel."

Jennifer began rolling up her sleeves, "So you want to fight, Amanda? Well let's fight now, or are you scared that I might ruin your makeup?" She was screaming at the top of her lungs now, "What shall it be? Rapiers? Guns? Fists? Knives? Anything you want! Nothing would give me more pleasure than to slit your lily-white neck or to pound your face until it was unrecognizable." Timothy reached Jennifer who was now backing Amanda to the wall. He grabbed her arm, "Let go of me, Tim. I want to kill her." She broke free of his grasp, lunging at Amanda, pulling her down to the floor, knocking over a small table which came crashing down on top of them. Jennifer got in a couple of good punches before Timothy pulled them apart.

"Jennifer, what the hell do you think you are doing?" The golden eyes looked at her in anger; he'd never seen her so angry.

The gown she was wearing had been torn, but she didn't give a damn, "Let go of me," she said calmly.

"Not until I get some answers."

"If you want answers, why don't you ask that trollop, Amanda."

He was slightly amused at Jenny's statement; he looked at Amanda, "Well?" Amanda just stared back at him.

Sirena looked at Tim, "It appears that Mrs. Bowmen has lost her ability to speak with her forked tongue." All eyes turned to the dark-haired woman, "She insulted your wife, and I must say, I would have reacted in the same way." Dante was amazed at Sirena's statement; he had never considered her a violent person; in all the years he had known her, she seemed sweet and innocent. That catty woman, Amanda, must have really said something personal.

Timothy looked back to Jennifer, "Apologize to our guest."

She looked at him, the green eyes shimmering as she cocked her head to one side staring at him defiantly, "No."

"Jennifer."

"I refuse. I want an apology from her."

"Jennifer," his patience was wearing thin, "You knocked her down and hit her."

Jennifer smirked, "That's true, and I enjoyed every minute."

"Apologize."

"No," Timothy's grip on his wife's arm tightened, "You want me to tell you what she said?"

"Yes."

"Fine, since I've already been embarrassed by that insidious, selfish, insolent, strumpet, then you should be, too." She stared at him in anger. How could he humiliate her and himself like this, "Very well then, Amanda Bowmen was my husband's mistress last year while I lie sick and almost dying from a miscarriage. Mrs. Bowmen," she took a deep breath to calm herself from shaking, "Mrs. Bowmen insists on throwing that up to my face every time she sees me. If you really must know, Tim, her exact words were that you were marvelous in bed and strong as an ox."

Now he was embarrassed. Robert and Molly looked at each other, realizing it was time to leave. Robert spoke in an angry voice, "Amanda, apologize for your behavior to Timothy and Jennifer. We are leaving."

Amanda still said nothing, the hatred she felt for Jennifer had increased two-fold. Robert took her by the arm and led her out of the room into the hall. Molly apologized for the commotion and left the room. Maggie followed her out, so she could get their cloaks and show them to the door.

Jennifer bowed her head, "Excuse me, please." She left the sitting room, running upstairs to her room. She had never been more humiliated in her entire life. Everyone now knew of Tim's infidelities, and she hoped he was satisfied. She sat down at the dressing table, looking at herself in the mirror. Her auburn hair, which had taken Maggie a good part of the morning to arrange, was disheveled from her brawl with Amanda. She began removing her hair pins, letting the auburn curls fall down her back. Her favorite gown, the mauve rose velvet, was torn at the bodice and shoulder. Turning away from the mirror, she stripped off the gown; standing in her petticoats, she gazed around the room; finding the rapier she was looking for, she grasped it in her hand. Taking the proper stance, she began fencing with herself, trying desperately to relieve the anger, humiliation, frustration and built-up energy which had accumulated inside of her in the last two hours. Timothy entered the bedroom and stood at the door watching her in all her anger. Her back was toward him, and she was so involved in her actions that she didn't hear him enter. With one arm flying in the air, she jabbed at the old rocker with such an intensity that she tore the chair from one corner to the other. "Take that, Amanda, you insufferable bastard; I hate you; I hate you." Timothy listened to her words, grinning at the sight of her. And a sight she was in her petticoats, holding a rapier. Suddenly she turned, "When did you get here?"

"A few moments ago." He paused, the lion-like eyes twinkling, "And I believe that the correct term is insufferable bitch."

She cocked her head to one side completely puzzled by what he said, "What?"

"You called Amanda an insufferable bastard."

She laughed, "Oh."

"I'm sorry for causing you embarrassment."

"You didn't," replied Jennifer.

"But I did. I should have known that Amanda was up to her old tricks, what with the way she was hanging over Dante and all." He sucked in his breath, "The Countess told me that if you hadn't slugged her, she most certainly would have done it. Why don't you find something else to wear and come back downstairs?"

She shook her head, "No, I'm too embarrassed."

"There is nothing to be ashamed of; everyone downstairs understands."

"Do they?" she glared at him.

"His eyebrows raised, "You are mad with me, aren't you?"

"You are damn right; I'm angry with you," replied Jennifer.

"Why?"

"Because sometimes, Tim, you are an arrogant bastard."

"Arrogant? Did you know that sometimes you act like a two-year-old?"

"What?" She turned her back to him.

"That's right. Any lady would have walked away from Amanda, but you would have to hit her."

Jennifer whirled around furious, "Oh, so now you're calling Sirena and me whores?"

"I didn't say that," Tim said firmly.

She walked closer to him, the rapier still in her hand, "Didn't you? According to you, we are not ladies, so in my eyes, that makes us whores. Sometimes I don't know why I love you so damn much, except for what Amanda said."

"And I don't know why I married a goddamn baby. Christ, Jennifer, I'm twelve years older than you, and sometimes I can't stand your childish ways. Like today."

"I don't see myself as being childish, and if you were so worried about our age difference, why in hell did you marry me?" She raised her rapier, waving it in his face.

"Put the sword down!" The golden eyes had taken on a menacing gaze.

Jennifer didn't flinch, "No. Answer my question."

"I thought you would grow up, but I guess I was wrong."

In anger she screamed, "Well then, why don't you divorce me?"

He was angry now, "Well if that's what you want, you'll hear from my attorney." He spun around, leaving the room, slamming the door.

Jennifer pulled the door open and raced into the hall in her petticoats waving her rapier. "Tim." He kept on walking, not turning around. The foyer filled with her house guests as she screamed again, "Tim, now who is acting like a child?" He kept walking, "Turn around and face me, you coward." He said nothing, but continued down the stairs, "If you wanted to end our marriage you could have done it a long time ago; I really don't know why I married you." She rambled on, "I would have been better off in the Barbary States. Just remember, I know who you really are!" He stopped, turning to face her, the golden eyes glittering. She knew she should have never said it; she regretted it the moment the words left her mouth, but she said it anyway. He started up the stairs after her; she raised the rapier while she backed down the hall, "Stay away from me."

He stalked her like a lion stalking his prey. Rick Jordan stared up the stairs, "Tim, wait, she's just upset."

Tim turned towards Rick, pulling a rapier off the wall, "Stay out of this Jordan; it's none of your business." Jennifer dropped her rapier as she fled to her bedroom, locking the door behind her. Tim reached the bedroom door, pounding on it. "Unlock this damn door, Jenny, or I'm going to break it down."

She looked around the room, grabbing a dress, she put it on quickly, knowing that she must leave through the passageway because if he came in, he would surely kill her. Taking a heavy cloak and some money out of her drawer, she touched the button on the door to the passageway. As she ascended down the stairs, she could hear Timothy still banging on the door.

Yvonne had cleared out the foyer, assuring everyone that Timothy and Jennifer's quarrel would soon be over, and everything would be back too normal. D'Mattea and Jordan were worried; Timothy was acting like a madman and Jennifer, well, she was acting irrational as well. Dante drummed his fingers on the chair, the banging had stopped. He jumped up, "Something's wrong, he's stopped banging."

Yvonne looked at Dante, "He's probably tired."

Rick looked at her, "Don't you think we'd better check?"

"No, it's their problem; they'll work it out." Yvonne answered.

Dante looked around, "I can't stand it anymore; I've got to check." He left the sitting room and entered the foyer in time to see Tim bounding up the stairs with an axe in his hand. He raced back into the sitting room, "Rick, Cliff, come quick, he's got an axe." Rick Jordan and Cliff McArnold jumped to their feet, followed closely by Sirena, Yvonne, Stefan and Daphne.

"Open this door, Jennifer, or I'm going to bang it down."

Rick looked at Dante, "I'm not going up there; he's furious."

Dante said worriedly, "What if he kills her?"

"He won't kill her; he loves her," said Yvonne in a worried tone of voice. They stood in the foyer and watched him hack at the door.

Jennifer had gone to the storage area and up the stairs that led to the kitchen where she found Gideon. Leaving a message with him, she went to the stables and saddled a horse, riding in the bitter cold to the *White Horse Tavern*. Tears rolled down her cheeks; she lost him forever; he would divorce her now.

Gideon had waited a short time as he was instructed and then took the note into the foyer where, after seeing Timothy in a rage, he handed the note to Yvonne. She opened it and read it. "Tim, she's not in her room," she yelled just as the axe hit the thick oak door, sending pieces of wood flying. He thrust his hand through the opening, unlatched the door, opened it and looked inside. Yvonne yelled again, "Tim, she left."

He turned around and went back to the staircase, "Where did she go?"

"Everything's in the note." Timothy ran down the stairs, taking the note from Yvonne, he walked briskly by the others into his study, slamming the door.

Timothy poured himself a large glass of brandy and sat down unfolding the note, "*Tim, I am afraid of you. I never was until today, except for one other time when you raped me onboard the Moonlight. I'm not telling you where*

I'm going; it's better this way. Get the babies a wet nurse for the time being. When I receive word that you have left on your next voyage, I will return to Lockwood to get the children, after which you can reach me at Weatherly." Seething with rage, he knocked all of the glasses off the table, including the wine. He overturned tables, chairs, breaking artwork, destroying expensive venetian vases, after his tantrum, he sat down at his desk and stared into space. His mind raced; where could she have possibly gone? She didn't know Newport or the surrounding areas at all. She wouldn't go to Robert and Molly's because she might run into Amanda. Perhaps she would return. Maybe she didn't leave the house. He rested his face on his hands, thinking over their argument; it was more than Amanda that caused her anger; it had to be because he was leaving. He wanted to hate her, but he couldn't because he loved her so damn much.

CHAPTER TWENTY-EIGHT

Geoffrey Lyndon, alias Steven Marshall, was sitting in the lobby of the *White Horse Tavern*, when a woman entered in a dark green cloak. Her hood fell from her head revealing a mass of auburn curls. He instantly recognized her as Jennifer Weatherly; rising from his chair, he stood close behind her just within hearing range.

"I would like to take a room for a week or so."

The tavern girl replied, "Your name please."

"Jennifer Weatherly, W-E-A-T-H-E-R-L-Y."

Noticing the plain gold band on her finger, the tavern girl said, "Will your husband be joining you, Mrs. Weatherly?"

She shook her head, "No."

"Very well then," handing her the key, she said, "Room 213."

"Thank you." She turned, leaving the lobby.

"Mr. Marshall, was there something you wanted?"

"I, ah, is there any mail for me?"

"No, sir."

"Thanks." Geoffrey wondered why Jennifer would come to the *White Horse Tavern* alone. Perhaps she and her husband had a falling out. Now would be the perfect time to strike; he would wait an hour and then go pay Jennifer Lockwood a visit. He went to his room to make his plans. A half hour later he told the desk clerk that he would be checking out, time to move on. He paid his bill in full and headed for Jennifer's room. Knocking, he waited for an answer.

"Who is it?"

"Room service."

"I didn't ask for room service," She answered through the door.

"I'm bringing towels, Miss."

"Oh, just a minute." Jennifer opened the door, then she stood in shock for a couple of seconds, before trying to slam it shut.

That couple of seconds was all that Geoffrey needed, as he pushed his way into the room, "It's been a long time, Jennifer."

"What do you want?"

"Payment, my dear. Payment!"

"I owe you nothing." She responded, her green eyes glittering.

"Ah, but you do, and you will pay me dearly."

"I am not going to give you any money, so you can forget it."

He grabbed her by the arm, "I'm not asking for money; you're coming with me."

Jennifer was furious as she tried to pull her arm away, and he tightened his grip, "If you plan to hold me for ransom, you can forget it. No one will give you a dime."

"That's not true; I understand your husband idolizes you; he'll pay."

Jennifer wanted to cry, but laughed instead, "Maybe once, Geoffrey, but we're getting divorced; he wouldn't give you a shilling for me."

"What do you mean divorced?" His entire plan had been shot to hell.

"It was agreed on today; you really don't think I would be here alone if it were not true."

His eyes narrowed, "Fine, then you'll come with me. I'll take you down south and sell you to the highest bidder, or maybe I'll sell you to a house of ill repute."

She held her ground, "I'll scream if you touch me."

He pulled a gun out of his belt, pointed at her and said, "If you scream, I'll kill you." She said nothing, "You will come with me, and by the way, I go by the name of Steven Marshall. If anyone asks you, we're old friends; if you say anything different, you'll get a bullet in your back. Now, get your cloak."

Jennifer obeyed, not because she wanted, but because she had no choice. This certainly turned out to be the worst day in her life. First her argument with Timothy and now meeting up with someone whom she feared greatly and had considered dead. She walked aside Lyndon, or Marshall, whatever he wanted to be called, without saying a word. He hired a carriage, and they were on their way. Jennifer dozed on and off; every time she awoke, he was staring at her in a lecherous smile, licking his lips. Deep down she knew that before she could escape or worse, be sold she would become his mistress. Morning came, and she pleaded with him to get them some food. He produced a package of hard rolls for her to eat.

"When are we going to stop?" she demanded.

"When we reach New York; we'll stop for a few days so I can purchase tickets on a ship."

"Where are we going?" questioned Jennifer.

"That, my dear, is none of your business."

It was futile talking with him; she wouldn't get any answers. How would she escape? Timothy would never find her, if he wanted to find her at all. Her heart ached; she probably would not see him or the children again. She rested her head against the wall of the carriage, staring out the window. The carriage ride to New York took three days; Geoffrey arranged for a room at a hotel which he locked Jennifer in while he went to arrange for passage on the next ship to New Orleans. Jennifer paced around the room waiting for Geoffrey to return, settling on looking out the window.

Geoffrey found Jennifer staring out the window when he entered the room, "I bought you some presents."

She looked at him blankly, "I don't want anything from you."

"Open them, it's a dress and a nightgown."

"I don't want it."

He glared at her, "Put the nightgown on and get into bed."

She stared at him defiantly, "No."

He crossed the room taking her roughly by the arm, "I said put it on."

"And I said no." The green eyes were fiery with anger.

He grasped the bodice of her dress tearing it down the front. She swung out her hand to slap him, but he grabbed her, "I wouldn't try it if I were you." He smiled, "Now, put on the nightgown. I expect you to be ready for me."

"I'll kill myself first before I sleep with you."

He laughed, "That is impossible my dear; there is nothing in this room to kill yourself with, I made sure of that."

She just wanted to kill him; the thought of him touching her made her want to retch. He left the room, leaving her to change. What choice did she have? She walked to the boxes on the bed; opening them. The first box revealed a bright red gown with a plunging neckline. A whore's dress, Jennifer thought to herself. Timothy had called her one, and Geoffrey was going to treat her like one. She tossed the dress aside, opening the other box. The nightgown was black in color and made completely of lace. She undressed nervously, putting on the nightgown, which barely covered her body. Climbing into bed, she waited.

Geoffrey returned to the room smiling, obviously pleased with what was about to happen. "You have no idea how long I've waited for this moment. Timothy Lockwood stole my life, and now I'm going to break the spirit of his woman."

"You are sick, Geoffrey. The thought of you touching me makes my skin crawl."

He crossed the room, slapping her across the face. He tore at his clothes, removing them quickly. His breathing had become harder and quicker. Jennifer glanced around the room; there was nothing she could grab to hit him. He pulled off his trousers revealing the small size of his penis, which still hung limply. Jennifer began to laugh, "What are you laughing at, slut?" She continued to laugh hysterically. He pounced on her, slapping her face, abusing her body with his hands. She held her legs tightly closed as she struggled with him, "You want to laugh at me? I'll teach you to laugh." One hand roughly grabbed one of her breasts, squeezing and massaging it. Jennifer willed her body not to respond as his lips covered her own. She bit him, tasting blood. He slapped her again, "I'll teach you, bitch." He tore the flimsy lace nightgown from her sleek body and immediately descended on her breasts, biting and sucking. She pounded on his back trying desperately to throw him off of her. His tongue played with her nipples, and her body betrayed her; she could feel the warm flush of passion filling her, the nipples were becoming peaked. She struggled, trying to get away as she felt his small erection against her thigh. He grabbed her hands from hitting him, pinning her hands down; he worked his knee between her legs, forcing them open. He penetrated her with one forceful thrust. Her body was not ready to receive him, and she felt as if her insides were being torn apart. A tear escaped the sea-green eyes as he plunged into her again and again, assaulting her in a way which no man had ever assaulted her previously, not even when Timothy raped her aboard the *Moonlight*. When he finished, he rolled off of her, "You didn't please me, Jennifer." She spit in his face, trying desperately to cover herself. Blood dribbled from the corner of her mouth. He grabbed her arm, pulling her toward him, "Touch me like you must have touched him." She shook her head, "I said touch me, or I'll kill you with my bare hands." She was scared as she reached out her trembling hand to touch his limp member. "You must be more skilled with your hands." She ran her fingers along his penis in fluttering motions, "If you are not that skilled with your hands, perhaps you're better with your mouth, whore." She tried to move away from him, but he grabbed her hair, pulling her down to his small, limp penis. "Take me."

"No." She said in a barely audible voice. "Please, anything but this."

Geoffrey began to laugh, and it sounded like that of a demented person, "I'm sure you did this for him, and now you can do it for me." He pushed her back down. Trembling, she began flickering her tongue, arousing him in a matter of seconds. A lump was rising in her throat as her tears rolled down her cheeks, dripping on him. She began to gag and for a moment she wanted to burst into laughter because he was so small compared to Timothy, and she had never gagged with him, even the first time when he taught her what to do. Her thoughts returned to Geoffrey and she began gagging more, as he demanded, "Take me in your mouth." Jennifer ignored him, sobbing openly now, "I said, take me in your mouth." She did so, still gagging; then something inside of her snapped and she sunk her teeth into him, causing him to scream in pain. He began shaking her shoulders, trying to free himself from her bite, and Jennifer could taste his blood which had mixed with her own. He succeeded in prying her off him, "You whore, I'm going to kill you, bitch."

She stared at him with no emotion in her eyes as she felt dead, "Go ahead, I've got nothing to live for now since you've degraded me to this level."

He slapped her across the face causing her nose to bleed. She touched her nose, the blood oozing between her fingers. She screamed as she dove at him; her fists found his face as she pounded. He slapped her again, sending her reeling backward across the room striking her head on the table knocking her unconscious. He picked her up, tossing her roughly on the bed. The damn whore could have maimed him for life. He washed himself off; she would pay for this. The packet ship he had booked them passage on was leaving at the end of the week. When they reached New Orleans, he would sell her to the worst whorehouse in the city. He would make sure that she would never be able to leave without a chaperone of some kind. Several hours later, Jennifer woke retching. Her head was spinning as she looked around the room. She put her hand to her nose, it was still tender. She looked around, her vision somewhat blurred, and she felt dazed. Jennifer knew she needed to be on guard because you could never tell what he was going to do. She smiled to herself; she did know one thing; he wouldn't be able to have sex with her or anyone else for that matter for a good period of time.

Geoffrey returned to find Jennifer wrapped in a sheet which she had pulled from the bed. "Get dressed, we're going to live on the packet in case anyone is looking for you; they'll never find you there."

Jennifer said nothing but obeyed him. Once she was aboard the ship, she might have more freedom. Then she would make her plans; she had some jewels that she could sell if she escaped, which possibly could buy her passage to Newport. She dressed quickly in the red dress he had bought her and tried to cover her bruises with some makeup. Once completely dressed and packed what little she had into the small reticule Geoffrey had bought, they left the hotel. He took her to a packet ship called the *Lady Liberty*. Jennifer grimaced, traveling on a packet would be slow compared to the clippers she had voyaged on in the past. She walked up the gangplank and was escorted to the stateroom for Mr. and Mrs. Steven Marshall. Spending the next weeks with Geoffrey would be tiresome; she would actually be glad to be sold to a bordello; at least in a bordello, she might be able to plan a quick escape. Jennifer looked around the stateroom which consisted of one large bed and a chest of drawers. A washstand stood in one corner, and a small desk was against the opposite wall. Once again, Geoffrey left her alone for which she was grateful. Jennifer went to the desk; opening the drawer, she found some stationary, a pen, and some ink. She sat at the desk, taking the pen and some stationary that bore the *Lady Liberty's* name; she began to write. *'To whomever finds this letter. My name is Jennifer Weatherly Lockwood, and I am being held against my will by a man who once called himself Geoffrey Lyndon and now goes by the name of Steven Marshall. I am from Newport, Rhode Island, and my husband's name is Captain Timothy Lockwood. Mr. Lyndon is taking me somewhere in the south and plans to sell me to a bordello. I am dating this letter so it can be checked against the ships log, so that if a search for me is conducted, at least an area of my whereabouts can be located. Please help me. Give this letter to either my husband or to whomever answers the door. They will know how to locate Timothy. I promise a substantial reward.'* She signed and dated the letter. Now the problem was what to do with it? She looked around the room; it had to be placed where Geoffrey might not notice but someone else might. She could place it under the bed, but what if no one ever found it. If she placed it under the sheets it would be found too soon and the Captain of the ship would question Geoffrey. Geoffrey would surely punish her; no, she couldn't do that. As she glanced around the cabin, her eyes fell upon a small bookcase which stood above the desk. Reaching up, she removed one of the books and flipped through it. Her mind raced; if she placed the letter in a book her only chance of it being found would be if someone picked that particular book to read. If she put it somewhere else, the chance of Geoffrey finding it would increase. She opted for the book; at least the letter would eventually be found. Placing it carefully in the book, she placed the book back on the shelf and waited patiently for Geoffrey to return.

She had become determined again; she could not allow him to break her spirit; he had come close to it earlier, but now she mustn't let him. She must stay strong and alert; it was imperative. Geoffrey returned with several packages, "There are some clothes for you in these boxes."

"What's the occasion?" She asked coolly.

"You must look presentable while we are on this ship and when we reach our destination."

Jennifer opened the boxes; all of the gowns had plunging necklines, "These are gowns for a whore."

"If the slippers fit my dear…" His voice trailed off, his eyes returning her icy stare, "Don't look at me that way."

"What way?" Jennifer asked

"Shut up. I've ordered a bath for you. I want you to be clean for tonight."

She didn't think he would be capable of sex, but he made her nervous, "Why?"

"We are dining with the Captain."

Luke Baker stood on the deck of the *Lady Liberty*; he was finally going home to New Orleans. He missed the south and his home; he watched the activity on the docks as he thought about New Orleans. The *Lady Liberty* was his ship; he had bought her two days ago from her original owners. He was in his early thirties, tall, thin and unmarried. His sandy blonde hair was a mass of long curls which framed his face. His green eyes scanned the docks; he had ordered the men to load the ship as they were sailing with the tide. He was anxious to return to New Orleans and see his family. He was the youngest of four brothers; his father had died several years earlier, and none of his brothers bothered with his mother or his two younger sisters, Carolyn and Rebecca.

Luke did not like the looks of one of his passengers; in fact, there was something strange about the man who called himself Steven Marshall; he didn't trust him. One of his crew said that the woman Marshall had with him was very bruised; Luke didn't tolerate men who slapped or hit women. If Marshall dared to do anything to the woman in his presence, he would kill him.

Jennifer stepped out of the now cooling water and towel dried herself. She decided on wearing the dark blue gown which was cut more modestly than the others. She applied some makeup to her bruised eyes and nose. The swelling of her nose had decreased considerably. Touching up the bruises had become a chore; she did not want to face anyone else who was traveling aboard the *Lady Liberty*. She heard a key in the lock, and Geoffrey strode in, "I see you are ready."

"Yes."

"Good. Remember to call me Steven, and try not to speak to anyone."

"I understand."

He leered at her, "You had better understand."

She said nothing because she was not in the mood to argue with the man. She watched him leave and heard the door lock. Once he was gone, she began to get dressed.

Geoffrey returned to the stateroom within an hour, "Are you ready?"

"Yes." Taking her by the arm, he led her out of the cabin and to the dining room where the other passengers had already gathered. The men in the room leered at Jennifer. She felt as if she was on display. She reluctantly sat down beside Geoffrey and across from the young Captain. The man that sat facing her appeared to be Timothy's age, perhaps younger by a couple of years. "Jennifer, this is Captain Luke Baker."

"How do you do, Captain Baker?"

"It is a pleasure to meet you, Mrs. Marshall." His green eyes scanned her face. The woman did have bruises which were covered with makeup. The only reason he noticed them was because her left cheek was still swollen. She was a beautiful young woman; Luke Baker couldn't see what she was doing with riff-raff like Steven Marshall. Baker made a mental note to keep his eyes and ears open concerning this oddly-matched couple. "Tell me, Mr. Marshall, what did you say you did for a living?"

"I didn't, but since you asked, I was once involved with a shipping company in London."

"I see. Your wife is most charming, although I must admit she appears to be only a child."

"Jennifer is a vision of loveliness, and she is quite young, but I assure you Captain, she's no child."

Marshall's answer disturbed Luke, as he didn't like the reference of not being a child which would suggest that she was rather worldly. Baker turned his attention to Jennifer, "Are you from London also?"

"Yes, Captain." She answered softly as the dinner was being served.

"I'm not sure. I thought perhaps I would offer my services to a shipping line as a manager."

Luke Baker was amused, Steven Marshall was not who he said he was, and he was just waiting for the man to make a slip with his tongue. As for the woman, he was sure her name was Jennifer, but he was just as sure that the woman was deeply afraid of Marshall. "Perhaps I can give you the names of some of the reputable firms in New Orleans."

Geoffrey smiled, "Yes, that would be ideal."

Jennifer was picking at her food, thinking. Perhaps she could get Captain Baker to help her once they arrived in New Orleans. She had her children to think of and by now, someone must be searching for her. She became oblivious to the conversation around her. What would Yvonne do if she was in a situation such as this? She'd fight to the death. But Jennifer couldn't get her hands on a sword. If she could, she would kill Lyndon. Dinner was over, and Geoffrey escorted her back to the cabin. Jennifer thought to herself at least she was safe from physical attack. He couldn't make her have sex with him because of what she had done to him, and she doubted that he would rough her up because he wouldn't want anyone to notice. Besides all of which, he wouldn't want her to have bruises if he was going to sell her. Geoffrey never kept any weapons in the cabin, yet she knew he had them. Where he kept them, she didn't know, but it didn't matter anyway. He would never leave her alone long enough for her to use any of them to her advantage.

CHAPTER TWENTY-NINE

Three weeks had passed since Jennifer's disappearance. D'Mattea and Jordan had discovered that she checked into the *White Horse Tavern* on December twenty sixth, paid a week in advance and was never seen again. They also found that a man who had been living at the *White Horse Tavern* for several months, suddenly paid his bill in full and left on the same day Jennifer had registered. They brought the information back to Lockwood. Timothy had been in a foul mood since that fateful day. He had sent word to the newspapers about the disappearance of his wife, offering a substantial reward for anyone who could inform him about her whereabouts. Yvonne hired a wet nurse for the twins, which caused security problems for the rest of them.

Prince D'Mattea felt something didn't make sense with the disappearance. This bothered him to the point where he was constantly in town to ask questions of people in the area. No one reported seeing her at all. He kept asking himself the question why would Jennifer pay for a week in advance and then leave on her own free will? He kept coming up with the same answer; no, she must have left under protest; otherwise, she would have contacted someone at the house by now. He was sure that she had enough money to book passage on a ship for London, and if she were to book passage on credit, it would affect her personal accounts, and there hadn't been any withdrawals in months. No, Jennifer didn't leave Newport on her own. The Prince definitely felt she was helped along. What about this Marshall person, the one who had checked out and paid his bill on the same day Jennifer checked in; perhaps he had something to do with her disappearance? Although Timothy had dismissed the idea of checking into Marshall, D'Mattea felt he should investigate this more; he left Lockwood and went into the city to the *White Horse Tavern.*

D'Mattea arrived at the *White Horse Tavern,* walked in and ordered himself a drink, "Can I get you anything else sir?"

He smiled, "Yes, what's your name?"

"Why do you want to know?"

"I was hoping that you could provide me with some answers."

Mattie stared at him, "That all depends on the questions, sir."

Dante reached into his pocket, withdrawing some gold coins, "If you answer the questions truthfully, it would be well worth your time."

She stared at the coins for a second, "Okay, but I won't have much time before the dinner crowd comes in." She sat down across from him.

"What do you know about a man named Steven Marshall?"

"Marshall? I think you mean the gambler. Not much; he was a strange one, always asking questions about the big mansion."

"Dante's eyes lit up, "What house?"

"The big one, Lockwood. Not that it's unusual."

"Why? Do a lot of people ask questions about Lockwood?"

"Yes."

"What do they ask?"

Mattie thought for a moment, "Let's see, they usually ask who lives there."

"I see; how was Marshall different?" replied Dante.

"He kept asking me questions about Mrs. Lockwood."

Dante's heart began to beat faster, "What kind of questions?"

"Why should I tell you? Everyone knows she's disappeared, or that's what they say."

"What kind of questions? I'm a friend of the Lockwood family."

She looked at him questioningly, not knowing if she should answer. The heat of his eyes was making her nervous as she answered him, "Okay, he wanted to know her first name. He said he thought he knew her, that he was a friend of hers from London. He also wanted to know if her husband treated her good, and I said he worshipped the ground she walked on."

"Were you working when she checked into the hotel?"

"No, it was my day off. But maybe the maid can be of help to you."

"Could you get her for me?" questioned Dante.

"Sure," she held out her hands for the coins. Dante put ten gold coins into her hands and watched her saunter off. Moments later she returned with a young girl, "This is Emily; she was working then."

Dante motioned for the young girl to sit down; she couldn't be more than twelve years old. "Emily, don't be afraid. I'm not going to hurt you; in fact, I hope you can help me." She nodded her head; he wanted to make her comfortable, "How old are you Emily?"

"Thirteen, sir."

"How long have you been working here?"

"Just about a year, sir. Please ask me your questions; I don't want to lose my job."

"You won't lose your job."

"You don't know him, sir," she said motioning to the big burly man behind the bar, "He's fired girls for less."

"How come your family lets you work in a place like this?"

"My parents are dead, sir. I work here for my room and board."

Dante was appalled, the poor child, "Don't worry about it. Tell me, do you know the big house called Lockwood?"

"Yes."

"Do you know what Mrs. Lockwood looks like?"

"Yes sir. She is beautiful; she was here."

"When?"

"The day after Christmas, sir. I've wanted to go tell her husband what I overheard the day she disappeared, but I haven't had a day off since," said Emily.

"What did you hear?"

"Well, I was in the room next door, straighten' out when I heard someone knock on Mrs. Lockwood's door. The man said it was room service, but we ain't got no men working on the rooms."

"What else happened?"

"Well, I listened at the wall and the man said, 'It's been a long time' and Mrs. Lockwood said, 'what do you want' and he said 'payment.' Mrs. Lockwood said she didn't owe him nothing, but he said she did. Mrs. Lockwood said she wasn't going to give him any money, and he said he didn't want none from her. He wanted her to come with him." Dante listened to every word the young girl said as she continued, "She said that he wouldn't get any money for her because she left her husband."

"Alright, Emily, get back to work." The burly man said as he approached the table.

Dante looked up, "I'm discussing something with the young lady."

The burly man spit on the floor, "And I said, she's got to get back to work."

Dante rose, "Listen, I'm discussing a matter of great importance with the young lady."

"If you're looking for a whore, sir..."

Before the burly man had finished his sentence, Dante drew his sword, the tip leaned against the man's throat, "Emily, get your things. I'm taking you with me."

Some men had risen, "Sir, behind you," said Emily. Dante whirled around.

Five men were approaching him with swords drawn, "Who do you think ye are?" one of the men questioned.

Dante didn't flinch, "Stand back gentlemen; this is not your fight."

Emily screamed, Dante looked over his shoulder, burly Sam had the young girl in his grasp. Out of the corner of his eyes, he saw one of the men charge at him; he whirled around, jabbing with his sword and feinting to the left. The other four began walking towards him. His mind was racing; the important thing was not to back into a corner; he glanced around, the safest way was up the stairs. They had backed him up the stairs, and he was successfully holding them off when Rick Jordan, Cliff McArnold and Yvonne entered the *White Horse Tavern.*

"What the hell," Jordan began, "It's D'Mattea."

Yvonne looked around, spying Dante on the stairs, Cliff and Rick drew their swords. Dante looked up; seeing them, he smiled and charged down the stairs, disarming one of the attackers as Jordan and McArnold attacked the rear. Dante picked up the sword from the man he disarmed, tossing it quickly to Yvonne, who lifted her skirts and joined in the fight. Dante yelled across the room to Yvonne who had just successfully disarmed and wounded an attacker, "Get the girl from the burly guy; she's got information about Jennifer."

Yvonne nodded, heading for the burly man, whose grip on the young girl had tightened. Emily squirmed, "Let the girl go."

"I ain't going to let no woman give me orders."

Yvonne chortled, "That's right; it is an order, and if you don't let her go, your blood is going to be spewing out of your body in a steady stream." The man didn't flinch; Yvonne moved in his direction; as she drew closer to him, he broke a bottle, holding it to the young girl's face. Yvonne paused, "Put the bottle down."

"Come a step closer, and I'll kill the girl."

A shot rang out; the bottle flew out of the man's hand, blood spurting out of the wound onto the girl. Yvonne moved quickly, grabbing Emily by the hand, pulling her away from the burly man who was whimpering behind the bar. Yvonne wondered who had fired the shot? Dante was still fighting off one of the men as were Rick and Cliff. Yvonne looked around; Sirena was standing in the doorway, her gun still smoking. Yvonne dashed across the room, "Sirena, take the girl and put her on the coach."

Sirena questioned, "What is going on?"

"Just hurry; I'll get the men."

Sirena took the girl to the carriage outside while Yvonne yelled to Cliff, "Get D'Mattea and Jordan; we're leaving."

He looked over his shoulder, all the while fencing with an attacker, "How can we leave; we sent the carriage back?"

"Sirena's here; she must have gotten our message," responded Yvonne.

"D'Mattea, Jordan, let's go."

Dante and Rick backed out of the tavern, running to the open door of the coach. Jordan looked at his friend, "Dante, how the hell do you get yourself in these predicaments?"

"The burly guy made a rude comment about Emily. Oh," he paused, "Let me introduce you to Emily." They all turned to the girl as Dante continued, "This is Rick Jordan, Cliff McArnold, Yvonne and Sirena. My name is Dante D'Mattea."

"It's a pleasure to meet you, Emily," said Yvonne.

"Mr. D'Mattea, what about my job? Sam will never want me back."

Dante responded, "Don't worry about it. You can have a job at Lockwood." He looked at his friends, "Who fired the shot?"

"I did," replied Sirena.

Dante looked at Sirena, "What were you doing at the tavern?"

"I got a note, saying to meet all of you there," she turned her attention to Emily, "Why are we taking this young girl with us?"

"She has information concerning Jennifer."

"Oh." The carriage stopped, and they piled out.

Dante opened the front door with the others following him. "Tim," he yelled.

Sirena interrupted him, "He's not here."

Dante turned around, "What do you mean he's not here?"

"He left, he pulled out about an hour ago with Mark Gregory before I left for the tavern," replied Sirena.

"Pulled out! Do you mean that they went to the Barbary States?" He gazed at her wild-eyed.

"No, they took the *Moonlight* and went to London to search for Jennifer," responded Sirena.

"Damn it!" Dante yelled at the top of his lungs.

Rick said, "Dante, calm down. What's wrong?"

Dante took a deep breath, "Everybody into Tim's study." Once inside Dante said, "The reason I went to the *White Horse Tavern* was to see if I could get any information about Jennifer's disappearance. The first person I talked to was the barmaid; she suggested that I talk to Emily." Turning to Emily he said, "Would you tell them what you overheard."

Emily began her story; everyone listened intently as she spoke, "That's what I told Mr. D'Mattea, but I never finished."

"What happened after she told him that she and Tim had split up?" asked Rick Jordan.

"He said she was going with him, and he would sell her down south to the highest bidder or to a bordello. Mrs. Lockwood said she'd scream if he touched her, and he said if she screamed, he would kill her." She paused, "He also said that he goes by the name of Steven Marshall, and if she said anything different, she'd get a bullet in her back."

"Did you see the man?" asked Dante.

"No, sir. I've never seen him."

Dante rose from his seat, poured himself a glass of rum, "So let's see, we know that Jennifer was taken by force and that she's being taken down south."

Sirena interjected, "We also know that this Marshall guy might try to kill her if she tries to escape."

"More importantly," Yvonne paused, "I've got a gut feeling that his real name is Geoffrey Lyndon."

"Geoffrey Lyndon? Who is that?" asked Cliff.

"He's the man who stole Jennifer before and sold her to the Barbary States. It has to be him; he's the only one I know of that would do something like this," replied Yvonne.

Dante was puzzled, "Why would he use the name Steven Marshall?"

Yvonne said, "To throw Timothy off his track. The day we arrived in Newport, Jennifer insisted that she saw Lyndon at Brick Market. Timothy checked it out and could not find a trace of the man."

Dante sipped his rum, "What should we do?"

Yvonne said, "With Tim not thinking straight and taking off to look for Jennifer in London, I say we take matters into our own hands."

Rick Jordan thought for a second, "Do you know what this guy looks like?"

Yvonne shook her head, "No."

Sirena rose from her chair, "But we know what Jennifer looks like."

Sirena approached Dante's side as he said, "If he's taking her down south, where would he take her?"

"The most logical place would be New Orleans," answered Cliff.

"Then we'll go to New Orleans," said Yvonne.

Dante shook his head, "Only two of us should go."

"I agree with Dante," said Cliff.

Yvonne looked around the room, "I think it should be D'Mattea and Jordan. This way, Cliff and I can take care of operations since we are more familiar with the cataloguing system, and the Countess can help us by keeping an eye out for any problems."

Rick Jordan poured himself a glass of rum, "I also think that Dante and I could gain admittance into the bordellos more so than you."

Yvonne laughed, "Good point!"

"What ship should they take?" questioned Cliff.

Dante looked in his direction, "If we take one of our ships, we are as good as dead. If this Marshall guy is Lyndon, then he would have checked into Timothy's firm, and those clippers will be easy to spot."

Rick agreed, "That's true. We will have to book passage on another ship."

Yvonne said, "What if you use my ship, the *Sea Witch*."

"No," Dante said quietly, "The *Sea Witch* is a known pirate vessel. We can't take that chance." He suddenly realized he had said the wrong thing, that Emily was still in the room.

Emily sat in stunned silence, these people were talking about pirates and the ship that belonged to a woman who must be a pirate. Rick said, "I don't see why we can't use her if we change the name of the ship."

Dante cleared his throat, "Sirena, why don't you take Emily to Gideon and see what she can do." Sirena obeyed, taking the young girl out. Dante turned to Rick, "I forgot that she was here."

"Didn't we all. I swear no one in this house has been thinking rationally since Jennifer disappeared," said Rick.

Yvonne said quietly, "For a group of men and women who are members of a powerful stronghold, we've fallen to pieces over the disappearance of Jennifer."

Cliff agreed, "That's true and we've been slipping up because of the considerable strain we've been under." He paused, "Like today, what happened in the *White Horse Tavern* should have never taken place, after all we're not in the Barbary States or the Caribbean. We've got to be careful."

"True," answered Yvonne.

"Alright, if Dante and I take the *Sea Witch,* we will have to rename her and get a crew together."

Yvonne thought for a second, "Most of the *Sea Witch's* crew is still aboard, so you need not worry about that."

"What do you want to rename her, Rick?" questioned the Prince.

"I don't know, something to do with our mission. You pick a name; you're good at that type of thing."

"What about *Green-Eyed Lady?*" said Dante.

Yvonne smiled, "It fits her."

"I like it," said Cliff.

"I do, too," answered Rick.

"Then it is the *Green-Eyed Lady,*" Dante paused for a second, "When do we leave?"

"Two days," responded Rick.

Yvonne poured rum for a toast as Sirena came into the study. Handing out the glasses, she raised her glass and said, "A toast to the *Green-Eyed Lady* and her two Captains, Prince D'Mattea and Rick Jordan. May they bring Jennifer back to Newport, safe and sound." They all raised their glasses in the air and then drank the contents down.

Sirena walked over to Dante, gazing deeply into his eyes. It appeared he could read her mind, taking her hand he said, "Excuse me."

Rick Jordan smiled, "I'll take care of Emily."

Dante and Sirena went to their bedroom. He pulled her to him the minute the door closed. She pulled away, "What's the matter?"

"I think you've misread my meaning. I want to talk to you, and I want you to listen to me."

"Whatever you like."

"Why do you have to go with Rick? Why couldn't Cliff go?"

He sighed, "Sirena, I think you know the answer to that; Rick and I are a team."

"Can I go with you?"

"No, it might be dangerous."

"I can take care of myself."

"I'm sure you can. You're a damn good shot Sirena, but in New Orleans you could be kidnapped."

"Not if I'm with you," Sirena said.

Taking her hand, he pulled her into his lap, "You're a beautiful woman, my friend for years, now my lover. If anything happened to you, I would die. And Sirena, you couldn't be with me when Jordan and I start the actual search of the bordellos." She frowned, her face flushing, "That's it, isn't it? You are jealous! I don't believe it." He kissed her, "I love you Sirena, and Jordan and I are not going to be sleeping with the women. We are going to be searching for Jennifer."

"I know; I'm sorry Dante for not trusting you, but I also realize that men have desires that need to be satisfied, and I couldn't bear that thought." She rose from his lap.

He pulled her back, "There are other ways to satisfy those desires, Sirena. I promise you that the only woman I'll look at is Jennifer, if and when we find her."

She kissed him lightly, "I love you. I guess you're right. You're always right."

Dante smiled, "Not always. Listen, there are some things that you can do here while Rick and I are away."

"What kinds of things?"

"Well, you can learn the system from Yvonne and Cliff; you can keep up appearances, and when Tim returns, you can tell him where we went."

She pressed closer to him, "Love me."

"I love you. Tonight will belong completely to us."

"Promise?"

"I promise. Get ready for dinner, I need a bath and then I'm going to talk with Jordan."

Rick Jordan sat in the kitchen talking to Emily as she peeled potatoes for dinner, "I'm terribly sorry that Dante caused you to lose your job, but you'll be better off here. I know that you overheard us talking about pirates and operations, but you need not worry about what you heard. It is important, though, that you not mention or discuss it with anyone. Do you understand?"

"Yes, sir. I'm just grateful to have another job."

"I'm happy that you could bring us so much information concerning Jennifer's whereabouts."

Dante entered the room, "Jordan, let's go into the library; I've got something to discuss with you."

Rick followed Dante to the library, "That was fast. I thought you and Sirena would be tied up all afternoon."

Dante ignored him, "I think that Gideon should come with us." They entered the library.

Rick said, "Gideon is needed here."

Dante shook his head, "No, with Emily here, Sirena and Maggie, I'm sure the women can manage. Besides, Stefan Weatherly has those two servants he brought with him, and there's Daphne."

"Speaking of Weatherly, I think we should tell him before we leave for New Orleans."

Dante stopped Rick, "Impossible. I saw Lizabeth upstairs and asked her where he was, and she told me that he and Daphne left for Boston earlier, and they won't be back until next week."

"I guess Yvonne can tell him when they return," replied Rick.

"I think if we have Gideon with us, the three of us can branch out every day taking an area of the city and report to each other every night."

"Okay, that makes sense; Gideon will come with us. Dante, can I ask you something?"

He poured himself and Jordan a glass of rum, "Go ahead."

Taking the rum from D'Mattea, he said, "Do you think we'll find her?"

He shook his head, "I don't know, Rick, but I do know we have to try."

"Do you think Tim will take her back?" questioned Rick.

He looked at Jordan in amazement, "You really don't know what it's like being in love with someone. He loves her, and she loves him, no matter what has happened between them." He paused, "Do you honestly think he would have gone to London to look for her if he didn't care?"

"He said he was going because of the children," said Rick.

Dante laughed, "He's lying; that's an excuse. If he didn't want to look for her, he wouldn't, kids or not."

Yvonne entered the library, "Oh, I'm sorry, did I interrupt something?"

"No, we were discussing taking Gideon with us," answered Jordan.

"Gideon? That means the three of you will be searching which is a good plan. I came to let you know that dinner is ready," said Yvonne.

"I'm starved; this afternoon's workout made me hungry," Dante said as he placed his glass on a tray.

Two days later, the *Sea Witch* had been renamed the *Green-Eyed Lady*. Gideon, Rick Jordan and Prince D'Mattea set sail for New Orleans. Sirena, Yvonne and Cliff stood on shore watching the *Green-Eyed Lady* pull out of port. Her destination was a mission to find Jennifer Lockwood.

CHAPTER THIRTY

Ginger Ashworth would be forever grateful to the Comte de Lucerne for supplying her with enough funds to reach New Orleans and start her own bordello. She was choosy about the women she employed, and recently, she had purchased a woman named Jennifer. She was a beautiful woman, a high-class whore, and since her purchase, the clients had doubled. Ginger had problems with the wench refusing to work, but she soon got the message that either you work or you don't eat. Ginger, herself, worked from time to time. Even as owner, she needed some excitement. The new girl Jennifer was bringing in money, and a few of the men had approached Ginger with offers to buy the girl from her. Ginger wanted to keep the woman for a while; besides, she had promised that Marshall guy that the woman would never leave the bordello and he had charged her a fortune for the girl. No, she would keep Miss Jennifer until she made her money back, then anyone who wanted to buy her had better offer a good price.

Jennifer's first days in the bordello were ones of loneliness. No one was allowed to talk to her, and she wasn't allowed to talk with anyone unless she was spoken to first. She was poked and prodded by the bordello doctor, a quack, who made lurid remarks about her body. Jennifer continued to be isolated as she was fitted for clothing suitable to her new trade and baths three times a day. Finally, she was allowed to associate with the other girls. When she was taken downstairs and introduced, none of the women seemed thrilled to meet her. There was one girl named Heather who came to Jennifer later and asked her if she had ever been on a ship bound for the Barbary Coast. Jennifer looked at her in amazement, could this plump girl be the same skinny, sickly girl that she had met, "Yes, I was once on a ship to the Barbary Coast."

"Then you're that Jennifer, the one I became friends with?"

"Heather?" The girl nodded her head, "I don't believe it; it's you, Heather!" She threw her arms around the girl; letting go, she began to cry, "I'm sorry."

"Come with me." Heather led Jennifer to her room. "What happened to you? I thought you were bought by Captain Bloodthirsty."

"I was," replied Jennifer.

"He sold you to Ginger Ashworth?" questioned Heather.

Jennifer shook her head, "No, I'm married to him." She started to laugh, a nervous, anxious laugh, as tears filled her eyes, "I was kidnapped again and by the same man."

Heather shook her head in disbelief, "I don't believe it, a second time?"

Jennifer ignored her question as her mind was racing, "Heather, listen to me, how can I get out of here?"

"You won't be able to get out. Madame Ginger paid a lot of money for you, so you'll never be able to leave until she gets that money back."

"Are you allowed to leave the bordello?" asked Jennifer.

"Sometimes," replied Heather.

"What if I wrote a letter, could you take it for me?" questioned Jennifer.

Heather hesitated, "Yes, but the mail is very slow, you could be here for weeks to come."

"What difference does it make?"

"I guess that's true," replied Heather.

"When are you going out next?"

"At the end of the week, probably Friday," replied Heather.

Jennifer smiled, "Friday, then. I will have the letter prepared for you to take."

Prince D'Mattea, Rick Jordan and Gideon pulled into port after being at sea for three weeks. Since they weren't carrying any goods, they had to pay a large sum of money in order to dock the *Green-Eyed Lady*. Their mission had begun, the city was divided into three parts. Each man was assigned to an area to search for Jennifer. After one week, only fifteen bordellos remained to be searched.

Rick was sitting in his cabin when there was a knock on his cabin door. He rose and went to the door wondering why any of the crew would be knocking. He opened the door to a young man, "Are you Rick Jordan?"

Rick was suspicious, "Why do you want to know?"

"I've got a message for Mr. Rick Jordan of the *Green-Eyed Lady*, a telegraph, sir."

"Then I'm him." The young man handed him the letter and was tipped with a gold coin. He tore open the telegraph message, *"Rick, stop. Tim's ship went down, stop. Yvonne."* Rick slowly sat down on a chair staring at the message.

Returning from a search that never seemed to end, Dante stopped by Jordan's cabin. He knew something had happened, "What's wrong?"

Rick stood up with a glass of rum in one hand and the letter in the other hand; he handed Dante the letter, "Read it."

Dante took the letter, read it, and placed it on the desk. He poured himself a glass of rum and sat down. He was exhausted, breaking his back looking for a woman he might never find, and now, one of his closest friend's ship went down. He looked up at Jordan, "We don't know if he's dead."

"Shit, think of it. Here we are in New Orleans and the *Moonlight* goes down with both Tim and Mark Gregory aboard. What do you think their chances are?"

"I don't know. Yvonne really hasn't supplied us with enough information," responded Dante.

"Oh, come on Dante, what should she have said, Tim and Mark were killed on a pirate ship? Do you realize that a statement like that over the telegraph would have brought everything we've worked for tumbling down?"

"Well, we've got to find Jennifer and go back to Newport."

Rick Jordan laughed, "We could be on a goddamn wild goose chase. She might not even be in New Orleans. That bastard could have changed his mind and taken her to St. Louis for all we know."

"We can't give up; that much I do know. There aren't many bordellos left to search. If she's not here we'll go back to Newport."

"Two days, Dante, and then we leave," said Rick.

"At least three days, Jordan, because if we find her, we're going to have to make a plan to get her out of the bordello."

Rick sighed, "Alright, three days, but no more."

Dante rose, "I'm going to bed, it looks like I may not get any sleep for the next few days." He left the cabin for his own, leaving Rick Jordan to drown himself in his drink. Dante wanted to make sure he would have a clear head for tomorrow. Now it was even more important to find Jennifer and bring her back to the children.

Jennifer was slowly beginning to hate herself; man after man assaulted her body in ways that she never thought were possible. If she ever left this hellish place, she could never return to Timothy, not like this, not after what she had been through. She lay in her bed, thinking it had been about two months since her abduction and no effort had been made to find her. The man she loved hated her; she was sure of it. A tear trickled down her cheek, one of sadness and total despair. She thought of taking her own life, but then she thought of the twins. If she ever did leave New Orleans, she might at least get to see the twins. Although, the more she thought of it, Timothy would never let her see them after the way she deserted them. The reality was, she hadn't planned on deserting them; she left to make Timothy realize exactly how much he loved her, she had thought he would have found her the following day and brought her back to Lockwood. Instead, in her misfortune, she ran into Geoffrey Lyndon. Her mind traveled back to her current circumstances; she wasn't certain how much more humiliation she could take; she did know that she had to leave Madame Ashworth's place of business. She woke early, after a night filled with nightmares. Jennifer put on her dressing gown and looked into the mirror. The dark circles under her eyes were more prominent, and she had lost a considerable amount of weight since her employment. She climbed into the bath tub and scrubbed her body as if to erase the men from the day before. She rose and stepped out of the tub, wrapping a towel around her and went to look at her meager wardrobe. All whore's clothes, everything from the dresses to her petticoats. What should she wear today? The black one with the red feathered trim.

Jennifer had just finished dressing when Heather burst into her room, "Jenny."

"Heather," she answered without looking at Heather, as she applied the finishing touches to her toiletry, she turned around, "I tried to cover the dark circles under my eyes. How did I do?"

Heather replied, "Fine. I brought some tea and cakes for us and yesterday's newspaper that one of the men left."

"The newspaper? What would I want to see the newspaper for?" questioned Jennifer.

Heather opened to a page, "What I am going to show you will upset you."

"Heather what could possibly upset me in a New Orleans newspaper?" Jennifer took the paper from her. The headline blared out at her,

Pirate Ship Goes Down. Suddenly her vision blurred for a moment and she felt lightheaded, she made her way to bed and sat down to read the newspaper. *Captain Bloodthirsty of the Moonlight went down with his ship outside of Tortuga. It had been reported that a Captain Mark Gregory was also aboard the Moonlight. There are no known survivors from the wreck. Both Gregory and Blood-thirsty were two of the most feared pirates of our day.* Jennifer began to shake uncontrollably, she whispered, "Tortuga." Tears began to stream down her face smearing the makeup she had just applied as the newspaper slipped to the floor. She wanted to vomit, her stomach was churning, and she felt as if she couldn't breathe.

Heather knelt to touch her hand, "Jennifer, I'm sorry."

Jennifer tried to regain her composure, looking up to meet Heather's eyes she said, "It is more important than ever that I get out of New Orleans, my children are in Newport, and I must go to them."

Heather shook her head, "There is no way-out, Jennifer. I'm sorry."

Jennifer shook her head, "I can't stay here. There must be a way of escape."

Heather realized that her friend was in shock and she tried to say something that would bring her back to reality, "You're a strong woman…"

Jennifer began to laugh a nervous laugh, "Strong? Oh no, Heather; I'm far from strong. I want to scream and cry. The only man I've ever loved might be dead," her voice cracked, "Not strong, but a survivor, and I'll survive through this nightmare."

"Jennifer, he is dead," said Heather softly.

Jennifer snapped, "No! If Tim was dead, I'd be able to feel it. The newspaper said no known survivors. He is alive; I can feel it."

Heather shook her head, "How can you be so sure?"

"I'm sure of it." Jennifer looked Heather squarely in the eyes, "Someday, when you find someone to love, to really love, you'll be able to understand."

The redhaired girl stared at her, "Jennifer, all of my life I've been at a man's mercy. I'm good for one thing, and that isn't respectability."

"Nonsense; when I leave here, you are coming with me," Jennifer said firmly.

"Listen, perhaps you may be able to escape, but I doubt the two of us will get away with it." She paused, her mind racing, "Do you know that you could pass for me?"

"Don't be ridiculous, Heather, I look nothing like you."

"I know, but if I got some color for your hair, and we made it red," Heather paused, "and then I could lend you some clothes, you just might be able to walk out of this place with everyone thinking that you are me."

"No, if I leave, so do you," Jennifer hesitated, "What will happen to you if they discover that I'm gone?"

Heather shook her head, the bright red curls bouncing, "Nothing. There wouldn't be any reason to think I had anything to do with you."

Jennifer was now pacing around the room; going to the window, she gazed out, "Not true," she turned her attention back to Heather; "Use your head for God's sakes, you are the only person that I talk to, and Madame Ginger would go directly to you when she discovered I was gone." Jennifer turned to look out the window again, she tilted her head slightly to the left, "My God!"

Heather raced to the window, looking out, "What's wrong?"

"Down there, I know that man."

Heather stood in the window, "What man?"

Jennifer pointed to the gentleman standing below the window, "There. That is Prince D'Mattea. Help me fix my makeup, I've got to go downstairs." Jennifer went to the table and began to quickly fix her tear-streaked face with Heather helping her. She looked at Heather, "I'm going downstairs." She rose and fled the room, racing downstairs to the main parlor. Her heart was beating, pounding in her ears; her blood pressure was rising. If her hunch was right, Dante was looking for her, which meant that Tim had sent him, and he still loved her. She reached the last stair facing the front door, which was being answered by Madame Ginger herself.

"Hello," said Dante smiling.

"Well, you are an early one," replied Madame Ginger.

Dante shook his head, "Not really, just a choosy one." He pulled a roll of money out of his pocket, "And I have a great deal of money to spend," he paused, "that is, if I find the right woman." Jennifer could hear the voices through the curtain which separated the main parlor from the front entry way.

"What kind of woman are you looking for?" Ginger asked. She liked this dark man with the European accent.

Dante smiled, "She must be tiny and I want her to have reddish hair."

"We have several that fit into that category," replied Ginger.

Dante glanced around the parlor, "She also must be strikingly beautiful with almond shaped eyes and a slight, slender nose."

"If I may ask a personal question sir, why are you interested in whores?" questioned Ginger as she looked at a very well dressed and educated man.

Dante laughed, a low easy laugh, "Aren't all men interested in a good time when they are away from home? I'm lonely and have a great deal of money to spend."

Ginger Ashworth was now laughing as well, "Well then, that is a sizeable bank roll you carry. I certainly hope you find the woman you like, but we do not open until this afternoon at four."

Dante thrust several of the bills into her hand, "Open for me now."

"I'm afraid sir, that it is impossible. Many of the girls had late evenings and are still asleep."

"Wake them. Listen, I'll throw in several more dollars and if I find a girl for me there will be an added bonus for you," his dark eyes appeared to be looking deeply into Ginger's.

She moved closer to him, "What kind of bonus?" Although she didn't fit the description of the type of woman that he wanted, she had to dream about bedding this fine specimen of a gentleman.

Dante replied, "Jewels." He saw her eyes light up, "Ah, I see you like jewels. Well? Will you open now for me?"

Ginger sighed, "Alright, but you must promise that you won't breathe a word of this to anyone."

Dante placed his hand over his heart, "I swear to you I won't."

Jennifer had taken a seat on one of the lounges facing the entrance way. She couldn't decide how she should sit, so she settled on just resting herself on one elbow. When Dante and Madame entered the room, Dante looked directly at Jennifer and their eyes met and locked. Dante kept a clear head and looked away from her. Jennifer also tried to pay no attention to Dante, but it was difficult. Her heart felt as if it was pounding out of her chest, and she was trying hard not to flush. Madame summoned all of the girls, many of which were angry at being awakened at such an early hour. All of the women fell into line, and Dante began at one end, looking the women over, every once in a while, hesitating on one woman before moving on to the next. When he reached Jennifer, he touched her hair, smiled at her and she smiled nervously back. Then, he moved to Heather, hesitating on her and then back to Jennifer, before being joined by Madame Ginger.

Dante sighed, "I like this one; she has the right coloring."

"Good choice sir. She's one of our newest and one of the most popular women in this house."

"I'm sure," he answered, sarcastically, staring at Jennifer who had hung her head in shame. Taking her by the arm, he said, "Show me to your room, woman." Jennifer led the way with Heather watching from the main parlor. Perhaps Jennifer's prayers had been answered in this dark man. Heather and the others went about their business, some going back to bed.

Once inside Jennifer's room, she threw her arms around him, "Oh Dante, thank you for finding me."

"Thank God I found you," Dante whispered.

"How are the children?"

"Fine, Jordan's with me and Gideon."

Jennifer went to pick up the newspaper, handing it to him. His eyes scanned the article; she knew about Tim. He looked at her and she said, "He's not dead, Dante."

Dante grabbed her and pulled her into his chest, holding her to him, "Let it out, Jenny."

She pulled away, "I'm not going to cry Dante, because he's not dead; I know it in my heart and soul."

The dark eyes marveled at this young woman standing before him pretending to be strong, when he knew she was on the edge. "At least this article gives Jordan and me more information concerning where he was when the *Moonlight* went down."

"You knew?"

Dante looked at her, "Yes. Yvonne sent a telegram saying Tim's ship went down, but that's all she said. We have to come up with a plan to get you out of here." He paused thinking, "What if I offer to buy you?"

Jennifer shook her head, "It will never work. She told Geoffrey that she would keep me for at least a year."

"Geoffrey? Is he going by the name of Steven Marshall now?"

"Yes," Jennifer replied before continuing, "I didn't think anyone would ever find me."

Dante was focused on Marshall, "Is this Marshall character still living in the city?"

"I don't know. Why?" questioned Jennifer.

Dante's mind raced; he would find the bastard and kill him with his bare hands, "No reason," he rose from his seat looking out the window. The drop to the ground wasn't that far, "I've got an idea."

"What kind of idea?"

"I'll get a rope long enough to reach the ground, and we'll steal you."

Jennifer's eyes opened wide, "Through the window?"

He smiled, "Yes, are you afraid?"

She shook her head, "No, but there will be someone else coming with me, a young girl, the redhead that was standing aside of me."

Dante looked her in the eyes, "Too dangerous."

"Please, she's been a good friend here and on the slave ship," Jennifer pleaded with Dante.

"Slave ship?"

"I met her two years ago on a ship to the Barbary Coast. The man who bought her sold her to Madame Ginger. I want to take her out of here, Dante."

He thought for a second, "Let me discuss this with Jordan; this afternoon, I'll be back with the rope and something for you two women to wear."

"How will you get it in?"

"Don't worry about that. Do you have any valuables that you want me to take to the ship?"

Jennifer rose going to the closet, "I've some jewels that I've successfully hidden in the hem of this cloak." She tore the hem open, the jewels spilling to the floor. Picking them up, she handed them to Dante, "This is all I have that is valuable to me."

Dante took them from her and wrapped them in the newspaper with the article of Tim's ship. He put them into his pocket, "My hour with you will be over soon, so I'll talk fast. I'll pay Madame what's her name for your services and reserve you for this afternoon when I bring you the rope and some clothes. You are to find a good hiding place and put everything I give you there for safe keeping. I would suggest that you tell your friend nothing until we finalize our plans."

"Okay." He turned to leave, "Dante," she walked towards him. "I love you. You've been a wonderful friend." She kissed him on the cheek.

"I'll be back green-eyed lady, and be careful." He left the room; she stood in the doorway, watching him amble down the hallway.

Dante reached downstairs and approached Madame Ginger, "Here you are my dear, payment plus a little extra. The girl was worth much more than you charge."

Madame Ginger counted the money, "Thank you, sir."

Dante raised one eyebrow as he said, "I'll be back this afternoon to see the girl, and when I return, I'll bring you your gift."

She smiled, "Thank you."

"You'll get the gift only if you save me that particular girl. I'm willing to give you triple the amount I just gave you."

Ginger Ashworth's eyes shined in greed, "You can bet I'll save her for you. In fact, I'll see to it when she's well bathed, perfumed and well rested for your return."

"Thank you." Dante sauntered out the door, hoping Rick Jordan had enough cash on him to buy the Madame an expensive trinket.

Rick Jordan was sitting at his desk when Dante burst into the cabin, "I've found her!"

Rick turned in his seat, "You've found her? Where?"

"Madame Ginger's. It's not far from here."

Rick rose, "What's the plan?"

Dante said, "We need long rope and some men's clothes small enough to fit Jennifer and another woman."

"Wait one minute, what other woman?" asked Rick.

"I don't know her name, but she's been a friend to Jennifer. And you know Jenny, she collects wayward people as if they were pets," replied Dante.

Rick shook his head in disbelief, "What do we need the rope for?"

"They are going to make their escape out the window," responded Dante.

"Out a window? Are you daft? What if Jennifer falls, those poor kids won't have any parents at all."

"Jennifer doesn't believe Tim's dead," replied Dante.

"You told her?" Dante shook his head no, as he pulled the newspaper package from his pocket, unwrapping the jewels. Rick's eyes opened wide, "Where the devil did you get those?"

"She gave them to me; they belong to her. But look at the newspaper." Dante handed the paper to Rick.

Rick sat down to read the article, "Tortuga? What the hell was he doing in Tortuga?" He looked up at Dante.

"My only guess is that perhaps he thought Jennifer might have been taken there if she was kidnapped."

Rick became inquisitive now, "What about Jenny? How does she look?"

Dante pulled up a chair, "She is very thin; overall, she looks fine, Jordan, but that's just a façade. I think deep down she's falling apart at the seams. She was happy that we came to rescue her, yet there was something else in her eyes, a sadness."

"That's to be expected, Dante. She probably feels she's been unfaithful to Tim. The feeling will pass."

"We can hope. How much money do you have with you?" questioned Dante.

"A considerable amount, why?"

"We've got to buy a trinket for Madame Ginger. I promised her a piece of jewelry."

"Jewelry? Why the hell did you promise her jewelry?"

"It was the only way she'd let me check out the girls this morning. I'm going back this afternoon, and I promised I'd bring her a gift."

Jordan went to the drawer of the desk withdrawing his money, "This is all I have. If you were asking me to do this for anyone else, I would have said no. But this is for Jennifer, and she's important."

"Where's Gideon?"

"He hasn't returned from the city."

"When he does, fill him in," Dante started to leave.

Where are you going?"

Dante looked at Rick, "I'm going to go buy the jewelry and see if I can find a certain man named Steven Marshall."

"Marshall? He's still in the city?"

"Jennifer thinks so," replied Dante.

"Wait a minute, I'll come with you. I want to kill the man."

Dante grinned at Jordan, "We'll share the pleasure of killing him."

"Perhaps Jennifer would like to watch us torture him," replied Rick.

"No, she's been through too much these last few weeks. We just have to make sure he's dead this time."

Rick's eyes became hard, "He'll be dead this time. Let's go look for him."

"No, let's buy the jewelry for Madame Ginger first, so we don't have to carry a large amount of money on us." Dante glanced at the table where Jennifer's jewels lay scattered, "I would suggest that we hide Jennifer's jewels."

Jordan looked at the table, "I guess that would be a good idea." The two men went to the table and began to pick up Jennifer's jewels. They decided to hide them in the false bottom drawer of the desk before leaving the ship.

CHAPTER THIRTY-ONE

D'Mattea and Jordan had purchased a bracelet for Madame Ginger which contained diamonds and rubies. Next, they purchased some clothes and a rope for the plan they would be putting in place to rescue Jennifer Lockwood and her friend. During the early afternoon, they found that Steven Marshall was holding a poker game at the Royal Palace Hotel. Anyone interested in playing was to be at the hotel by seven o'clock.

Jordan and Dante went back to the ship before Dante returned to Madame Ginger's. Dante was wearing his heavy cloak which enabled him to conceal the clothes and the rope he had purchased for the escape. Making his way to Madam Ginger's he stopped at the Royal Palace to look at the hotel and to check the exits. Once that was done, he continued to Madame Ginger's.

Madame Ginger answered the door, "You're back."

The dark eyes bore into her, "Yes," reaching into his pocket he withdrew a small gaily wrapped box, "What I promised you."

She took the box greedily out of his hand, tearing open the paper with her small, thin fingers, she gasped at the bracelet, "This is most beautiful sir; you must be a rich man, a very rich man." He smiled at her remarks, "The girl you requested is waiting for you upstairs; you know where she is." She turned the bracelet so it hit the sunlight streaming in from the window, looking at the details in the gold. Each diamond was placed in the center of several rubies to give the appearance of a series of flowers. She felt quite pleased with the present.

Dante made his way to Jennifer's room, knocking, "Who is there?"

"Dante the man who was here earlier, little one." He said in a loud and clear voice in case anyone was listening. "I'm dying to touch your soft body and smell the sweetness of your skin; open the door, please."

Jennifer stifled a laugh from inside her bedroom as she opened the door, Dante faced her grinning from ear to ear, "Please come in," she said. He entered the room shutting the door behind him, "You didn't have to lay it on so thick, Dante."

He put a finger to his mouth, silencing her as he approached her so she could hear his whisper, "Answer whatever I say, do you understand?"

"But?"

He placed his finger tips to her mouth, as he whispered, "Someone is outside the door. How good of an actress are you?"

She shrugged her shoulders, shaking her head, "I don't know."

"Oh, but you are such a beautiful woman, such intriguing eyes, and your kiss, you have no idea what it does to me, you green-eyed vixen," Dante said loud enough for anyone outside the door to hear.

Jennifer purred in a sultry voice, "And you sir, are man enough for ten women."

"Ah, but I only want you in my bed, you vixen. You know how to please a man as you proved to me this morning."

Jennifer blushed, just yesterday another man told her the same thing, "Help me remove my dressing gown."

"What beautiful breasts. They were made for me, I'm sure of it."

She began breathing a little heavier, "Kiss me again, there, ooh."

Dante quickened his breathing, "I need you, woman. Look what you've done to me. Look at my trousers. Hurry," he gasped, "help me out of my restrictions; free me of my bondage, you vixen." He paused, taking her by the arm leading her to the bed, he moaned loudly, "That's it." He motioned for her to sit.

Jennifer sat on the bed, she moaned, somewhat like a little scream, "Take me now. You are driving me wild."

Dante pushed her down on the bed and lay beside her, whispering in her ear, "Bounce up and down on the bed so it squeaks; every once and awhile, moan. When I tell you, scream as if," he paused. "You know what I mean." He was slightly embarrassed talking to his good friend's wife in this manner, "I'll do the same."

The two of them sat on the bed, bouncing up and down, each moaning. This continued for some time until Dante gave Jenny the signal to scream with pleasure which he followed with his own moaning. He whispered to her, "I'm going to check the door." He rose from the bed, removed his shirt and walked to the wash basin, wetting his hair and chest with the water. He kicked off his boots and removed his socks, unbuttoned and unzipped his pants as he sauntered over to the door. He opened the door quickly to find a redhaired woman standing outside, it was the woman Jennifer wanted to take with her. Dante pulled her inside the room, "What the devil, have you been standing out there this past hour?" He slammed the door waiting for her to answer, "Well?"

Heather looked at this dark-haired man with the very dark eyes, who was supposed to be Jennifer's friend, yet it appeared he had his way with her, she shook her head, "No, but I did see Madame Ginger with that man, the one who brought Jennifer here."

"Were they saying anything?" questioned Jennifer.

"No, they," she paused, "did you lay with him?"

Jennifer shook her head, "No, it was, never mind. Did they say anything?"

Dante had put his socks and boots back on, zippered and buttoned his pants. He had put on his shirt and was buttoning it as Heather answered, "Yes, I did hear him tell Madame Ginger that he wanted you back. But she said it was out of the question."

Dante asked, "What did he say?"

Heather looked at him, "He said he'd give Madame two days to change her mind and if she didn't, he would force his way in there and take her."

Jennifer looked at Dante, "Does he know you?" Dante shook his head, "Did he ask Madam who was in here with me?"

"No, he did say," Heather hesitated, "He said it sounded like you've improved as a lover and that was why he wanted you back."

Dante mumbled under his breath, as Jennifer urgently said, "Dante, you've got to get us out of here."

He looked at Jenny, "Tomorrow night at nine o'clock. Hide the rope and the clothes. I'll come here," he turned to Heather, "Make sure you're here in this room and ready to go." Heather nodded her head as he continued, "Both Jordan and Gideon will be under the window to help with the escape. If you two get separated, you are to go to the docks and board the ship called the *Green-Eyed Lady*, can you remember that?" Both women shook their heads yes. "Good, once we are on the ship, we'll leave immediately. My only regret, Jenny, is that I have to leave you here another night. I'm truly sorry."

Jennifer smiled wanly, "I'll survive. I've survived this long."

Dante kissed her forehead, "Take care of yourself; be careful, and I'll see you tomorrow evening at nine."

He began to leave the room, "Dante, wait," she rose from her chair crossing the room, "Thank you."

He looked deeply into her green eyes, "I haven't done anything yet; thank me when we're safely out to sea." He turned and left the room.

Evening approaching rapidly, Rick Jordan and Gideon waited for Dante's return. Gideon paced around the room, partly from nerves and partly due to finding out about Tim's ship going down. Timothy Lockwood had been like a father to him. He was beginning to make Rick Jordan extremely nervous, "Gideon, will you please sit down. I'm anxious enough, and you're making me nervous which is not a good thing considering Dante will be here momentarily, and we are supposed to play poker with Marshall."

Dante entered the cabin shouting, "That bastard wants to buy her back from Madame Ginger."

Jordan's eyes widened, "How do you know?"

"Never mind about that, are you ready to go into the city for dinner? I can't wait to stick my sword through that animal. I might even do it before the card game."

"Dante, calm down. How can you possibly do it before when you don't even know what the bastard looks like?" Rick turned to Gideon, "Are you coming for dinner?"

"No sir. I'll make myself something and get to bed early."

"Fine. Dante, let's go," Jordan placed his sword in its sheath and stuck a small pistol into his pants. Rick felt that if Lyndon pulled a gun, he wanted to be prepared. The two men left the *Green-Eyed Lady* for the Royal Palace Hotel, where they would have dinner and then play cards with one Steven Marshall, alias Geoffrey Lyndon.

The poker game began promptly at seven o'clock. Marshall obviously was a gambler, a professional gambler, but tonight he didn't seem to have the luck needed to beat this Jordan man. Dante dropped out of the game early on, letting Rick play his best poker with a little help from marked cards. Lyndon was obviously at a loss as to the way the cards were falling in the game. When he suggested to Jordan that they change decks at about eleven, Rick agreed since only he and Marshall were left playing. The others had left the room except for Dante who sat quietly in the corner watching the game.

New cards were substituted for the original deck, yet Marshall still had no luck with the cards. At quarter to twelve he said, "That is it, Mr. Jordan. I'm cleaned out tonight."

Rick smiled, "Are you sure you wouldn't like to borrow some money? I'll give you a loan."

Marshall shook his head, "No, I've never borrowed money from another gambler."

Rick rose from his seat, "Let me buy you a drink then." Marshall shook his head; Rick said, "Why don't we go to my ship. I've got some Jamaican rum that will make you forget your losses."

Marshall was hesitant, "I don't know. It's late."

"Come on, the ship's not far from here."

"Alright, I guess one drink wouldn't hurt." Marshall rose from his seat, and the three men left the Royal Palace for the *Green-Eyed Lady*. Dante walked aimlessly behind, clenching and unclenching his fists in anticipation. Marshall was a damn fool that he trusted them in taking him to their ship. Once aboard the *Green-Eyed Lady*, the three men went to Rick's cabin. "This is a nice ship."

"Thanks," Rick handed him a glass of rum, raising his glass he said, "To a good and prosperous game next time, Mr. Lyndon."

Geoffrey choked, "How do you know my name?" Dante had already drawn his sword.

Rick Jordan, held a pistol in his hand, aimed at Lyndon, "That doesn't matter, you bastard."

"What have I done to you?" Geoffrey began to sweat.

Dante placed the tip of his sword against Geoffrey's throat, "It's not what you've done to us that angers us." Lyndon began to shake as Dante continued, "We are going to have revenge for the two people that are important to us. Do the names Timothy and Jennifer mean anything to you?"

Lyndon turned an ashen white, the color draining completely from his face. Rick Jordan laughed sadistically, "I see you're upset, and you should be, because before we kill you, we're going to torture you. I think that will be just punishment."

Dante grinned cruelly, "Let's take him to the hold, I can't wait to see him bleed."

"Please, I'll give you money, anything you want. Let me go. I beg of you have mercy," Geoffrey cried.

Dante screamed, "Let you go? Have mercy on you? You can't be serious; did you have mercy on Jennifer when you stole her not once, but twice?"

Rick said, "You are a piece of slime, Lyndon, the lowest of all life forms."

"Did you rape her?" screamed Dante. Geoffrey said nothing as Dante's rapier tore Geoffrey's shirt and the blood oozed from his arm, "Answer me or you'll be spilling more blood."

"Yes," cried Lyndon.

Rick jumped at him, twisting his arm behind his back, "You die tonight after we torture you."

Jordan and D'Mattea led him down to the hold, stripped him of his clothes so he stood naked before them chaining him like an animal to the wall. Dante took the whip from the wall and began to whip his back. Geoffrey screamed in agony, waking Gideon, who raced down to the hold.

Gideon entered the hold to find Rick and Dante whipping a man who was chained, "Who is he?"

"The man who is responsible for Jennifer," replied Rick.

Gideon's eyes opened wide, "Can I watch?"

"Sure," replied Rick.

Dante continued with the lashes, on the fifteenth one he stopped. Geoffrey was nearly unconscious, so Dante grabbed a bucket of water and threw it on him, bringing him back to reality, "Please," screamed Lyndon.

Jordan said, "Let's turn him around." He and Dante unchained him and then rechained him so his back was to the wall. Jordan began to laugh, "Well, well, look at this. Dante, we've got a real sick one on our hands." Dante's dark eyes followed Rick's pointing finger to Geoffrey's erection, "I see that a beating gets you excited." Geoffrey hung his head, "It really doesn't matter because you will never use it again. Gideon get him some water to drink, I want him fully awake when we castrate him."

Geoffrey's head snapped up, his eyes were wild with fear as Dante said, "It won't hurt, because you must be in considerable pain now from your back, so what's a little more. My only regret is that neither Jennifer nor Timothy will have the pleasure of watching you die." He began laughing uncontrollably, the madness of what he, Rick and Gideon were about to do hit him. They were all pirates, it was true, but they had never tortured anyone even before they joined Tim's stronghold. Were they sick with madness over what had happened to their friends? Or were the true natures of their personalities coming to the surface? Dante tried to reason with himself that the man deserved every-thing that was coming to him, but he still felt guilty as he was about to murder someone who couldn't defend himself.

Gideon returned with the water for Geoffrey to drink. Gideon held the glass as he drank. Dante had stopped laughing and was staring at Rick who was approaching Geoffrey with the sleek rapier. He held the rapier over the now limp member; he grinned, "You have no idea how much pleasure this one downward movement is going to bring me." Geoffrey fainted as Rick raised the sword. Dante's eyes opened wide, not wanting to believe what he was about to see, at the last second, he turned away; this revenge he could not watch. He heard the whoosh of air as the rapier came done. Geoffrey screamed as the rapier hit its mark, blood spurted out, hitting Rick's face and shirt. A steady stream of blood flowed smothy from the wound. Gideon shut his eyes when the sword struck Geoffrey. Dante turned around, the sight before him had sickened him, he retched everything he had eaten during the day. Rick stood mo-tionless for a few seconds, the sword still in his hand. "My God! Dante, what have I done?" Rick turned to stare at Dante who had broken into a cold sweat and now slumped against the wall. Gideon began to throw up.

Dante looked at his friend, his comrade. He swallowed hard, the taste of bile still in his mouth, "You've killed him and if he isn't dead yet; he will be soon." Dante, who had been kneeling while vomiting, strug-gled weakly to his feet. "I've got to get out of here, the stench and sight of him is killing me." He stumbled up the stairs gasping for fresh air. He had to get control of himself, he had to for sanity's sake. Once on deck, he strolled along the railing. Tomorrow couldn't come quick enough for him; he wanted to leave New Orleans, and the sooner the better. He tried to think of Sirena, thanking God that he didn't allow her to come with him. He heard a loud splash and then footsteps approaching him, he turned to see Rick in the moonlight. His shirt covered in blood. Dan-te paled.

"What's wrong D'Mattea?" Rick asked as if it was a normal day.

Dante stared at him in disbelief, tears came to his eyes, he blinked them back, "What's wrong Jordan? How can you have asked me something like that?"

"You act like you've never killed anyone before," replied Rick.

"Not like that. I've only killed in self-defense, when my own neck was on the line. But tonight, that was sick, we didn't even let him fight. The whipping was bad enough, but after…" Dante's voice trailed off.

Rick grabbed his friend, "Don't fall apart on me, Dante."

"I'm not falling apart, Jordan. It's just that I can't believe what we've done. How cruel we've become. How angry we were to do something like that. And for what?" He paused long enough to catch his breath, "A woman neither of us will ever have because she is bound to one man." Dante began to laugh, "Timothy Lockwood would have enjoyed tonight, I'm sure. I know Captain Timothy 'Bloodthirsty' Lockwood has been involved in similar escapades. I have heard the stories as I'm sure you have as well."

Rick Jordan slapped him across the face, "Get a hold of yourself, Dante. You stay like this, and you won't be any help for Jennifer."

"Jennifer, that lady has the guts to go through with the scheme herself if we don't show up. We've done all of this for Jennifer, and I ask you why?" Dante continued to rattle on, "It's not because of Timothy you know. She's a beautiful woman, a desirable woman. I've seen the way you've looked at her when you've thought no one was looking. It's the same way I do; we are lusting after another man's wife." Rick Jordan was speechless as Dante continued, "Do you realize that this whole thing has been a game?"

Rick stared at his friend, "A game?"

Dante began heading back to the main cabin, with Jordan at his heels, "That's right a game. It was a race to see who could find her first." He stopped short and turned to Jordan, "And I won. But what's the prize? It's not Jennifer, because the only man she wants is Timothy."

"What about Sirena?"

"What does she have to with this?" questioned Dante.

"I thought you loved her."

"I do." He continued on to the cabin, leaving the door open for Jordan. He poured two glasses of rum, handing one to Jordan.

"Then why do you want Jennifer?"

Dante smiled, "Don't you? No, don't answer that, of course you do; otherwise, you wouldn't be here to rescue her. Jennifer is a beautiful woman, a sensual woman; she would have to be in order to make Tim love her the way he does. I love her, Jordan, but not in the same way I love Sirena. I love Jennifer as a friend, and I won't be a hypocrite by saying that I don't desire her, because I do. I want to know what it's like to love her, to feel her body pressed close to mine, but I would never want anything more from her. Jennifer is the type of woman that is your mistress and Sirena you marry."

"I'd like the same thing, I'll admit it. Timothy Lockwood is a lucky man, but she belongs to him even if he's dead; she'll belong to him in spirit," replied Rick.

"What if he's dead? What happens to the stronghold?" asked Dante.

"That little lady we're going to rescue tomorrow night will probably take it over and have all of her employees falling at her feet."

"What did you do with Lyndon's body?" queried Dante.

"Threw him overboard," replied Jordan with no emotion.

"Was he dead?" questioned Dante.

"Yes."

"Are you sure?"

Rick looked at his friend, "If he wasn't, he will be when he drowns."

Dante paled again, putting down his glass, he said, "I'm going to try to get some sleep. It must be daylight already and we've got an important mission tonight."

"Good idea; let's get some rest."

Dante left the cabin for his own. Who was he kidding? Sleep wouldn't come easy at all. Not now, not after last night. He reached his cabin and lay on the bunk fully clothed. As he suspected, sleep did not come easy. He tossed and turned endlessly on his bunk; every time he closed his eyes, he saw Rick raising the rapier. It would be a long time before he got over the trauma. Several hours later, Dante rose and washed his face, changed his clothes and went topside. It was close to seven o'clock in the evening, and he was nervous. He paced around the deck like a cat, stopping every once in a while, to gaze out into the city of New Orleans. His jitters were getting the best of him as he walked to Rick's cabin, entering without knocking. Jordan was still asleep; it appeared that nothing bothered him. Dante shook him, "Jordan, get up; it's quarter to eight."

Rick rubbed his eyes, "What?"

"Get up, it's quarter to eight. We've got to get Gideon and go to Madame Gingers."

Jordan sat up, "Right." He ran his hand through his hair, "Let me wash my face, and you get Gideon. Meet me back here."

Dante left Jordan and went to find Gideon. Gideon was in the galley stocking shelves. "Gideon, where did this come from?" Dante asked, pointing to the crates of food.

"I went into the city this afternoon and purchased it for our voyage," responded Gideon.

"Good thinking. It's almost eight o'clock; we've got to get Jordan and go into the city for Jennifer."

"I can leave these here and take care of it later. I'm ready." Gideon followed Dante to Jordan's cabin.

Rick met them at the door, "Okay, D'Mattea, what's our plan?"

Dante shut the door, "This is it. Jennifer and the other woman will be dressed as men. Rick will stand outside the window, and Gideon, you will stand at the top of the alley to make sure no one sees us." Dante paused, "Then, at nine-thirty Jennifer and her friend will shimmy down the rope. Then," he pointed at Jordan, "you walk with them until you reach the ship."

Rick asked, "Where will you be during this time?"

"I'll be in Jennifer's room. At ten o'clock, I'll go downstairs, pay Madame Ginger and head straight for the *Green-Eyed Lady;* when I get to the ship, we will leave."

"Fine, let's go," said Rick.

The streets of New Orleans were busy during the evening hours, especially those streets near Madame Ginger's establishment. The three men reached Madame Ginger's at quarter to nine. Gideon and Rick continued walking past the building. Gideon paused at the corner, and Rick turned down the alley. He looked around; windows lined this side of the building. D'Mattea never told which window except that it was on the second floor. He sighed; the only thing he could do would be to wait until a rope dropped from one of the windows.

Dante made his way into Madame Ginger's; men filled the establishment tonight. Madame Ginger saw him, "Well, I guess you are here for Jennifer."

He smiled, "Busy tonight."

"Yes, we are quite busy. Jennifer's upstairs waiting," replied Madame Ginger.

Dante winked, "Thanks." He walked through the crowd and up the stairs to Jennifer's room. He knocked.

"Who is it?" asked Jennifer, though she knew it would most probably be Dante.

"It is me, Jennifer, Dante, the gentleman who was here to see you yesterday."

She opened the door, "Come in."

Dante entered, noticing the other girl wasn't in the room, "Where's your friend?"

"She'll be here."

He looked Jennifer over, the clothes he had bought her, fit her snuggly, showing too many curves, "Those clothes will never do."

"Well, I'm not going to shimmy down a rope in a gown."

"No, I guess you can't. But everyone will know that you're a woman."

"Then Rick Jordan will give me his cloak."

"It'll never do. It would be dragging on the ground."

"Then I'll have to take my chances dressed like…" she was interrupted by a knock. "Who's there?"

"Heather." Jennifer opened the door, "I thought for sure I was going to get caught."

"Are you ready?"

Heather replied, "As ready as I'll ever be."

"The two of you sit down and listen," said Dante. Jennifer and Heather sat side by side on the bed. "The two of you are going to shimmy down the rope. When you get to the bottom you're going to leave with Rick and Gideon for the *Green-Eyed Lady*. I'll wait a half an hour and then leave. This will give you plenty of time to escape."

"When are we leaving?" asked Jennifer.

"In just a few minutes, where is the rope?"

Jennifer went to the closet, got the rope and handed it to Dante. He unraveled it and tied one end to the bed and other out the window. "Heather, I'll go first, then you follow." Heather nodded her head.

Dante looked out the window to see Jordan standing at the foot of the rope. "Jenny, are you ready?" She shook her head yes, "Then let's go." He helped her climb out the window. Jennifer clung to the rope inching her way steadily down.

When she reached the bottom, she threw her arms around Rick Jordan for a few seconds then released him to watch Heather make her way down the rope. Dante stood in the window trying to keep the rope still. After several minutes, Heather reached the ground. Dante watched Heather, Jennifer and Rick join Gideon and begin to make their way to the *Green-Eyed Lady*. Going to the bed, he untied the rope and let it drop to the ground. He then mussed up Jennifer's bed and sat down to wait. After a half-hour he made his way downstairs, paid Madame Ginger and left. Once outside Madame Ginger's, he took a deep breath and walked briskly in the direction of the harbor. After a few minutes, he heard some yelling, which told him that Jennifer's room had been found empty, and now they were looking for him. He continued to walk unnerved, because the least variation in his walk would draw attention to him. As he hit the waterfront, he broke into a run for the *Green-Eyed Lady*. Reaching the ship, Jordan was standing on the deck waiting for him. The two of them pulled up the plank and then helped Gideon with the anchor. They could see some men running towards the docks. The *Green-Eyed Lady*, manned by her pirate crew, raised her sails and slowly backed out of the port of New Orleans on their way home to Newport.

CHAPTER THIRTY-TWO

Sweat poured from the two muscular bodies as they unloaded the black pirate ship. Timothy Lockwood and Mark Gregory had never been more humiliated in their lives as they were now. The *Moonlight,* carrying an empty hold, was attacked by Torreya, the most feared Caribbean pirate. Taken-off guard was humiliating in and of itself, but when the *Moonlight* sunk with relatively little fight, it was embarrassing.

Torreya was a dark man, thin and tall. He was known mostly for his slave trade and his capture of innocent people; both Timothy and Mark would have given their lives for his capture. The slave trade in the Caribbean would virtually be at a standstill if Torreya had been out of the way courtesy of Tim and Mark, but instead, they were the captives. Their only hope now was if the stronghold attacked Tortuga, but the prospect of that happening was virtually impossible. Torreya kept a watchful eye over both Timothy and Mark, knowing full well whose ship he had brought down and who his most prized prisoners and slaves actually were, and he couldn't believe his good fortune. Another reason he kept a good watch over them is that he didn't trust the two men because together they could easily overtake a ship and pull out of port and Torreya could not have that happen. He had plans for the two Barbary Captains, his full intention was to put them to work on his ship the *Raven*. With Lockwood's knowledge of the water, the *Raven* could easily sneak into any port in the world at any given time unnoticed.

Mark and Timothy had plans for Torreya; they knew he would probably try to use them to get into ports not usually accessible to him, and they would help him get into the ports he wanted. After several times, Torreya would trust them, and they would lead him straight into an enemy port, one that the stronghold would be in, and then they would gain their freedom. Timothy and Mark had finished for the day and were taken by guards to their residence aboard the ship. The two guards posted themselves outside the door. Timothy paced around the room like a nervous caged lion. Since his capture, he spent a great deal of time thinking, "Mark, when do you think Torreya will make his visit?"

"We've been here for three weeks now," he paused, "and we've done everything we were told to do plus a little extra. I'd say that he'll come to us any day now," replied Mark.

The door opened and in walked Torreya's servant, Sebastian, who was an approximately six-foot seven giant man. "Torreya has requested your presence at his home. You are to come with me." The two men followed him off the ship to a waiting carriage where the three of them sat together on a bumpy ride to Torreya's home. The house was a large white Spanish-style home.

Torreya met them at the door, "I'm glad you could come, gentleman." Timothy thought quietly to himself that they had no choice. Torreya directed his comments to Mark, "So we meet again, Captain Gregory." Timothy looked at Mark in surprise, he had never mentioned knowing Torreya. "This time it is under my terms."

"That's true, Torreya," replied Mark flatly.

Torreya threw back his head and laughed loudly in an attempt to get a reaction from either of the men, yet neither moved. Torreya looked at Mark, "But it's not you I'm interested in, it's your young friend, here. It seems I've captured the most feared Barbary pirate since you were operating steadily. A lucky break for me!"

Timothy's golden eyes were smoldering in anger, "Get to the point, Torreya, what do you want from me?"

"I want your services as a navigator. I understand that you are the best in the world with Mr. Gregory a close second," replied Torreya.

Timothy couldn't resist, "And we know that you couldn't navigate yourself out of your own home." Sebastian, who had been standing against the wall, began to approach Timothy, who was not afraid of the giant.

"Sebastian, don't touch him," he turned his attention to Timothy, "That's true, Captain Bloodthirsty, may I call you Tim?"

Tim raised one eyebrow, staring at him in disbelief, "No, you may call me Captain Bloodthirsty."

Torreya sat down behind his desk, "Whatever you wish." Turning his attention to Sebastian he said, "Get me some brandy and rum for our two guests. When you finish, check to see if dinner is ready."

Mark said, "When do you want us to start working for you?"

Torreya smiled, "I didn't think you would agree so quickly."

Timothy interjected, "Navigating a ship is better than taking crates off of one."

"True, Captain Bloodthirsty. I can see where something like that would seem menial to you." Neither Timothy or Mark spoke as Torreya continued, "Well then, we ship out tomorrow morning."

"What is our destination?" asked Timothy.

"New Providence," replied Torreya.

"New Providence is a neutral port and a very easy one to get into," said Mark.

Torreya smiled slyly, "We will not be entering New Providence through its regular port, we will be entering at the other side of the island." Timothy ran his hand through his hair. New Providence, what luck! Perhaps Jack Webster and Devlin Jones ships would be in New Providence or the surrounding area. If the *Raven* was spotted, both ships would attack and if they weren't in port then some other plan must be made. Torreya said, "Captain Bloodthirsty, what are you thinking?"

Tim looked him straight in the eyes, "I'm thinking that where you wish to land your ship is an area which is very heavy in coral. But if we navigate the area correctly, we should not have a problem."

"Then you think you could get me into New Providence and my men could circulate in the city without anyone knowing we are there?"

"Yes, it won't be a problem," Tim paused, "I know the perfect cove in which to hide the ship."

Torreya was excited, "Excellent!"

Sebastian entered the room, "Dinner is ready, sir." All three pirates followed Sebastian into the elaborate dining room.

"Ah, Concetta, I'm glad you could join us for dinner. I'd like you to meet my guests."

"Torreya, you mean your prisoners?" she replied.

"Now, now Concetta, haven't I treated you well? I'd like for you to meet Captain Timothy Bloodthirsty and Captain Mark Gregory." Timothy noted the fact that she, too, must be a prisoner.

The young, dark-haired woman stared at them; the younger man was extremely handsome, "How do you do, gentleman?" Both nodded to her waiting for her to take a seat so they could sit.

Later that evening, Mark and Timothy paced around the hut that had become their home on Torreya's property. Mark whispered, "Do you think Webster and Jones will be in the area?"

Timothy looked at Mark, "It's possible, very possible, as is the possibility of the Brentwood Brothers being in the area."

Mark frowned, "But they would never know we were on the *Raven.*"

"That doesn't make a difference. They know if they see the *Raven* they are to attack." Timothy paused, "Mark, we can't depend on them; we've got to try to escape in New Providence."

Mark shook his head, "You know damn well that Torreya will have Sebastian watching us like a hawk."

"That's good. While he's watching us, we'll watch him. At some point we will catch him off guard," replied Timothy.

"Then what? Do you honestly think we'll get off that ship?" questioned Mark.

Timothy smiled, "Of course we can. When was the last time you went for a swim?"

"A swim?" Mark looked at him in amazement.

Timothy shook his head, "Yes, a swim. We'll go over the side and swim to shore."

"Here we are making plans, and we don't even know if we'll get away with it."

"We will." Timothy replied; he was positive. Sebastian could be handled easily. In fact, Torreya himself said that his crew would be going into the city, and that was when he and Mark would attempt their escape.

The following morning, Timothy and Mark were led to the *Raven* being met by Torreya himself who was standing on deck, "Good Morning."

Timothy nodded as did Mark who said, "Where will our cabin be?"

Sebastian came forward, "You will be bunking with me."

Timothy raised one eyebrow, "I see."

"Come gentleman, I'll show you where you will be working." Torreya led the two of them into the navigation room.

Timothy looked around, amazed. No wonder Torreya had problems navigating, his maps were either incomplete or crude drawings with little markings. His golden eyes stared into Torreya's black ones, "These maps are not the best, but they will do."

Torreya stared back at Timothy, "Please feel free to make your own maps."

Mark looked at him, "Torreya, when we get to New Providence, how long will your men be staying ashore?"

"Until they collect enough people to be used as slaves."

"I see," replied Mark.

"Well gentlemen, I'll leave you to your work. Sebastian will be outside the door." Torreya left them in the navigation room.

Timothy and Mark looked at one another. Mark's eyes scanned the room, "Do you think he wants us to navigate the entire trip?"

Timothy shrugged, "We've got nothing better to do with our time."

"Tim, navigating from Tortuga to just outside of New Providence will take us five minutes."

Timothy grinned, "I know, but we'll only plot our course in sections and give them only a day's navigation to work with at a time."

Mark wanted to laugh because Torreya had no idea how navigation worked, nor would he know that it didn't take them days to do this navigation. "Let's get to work." The two men worked side by side plotting the course for the ship to travel. The minutes turned into hours as they plotted the three weeks of travel on separate pieces of paper. Then they took a larger sheet of paper to plot the entire course up to the area surrounding New Providence.

Timothy looked up from his work, "Mark, in this area," he pointed to the map he was drawing, "we should be able to get this tub of a ship into this cove. What do you think?"

"Isn't that cove visible from these two areas?" Mark asked as he pointed to the map.

Timothy grinned, "Exactly right, and if we get this ship into this cove one of our ships, either the *Delta Blood*, *The Devil's Lady*, *Sea Bird*, or *Caribbean Lady* are in the area, they will be able to spot the *Raven* from either area," Timothy said as he pointed to the two areas. "Once the *Raven* is spotted, they will attack, and the *Raven* will have nowhere to go. She will be trapped."

Mark replied, "And if any other ship such as a privateer spots her, she will be attacked. Everyone wants Torreya."

Their discussion was interrupted by Sebastian, who entered the cabin with a tray of food, "Torreya has sent you lunch. You will be taking your meals here unless Torreya requests differently." Timothy covered his maps and rose from the drawing table to join Mark at the makeshift dinner table. Sebastian watched them quietly for a few minutes before leaving the cabin.

Timothy played with his food while Mark ate hungrily. Every once in a while, he would take a mouthful. His mind was elsewhere. Mark looked at him, "Tim, what's the matter?"

He looked up from his plate, "Tomorrow, Jennifer and I would have been married one year." Tim ran his hand through his hair nervously.

Mark continued to eat, "One year already."

Tim's face was expressionless, "I've lost her, Mark; in my fit of rage, I lost her."

Mark looked across the table at Timothy, "She's probably home already."

Timothy shook his head, "No, I've lost her; she would have contacted me. I've hurt her so many damn times that I know that it was the last time. She's gone forever."

Mark rolled his eyes, "I forgot that you can be dramatic from time to time. I don't think so; she's probably worried to death over your disappearance. Tim, you can't worry about her, not now. We've got to worry about ourselves and how we're going to get out of this mess."

"I know," Tim replied solemnly.

"So, eat, the food is good, and you've got to eat."

Timothy looked at his dish, frowned and began to eat. Mark was right; there wasn't any time to worry about Jennifer, but he couldn't keep his mind off of her. She filled his dreams and his thoughts. He wished he could smell the freshness of her hair and touch the softness of her skin. Deep down, Timothy knew that he was one that was solely responsible for the two of them being captured. His mind was constantly on Jennifer and that made him lower his guard and not pay attention, which resulted in their capture and the sinking of the *Moonlight*.

One week had passed, and Torreya never once came by to see how work was progressing. Sebastian carried all of his messages to Timothy and Mark and watched over them. In turn, Timothy and Mark watched Sebastian; they learned his every move. They watched his movements, so they would know when they could take him off guard. Timothy had put Jennifer in the back of his mind. He couldn't think about her because it upset him, and he did not work well when he was upset. Instead, he thought of the *Moonlight* going down without a fight. He and Mark were two of the most feared Barbary pirates and their ship went down with no fight at all. The more he thought of it, the angrier he got. He lost some of his best men when the *Moonlight* sunk at Torreya's hands. He vowed to himself that if he and Mark got out of this predicament alive, he'd have the stronghold attack Tortuga and bring Torreya alive, so he would have the pleasure of killing him. White slavery would become nonexistent in the Caribbean with Torreya dead. The only problem would be in the Barbary States, which was much too large an area to stop white slavery altogether, but he could put a tight rein on the area.

Mark worked steadily on a map of New Providence; he plotted the rivers, valleys, and hills. If he and Timothy jumped ship, they would have to know the area for a perfect escape, and once they did escape, they would have to hide in the wilderness. Neither of them had any money or valuables since both went down with the *Moonlight* and Torreya took whatever remained. They would have to wait on land until a search for them had been conducted.

The *Raven* arrived in New Providence late in the evening while both Timothy and Mark were asleep. They were awakened by a large crash, which jolted them out of their bunks and onto the floor. Timothy rubbed his eyes, "Damn, we've hit either a sandbar or coral and I'd go with the coral from the sound of the crash."

Mark searched around the dark room for the candle, "Do you think we're close to shore or still out?"

"If we hit coral, we're close to shore, probably too close. No wonder Torreya has trouble with navigation. No one on this damn ship can read an easy map."

Mark lit the candle as Sebastian entered the room with Torreya, "Wake up gentlemen, we've got a problem. It seems we have hit..."

Before Torreya could finish his statement, Timothy said, "Coral, because your crew cannot read a simple map."

Mark continued, "If we were so close to the island, why didn't someone wake us if they couldn't read the map?" He stared at Torreya.

"Your maps must be wrong," said Torreya sternly.

Timothy's golden eyes flickered dangerously, "Our maps are not wrong. Your men cannot read. I suggest if you can move this tub of a ship out of this coral reef, that you dock it in the cove before we sink."

"That is what you are here for, Captain Bloodthirsty. I want you to get us out of this mess."

Timothy threw on his shirt, wondering how Torreya with his simpleminded crew could have lasted in the Caribbean as long as they had without being captured. "Let's go." He followed Sebastian. When they reached the wheel of the ship, Timothy began to bark orders at the men who refused to listen to him. He looked at Torreya, "Tell your men to do what I say, or this ship will sink."

Torreya spoke in Spanish to several of the men, ordering them to follow Timothy's directions. Timothy maneuvered the ship carefully out of the coral reef and into the cove. Once inside the cove, he ordered the men to drop anchor. Torreya was satisfied with Timothy's skills, "Captain Bloodthirsty, you are indeed an asset to my crew." Timothy said nothing. "Sebastian, bring him back to his cabin."

The giant led the way to Timothy's cabin where Mark had been waiting for nearly an hour. Timothy entered the room, "We're in the cove."

"How much damage do you think was done to the ship?" questioned Mark.

"Hard to tell." The golden eyes were tired, "What I can't believe is the fact that Torreya and his crew have never been captured."

Mark looked towards the door, "Sebastian still outside the door?"

Timothy nodded, "I'm sure he will be for a long time. Did you finish those terrain maps you were working on?"

"Yes, I've hidden them in a piece of oilskin, if they get wet nothing will happen to them."

"Good. I've been saving bread and some dried meat, but we'll have to depend on fish or small animals if we're hiding for more than two days."

Mark nodded, "We certainly will need luck if we jump this ship, and you can be sure they'll look for us."

Timothy turned to face Mark, "Sebastian carries both a sword and a pistol. If we knock him unconscious, we'll take his weapons." Timothy walked to his bunk, sat down and sighed, "I've got to get some rest. I would suggest you do the same."

Several hours later, Sebastian and Torreya entered the cabin where Timothy and Mark were working on reproducing maps. Torreya's cold eyes showed little emotion as he spoke, "Captain Bloodthirsty, you did an excellent job, earlier. I must commend you on your expertise."

Timothy rose from the desk he was sitting at, "What are your plans, Torreya?"

Torreya laughed, "Come, Captain, you must be more specific. Do you mean my plans for the two of you or my plans for the future? Or perhaps you mean my plans for the present."

Mark lost his patience, "You know damn well what Tim's talking about, Torreya."

Torreya gazed at Mark Gregory for a second before turning to Sebastian, "This evening, see that the two of them are kept quiet." He turned, leaving the cabin.

Tim turned to Sebastian, "Why do you have to watch us closely tonight? What is Torreya planning?" Sebastian stared at him blankly, turned and left the room. Timothy looked at Mark, "What do you think?"

Mark smiled, "I think Torreya and his men are going into the city tonight, and Sebastian is being left to watch over us."

Timothy grinned, "Exactly what I thought. How well have you looked at this ship?"

"Hardly at all. Most of the time Torreya has called for me at night when I could hardly see, but if there are only three people on board," he paused, "We're home free once we take care of Sebastian."

"Sebastian is going to be a problem, considering we don't have any weapons."

"I've been thinking about that Tim, and I think we'll have to use brute strength. Of course, it must be your strength." He looked at Tim sadly, "I'm in my fifties now, Tim; I'm getting old, and you're young and strong."

"Mark, I've seen you fight with the best of them."

"That was over ten years ago, Tim. I've never told anyone this, but since you left my crew, we've been docile. We've been living off of smaller booties and money we've had for years."

Timothy shook his head no, "I don't understand Mark, a little over six months ago when the *Rogue* was under attack, I was the one who was off guard and vulnerable; you fought like the old days."

Mark closed his eyes for a moment. How could he tell Timothy Lockwood that he was not the person he was years ago because of an injury similar to Timothy's, "You thought I fought like the old days because I wasn't injured. But that was because my crew protected me. Tim, right after you left my crew, I sustained two injuries, one of which was similar to yours and the other injury severed some of the nerves in my hand and arm. I can hardly hold a sword."

"Mark, I'm sorry."

"There's nothing to be sorry about; I've lived a full life. I'm an old man Tim; in order for our plans to work, it's going to be up to you."

Timothy's golden eyes darkened, "Do you have a suggestion?"

Mark frowned, "What if we make your bed look like you're asleep, and you can hit him over the head, knock him out."

Timothy began to laugh, "And Mark what do you suggest I knock him out with? My fist?"

"No," Mark looked around the room spying a loose floor board. He walked over to it, bending down to see if he could pry it from the floor, "Here, Tim, help me."

Timothy walked to where Mark stood. The two men worked together in order to pry the floorboard loose. Finally, it came loose with a crack of the wood. Timothy smiled, "This piece of wood will make a fine weapon."

"Ideal. Now we've got to cover this hole so Sebastian doesn't see it."

Timothy looked around the room, "Let's take that rug and put it over the hole." He reached for the rug, pulling it so it covered the hole left by the floorboard. He looked at Mark, "Perfect."

"Tonight, we strike," said Mark.

"Tonight," answered Timothy, his topaz eyes twinkling. Tonight, they would make their escape from the *Raven*. Torreya would be surprised to find his giant unconscious and tied up in the cabin formerly occupied by his prisoners.

CHAPTER THIRTY-THREE

Torreya stood at the railing of the *Raven* watching the sun set in brilliant patterns of reds and purples. Within the hour, he and his crew would be leaving the ship for the city. Sebastian would be staying behind to watch the prisoners. Timothy and Mark paced around their cabin, every once in awhile, they would stop and look out of the porthole. Timothy knew that Torreya wouldn't leave the ship until the sun had set completely. He figured that would be in about an hour, and at that time, Sebastian would bring them dinner, and they would strike.

Sebastian was summoned to Torreya's cabin, "Sebastian, we will be leaving within the next few minutes. Please make sure the prisoners are kept quiet and are well fed."

"Yes, sir. How long will you be gone?" questioned Sebastian.

"Just tonight. All of our expeditions will be at night. It is much safer that way; besides, we can use the daylight to repair the ship."

"I will take good care of the prisoners."

Torreya stared at him, "I have no doubts in you Sebastian. Now," he rose from his seat, "I must join the crew for our expedition."

Sebastian followed his Captain out to the row boats and watched the crew and Torreya leave. He stood watching them for approximately fifteen minutes before going to check on the prisoners.

Timothy had been squatting in the corner of the room with his wooden weapon. His legs were beginning to tire; he started to get to his feet to stretch his legs when he and Mark heard a key rattle in the door. Timothy looked at Mark; putting a finger to his lips, he rose quickly with the board in his hands.

The door opened, and Sebastian strode into the room. Timothy raised the plank of wood and crashed it over the giant's head who stumbled and fell. Mark took his sword and pistol. He put the pistol in his pants and handed the rapier to Timothy. Then, Mark began tying the giant with the sheets they had shredded earlier in the day to use for rope. Timothy walked to the open door; the warm breeze hit his face. He could smell the sea air; he looked around the deck; it was deserted.

Timothy ran back to the cabin; "Mark, the giant is the only man on the ship."

"Good," replied Mark.

"Do you think Torreya has any of our things on board?" questioned Timothy.

Mark stared at Timothy, "I know what you are thinking. You want to see if your sword is on board."

"Right." Timothy answered, "I want that sword, Mark. I had always planned to give it to my first born, and it will belong to Lion someday."

"We'll search his cabin. Come on, let's go." The two men left Sebastian on the floor of their cabin, tied up. Once inside Torreya's cabin, they made a complete search. Timothy found his ivory handled sword in the corner of the room still in its sheath. He put it on his belt.

Mark was busy forcing open a desk drawer. "Damn."

"What's wrong?" Asked Timothy, crossing the room.

"Torreya must have money in this drawer." He looked up at Tim, "If I can get it open, we certainly can use the money."

Timothy knelt beside Mark and two of them worked on the drawer, finally forcing it open. Inside were loose gems, pieces of jewelry and money. Timothy grabbed a handful of the gems and began to load his pockets. Mark followed his actions. Next, they put the coins in pouches, which were in the drawer and tied them to their belts. Timothy rose, "That's enough. I think we have enough to buy us passage to Newport."

Mark laughed, "More than enough. Torreya will certainly be surprised.

Timothy grinned, "He sure will. Let's go before they return."

They made their way to the decks to find that not a single row boat was left. Timothy ran his hand through his hair. Mark said, "Well, what now?"

Timothy thought for a few moments; as much as he hated swimming in the darkness, especially in an area which was heavily infested with sharks and coral, they had no choice. "We make a swim for it."

Mark looked at Timothy, "I'm game, Tim, if something should happen, promise me, you'll continue."

Timothy stared at Mark; he knew his friend was talking about the sharks. "Only if you promise the same," he paused, "And Mark, if anything should happen to me, promise me you'll see to my children and Jennifer."

Mark nodded, "I promise."

Timothy looked Mark in the eyes, "You ready?"

Mark shrugged, "As ready as I'll ever be."

Timothy tied a rope to the railing of the ship and dropped it overboard; hearing it splash in the water, he climbed over the railing and shimmied down the rope, hitting the cool water. Mark followed him down the rope, and the two men began swimming. Timothy's strokes were long and forceful; Mark's strokes were short and choppy as he struggled with his bad arm. Timothy was approximately one hundred and fifty yards ahead of Mark when Mark called out to him, "Tim, sharks!"

Timothy turned around and began swimming towards Mark who was being surrounded by sharks. Timothy yelled across the water, "Don't move, Mark. I'm coming."

"No," Mark yelled in a barely audible voice, "Go on, you have a wife and children to think of…" suddenly, Mark screamed, and Timothy knew instantly that a shark had attacked.

Tears filled Timothy's eyes as the screams filled the night air. He had been treading water when he looked back towards shore, another seventy or eighty yards. Mark was screaming in the distance, and Timothy couldn't bear it any longer; there was nothing he could do for him. He began to swim quickly with what little energy he had left. His ears were filled with the screams of a close friend, a man who had become a father to him. He reached water where he could stand, he stumbled into shore, his clothes and hair plastered to him. He could taste the salt water on his lips, when mixed with the salt of his tears. Timothy sat on the sand, staring out into the sea. Mark had died because of Torreya, and now Torreya would pay. Timothy was furious; he would bring Torreya down with the help of the stronghold. He would destroy the man who had murdered his friend and the only father figure in his life.

Timothy stood up weakly and looked around. He didn't know the island as well as Mark, and Mark had the map of the island. He sighed; he needed a place to spend the night. He looked around and began to walk slowly in the direction of the thick forest. Timothy had been walking for about an hour when he came across a small cave. His clothes were still damp, and it was getting cold. He had stolen a knife from Torreya's cabin; he held it in his hand staring at it before he began to cut some of the nearby brush. He found some bananas and coconuts, which he put in the mouth of the cave for later. Then, he began dragging the brush to the mouth of the cave in order to conceal it from any intruders. Next, he back tracked and began wiping out his footprints. He would be safe for the next few hours. Timothy stripped down until he was naked and laid his clothes around the cave so that they would dry. He looked around and settled on leaning against a wall facing the entrance as he closed his eyes. His thoughts were of Mark, his children and Jennifer. He finally dozed off.

While Torreya and his men rowed the boats back to the *Raven* in the wee morning hours, Torreya noticed several sharks in the area, which was concerning to him, and he reminded everyone to be cautious. When they neared the *Raven*, he saw the rope hanging over the railing of the ship. He instantly knew something had happened; Gregory and Bloodthirsty had tried an escape. Torreya glanced around the water at the sharks; from the number of sharks in the water, he assumed they didn't get far and perished by being shark bait. Once aboard the ship, he and several of his men went directly to the prisoners' cabin. Sebastian was still unconscious and tied, "Wake him up and take him to my cabin." Torreya stormed off in the direction of his cabin, leaving several of his men to the giant. When he opened his cabin door, he found the room in shambles. His eyes instantly went to the desk. The drawer had been forced open. He crossed the room to look in the drawer; he sucked in his breath. Most of the loose gems were gone as were every coin. He slammed the drawer closed and poured himself a glass of rum. All of the gems and coins now sat in the stomachs of sharks. Torreya threw his glass across the cabin, and it shattered in millions of pieces when it hit the wall and fell to the ground. Sebastian had some explaining to do. He poured himself another glass of rum while he waited. Several of the men brought Sebastian into Torreya's cabin. "Here he is, Captain."

Torreya stared at him coolly, "Well, how did you allow this to happen?"

The giant hung his head, "I don't know, sir."

"You don't know?" Torreya screamed as he put his glass down. He turned to the other members of his crew. "Take him, and follow me," Torreya led the way to the railing of the ship where the sharks were still milling around. "Throw him overboard; he's of no use to me." He stated angrily.

Sebastian looked at the sharks, his eyes wild with fear, "Please, sir," he began to beg.

"Throw him overboard, now."

Four men grasped the giant's arms and legs and hurled him overboard. A large splash was heard as Torreya stood close to the edge of the railing to watch the sharks attack Sebastian, who was screaming the moment he hit the water. Torreya turned to his other men, "Take note, gentlemen." None of the men said a word as Torreya walked off in the direction of his cabin.

Timothy woke in the early morning; he rubbed his eyes as he rose to his feet going over to his clothing which had dried. He put his clothes back on which felt stiff, and he knew they would loosen after a period of time. Taking out the knife he began cutting a hole in the coconut; succeeding, he drank the milk before splitting the coconut in half to eat its meat. He reached for a banana and proceeded to eat it. He thought of what he could do; he knew he must move on as that much was clear, but how much further was the city? He removed the pouch from his belt, emptying the coins into the sand and began to count them. He had one hundred and fifty gold coins which would be enough to get him some new clothes, a room at a hotel, a bath and hot meal and possibly passage to New York or Newport. He felt his pockets, the gems were still there. He would sell the gems in New Providence before he left the island. Timothy made his way out of the cave; the sun was hot for so early in the morning. It was important that he reach the city within the next few hours, or he would bake in the sun without a hat. He began to walk; he didn't even know if he was traveling in the right direction. He was exhausted after walking for an hour and half in the hot broiling sun; he wanted to stop, but he knew that would be disastrous. The only thing that kept him moving was his thoughts of Jennifer and the children. Timothy was beginning to get thirsty; his mouth was dry. Looking around for another coconut tree, he found one. He climbed the tree and cut down a couple of coconuts; cutting into them, he drank the milk. Suddenly he saw smoke in the distance, perhaps from the city. He continued to walk, the sweat trickling down his neck and face. Timothy stopped to remove his shirt, which was soaked with perspiration. He tied the shirt to his belt. The sun was getting hotter, and he could feel the skin on his back burning. It had to be after twelve o'clock; he stopped to draw a sundial in the sand. It was one thirty; how long had he been walking? It seemed like days, but it was only a matter of hours. He put his shirt on again and continued walking. Two hours later, he reached the outskirts of the city; in a little while, he would be able to rest. He was too tired to run, but the speed of his walking increased. He reached the city in a matter of minutes; it was a busy city; people filled the streets, and no one seemed to notice him, or if they did, they were not paying any attention to him. He walked into a store and purchased himself some clothes which cost him thirty gold coins. The *Rosewood Inn* appeared to be a nice hotel from the outside. He entered the building and went to the desk.

"Can I help you, sir?" asked the man behind the desk as he looked over the condition of Timothy's clothes.

"Yes," The gold eyes seemed to bore right into the man behind the desk, "I would like to have a room, a hot bath and a hot meal."

The hotel clerk was nervous, "How long will you be staying, sir?"

"At least a couple of days."

"You must pay in advance for the room."

"How much?" asked Timothy.

"Let's see, two nights?" He looked at the golden eyed man, "Twenty gold coins."

Timothy felt the price was a little high, but he was not in the mood to argue. He opened his pouch and withdrew the coins, placing them on the counter, "Where is your register?"

The man behind the counter put the register in front of Timothy who had decided to sign it Timothy Weatherly, in case Torreya came looking for him, "I hope you enjoy your stay Mr. Weatherly. Here is your key."

Timothy took the key, "Thank you. I'd like to take a bath and have a hot meal."

"The dining room will be open in an hour."

"Have whatever the specialty is sent to my room," requested Timothy.

"Certainly, sir."

Timothy walked up the stairs to find his room. He opened the door; it reminded him of the one he and Jennifer shared in Java. Closing the door, he put the packages on the nearest chair; seconds later, a maid knocked on the door with the hot water for his bath. She filled the large tub with several buckets of water, "Is there anything else, sir?"

"No, that will be all for now." The young woman bowed to him and left the room. Timothy undressed; he felt the hot water with his hand. It would be good to be clean again. He sank into the tub and lathered his body with the soap. The young woman had left two buckets of fresh water for him to rinse the soap from his body. Timothy rose from the soapy water, rinsed himself and began to dress in the new clothes he had bought. He looked at himself in the mirror, a bearded man dressed in fine burgundy waistcoat and grey trousers stared at him. He smiled; not many people would recognize him. A knock on the door startled him, "Who's there?"

"Dinner, sir."

Timothy walked to the door, opened it and a maid brushed past him with a tray of food. She placed it on the table, "Will there be anything else, sir?"

The golden eyes stared at her as she reminded him of his wife, he blinked, "No thank you." She turned and left his room, shutting the door behind her. He walked over to the small table and lifted the cover from the steaming food to smell the aroma. He sat down. One of the bowls contained a mushy substance which he picked up to smell, it smelled sweet. Tim had no idea what it was, so he picked up the spoon and tasted it; it was good and so hot that it burned the roof of his mouth. Next, he tried the fish, which was good but contained too many bones for his liking. The wine was a dry sweet one, but was pleasant enough to wash the food down. When he completed his meal, he put the tray outside the door, keeping his glass and the bottle of wine. Making sure the door was bolted, he sat at the window staring into the street thinking that Torreya and his men would be coming into the city. The fact that Torreya would be taking innocent people as slaves sickened him. He finished his bottle of wine, undressed and got into bed. A real bed felt so good, and he was exhausted; between the bottle of wine and his exhaustion, sleep came quickly.

The following morning, Timothy rose at ten, had breakfast and went on his way to see if he could book passage on a ship bound for New England. The docks were busy with men working, unloading cargo ships. Timothy was secretly hoping that one of his ships would be in port, but he couldn't be that lucky. Most of the ships were bound for other Caribbean islands, which were of no use to him. He needed a ship going to the New England states. He stood on the docks counting the ships that remained, six in all and one of them had to be going to New England. He approached a Captain he saw yelling orders to inquire if he knew of any ships bound for New England. The Captain told him that the *Lady Liberty*, the ship moored aside of his, usually traveled to New York.

Luke Baker hadn't planned on traveling to the Caribbean, but his sister wanted to visit some friends before her upcoming marriage. Luke had agreed to take her to New Providence, buy some goods and take them to New York while she visited her friends. He would then return to pick her up, and they would go home to New Orleans.

Timothy was met at the gangplank by the first mate, "I would like to see your Captain."

The first mate looked over the finely dressed man, "Does he know you, sir?"

Timothy shook his head, "No, he doesn't, but I would like to talk to him about booking passage on this ship; it is going to New York?"

"Follow me." Timothy followed the man to the cabin. He knocked, "Cap'n Baker, there's a man here would like to speak with ye, sir."

Luke Baker opened the door of his cabin to face the tall man with the strange gold eyes, "What can I do for you, Mr....."

"Lockwood. Timothy Lockwood."

"Mr. Lockwood," Luke extended his hand to Timothy. The two men shook hands.

"I am looking to book passage aboard this ship if you're bound for New York."

Luke stared at this stranger for a moment, "As it happens, Sir, we will be leaving for New York within two hours."

Timothy's eyes brightened, "Perfect, do you have room for me?"

"We have one cabin available; it's one of our larger ones so it will cost you a pretty penny."

"It doesn't matter. How much do you want?"

"Seventy-five gold coins," responded Luke.

"Does that include meals?" questioned Timothy.

"Yes."

Timothy thought it was a fair price. That would leave him with twenty-five gold coins and the gems. Opening the pouch, he counted out the coins and paid Luke Baker. "I will return within the hour."

Baker took the coins and put them in his pocket, "We leave within two hours."

"I understand perfectly. I will be back within an hour." Timothy turned, leaving the ship for the hotel.

When he reached the hotel, he picked up his packages from the room and left without officially checking out of the inn. On the way back to the *Lady Liberty*, he decided against selling the gems until he got to New York. When he reached New York, he would book passage on credit and pay when he reached Newport. The gems could be sold while he was waiting to book passage in New York. Once aboard the *Lady Liberty*, he was shown to his cabin. Moments later, Luke Baker knocked on his door, "I'm sorry to bother you, Mr. Lockwood, but do you have anything to do with the Lockwood-Gray firm in Newport, Rhode Island?"

Timothy was surprised, "Yes, I do. Why?"

Luke continued, "After I stop in New York I was planning on a trip to Newport to commission your firm for a new clipper. I understand that you've recently developed a ship that travels at speeds much faster than the McKay clippers."

"That's true, but why would you be interested in one of our ships?"

Luke sat down at the table in the center of the room, "I need a fast ship, Mr. Lockwood." Timothy joined him at the table was he continued, "My reasons are somewhat secretive; in fact, what I'm planning will endanger my life."

"What are you planning, Mr. Baker?" If your plans are illegal, perhaps it would be in your best interest to deal with me, rather than my partner."

"Smuggling," replied Luke as Tim's eyes widened, "Human beings."

Timothy smiled, he knew he liked this man, "Where are you smuggling these people to?"

"They are blacks, Mr. Lockwood, many of which are slaves on plantations in New Orleans. I would like to transport them into the northern states and set them free."

"It appears that you and I have a common interest, Captain Baker. You see, at the present time I am involved in a similar situation. It is important that you be secretive. It is also important that you deal directly with me because my partner knows nothing of my escapades," replied Timothy.

"I understand completely, Mr. Lockwood, and your secret will be safe with me."

"Good. The clipper ship you wish to purchase was designed for speed. These ships can out run any ship that they come up against. Since you are continuing on to Newport, may I stay aboard when we reach New York?"

"Of course."

"I will pay you the balance when we reach Newport."

Luke Baker rose, "No need, sir, let that part of the voyage be on me."

Timothy shook his hand, "Mr. Baker, you are a life saver. If you have any navigational problems on this voyage, please call on me."

"I trust you will dine in my cabin this evening?"

Timothy grinned, "Most assuredly."

"I'll see you later this evening."

Timothy nodded as Baker left the cabin. His thoughts were on his home in Newport, Jennifer and the children. He began to pace around the room; every once in a while, stopping to gaze at the books which sat on a shelf above the desk. He sighed, perhaps he should choose one of the books and read it to get his mind off of Torreya and Newport. This would be a long voyage, maybe he should start with one book and read through the six of them. He started to walk to the book case to look at the books, then changed his mind. He would go topside and see if he could help out with anything.

CHAPTER THIRTY-FOUR

The *Green-Eyed Lady* sailed into Newport harbor on a warm day at the end of March. Jennifer and Heather were standing at the rail of the ship when Rick Jordan approached them, "Glad to be home, Jennifer?"

She turned to look at Rick, "Yes and no."

Rick Jordan looked at her in amazement, "What kind of an answer is that?"

Jennifer tilted her head, "An honest one. It is true I'm happy to be back in Newport, but my real home is Weatherly."

"What about Timothy?" questioned Jordan.

Jennifer's eyes brimmed with tears, "I've been lying to myself, Rick. Just as you and Dante have been, if Timothy were truly alive, we would know." Heather placed her arms around Jennifer's shoulders.

"Yvonne may have tried to reach us after we left New Orleans. I bet he's waiting at Lockwood for our return."

"Don't you see, Rick, we are grasping for straws."

None of them heard the Prince approach them, "Jennifer is right."

Jordan turned to face his friend, "We don't know for sure, Dante."

"Jordan, stop. We all must face the realization that Timothy Lockwood is presumed dead. When we reach the estate, we will have a meeting between those members of the stronghold that are in port to decide on our fate." He paused for a moment before continuing, "Jennifer, you must make the final decision. I think Timothy would have wanted it that way."

She nodded, her mind racing. There were so many decisions to be made. "Can we have this meeting tomorrow?"

"Certainly," answered Dante. "As of right now, you are the boss."

Jordan said, "I'll hire a carriage to take us to Lockwood." He turned leaving by the gangplank which had been lowered by Gideon.

Jennifer said, "If you would excuse me, I wanted to gather what little things I have aboard ship. Heather, are you coming?"

"Yes," replied Dante.

Dante watched the two women leave for their cabin. His thoughts were of Sirena; he couldn't wait to get back to Lockwood. He felt as if his entire world was falling apart, and he needed to be held by her. Moments later, Rick Jordan returned, "The carriage is ready. Where are Jennifer and Heather?"

"They went to get their things. I'm going to get mine, are yours ready?"

"Yes, I'll wait for the women. Would you pick up my bag for me?" asked Rick.

"Sure." Dante walked away.

Jennifer and Heather reached the cabin they were sharing. "Jennifer, what was all the talk about the strongholds and decisions?"

Jennifer smiled wanly, "I have a lot of decisions to make. When we get to the house, someone will show you to a room, and I will be taking many of my meals alone. At least for today, I would like to spend time with my children."

"I understand," Heather answered as she threw her last belonging into the small reticule, "You have everything?"

Jennifer looked around the cabin, "I think so. Let's go."

They met Jordan and D'Mattea on deck. Rick took Heather's arm and led her down the plank with Jennifer walking slightly ahead of Dante. They boarded the carriage for the ride to Lockwood. Jennifer stared forlornly out the window; her thoughts jumbled. She watched the countryside pass by slowly; it seemed they were taking an eternity to reach Lockwood. The carriage stopped in front of the large house. Heather sucked in her breath; she had never seen a house so large. D'Mattea paid the driver while Rick carried the baggage.

Jennifer opened the front door, walking into the main hall. She was met by her cousin, Stefan. "Jenny, what has happened to you?" He had never seen his cousin dressed in rags before; she said nothing, "Jenny, where have you been?"

"Away," she answered quietly. She had forgotten about Stefan being in Newport. Yvonne and Sirena were coming down the stairs laughing when they spotted Jennifer standing in the hall. A strange woman was entering the house with Rick and Prince D'Mattea. Sirena ran down the rest of the stairs to him. Yvonne made her way to Jennifer who was in some kind of trance. She put her arm around the young woman's shoulder; Jennifer looked at her, "Yvonne, is he here?"

She shook her head, "I'm sorry."

Jennifer turned slowly, "Would you see to it that my friend Heather has some new clothes, a hot bath and a room."

"Sure," Yvonne replied.

"When there's time, I'd like a hot bath," She paused, "Where are my children?"

"The twins are asleep, and Lion is being tutored."

"Tutored?" questioned Jennifer.

"I took the liberty of hiring a governess," responded Yvonne.

"Oh, when his classes are finished, have him sent to my room," replied Jennifer her voice flat.

Yvonne was concerned as Jennifer was not herself; "I will do that; will you be joining us for dinner this evening?"

"No, have my meals sent to my room." Jennifer walked up the stairs to her bedroom. All eyes followed her up the stairs.

Stefan approached Rick Jordan, "What is the matter with my cousin? Where has she been?"

Jordan looked at Dante who was still holding Sirena to him, "I think Jennifer should answer those questions when she's ready." Turning to Yvonne, he said, "See to Heather's room. Is Cliff here?"

Yvonne glanced at Stefan, "No, not right now."

Jordan had forgotten about Stefan Weatherly, "Meet me in the study after you take care of Heather."

Yvonne looked at Heather, "Come with me."

Dante smiled and said, "I'm going upstairs, Rick."

"I think I will too. I want to change my clothes," responded Rick.

Jordan, D'Mattea and Sirena left Stefan Weatherly standing in the hall staring after them. Stefan turned and went to the kitchen where Daphne, his future wife, was instructing the cook for lunch and dinner. "There will be four more for dinner." He said upon entering the kitchen.

Daphne turned around, "Four more?"

He nodded, "D'Mattea, Jordan, Jennifer and a woman named Heather have returned."

"Jennifer's home! I must see her." She started to leave the room, but Stefan caught her arm, "What's wrong?"

"She said she wanted to be left alone. Why is it that I get the feeling that everyone knows what is going on in this house except me?" questioned Stefan.

Daphne frowned; he had been asking a lot of questions lately, "Don't be ridiculous. There is absolutely nothing going on in this house."

"Daphne, I happen to think something is going on and that you know what is going on in this residence."

"How many times do we have to discuss this, Stefan? I don't know what you are taking about," replied Daphne.

"I'll find out what is going on in this house, if it is the last thing I do," said Stefan angrily.

Daphne thought to herself, it just may be the last thing you do if you keep pressing for answers, but said instead, "Why don't you find Maggie and tell her that Jennifer is back. I think she's in the library."

"Don't try to change the subject on me. I want some answers to my questions," replied Stefan.

Daphne looked at him for a moment, "I'm not trying to change the subject because there is no subject to change." She could understand Jennifer's reasoning as to why Stefan shouldn't be told. He was much too law abiding, and he wouldn't be able to tolerate the fact that his beloved cousin, her husband, his fiancé and a series of others were involved in something both dangerous and illegal.

"We'll discuss this later." Stefan began to leave the kitchen; Daphne called out to him, but he ignored her calls. His thoughts were on his cousin and her whereabouts the last three months.

Jennifer had finished her bath; standing in front of the full-length mirror, she examined her fine body. Sighing, she began to dress before Lion came to visit her. After dressing, she sat at her dressing table and began to brush the long auburn hair in quick, hard strokes. Staring at herself in the mirror, she noticed she had changed. There was something different about her, not really her appearance, but something in her eyes, a new maturity; she wasn't seventeen years old any more; in fact, she would be twenty soon, which was still a young age, but she had learned a lot in the three years she had known Tim.

Lion knocked on the door and entered; at ten years old, he was a miniature of his father. He was tall for his age, and his eyes were slightly darker than Timothy's, yet his movements were those of his father's. He knew Jennifer wasn't his mother, but she was nice and pretty; "Mother, you are home." He hated calling her mother, but his father insisted that he did.

She stared at him, cocking her head to one side, "Lion, how are you?"

"Fine, but I would like to know where my father and you have gone to for these last months."

The child talked like an adult, which should probably be expected since he had been around adults for the last three years, "Well, I've been in New Orleans."

"Where's New...."

"Orleans," Jennifer finished his question, "Well it's in the southern part of the country."

"What were you doing there?"

"I," she paused. What could she say to this man-child? Lion stood before her with his hands on his hips and staring at her so intently that he appeared to be looking into her very soul much like his father had on several occasions. "I was taking care of some business matters for your father."

Lion ran his hand through his hair like Timothy. Jennifer smiled at that reminder of her husband, "Where is my father?"

Jennifer chewed on her bottom lip nervously, "He's away."

"I know that, but where? I heard Aunt Yvonne crying; she was saying something about my father, but I couldn't understand her." His golden eyes had darkened.

"Your father is away on business. He doesn't tell me where he's going, and I don't ask him."

"You're lying."

"Lion, I'm telling you the truth. I don't know where your father is at the moment." This little boy was making her nervous.

He shook his head, tossing his long dark curls from side to side, "You aren't lying? You left without telling my father where you were going. I saw what you did to him. You drove him crazy, and he went looking for you."

Jennifer sat on her bed and motioned to him, "Come here, Lion."

He tapped his foot on the carpet, "No, I will not! My father's dead, isn't he?"

Jennifer shook her head, "No."

"Yes, he is. That's why Aunt Yvonne was crying, and it's all your fault. I hate you, and my father hates you." He turned and ran out the door banging into Rick Jordan who grasped him by the shoulders, but Lion squirmed away from him and ran down the hall.

"Jenny, what's wrong?" asked Rick.

She rose from the bed, "Damn that little brat; he knows how to get to me just like his father did." Turning to Rick she said, "In the three years that I've been his stepmother, I have tried so hard to get him to like me. But now he hates me; he blames me for his father's death."

Rick looked at her surprised, "You told him?"

She shook her head, "I tried to deny it, but he knew. I think the child sneaks around the house listening to the conversations of the adults."

"I'll be damned," Rick replied.

Jennifer was frustrated, "He's so much like his father, that I can't stand it."

"I stopped by to ask how you were?" questioned Rick.

"Come in and shut the door," Rick closed the door behind him, "I'm fine."

"Your cousin is asking a lot of questions, too many."

Jennifer was standing near the window, "One of our ships is coming in."

"What should we do about your cousin?"

"Be careful, and don't answer any of his questions." She turned to face him, "Perhaps you should go downstairs to see what ship is here."

"I'll get D'Mattea, and we'll go to the caves," replied Rick.

Jennifer frowned, "No, let Dante have this time with Sirena."

"Okay, let me get downstairs." Rick left Jennifer's room.

Sirena lay in the security of Dante's arms. She didn't understand him anymore; he had changed. Something had happened to make him change, but he was not willing to discuss it. He didn't want to make love to her, not yet at least. He just wanted to be close to her, feel the warmth of her body pressed against him. They had been laying there for over an hour when Dante turned on his side, propping himself up on his elbow. Sirena stared at him, not knowing if she should talk or not. His other hand, which rested on her stomach, slowly moved to touch her hair. His fingers played with the dark silky strands. He thought of how he loved her, truly loved her. Her dark eyes searched his face, he smiled. It was so quiet that she couldn't stand it any longer, "What are you thinking?"

"I'm thinking how much I love you and need you, Sirena. I'm not talking about needing you sexually, I mean I need you emotionally as well as sexually."

She turned to her side to face him, "I need you in the same way; I think I always have."

"How did you put up with me?" questioned Dante.

Sirena smiled, "What exactly do you mean?"

"You were my friend for such a long time; even when I was involved with a variety of women and illegal activities, you remained my friend," Dante paused, "I guess you were a true friend."

She thought for a second, "I am a true friend; nothing has changed on that score."

"Our relationship has changed, Sirena."

She ran a slim finger along his jawbone, "That's true, Dante; we've become lovers, but we can still be friends. In fact, I believe we are closer friends than we ever have been."

He pulled her closer to him, "You are my friend, Sirena; you are also my love and my life."

"No, never say I'm your life, that makes you vulnerable, and you can't be vulnerable in this business," replied Sirena.

"I want to marry you, Sirena."

"I know, but we can't until my divorce. Don't ever become vulnerable, Dante, promise me. I don't want you to end up like Tim."

Dante leaned forward and kissed her, "I promise to try not to be vulnerable."

"What do you think Jennifer will do now that Timothy's gone?" questioned Sirena.

Dante's eyes saddened, "I don't know."

"Can I be with you when she has the meeting tomorrow?"

"Of course," replied Dante.

"Thank you."

"Don't thank me, Sirena; you are a part of this just as anyone else." A knock interrupted their discussion, "Who is it?"

"Rick."

Dante sat up, "What do you want?"

"I'm not yelling through the door, so open it."

Dante rose from the bed to open the door, "Well?"

"I'm going to the docks; one of our ships is coming in."

Dante picked up his jacket, "I'll come with you."

"No. Jennifer said to give you this time with Sirena."

Dante looked at Sirena, who was sitting on the bed, "I don't mind if you go; in fact, I'll come with you."

Rick looked at the two of them, "I'm going to my room; we've got to be extra careful because Jennifer's cousin is asking too many questions."

"We'll use the passageway," said Dante.

"I'll meet the two of you downstairs," replied Rick.

Two days later, Jennifer had come to her decision at two in the afternoon. She assembled Rick Jordan, Dante D'Mattea, Sirena, Yvonne, Devlin Jones, Cliff McArnold and Jack Webster into the library once she had made sure that her cousin was not in the house. Once satisfied that he had gone out with Daphne, she entered the large room, shutting the heavy oak doors behind her. She walked to the desk and sat down behind it. "Please sit." She waited for her audience to sit before speaking, "I have assembled you here to discuss the future of the stronghold and the decisions that I have made. Please listen to everything I have to say before any comments. You will have plenty of time to comment when I finish." She paused, "I have decided to take the children and return to London."

Yvonne stared at her in disbelief, "Why?"

Jennifer took a deep breath, "There is no reason for me to stay here. Rick Jordan, Dante D'Mattea, and you, Yvonne, will be entrusted with making sure the stronghold stays together unless there are objections?" Jennifer looked at the three of them, none of them said anything, "You have my permission to work out of this house and the profits will be redivided among the ten of us which includes Yvonne, Jack, Devlin, Jacques, Joseph, Michael, Cliff, Dante, Rick and myself. Approximately twice a year I will return to Newport to check on the stronghold. I think if Timothy had to pick someone to take over, he would have chosen the same individuals as I."

Devlin Jones was the first to speak, "Mrs. Lockwood, there is always a chance that he and Mark are alive."

Jack Webster chimed in, "That's true. Why, he and Mark Gregory are strong men, powerful men; I bet they are alive and stuck on some Caribbean Island trying to bribe the natives into building them a ship."

Jennifer raised her eyebrows, "Those are nice thoughts, gentlemen. I know how much you all care about them, but those thoughts are unrealistic."

Cliff McArnold said, "When will you be leaving for London and more importantly, will your cousin be coming with you?"

"I'll be leaving within the next two days and Stefan, Lizabeth, Harris and possibly Daphne will join me, along with the children."

Rick Jordan looked around the room and then at Jennifer, "Would you like to take any of the servants with you?"

"No, I'm sure Maggie will want to stay here, and Yvonne, I think we should release the governess from her duties and give a month's salary."

Yvonne said, "Of course, Jennifer."

Jennifer turned to look at Dante and Sirena, "It would be a great honor if Prince Dante D'Mattea took me home on the *Italian Princess*. Of course, in requesting this I must also request that Sirena and he stay at Weatherly, so I can show them London. Please say yes, Dante."

He flashed a smile, "Of course, Sirena and I would be more than honored to spend some time in London, but it can only be for a few days."

"Fine." The green eyes twinkled, as she turned her attention to the others in the room, "All of you are most welcome to visit me in London, especially if any problems occur here."

"What about Robert Gray?" asked Yvonne.

"I will tell Robert that I am meeting Timothy in London and we've decided to live there. I will also tell him that all of our correspondence will be through Rick," responded Jennifer.

Rick was pouring rum into some glasses for the others; he paused for a moment, "Do you think Robert Gray will accept that?"

"Probably not, but he'll have no choice," answered Jennifer.

Yvonne looked at the auburn-haired beauty who was in total control of her emotions and thoughts, "Jenny, why don't we go and see Robert this afternoon."

"Good idea. I think it would be wise if Rick accompanied me to Robert's office."

"I'll get my jacket. Will you be ready within an hour?" asked Yvonne.

"Certainly," replied Jennifer. "And when I return, we'll have a late dinner."

Jack Webster said, "I've got an idea, Mrs. Lockwood." Jennifer's attention turned to Jack, "I bet you didn't know that Devlin and me were good cooks."

She smiled, "No, I didn't."

"Well then, we'll make this your farewell dinner. We'll cook a surprise for everyone," responded Jack.

Sirena said, "I'll help. I happen to know an Italian dish that I think you'll like." She turned to Yvonne, "I'm sure you know a Dutch dish that you can make."

Yvonne smiled, "Sure, if we have the ingredients."

Dante began to laugh, "It appears that we are going to have an international dinner. While all of you are cooking, I'll see to it that *Italian Princess* is prepared for voyage and docked in Newport Harbor." Dante was the first to leave the meeting, followed by Yvonne, Sirena, Jack and Devlin who all went to the kitchen to begin preparations for the dinner that was to take place later in the evening. Cliff McArnold returned to the cataloguing of goods, leaving Rick and Jennifer alone.

"You are a strong woman."

Jennifer stared at him, "Am I strong? I just did what I had to, it's time I took control."

"Tim would have been proud," Jordan said quietly.

"Thanks," Jennifer replied with tears welling up in her eyes, "Would you excuse me? I would like to freshen up before we go to Robert's office."

"Of course." Jennifer rose from behind the desk, and Rick watched her leave the room. Pouring himself a glass of rum he walked over to the large desk, Tim's desk. He pulled out the chair and sat down to look over some papers.

An hour later, Jennifer and Rick Jordan sat in Robert Gray's office waiting patiently for Gray to return from the factory. They had been waiting a little over twenty minutes when Gray returned to his office. "Jennifer, Mr. Jordan, I'm sorry to have kept you waiting."

Jennifer smiled, "It's no problem, Robert."

"What can I do for you, Jennifer?"

She removed her gloves, placing them neatly in her lap, "Timothy, as you know has been away on business for the past several months."

"Yes, has he returned?" asked Robert.

Jennifer replied, "No, he hasn't; however, he's written me a letter requesting that I take the children to London to meet him."

"Oh, you're going on a holiday."

Jennifer shook her head, "No, Robert. Tim has decided to move the family to London."

Robert was shocked, "This is sudden, isn't it?"

"Not really. I've wanted to return to my native country for months now, and he is involved in some important business matters in Europe. In fact, he's written that they've asked him to take seat in Parliament." Jennifer lied because Robert would never be able to find out the truth. Rick Jordan tried not to show any expression on his face, but Jennifer had just blatantly lied to Robert.

"Parliament?" questioned Robert.

"Yes, Robert, that is part of our government," responded Jennifer.

"Yes, of course."

Jennifer continued on with her lie, "Taking a seat in Parliament would require him to remain in England."

Robert was visibly upset, "I see. What about his partnership with me?"

Jennifer smiled, "That is where Mr. Jordan comes in," Robert looked at Rick Jordan, "Timothy has a partnership with Mr. Jordan and several other people."

"What kind of partnership? I've noticed all kinds of people on your land."

Jennifer continued, "That's not important. What is important is that Timothy will let Mr. Jordan take his place here. Mr. Jordan will remain at Lockwood and take care of the house for us in the event we wish to return."

Robert turned to Rick Jordan, "I am to assume that you are to be my partner in the shipping business for all purposes intended?"

Rick replied dryly, "Yes, I am."

"Well Mr. Jordan, I wish to know your background."

Rick smiled, "Certainly, what do you want to know?"

"What country are you from? Your accent is hard to place."

Rick wanted to laugh at that moment, as this was not the kind of question that he would ask a prospective partner, "Well, let's see. I was born in England, but I left there when I was six years old. I've done a great deal of traveling, in the Dutch Indies, Northern Africa and the Caribbean."

"Are you married?"

"No, I'm not, although I've been told that I'm quite the ladies' man, but there is no special woman at the present time," responded Rick as he smiled.

"Who else will be residing at Lockwood with you?"

Rick didn't like this questioning, as he found Robert Gray to be nosey, "Really, Mr. Gray; I do not find that to be any of your business."

Jennifer interrupted, "That's true, Robert, I can assure you that all those living at Lockwood are respectable people."

Robert looked at her; this young woman was virtually telling him what to do. "And when will you be leaving to join Tim?"

"In two days," responded Jennifer.

Robert asked, "Which ship will you be traveling on?"

Jennifer replied, "The *Italian Princess*."

"I did not notice such a ship in our local port."

Jennifer was becoming angry; he was beginning to ask too many questions. "Do you know every ship that is in port, Robert?"

"No, of course not."

"Well then I can assure you that the *Italian Princess* has been in port for several days; in fact, her Captain is a good friend of Mr. Jordan's"

Rick had had enough of the questioning, and he interrupted the two of them before Jennifer went into a rage and blurted out something she should not say. "Excuse me, but we didn't come here to discuss which ship Jennifer was taking to London or how I got my accent."

Jennifer took a deep breath, attempting to control her temper, "That's true. Rick has the qualifications needed to fill Timothy's position here."

"I'm sure he does, but I don't understand why I can't send reports directly to London."

Jennifer looked Robert Gray directly in his eyes and said coolly, "Because Timothy has requested that we let Rick control this portion of his business."

"I guess I can't argue with you since Timothy owns more of the business than I do," Turning to Rick Jordan, he extended his hand. Rick grasped Robert's hand, "It will be a pleasure to work with you, Mr. Jordan."

"I'm sure we'll work together quite well, Mr. Gray."

"When should I expect you to fill Timothy's office?" asked Robert.

"Tomorrow morning," replied Rick.

"I'll see you tomorrow then." Turning to Jennifer, Robert said, "When do you expect to leave?"

"Within a couple of days," responded Jennifer.

"Have a safe trip."

"I'm sure I will." Jennifer smiled as she put her gloves on and rose to leave.

"Tell Timothy I said hello, and I will miss him," replied Robert.

"I will." Jennifer turned to Rick, "Come, Rick, we must get back to Lockwood." The two of them turned, leaving Robert staring after them.

Robert Gray stood in his doorway watching Rick Jordan help Jennifer Lockwood into their carriage. He wondered if Jennifer realized that she was causing a scandal in Newport's fine society by having male visitors in her home while her husband was away. His thoughts turned to Timothy; something must be wrong. Timothy had always kept his other business dealings very secretive, too secretive for Robert's liking. Something was going on at the Lockwood estate; he was sure of it, but what was it? He had tried to find out when Timothy was away, but everything appeared to be normal. Now, with this Jordan character in control, he might never find out what all those people are doing at Lockwood. They were all Captains, yet where were their ships in Newport harbor? He would have to check the other harbors in the area. After all, these ships couldn't just disappear. He sighed and returned to his office.

CHAPTER THIRTY-FIVE

Stefan was upset that his cousin ordered him to return to London and that she would be taking the three children to live there. He was angered that she wouldn't answer his questions about Timothy, the estate, or any of the other characters that appeared to have free reign of her home. Neither would she answer questions about her whereabouts before she returned to Newport. She demanded to know his intentions with Daphne Charbonneau. Jennifer wanted to know if he was planning on marrying Daphne, and if he was, then she insisted that he do it today before they returned to London. He finished adjusting his ascot and looked into the mirror. He didn't like being ordered around by anyone, especially a woman who was two years younger than himself. He wanted Daphne to have nice wedding with many guests, but Jennifer was forcing him to marry her today before leaving for London tomorrow. He combed his hair for the third time before going downstairs where Harris would be his best man, and Jennifer would be the other witness. There was a part of Stefan that was happy that he was getting this wedding over with, but he didn't appreciate his cousin forcing him. Jennifer had changed dramatically since she met Timothy Lockwood and his group of friends. There was a time that she told Stefan everything, and now she was cloaked in secrets, and it angered him.

Jennifer assumed complete responsibility for the wedding. She and Daphne were in Daphne's room, and Jennifer helped her into the very dress that she wished she had worn on her wedding day. Thinking about her own wedding day, she became teary eyed, blinking back the tears staring at the white satin dress with the delicate lavender flowers, oh how she had wished she had worn that dress. Her heart ached for Timothy; their parting had been so violent, and she hated the thought of him dying with the knowledge that his childlike wife left him. Jennifer took a deep breath and moved away from Daphne, "There, don't you look beautiful."

"I'm so nervous."

"I guess you would be as it is your wedding day." Jennifer answered in a matter-of-fact way.

Daphne looked at her in amazement, "Weren't you nervous?"

Jennifer shook her head, "No, but of course the situation was a little different."

Daphne sighed, "I guess you're right."

Jennifer smiled, "Are you ready?"

"Yes," replied Daphne nervously.

Jennifer opened the door which signaled Yvonne who was standing down the hallway. Yvonne waved to Rick and then motioned to Jennifer that they were ready. Jennifer hustled Daphne out of her bedroom and down the corridor. Yvonne walked behind Daphne, and Jennifer walked in front of her. When they reached the main hallway, Jennifer entered the sitting room first, taking her place beside Harris. The room was filled with fresh flowers and friends of Jennifer and Daphne. Jennifer looked at her cousin; he was handsome standing beside the minister in his grey suit and grey waistcoat. Daphne entered the room and everyone's eyes fell on the bride. She was beautiful; Jennifer took a deep breath; she hoped that Daphne and Stefan would lead a more normal life than she and Timothy. Daphne reached Stefan, and he took her hand as the minister began the ceremony. Yvonne watched Jennifer's face change with a variety of emotions. Jennifer's mind was elsewhere now; she was in the Barbary States, sweating and ashamed when a tall, golden eyed man who she knew bought her. Next, she was in Java running for her life when, once again, she was saved by the topaz eyed man.

The ceremony was over, and Jennifer remained sitting. Yvonne crossed the room, placing her hand lightly on Jennifer's shoulder. "Jennifer, are you alright?"

Jennifer turned, "Yes, why?"

Yvonne smiled, "You seem to be in another world."

"The ceremony is over?"

"Yes."

Jennifer rose, smoothing her deep purple silk dress, "I must congratulate them." She made her way over to her cousin and Daphne. Hugging both of them, she wished them the best of luck.

Several hours later, Jennifer packed the last of her dresses in her trunk. Some of her clothing would be left behind, so she could travel lightly when she periodically returned to Newport. Next, she packed the twin's clothes; when they got to London, she would have to buy them some new clothes; they were growing up so quickly. Jennifer looked around the room; everything that she wanted to take with her was packed. Her eyes focused at the closet; crossing the room, she opened the closet door. Timothy's clothes hung neatly in the closet; she touched his black velvet jacket and matching trousers. That suit had been the last thing she had seen him wearing. She took it from the hanger and held it in her arms. His scent was still on the jacket; she could smell him. Tears were welling in her eyes; she blinked a few times to try to keep them from falling down her cheeks. She held the jacket close to her, and she wanted to feel his arms around her; she wanted to feel close to him no matter where he was in death. She walked over to the bed and sat down. She smoothed the jacket over her lap; as she did, she felt a hardness in the jacket pocket. Jennifer reached in and pulled out a small box wrapped in a pretty paper. A small tag with her name; unwrapping the box, she opened it, finding a sapphire ring. Taking it out of the box, she put it on her finger; she couldn't hold back the tears any longer; they streamed down her cheeks. She felt as if her chest was going to burst open as the tears flowed freely. She wiped the tears with the jacket sleeve, composed herself and took the ring off, placing it back into the box and back in the jacket pocket. She rose from the bed, put the jacket into the closet and lay down on the bed which seemed so big. It took her a long time to fall asleep. She slept restlessly, tossing and turning with her dreams. Dreams of Timothy, mixed with nightmares of Geoffrey, the Barbary Coast and Madame Ginger's. She woke with a start; realizing it was still early morning, she dressed and went downstairs.

Rick Jordan and Dante D'Mattea were sitting in the library having a cup of coffee when they heard a noise. The two men looked at each other and drew swords before entering the foyer. Upon seeing Jennifer, Dante asked, "What are you doing up at this hour?" He put his rapier into its sheath, as did Jordan.

"I couldn't sleep." She stared at the two of them, "What are you two doing up?"

Rick replied, "I've been up all night, and Dante always gets up this early."

"That's true," replied Dante, "Why don't you join us for coffee?"

"Sounds good." She followed them into the library. The three of them sat in a circle as Dante handed Jennifer her coffee. "Who made the coffee?"

"Jordan, although I must admit, I like espresso better."

Rick said, "Dante and I were just saying that you've done a great job in coping with the problems we have had lately."

Jennifer sipped her coffee, "Thank you."

Dante sighed, "Are you sure you wouldn't like to stay in Newport?"

She shook her head as Rick Jordan said, "We're going to miss you, Jennifer."

"And I'll miss all of you. Would you promise me that you'll be careful?"

"Aren't we always careful?" asked Dante.

Jennifer replied, "I mean with Robert Gray; he asks a lot of questions. Don't provide him with any answers."

"I promise you that Robert Gray will not learn any information from me."

Dante added, "And you don't have to worry about me since I won't really be dealing with him, and if I do, rest assured that I won't spill any secrets."

Sirena knocked on the library door, "I wondered where you went to, Dante."

"You're awake," he crossed the room to kiss her good morning, leading her back to his chair, he pulled her into his lap.

Sirena squirmed out of his arms and pulled a chair over, "What's going on?"

"Nothing," answered Rick.

Jennifer said, "It appears that none of us could sleep." She paused, "Sirena, why don't we prepare breakfast."

"Sure," she started to rise from her seat when Dante grabbed her arm, "What's wrong?"

"Nothing, I just wanted to make sure that you didn't get your gown caught in the chair; I saw it was wrapped under the leg," he said as he pulled the chair up, releasing her gown from under it.

"Thank you," turning to Jennifer, she said, "Come on, let's go make breakfast."

Jenny rose to follow Sirena out of the library, leaving Jordan and D'Mattea alone again. Dante looked at Rick, "Are you sure you can handle everything for a couple of weeks?"

"Positive. You and Sirena have a good time. I've always said, if the opportunity presents itself, take it." Rick smiled thinking about Heather as he spoke.

"What are you grinning about?"

"Nothing," smirked Rick.

"You are, and I know what it is!" exclaimed Dante.

Jordan teased him, "You know what? What is it?"

Dante narrowed his eyes and smirked, "I saw her leave your room, Jordan, earlier this morning."

"You saw who leave my room?" questioned Rick thinking to himself that D'Mattea couldn't have seen Heather leave.

Dante smiled, "Heather."

"Heather wasn't in my room," replied Rick with a straight face as he tried to appear unrattled by Dante's words.

"You can deny it if you like, but I saw her with my own eyes."

"And what were you doing out of bed at that hour?" questioned Rick, still not indicating what Dante was saying was true.

"Sirena and I had just finished," he stopped in midsentence, "We heard a noise, and I went into the corridor to check."

"Spying on me, are you?"

Dante grinned, "No, I've just got good ears as my lady does. Frankly, Rick, I don't give a damn whether you sleep with her or not."

"Good, because it is none of your damn business."

"That's true," Dante raised one eyebrow, "But I have a word of warning for you. Be careful she doesn't fall in love with you."

"What does a woman like her know about love? She's prostituted herself for years."

Dante was shocked at his friend's words, "Did you pay her for sex?" Jordan was quiet, "You didn't pay her, so that means it was a mutual coupling, so are you trying to convince yourself that you slept with a prostitute and not a woman who just might be interested in having a normal relationship for once in her life. And to answer your question, she probably knows more about love than any of us put together."

Rick was slightly embarrassed about Dante's chastising yet remained nonchalant, "I doubt she will fall in love with me."

"I'm just warning you; strange things happen." Dante rose from his seat, "I'm going to see how Sirena and Jennifer are doing in the kitchen.

"Go ahead. I'll be there in a few minutes." He watched Dante leave. He was angry that Dante saw Heather leave his room.

Later that morning, the trunks were loaded into one carriage and the twins, Jennifer, Stefan, Daphne, Sirena, Dante, Harris, Lizabeth and a reluctant Lion were taken to the ship on two other carriages. Lion Lockwood was angry at Jennifer for taking him away. He'd rather stay with Aunt Yvonne and Uncle Rick. He threw a temper tantrum, but Uncle Dante picked him up from the floor and gave him a spanking, which made him furious. He wouldn't cry because he didn't want them to think that it hurt. His golden eyes darkened in anger as he watched Aunt Yvonne and Uncle Rick fade in the background. Jennifer had also watched Lockwood fade into the distance. She remembered the first day she had seen the massive house and the happy times spent there as well as the bad. She would return, that much she was sure of, and when she did, she might be ready to take total control of the stronghold. The carriages reached the docks, and the men from the *Italian Princess* unloaded the carriage with the baggage as Jennifer dragged a screaming Lion aboard. Dante began shouting orders to his crew, which began working at full force to get the *Italian Princess* moving. Within an hour, Newport harbor was in the background. Lion occupied himself by asking various questions of the crew and watching the waves roll by the clipper ship. Jennifer went to her cabin and unpacked a portion of the trunk which contained some clothes for the twins who were going to be five and a half months old. Both Timothy and Arianna were asleep; the rocking of the ship was making Jennifer drowsy. She decided to lie down, considering she hadn't sleep during the night.

Daphne and Stefan unpacked part of their clothing. Every once in a while, Daphne would look at Stefan and wondered what he was thinking. She worried about Jennifer coming to London with them; Stefan would want to know everything Jennifer was doing and why she would have to correspond so often with Rick Jordan. She was also afraid that she couldn't live up to Stefan's expectations of her. He was very rigid and very proper, and he expected her to be also, but since meeting so many free-willed people, she couldn't possibly be that rigid and law abiding.

The days passed quickly aboard the *Italian Princess,* and London could be seen in the distance. Jennifer stood at the rail of the ship, staring out into the ocean. It seemed everything she did lately brought memories back to her. She stood at the rail for a long time, what seemed like an eternity as tears filled her eyes.

Sirena approached Jennifer and stood beside her. She sighed, "Do you know that my husband might be in London with his newest trollop?"

Jennifer blinked back her tears and sniffled, "Maybe while you're here you can convince him to give you a divorce, so you could marry Dante."

"You mean if I find him."

Jennifer's green eyes darkened, "Do you know that almost every man I've known or loved has brought me pain or stood in my way for something I wanted?" She stared directly at Sirena now, "Don't let your husband do that to you. You want to marry Dante, and I'm sure you will."

"I have to marry him soon, Jennifer."

"Why? Are you afraid that you'll lose him?"

"No, I'm not afraid of losing him. In fact, I truly believe that he loves me and that our love is stronger than most people. The truth of the matter is that I'm pregnant and I don't know what I want to do."

Jennifer wasn't surprised by the admission from Sirena; in fact, she thought she saw a new look about Sirena, "Have you told him?"

Sirena shook her head, "No. I can't tell him because I don't know if I can take the scandal."

Jennifer put her arm around Sirena, "Come on; let's walk along the deck." Sirena walked with Jennifer as she said, "Why should you care what people think? You love him, and you are carrying his child. That is what is important. I know because I've been through it myself."

"What do you mean?" questioned Sirena.

Jennifer sighed, "Before I had the twins, I had a miscarriage and almost died."

Sirena stopped walking and grabbed Jennifer by the arm to stop her from going further, "I'm so sorry; that must have been horrible."

Jennifer said, "No need to be. Timothy and I weren't married. I was seventeen years old, and my only thoughts when I lured him into my bed were what would it be like? The only thing I cared about was becoming a real woman." She paused, taking a deep breath, "Who thought of the consequences? Certainly, I didn't, and actually, I had made Timothy my goal, which was wrong."

"Are you saying that you didn't love him?" questioned Sirena as they continued walking in the direction of the cabins.

Jennifer looked away and then back at Sirena, "In a way, yes; I was attracted him; he was so handsome, but I wasn't in love with him yet."

"I do love Dante, but I don't know if I'm ready to give him a child or if he wants one."

Jennifer's green eyes twinkled, "Let me tell you a secret; all men want children. They have this feeling of really being a man, of continuing their lineage. I'm sure that Dante will want the child." Sirena said nothing as Jennifer said, "I can't tell you what to do and whether you tell him will be your decision."

"Oh, I know that," responded Sirena.

"And remember, who at Lockwood would make a comment about your pregnancy?"

Sirena smiled, "I guess you are right, Jennifer." They reached Sirena's cabin, "I'll go in now and try to make a decision as I pack our clothes."

Jennifer hugged her, "I know whatever you decide will be best for you."

"Thank you. I'll see you later."

Jennifer made her way to her own cabin to put the rest of her things in order for her trip to Weatherly. It would be good to be home again after being away for such a long time.

The *Italian Princess* docked in London, and Stefan hired several carriages to take them to Weatherly. Jennifer's eyes scanned the docks as they had years before, catching sight of a blond woman walking with a man and a small child. They were laughing and appeared to be very much in love. Jennifer was sure she recognized the woman; she looked like Laura Harrington. Jennifer turned to Dante and said, "Excuse me for a minute. I think I see someone I know." Jennifer crossed the road and began walking towards the woman.

The blonde woman looked in Jennifer's direction and the happy expression on her face turned to one of shock. Jennifer drew closer and said, "Laura, Laura Harrington?"

The gentleman she was with stopped talking, Laura took a deep breath, "I'm sorry. Do I know you?'

Jennifer cocked her head to one side, "Jennifer Lockwood. You are Laura Harrington, aren't you?"

Laura became nervous by the piercing green eyes and the young woman that stood before her, "No, you've made a mistake. My name is Laurel Thompson."

Jennifer was surprised; she had to be Laura Harrington, "I'm sorry. I guess I have made a mistake." She glanced at the little boy, "What a cute little boy. What's his name?"

The man answered, "Geoffrey."

Jennifer's eyes opened wide, she knelt before the small child, "Hello Geoffrey." He backed away from her, and Jennifer rose to her feet. "I'm terribly sorry." She turned and began walking back to Dante who was coming towards her. Laura followed Jennifer with her eyes as Jennifer walked back to a man who was obviously not Timothy Lockwood, and who took Jennifer by the arm and led her to the waiting carriage.

Some servants still occupied Weatherly, and Sirena and Dante were impressed with the size of the house, which clearly testified that Jennifer came from wealth. Daphne walked around the foyer, and Jennifer went into her father's library. She thought of her mother at the Bryant Sanitarium; she never went to see her before Timothy swept her away to Newport. Now that she was home again in her beloved London, she would make every effort to contact the sanitarium to ask permission to visit with her mother. She ran her hand along the desk and sat in the large chair. Her thoughts turned to Laura Harrington, who was obviously still telling lies. Jennifer was positive that the woman who called herself Laurel Thompson was indeed Laura Harrington. She was also sure that Laura had the man she was with charmed into believing she was Laurel Thompson. Jennifer sat back in the chair, tears filling her eyes. At least Laura had someone to be with, someone who probably cared about her. Jennifer thought of the time Timothy had stolen into her house because he needed her help. She missed him terribly; for the first time, she truly broke down sobbing for her loss of her husband and lover, for her children and for Timothy who must have died thinking she hated him. Jennifer dreaded going into her old bedroom. She wiped the tears from her cheeks, took a deep breath and pulled herself together. She had to stop crying; it was too late for tears; she must be strong. Taking another deep breath, she went to her bedroom to face lost memories.

The days passed quickly as she entertained Dante and Sirena, giving them the grand tour of London. Sirena had inquired as to whether her husband was in the city but found he had left for France. It was just as well because she had an important decision to make. Dante should be told about the child and perhaps she should tell him while they were in London. She knew she would have to tell him eventually, seeing she was two months along. She sat on the edge of their bed staring at him while he slept. He was handsome, and she wasn't sure that she deserved this man.

He stirred, his eyes opening slowly. He smiled and in a sleepy voice said, "What time is it?"

"Early; it's not even dawn."

Dante struggled to a sitting position, the sheet falling to his waist, "What are you doing sitting on the edge of the bed?"

"Thinking."

He patted the space aside of him, "Come and think close to me." Sirena crawled up the side of the bed and under the covers. He turned to face her, "What are you thinking that has you up in the middle of the night?"

Sirena smiled weakly, "Oh a lot of things."

"It must be important. Have I done something to make you upset?"

She shook her head, "No, I have something to tell you, and I don't know how to tell you."

Dante stared at her in the darkness of their room, showing no emotion as he spoke, "This thing that you have to tell me is obviously important and upsetting to you; otherwise, you wouldn't be up in the middle of the night."

"You might be angry, and I never wanted to hurt you."

"Sirena, the best way is to just tell me."

She looked into his almost black eyes, as she began to ramble, "I never meant for it to happen; I never thought it would, but it did, and I guess I can't do anything about it, except hope that you'll forgive me and still love me and most importantly remain my friend."

Dante looked at her in confusion. What was she talking about? Love? Friendship? Hurt? She was making his head spin, "Sirena, get to the point."

In a muffled voice she said, "I'm with child."

He couldn't make out what she said; he looked at her, "Speak clearly. I didn't understand what you said, and will you look at me?"

She moved so that she tilted her head towards him, "I'm pregnant." He didn't say anything, and his expression didn't change as he blinked his eyes a couple of times. "I knew it! You're upset with me. I wanted to get rid of it, but Jennifer talked me out of it. I know this is going to come between us." She paused, realizing that she wasn't giving him a chance to talk, but he still said nothing.

Several things were running through his thoughts. How could she possibly consider destroying a child? How could she doubt him? He looked at her face; she was upset, her eyes frantically searching his face waiting for him to speak. When he found his voice, he spoke slowly, "How could you ever think I would be angry at you for being pregnant with my child?"

"Because we're not married."

"What the hell difference does that make?" The dark eyes searched her face.

"The scandal."

"What scandal? I love you, Sirena. How could you ever doubt me?"

"You've changed, Dante, ever since you came back from New Orleans, you've withdrawn. I thought you were tired of me."

"Never," he leaned towards her, drawing her, face to his and kissed her long and hard, "You are the only woman I've ever really trusted; you are my lover, and you are my friend." He paused, "Something happened in New Orleans that I don't wish to discuss, but that is not important. What is important is us and our child," he looked at her questioningly.

"You want the child?" Her eyes opened wide as she questioned him.

"I want the child; it's part of you and part of me, and we don't need the blessing of the church."

"Hold me, Dante, please. I was just so afraid that you would hate me, that you would accuse me of trying to trap you into a stable relationship."

"We have a secure relationship, Sirena. In fact, when we get to Newport, I'll buy you a house instead of living at Lockwood."

"No," she shook her head, "I'll feel like your mistress."

"Sirena, you are far from a mistress. We'll tell everyone that you're Princess D'Mattea, and when you get your divorce, we'll sneak off somewhere and get married."

"I'm sorry."

"For what?"

"For doubting you."

"Everyone has doubts sometimes, and I was preoccupied when I returned from New Orleans. I'm sorry I caused your doubts." He leaned over again to kiss her. His eyes twinkling, he said, "I thought I noticed more fullness in your breasts."

Sirena blushed, "You are happy then?"

"I've never been happier." Dante kissed her again drawing her closer to him.

She broke off the kiss, staring into his eyes she said, "I love you. Just hold me close, I'm so tired." He smiled and held her in his arms, thinking about the child she was carrying. Sirena fell asleep quickly, and he lay awake thinking.

Sirena woke first, giving Dante a light kiss on the cheek. His nose twitched as she touched his face. He opened his eyes slowly, "Good morning."

"Good morning."

His hands went to his eyes and he rubbed them; his right arm was still asleep from Sirena's head being on top of it all night. "I hate to end our holiday, but we have been here three weeks, and we really must return to Newport."

"I know. I hate to see it end, but I'm anxious to return. You did mean what you said last night about the house?"

"Yes, I meant it. In fact, I meant everything I said last night."

"I'm glad."

"So am I."

"Let's get dressed and go downstairs to breakfast."

Dante drew her close to him, "Not yet. Let's just stay here for a few moments, so I can enjoy your beauty." Sirena giggled as she snuggled close to him.

Jennifer sat in the library going over some mail that had come from Newport. All were business matters which needed answers as soon as possible. She sat there wondering if she would make the same decisions as Timothy might have; it was important that she did, so Robert Gray would believe that Timothy was in London. Also enclosed with Gray's letters were letters from Rick discussing the stronghold.

Lizabeth interrupted her reading of Jordan's letter, "Excuse me, Miss Jennifer, but there is a woman in the sitting room with a small child. She wishes to see you."

Jennifer put the letter on the desk, left the library and went into the sitting room. Laura Harrington or Laurel Thompson sat before her with the small boy named Geoffrey. "Mrs. Lockwood, I'm sorry to bother you at home."

Jennifer stared at her, "Not at all, Miss Harrington, or Mrs. Thompson, whatever you prefer."

"It is true, I am Laura Harrington, but I've got a new name and a new life."

"So why are you here?" Jennifer's eyebrows raised as she spoke.

"I'm going by the name of Laurel Thompson, and the man you saw me with three weeks ago is my fiancé," she paused, "You see the only way I could explain my son was if I told him I was a widow."

"Which of course, you did. Lying has always come easy to you, doesn't it?"

Laura looked at Jennifer coolly, "You still hate me, and I don't understand why? You have your husband, the man who should have been mine, but he was too bewitched by your red hair and cat's eyes to notice me."

"At least I wasn't going behind his back and having an affair with a slimy, disgusting, money-hungry monster," replied Jennifer.

"Geoffrey may have been all those things to you, but he did it because of me. He was good to me."

"Well, he wasn't good to me!" Jennifer replied angrily, "In fact, I sincerely hope he is dead after what he's done to me and probably other women. I hope he rots in hell." She turned to the small child, "Is that his son?"

"Yes."

Jennifer's green eyes flickered in the light with her anger, "I suggest you pray to God that he doesn't turn out like his father. As far as I am concerned, should I pass you on the street I shall not speak to you, Laura Harrington no longer exists. Good day, Mrs. Thompson." Jennifer turned and left the sitting room. Upon seeing Lizabeth in the main foyer, she said, "Would you please show Mrs. Thompson and her son to the door." Jennifer continued across the hall to the library.

The library door was closed, and she didn't remember shutting the door. When she opened the door, she saw Stefan sitting at the desk reading Rick Jordan's letter. She approached the desk and grabbed the letter from his hands, "What do you think you're doing?" She stared at him coolly.

"Jennifer, you are living in my house now with your three brats, and I demand to know what you are involved in?"

She was furious, "Your house? Half of this house is mine, and the truth is my father felt badly for you, so he let you have half, but the reality is it should have been all mine! And it is none of your damn business!"

Stefan had jumped to his feet and grabbed her by the arm. Her father had been right, she was too free as a child; she thought like a man sometimes. His cousin Jennifer needed to be controlled, "It is my business. They are all pirates, aren't they?"

Her green eyes became very angry, "Let go of my arm, Stefan." She said in a gritty voice.

"Not until you answer my questions. All of them are pirates! You and Timothy are involved with them, aren't you?"

"Let go of me, and you don't know what you're talking about!" She wrenched her arm away from him rubbing it.

"Timothy's one too, isn't he?" He slapped his forehead, "That's how he knew so much about pirates and that woman, Yvonne, is the pirate he told us about. That's how he knew where to look for you when Lyndon kidnapped you. This is finally beginning to make sense." He stared at his cousin whose face showed no emotion, "That's why all the activity at Lockwood, those special ships Timothy designed, the strange men appearing out of nowhere. What have you gotten yourself into?"

"Stefan, you are talking out of your head." It was futile attempt, but she tried anyway, "It's your imagination; there is nothing going on at Lockwood."

"Stop, Jennifer, I'm not a little boy anymore." He crossed the room and locked the library doors, turning to face her he continued, "I want answers, and I want them now."

"No," Jennifer shook her head, "I have nothing to tell you."

He grabbed her arms again, this time his grip was much tighter, "I'm going to ask questions, and you're going to answer them, otherwise I'll break both of your arms."

"What's wrong with you, Stefan? Let go of me." He was beginning to frighten her; the last few months he had become irrational, but now he was beginning to act like a madman.

"Not until you answer my questions."

The tears sprung in her eyes; her fingers were beginning to tingle from the loss of blood flow to them, "Alright, but let me go."

He released her, and she sat in a chair, "Where's Timothy?"

She looked at him angrily; she would be damned if she let him see her weakness and any tears, "He's dead." She responded with no emotion.

"Dead? How?"

Icily she replied, "We don't know the details except that the *Moonlight* went down outside of Tortuga with both Timothy and Mark Gregory aboard."

"Where were you those weeks you were missing?"

"It is not important," she responded flatly.

"Answer me." He raised his voice.

Jennifer looked up at him as he was now standing over her; the green eyes were very cold, calculating as she tipped her head to one side; she licked her lips and said very calmly, "I was in a bordello. I was working in a bordello to be exact; are you shocked?"

Stefan was horrified, but he tried to remain calm, "I wouldn't be shocked at anything you do. Did Timothy take you there? He asked sarcastically.

Jennifer rolled her eyes, "Of course not."

"What is going on at Lockwood?"

Jennifer rose from her seat, "That, Stefan, is none of your damn business. It doesn't concern you."

"If you are living in this house, it is my business."

"You seem to keep forgetting that half of Weatherly is mine."

"I'm not forgetting, Jennifer, but if you are involved in something illegal, I would prefer that you go back to Lockwood. We Weatherlys are important people in London, and I will not tolerate a scandal."

"That's all you care about, isn't it? What people say or think or do? Don't you have a passion for something? A goal? She stared him directly in his eyes, "You want truths, Stefan? I'll tell you truths! Yes, we are all pirates!" She screamed it at the top of her lungs, "In fact, when Dante and Sirena leave, I'll be going with them. I wouldn't want to destroy your concept of honesty and humanity. At least one Weatherly in this house has some backbone! Now open the door, so I can pack."

"Jennifer, I'll have to turn you and your friends into the authorities," Stefan stated.

Jennifer whirled around, "The authorities? How dare you? You do not belong in Newport or anywhere in the states, nor should you be reporting to any authorities. Just let us leave! Open the door, Stefan; it will be better this way. After all, I do not want to disgrace the family name, nor do I want to arrange for my once beloved cousin to meet with an untimely end." Stefan was shaken to his core as he opened the door, and Jennifer stormed up the stairs to Dante and Sirena's bedroom as she walked down the hall; she realized that Stefan might take this out on Daphne, especially if he found out about her involvement at Lockwood. Jennifer turned and went to Daphne's first to warn her of Stefan's outrage. Something in her cousin's head had definitely snapped. He seemed so bitter and angry. Jennifer was positive that it had absolutely nothing to do with his lack of knowledge over her affairs. It appeared that her cousin was suffering from the same maladies as her mother, mental illness. God help her as she thought about it; did it run in the family?

CHAPTER THIRTY-SIX

Daphne was happy that Jennifer warned her about Stefan; at least she was prepared when he returned to their bedroom. When he opened the door, she pretended to be asleep. He shook her a couple of times, and she moaned, opening her eyes slowly, "Get up, I have to talk to you."

Daphne rubbed her eyes, yawning she asked, "What's wrong?"

"Tell me the truth Daphne, what do you know about Lockwood?"

"Lockwood?"

"How much do you know?" asked Stefan.

"Nothing, Stefan. What are you talking about?"

"Did you know that Lockwood is being used by a group of pirates to bring in smuggled goods and God knows what else?"

"No," Daphne shook her head, "I didn't. Are you sure?"

He paced around the room, "How did you and my cousin meet?"

"My uncle is Devlin Jones, and when both my parents died, I begged him to take me to New England." She paused wondering if this lie would back fire on her, "He knew that Timothy Lockwood's wife was pregnant and had to stay in bed, so he thought I would make a good companion for her. I assure you Stefan that my uncle is no pirate."

"Can you be sure?" His stare was frightening.

Daphne kept her composure; if there was one thing she learned from her pirate friends is to never play your hand if you can help it,

"Yes, he owns and operates a small trading store in Massachusetts. You can check it out if you wish."

"What does he have to do with Timothy Lockwood? How does he know him when Timothy's from Rhode Island, and he's from Massachusetts?" Stefan's eyes had a strange wild look.

Daphne got out of bed, "How am I supposed to know?"

"You should know things like that; he is your uncle."

Daphne crossed the room and stood before him, "There's a lot that I don't know about you either. And I married you."

"I believe you, Daphne. If Jennifer's my cousin and didn't tell me anything, she certainly wouldn't tell a stranger."

He believed her, and that was good; it was important that he didn't know anything of her involvement in Newport, "Is breakfast ready?" Daphne asked trying to change the subject.

"Lizabeth was preparing the table when I was on my way upstairs."

"Why don't you go down, and I'll be there in a few minutes."

He kissed her, "I'll see you later." Turning, he left her alone to dress; she looked around the room spying paper and she quickly wrote a note to Jennifer letting her know what she told Stefan in case he checked her story. Daphne dressed quickly, leaving the room to slip a note under Jennifer's door before going down to breakfast.

Jennifer knocked on Dante and Sirena's door. Dante was just buttoning his shirt and Sirena sat at the window looking out. Dante opened the door, "Jennifer, how are you?"

"Not very good. May I come in?"

"Certainly," Jennifer walked past him, and he shut the door, "What's wrong?"

"My cousin has put his nose where it doesn't belong. He went into the library and read a letter from Rick; then, he tried to trap me into telling him what was going on in the house. But I didn't have to tell him a word because the letter said enough. He threatened to break my arms if I didn't tell him the truth, so he knows we are all pirates and that we are involved in something which he considers to be illegal." Jennifer thought about her cousin; he was correct in that what they were doing was illegal but they were also doing good as well by saving people from being slaves.

"I can't believe Rick would be stupid enough to put so much into that damn letter." He paced around the room, "Did he ask you about anything else?"

"My whereabouts when I was missing and Timothy. The point is, I certainly can't stay here as it is too dangerous."

Sirena spoke for the first time, "Then you'll return with us?"

"The sooner the better," replied Jennifer.

Dante put his jacket on, "I'll go to the *Italian Princess* and prepare the crew. I think it would be best if we left this evening, if you can be ready."

He crossed the room to kiss Sirena goodbye; I'll see you later." He left the two women alone.

Sirena looked at Jennifer, "Well, the holiday in London has ended. Fortunately, I've been packing all week, and I have only a few things to put into the trunks. When I finish, I'll help you with your things and the babies."

Jennifer knelt next to Sirena's chair, "Have you told him?"

"Last night."

"Well?" asked Jennifer.

"He was sweet. He doesn't want me to worry. In fact, he said he would buy us our own home in Newport once we returned."

"That's wonderful! Why don't you get dressed and meet me downstairs for breakfast in fifteen minutes? I really don't want to face Stefan alone," said Jennifer.

"I just thought about something. What about Daphne?" asked Sirena.

"I've talked with her, and she said she'll deny knowing everything."

"That's good," replied Sirena.

"See you in fifteen minutes," said Jennifer.

Sirena smiled, "Yes."

Jennifer left the room and went to her own room. When she opened the door, a note lay at her feet. Picking up the envelope she read it and placed it in the pocket of her dress. Daphne's secret would be safe with her. She opened up the trunk, which stood at the base of her bed and began throwing the clothes into the trunk.

Sirena came to Jennifer's room when she finished dressing, "I didn't want to go downstairs alone without Dante or you."

"I don't blame you. Let's go." The two women went downstairs. When they entered the dining room, both Stefan and Daphne were already eating. Jennifer walked to the buffet and handed Sirena a dish. They filled their plates and sat down at the table, "Good morning."

Daphne smiled and said, "Good morning, Jennifer, Sirena."

"Sirena gazed quickly across the table at Daphne, "Good morning.""

Stefan asked, "Where's D'Mattea?"

Jennifer's green eyes glared at him, "He went to his ship."

"I assume that you are still leaving at the end of the week?"

Jennifer looked across the table, "No; in fact, we will be leaving today."

"Today? You couldn't possibly leave today," Stefan said.

"Why not? You certainly can't keep me here or Sirena for that matter," snapped Jennifer.

Stefan laughed, "I can, you see I've sent for the authorities."

"The authorities?" Jennifer stood up and Daphne looked at Stefan in amazement, "You've sent for the authorities?"

Stefan smiled with a maddening look in his eyes, "I'm going to have your children taken away from you and have them made the wards of the country of England."

Jennifer stood up, "You can't do that, Stefan."

"Of course I can; sit down, Jennifer. You, my dear cousin, are an unfit mother."

Jennifer yelled at the top of her lungs, "I am far from unfit! We are leaving, isn't that good enough for you?"

"No," replied Stefan, "You're a whore, Jennifer. Everyone in this house knows that you seduced Timothy Lockwood into your bed. All of the women at Lockwood are whores."

Sirena stared at him, "Do you know that I am the Countess of Lucerne...."

Stefan cut her off, "I really don't give a damn. You, too, are a whore." Sirena wished Dante would return, as this man was frightening.

Daphne had become frightened; she spoke timidly, "Then you are calling me a whore also because I lived at Lockwood."

He looked at her sternly sending chills down Daphne's back, "Of course not, my dear. You were a virgin when I took you. But my cousin here," he paused, "she's slept with men before marriage and has even worked in a bordello."

Jennifer was furious, "I slept with Timothy who became my husband, you ungrateful bastard. I am a Weatherly, Stefan, and I am not as dispassionate as you. Lizabeth?"

The maid appeared, "Yes, Miss Jennifer."

"Get my children ready, I am leaving."

Lizabeth replied, "Yes, Miss."

Stefan stood up, "Lizabeth, don't you touch those children." Lizabeth looked at Stefan, wondering what was wrong; it was obvious that he was angry as was Miss Jennifer.

"Never mind, Lizabeth. Sirena, would you please get the children?"

Sirena nodded as she ran out of the room to get the three children. She didn't know Jennifer's cousin that well but decided he was very dangerous. She dressed the twins quickly while Lion got dressed. Sirena said to him, "We are going back to Newport."

"Why?" he asked.

"Never mind why, but as soon as you are dressed, you wait for me. If Jennifer or I tell you to run, you run. Do you understand?"

"Why?" his golden eyes stared at her.

"Stefan wants to take you and the twins away from Jennifer and give you to England."

"I don't understand," said Lion.

"Don't worry about it. You'll understand when you are older. Just do what we say," replied Sirena. Lion shook his head yes, "Good, let's go."

Jennifer knew that it took an hour to get to the authorities and an hour to return. She had no idea when Stefan had sent for them or if he even did, as he could be trying to terrify her; however, after everything she had been through, it would be difficult to terrify her. Stefan left her no choice; she must take matters into her own hands. Stefan had sat down smugly after his announcement that he would be having her children removed from her care, and Jennifer had remained standing.

Daphne excused herself to go upstairs; on the way, she met Sirena, the twins and Lion. "I'm coming with you," said Daphne.

"What?" asked Sirena.

"I can't stay here. I'm coming with you. I'll get a couple of things together," replied Daphne.

"That's probably what Jennifer and I should do," replied Sirena.

"Take the children into the library. Let Lion watch them; then, you could go upstairs and put some clothing and valuables together."

Sirena continued down the stairs; she put the children into the library and returned upstairs. Fortunately, she had been packing every day and most of her and Dante's things were already on the ship. She went into the bedroom, taking her heavy cloak, their jewels and money tossing them into a small reticule. Next, she went to the children's rooms taking a couple of outfits for each child and some favorite toys. Daphne came to the children's room.

"I can fit a few things into this reticule. I'm not taking much with me."

Sirena looked up, "Take some more clothes and the rest of these toys if you can fit them."

Daphne put them into her bag as fast as she could. The two women continued on to Jennifer's room. They took her cloak, her jewels and two dresses. They went downstairs to the children. Daphne stood with the children while Sirena went back to the dining room. She opened the doors to see Jennifer holding a knife to protect herself, "The children are ready."

Not taking her eyes from Stefan, Jennifer replied, "Good. Thank you, Sirena."

"When Dante gets back, we will go," said Sirena.

"I'll send the authorities after all of you," screamed Stefan.

"I wouldn't try it, Stefan. I don't understand why you've changed so much. I'll just be glad to be out of the house." Turning her attention to Sirena she said, "Would you please get my jewels."

"It's already taken care of," replied Sirena.

"Go to my room and get the packet of papers at the top of the trunk," said Jennifer.

Sirena left the room, when she reached the hall, Dante was coming in the door. She ran to him, "We've got a problem. Stefan sent for the authorities."

"The authorities?"

"He wants to take the children away from Jennifer," replied Sirena.

Dante glanced around the foyer and the staircase, "Where is Jennifer?"

"In the dining room, holding a knife to her cousin. The children are in the library with Daphne and a few bags of clothing. I have to get a packet of papers from Jennifer's trunk."

His dark eyes glanced around again, "I'll put the reticules into the carriage I've hired from town. When you come downstairs, go right out to the carriage." She nodded and went on her way. Dante turned and went into the library.

"When Daphne saw Dante she said, "Thank God you are here, Stefan has gone mad. I'm coming with you."

"Take the children to the carriage outside. I'll bring the reticules."

Daphne picked up the twins, and Lion carried a small bag after her. Dante carried the rest of the bags. He spoke to the driver in a low voice, and Daphne couldn't make out what he was saying. He turned to Daphne, "When Sirena gets here, tell her to stay in the carriage." Daphne nodded.

Dante walked back into the house, drawing his sword, he walked into the dining room. "Jennifer, your cloak is in the foyer, go out to the carriage. I'll take care of him."

Jennifer, put the knife down, "Don't hurt him, Dante."

"I won't. Now go to the carriage." Jennifer left, and Dante looked at Stefan, "She's your cousin and you called the authorities?" He shook his head, Stefan said nothing as Dante continued, "When they get here, I suggest that you tell them you've made a mistake."

"Why should I?"

Dante moved closer to him, the tip of his sword close to Stefan's neck, "If there are any problems in Newport because of you, you'll pay with your life." In one quick move, he cut the ties from the curtains to use as a rope. He motioned for Stefan to sit in a chair, and he tied him to the chair, "Arrivederci, Mr. Weatherly." He turned, leaving Stefan tied to the chair. Dante hurried out of the house and motioned to the driver that they were ready to leave. The horse drawn carriage sped down the gravel road and out of the estate. Within a half hour the carriage reached the docks, and Dante paid the driver. Jennifer, Sirena, Daphne and the three children boarded the *Italian Princess*. The planks were pulled up, and Dante shouted orders to his crew. The fast clipper began to move out to sea leaving London behind it. Five and half days, later the *Italian Princess* entered the cave at Lockwood. They were met by Rick Jordan who was surprised to see Jennifer and Daphne returning. He looked at Dante and then Jennifer for an explanation.

"Rick, we'll discuss it after I put my children to bed." Jennifer was carrying one of the twins, and Daphne had the other. Lion followed along.

When they reached the kitchen, Jennifer gave Arianna to Maggie, and Daphne followed her with Timothy. Jennifer and Sirena crossed the hall and went into the sitting room, closing the door behind them, "Sirena, would you like some sherry?"

"That would be nice," replied Sirena.

Jennifer poured the sherry; D'Mattea and Jordan came into the sitting room; Jennifer handed Sirena her sherry, "Would the two of you like some rum?" Both men nodded, and Jennifer poured it into two glasses, handing one to Rick and one to the Prince.

Rick Jordan said, "Dante has filled me in Jenny, and I'm sorry."

She sipped her sherry, "Not half as sorry as I am. I don't know what is wrong with him."

"Do you think we should worry about him taking action against us?" questioned Rick.

Dante said, "No, I've warned him, and I don't think he'll try anything."

Sirena signed, "I feel bad about Daphne."

"Has she said anything about divorcing him?" questioned Rick"

Jennifer shook her head, "No, but I can tell you that she's frightened of him."

Dante looked at Sirena and then Rick and Jennifer, "Now is a good time to tell you that Sirena and I are going to buy our own home. It'll be close by because of things here."

Rick was surprised, "What prompted this decision?"

Dante smiled, "Sirena's pregnant."

"Congratulations, to the both of you," said Rick and Jennifer as they raised their glasses in the air.

Jennifer asked, "Where's Yvonne and Cliff?"

"They left for the Barbary Coast this morning," answered Rick.

"And Heather?" questioned Jennifer.

"Heather is on a shopping spree. She should be back soon."

Daphne entered the sitting room, "Maggie and Gideon are preparing dinner."

"I'm famished," Sirena said, "But first I would just like to lie down for a little bit."

Dante rose with her, "It's been a long trip. I think I'll take a nap myself."

Daphne sat in a chair near the window and stared into space thinking. The room grew quiet as Dante left to do some paperwork, and Jennifer stayed behind not wanting to leave Daphne alone in case she wanted to talk. Jennifer paced around the room like a nervous cat while Daphne remained silent looking out the window.

Several days later, Jennifer was even more jittery. She had the feeling that someone was watching her. Yet, both Dante and Rick searched the grounds and found nothing. Dante and Sirena bought the house and property next to Lockwood and were preparing to move into it within the next three weeks.

Robert Gray stopped by the house to see Rick Jordan about a matter at the shipping offices. Jennifer hid in the hallway until he was gone; it was important that he didn't see her. Later that evening, Jennifer took a walk along the grounds; as she walked, she thought of Timothy and how she had loved him. She vowed to herself that she would never love that desperately again. No man would ever possess her again; she wouldn't allow it. Walking around the grounds had become a favorite pastime for her as she couldn't go into Newport for fear of being seen by Robert or someone else who knew she moved to London. She went into the barn deciding that she would go for a ride today. She had her horse saddled by Gideon earlier in the day and decided to ride along the cliffs, looking out to sea and wished that someday she would see the *Moonlight* coming in and that Tim and Mark would be safe. She suddenly felt as if she was being watched; turning the horse around, she saw a man run into the bushes. She kicked the horse and rode swiftly back to the barn, dismounted and left the horse fully saddled as she ran back to the house.

Rick Jordan was just on his way to look for her when she ran straight into him, "Jennifer, what's wrong?"

Her green eyes were wild with fear, "Someone is outside on the grounds Rick, and he was watching me. I saw him."

Rick put his arm around her and took her back into the house, "Calm down, I'll go out and look."

Jennifer grabbed his arm, "No, he ran."

"It was probably a prowler. I think you should carry a weapon with you from now on just in case."

"In case of what?" she looked up at him.

"In case I'm not here; you could protect yourself if someone does try to break into the house," responded Rick.

She nodded, "I'll carry a knife and a pistol."

"I think you should have a rapier with you at all times, Jennifer," replied Rick.

"It's too large. A knife and a pistol would be better," Jennifer said very nervously.

Rick shook his head no and said, "A man could overpower you if you had a knife for a weapon, and with a pistol you would need perfect aim," he paused, "but with a rapier, you could hold him off and possibly kill him."

Jennifer shuddered; the thought of having to protect herself in her own home disturbed her, "I'll be okay. When I'm in the house alone, I'll have a sword nearby, or when I go for a walk, I'll carry a rapier."

Rick looked at Jennifer and could completely understand the attraction that Timothy and she had, as she was just as stubborn as Tim. "I would suggest that you try not to go for walks at night. During the day isn't bad, but at night, an intruder is more likely to attack." He paused, "Why don't you go to your bedroom and rest."

"I left the horse in the stable with his saddle on," replied Jennifer.

"Don't worry about it. I'll send Gideon to take care of it."

Jennifer nodded and began going upstairs; Rick watched her go up the stairs. Lately, he and Dante thought she was seeing things, that all of the stress she had been under was taking its toll on her. Every time they went to check the area, they found nothing, no clues as to anyone being there. He decided to check the horse himself; leaving the house, he walked to the stables. When he reached it, all of the horses were in their stalls and not a single one was missing or still saddled. Rick looked around the stable, making sure no one was there. They didn't have stable hands which meant that someone was either in the barn at this moment or had been in the barn. He didn't like this at all; someone has to be watching Jennifer, and he couldn't help think that her cousin was involved. Rick left the stables and returned to the house.

D'Mattea was sitting in the library going over his financial statements which had become a pastime since he and Sirena bought the house. He and Sirena would finally move in tomorrow. Rick entered the library; Dante looked up, "Jordan, what's wrong? You look disturbed."

Rick poured himself a glass of rum, gulped it and poured another one before sitting down across from the large desk that D'Mattea occupied, "Something strange is going on, Dante."

"What are you talking about?" questioned Dante.

Rick stared at his friend, "Someone is watching this house."

"Now you sound like Jennifer; look Jordan, we've all been under considerable strain wondering whether or not Stefan Weatherly would send the authorities here. It is making us all crazy, and because of it, every time we see a shadow, we think it's a person."

"Not this time. Jennifer saw a man standing in the bushes near the cliffs watching her. She rode the horse back to the stables and left it there, saddled," stated Rick in a low tone.

"It was probably her imagination," Dante did not want to think of this possibility, as it could mean problems for all of them; better to be Jennifer's imagination.

"I don't think so," Rick gulped his rum again, "I went out to unsaddle the horse, and someone had already done it."

Dante thought for a minute, "Are you positive that you checked every stall?"

"Yes, but Jennifer left the horse out in the open and not one horse was missing. It is as if whoever is doing this is trying to undermine Jennifer's credibility and the status of her mind with us," replied Rick.

"Who do you think it is?"

Rick looked at his friend, "I don't know, possibly her cousin? Or maybe a private bounty hunter of some kind? The truth is I don't know, but I think we all should be wary of strangers on the property or at the door, or even people trespassing for that matter. If we don't, everything we've worked so hard for will crumble."

Dante said, "If this person is after Jennifer, I would suggest that she carry a weapon."

"I told her that tonight. She was pretty shaken up."

"Did she say if she knew him?" questioned Dante.

"No, she didn't say and if she recognized him; she would have said something."

"You know that Sirena and I are moving out tomorrow." He paused, "If you need me for anything, I'll only be fifteen minutes away."

"I know." Rick rose from his seat, "I'm going to my room."

"I think I'm going to retire for the night also." Both men left the library together.

Outside, a man stood next to a tree watching the house grow dark. He pulled a cigar from his pocket and lit it, smiling sinisterly as he gazed at the dark house and its inhabitants. He turned and walked in the direction of the horse he had hidden in the woods. The following day he was back in his spot watching. He had a close call the night before with Jennifer, but he was sure that she didn't recognize him. He watched a carriage being loaded with trunks; someone was going somewhere. Next, he saw D'Mattea with a woman he didn't recognize get into the hansom cab while Jordan, Jennifer and two other women waved goodbye. Thinking to himself that D'Mattea would be out of the way, he would have to deal with Jennifer and Jordan. When D'Mattea returned, he would take care of him. He sat in the trees watching the house, an hour later Jordan left as he did every morning. For the past month the house had been watched. This morning he would follow him to see where he was going.

Rick Jordan rode his horse into town; today he would be meeting Robert Gray to discuss the finances of the Gray-Lockwood firm. Rick felt uneasy as he rode into the city, having the feeling he was being followed, yet every time he glanced over his shoulder, he saw nothing. The man followed Jordan to the Gray-Lockwood firm and watched him go inside. He watched for two hours before returning to his hotel room.

It was getting warmer as the days went by; Jennifer was outside playing with the children when Rick returned, "Rick."

"Jennifer, what a beautiful day today."

"It's awfully hot for the middle of April," responded Jennifer.

"I think it's going to be one of those years when we don't have a spring and go into summer," said Rick.

"I had a letter from Yvonne and Cliff today."

"Where are they?" questioned Rick.

Jennifer smiled, "Ibiza, Spain. They got married."

"Married," replied Rick, "I'll be damned."

Jennifer continued, "They are honeymooning in Ibiza; Yvonne has a home there."

"Did they say when they are returning?" Rick questioned as he would feel more secure with Yvonne and Cliff around as well. The uneasiness he was feeling in his gut kept telling him that there were going to be some problems.

"No," said Jennifer, "Would you help me with the twins?"

Rick picked up Timothy and Jennifer picked up Arianna, "Lion, it's time to go inside."

Lion ran to Jennifer, "Why?"

"You know you can't stay outside by yourself," responded Jennifer.

"Please," his golden eyes focused on her.

Rick said, "Lion, why don't you come in the house, and I'll teach you a special game while your mother puts the twins to bed."

Lion ran his hand through his hair, "A grown-up's game?"

Rick smiled at Lion; he couldn't help being reminded of Tim every time Lion ran his hand through his hair as Tim would do, "Sure."

"Okay." Lion followed aimlessly, thinking that Uncle Rick would probably teach him something he already knew.

Jennifer took the twins upstairs to change them and put them to bed, while Lion followed Rick into the library. Jennifer couldn't help wonder if she was being watched today. All afternoon she kept glancing around and deliberately stayed close to the doorway in the event she saw someone, so she could get the kids in the house and bolt the doors. She had to remember to keep her rapier close by for protection.

CHAPTER THIRTY-SEVEN

The *Lady Liberty* had her share of problems the last month and a half; twice they were blown off course by storms, each time causing damage to the ship. Timothy and Luke Baker had to make a three week stop in Bermuda for repairs after the first storm. The second storm was off the coast of New York. This last storm caused considerable damage, which put them in New York harbor for four weeks. Now they were one hour from Newport harbor, and Timothy was as nervous as a caged lion. The tall, topaz-eyed man paced around his cabin; he walked to the desk and picked up a small jade statue; he stared at it for a moment and put it down. He glanced up at the bookcase; one of the books was pushed further in than the others. Timothy reached up and withdrew the book; when he did, a paper fell from the pages. He picked up the paper from the desk, and when he did, his heart began to pound so loudly that his head felt like it was going to explode, he recognized the handwriting, '*To whomever finds this letter. My name is Jennifer Weatherly Lockwood, and I am being held against my will by a man who once called himself Geoffrey Lyndon. He now goes by the name of Steven Marshall.*' Timothy's eyes began to read faster, '*I am from Newport, Rhode Island, and my husband's name is Captain Timothy Lockwood. Mr. Lyndon is taking me somewhere in the south and plans to sell me to a bordello.*' A bordello in the south! Timothy was furious; when he found Lyndon, he would kill him, destroy him with his bare hands. '*I am dating this letter, so it can be checked against the ship's log; if a search for me is conducted, at least an area of my whereabouts can be located. Please help me. Give this letter to either my husband, or to whomever answers the door.*' Timothy didn't read any further as he ran to Luke Baker's cabin with the letter in his hand.

"Baker," Timothy pounded on the door.

Luke opened the door, shaving soap still on his face, "What's the matter?"

"Do you remember a small woman with dark green eyes and reddish hair traveling with a blonde man who is going bald?"

"Yes, I remember her. Why?" questioned Luke.

Timothy ran his hand through his hair, "She was on this ship?"

"Yes, why?" questioned Luke again.

"Where did you take them?" questioned Timothy.

"New Orleans; will you tell me why?"

"She was my wife, and she's been missing for months," Timothy was sick to his stomach wondering what had become of Jennifer in New Orleans if Lyndon did sell her to a bordello.

Luke Baker remembered her, "The guy's name was Marshall; in fact, I didn't trust him. The girl had some bruises when they first came on the ship."

Timothy ran his hand through his black hair again, "When we get to Newport, I'll assemble my men, and I'll go look for her."

"We've got about an hour before we dock."

"I'll be in my cabin." Timothy put Jennifer's note into his pocket and returned to his cabin to think about making plans for New Orleans.

Jennifer had woken from her nap and went downstairs; she was met in the hall by Heather. "Jennifer."

"Jennifer smiled, "Are you going somewhere?" Jennifer asked, noticing Heather's attire.

"I thought I would try to get Rick to take me into town for dinner, if you have no objections to staying alone?"

"Go ahead," responded Jennifer, "I won't be alone; Daphne and Maggie are here."

Heather looked at her friend, "Not really; Daphne went over to help Sirena decorate while you were napping, and Maggie is asleep, she hasn't been feeling well."

"Maggie's here and that's all that matters. If Rick and you want to go out to dinner, please do. I can always make something for myself and Lion."

Rick came out of the library, "Did you have a nice nap?"

"Yes," replied Jennifer.

He turned his attention to Heather, "You look lovely."

"I was hoping that you thought so," responded Heather. "How about you take me to town and out to dinner?"

Rick looked at Jennifer, "We can't leave Jenny alone."

"Don't be foolish," responded Jennifer. "I'll be fine; Maggie's upstairs, and I promise to keep my rapier with me at all times."

"Are you sure?" questioned Rick.

Jennifer smiled, "Positive. The two of you go ahead and have a good time."

Rick turned to Heather, "Let me get my jacket, Heather, and then we can leave." He left the two women standing in the foyer.

Heather looked at Jennifer, "Are you positive you're going to be fine?"

"Positive, don't worry about me. Have a good time; I think I'll make something to eat for myself and Lion," responded Jennifer.

"I meant to tell you that Lion is with Daphne at Sirena and Dante's, but they should be home soon."

"If you will excuse me then, I'll make myself something to eat." Jennifer walked off in the direction of the kitchen.

Rick came downstairs, and he and Heather left for the city. He was worried about leaving Jennifer alone, but he was sure that she would be fine as lately there had not been any suspicious activities or feelings of being watched.

The man was hiding in the trees again, watching the large house. Many people left the house and hadn't returned. Now Jordan and the woman he didn't know left the house, meaning Jennifer was alone. From what he could tell, she was the only one in the house. He would wait a few minutes and then make his move. He watched for fifteen or twenty minutes before going closer to the house. He walked around, looking into the ground floor windows. He saw Jennifer in the sitting room eating. He looked around and decided that the back entryway was the best way to enter the house. Breaking the glass with his gloved hand, he entered the house. The kitchen had two doors, the first one he opened brought him into total darkness and a flight of stairs. The second door led to a corridor; he made his way slowly along the hall. Jennifer had finished eating and went into the library to get a book to read. After choosing the book, she returned to the sitting room; she opened the book to read, but her mind drifted as she began to doze off thinking about Timothy.

The *Lady Liberty* had come into Newport harbor and as soon as the plank was lowered, Timothy hired a landau to take him to Lockwood. The ride seemed to take forever this dark misty night; in fact, he had never seen the fog so thick.

The intruder silently made his way along the corridor and into the sitting room where Jennifer drifted into a light sleep. She thought she heard the floorboard squeak; her hand instantly grabbed the hilt of the rapier as her eyes flew open. The room was completely dark, and she could hear someone breathing very close to her, yet she couldn't see anyone. She began to panic as she rose quickly, knocking over a vase which crashed to the floor in a million pieces.

"Jennifer, I've come back for you."

Her green eyes opened wide with fear; she knew the voice, a horrible, sinister voice. In a barely audible voice she said, "Geoffrey?"

He laughed in ripples, "I see you haven't forgotten." Jennifer lashed out with her rapier in the direction from which his voice came and he laughed again, "I'm not stupid enough to be that close to you."

Trying to quiet her fear she yelled, "What do you want Geoffrey? Money?" Jennifer prayed that Maggie would hear her.

"I want you to be punished for what your friends did to me."

"My friends?" She started to back towards the door, certain he was near the fireplace. She kept her rapier extended in front of her whipping it to and fro, hoping that she would stab him if he came near her. "What friends are you talking about?" She was almost at the door when someone grabbed her from behind. He grasped the hand which held her sword, and it fell to the floor after a small struggle. It was completely dark in the room, and she could smell his foul breath.

"You always thought you were so smart, Jennifer, but I've always been smarter."

She tried to wriggle away from him, yet he held her arms tightly. They fell to the floor in a struggle, knocking over a table. He straddled her as her legs flailed in all directions, "I'll give you money, as much as you want."

"Money could never buy back what those animals took away from me," Geoffrey said in a gritty voice.

"I don't know what you're talking about." Her only hope was if Dante took Daphne and Lion home or if Rick and Heather returned.

"They took my manhood from me and now," he began to laugh uncontrollably as he tied her hands behind her head, "Now I'm going to kill you. But I'm going to do it slowly so that you will be tortured as your friends tortured me. The best part is that I'm going to let you suffer."

Timothy's carriage pulled up to Lockwood; as he climbed the steps to the front door, the house was completely dark, which he thought was strange. When he tried the front door, he found it bolted so he made his way around the house in the fog. The back door was wide open and the glass broken; he instantly drew his sword. In a loud roar he yelled, "Jordan, D'Mattea."

Geoffrey, who had finished tying Jennifer, looked at her wild eyed, "What was that?"

"I don't know; someone must be here." She could hardly hear the voice and had no idea what they were saying or who they were looking for; in all probability, it might be Maggie.

Timothy checked all of the doors in the hallway as he moved easily towards the front entrance. Something was wrong; the house was too dark. He reached the foyer and heard a noise on the stairs. He whirled around to see Maggie in a dressing gown.

Maggie froze in shock on the stairs, "Captain, we thought you were dead."

He climbed the stairs to meet her as she looked suddenly pale from the shock of seeing him quite alive and he feared she would faint, "Where is everyone?"

She shrugged, "Prince D'Mattea just moved today, but Mr. Jordan and Mrs. Lockwood should be here."

Timothy's yellow eyes opened wide in surprise, "Mrs. Lockwood, she's here?"

"Yes, sir."

He grinned. Jennifer had always been a fighter. Just then they heard a crash from downstairs. Jennifer and Geoffrey were rolling around on the floor. He had tied her hands together, but didn't secure them to anything else and in the moment in which he shifted his body weight, she threw him off of her. Timothy raced down the stairs and into the dark sitting room, "Jenny?"

Jennifer blinked, it was his voice, but it couldn't be his voice. She was dreaming or must be delirious from hitting her head when she and Geoffrey had fallen to the floor. She called out to him in a weak voice, "Timothy?"

"Where are you?" Timothy bellowed.

In order to protect himself Geoffrey scrambled for Jennifer's rapier. Jennifer struggled to her feet, "Light one of the lamps; Geoffrey's in the room, and he has my rapier."

Maggie had come to stand behind Timothy with her lantern, throwing enough light on the room so Timothy could see both Geoffrey and Jennifer; in that split second, Jennifer ran towards Timothy as he raced to Geoffrey with his sword extended.

Jennifer looked at Maggie frantically. Her clothes were torn, her hair was disheveled, and she felt as if a ghost was there. "Maggie, light

the lanterns in this room, hurry." Maggie entered the sitting room timidly. She lit the lantern on the right wall and then on the left wall.

Timothy charged at Geoffrey, their rapiers meeting with a clash.
He feinted to the right and left with short jabs. Geoffrey was not as
skilled a swordsman, and his arm was quickly getting tired. The two
women watched in awe as Timothy disarmed Geoffrey, the rapier flying
into the middle of the room. Timothy had him at swords point, "You
will die this time, make no mistake about it as I will kill you."

"Please," whimpered Geoffrey.

Timothy's golden eyes darkened in anger, "This time I'll make
sure that you're dead."

"You can't kill an unarmed man," cried Geoffrey.

Now it was Timothy's turn to smirk, "Watch me."

Prince D'Mattea was taking Daphne and Lion home when he
noticed the landau in the front of the house. He told Daphne and Lion
to stay put in his carriage. Dante walked up the stairs trying to enter the
front door; he couldn't budge it. Taking out his pistol, he shot the lock
and pushed the door open.

Jennifer, whose hands were still tied, ran to the front door and
saw Dante entering with pistol in his hand, "Dante."

He looked at her hands and clothes, "What happened?"

"Hurry, Timothy's in the sitting room with Geoffrey."

Dante was taken aback, both of them alive? He was certain that
both of them were dead. Dante sprinted into the sitting room. Timothy
still had Geoffrey at swords point. "Tim?"

"Dante, take him downstairs and tie him up."

"Let's go, Geoffrey." He held the pistol to Geoffrey's back as
they left the sitting room.

Timothy turned to face Jennifer whose face was stained with
tears and a little bit of blood near her mouth. He quickly strode across
the room just as she fainted in his arms. Maggie ran to get some water,
and she and Tim revived Jennifer. Jennifer threw herself into Tim's arms
sobbing. Tim motioned to Maggie to give them some privacy, and she
left the room shutting the door behind her. Timothy grasped Jennifer's
face, wiping the tears and blood away, "Tim, am I dreaming?"

Timothy smiled, "No, but if you were dreaming, I'm having the
same dream." He leaned forward and drew her into a deep kiss, tasting
her.

Jennifer pulled away, "We thought you were dead; when I saw
the newspaper article, my heart broke."

He looked at her, "I think the two of us need to talk." She shook her head, not saying a word, "Why don't you change your dress and meet me in the library in a half hour. I must take care of something first." She nodded and watched him leave the room, knowing he was going downstairs to deal with Geoffrey.

Timothy reached the cellar and found Dante and Geoffrey in the cataloguing room. Geoffrey was tied to a chair, and Dante sat opposite him. Dante rose when Timothy entered the room. "Mr. Lyndon, I can't tell you how displeased I am with you." Geoffrey was gagged so he couldn't say a word. "Several years ago, I thought I killed you with my bare hands." Timothy walked closer to Geoffrey's chair, "This time you will be dead because I'm going to snap your neck." The topaz eyes grew darker in anger, as his hands encircled Geoffrey's neck. His thumbs were pressed strategically on Geoffrey's Adam's apple as he began to squeeze. He squeezed tighter and tighter until Geoffrey's face began to turn blue. Within minutes Dante and Timothy heard a loud snap. Timothy released Geoffrey whose head fell forward. Timothy noticed the front of Geoffrey's pants were soaked with urine, however he checked to see if Geoffrey had a pulse to make sure the bastard was dead this time.

Dante was the first to speak, "What do you want to do with the body?"

Timothy looked at him, "When Jordan returns, I want the two of you to take him behind the house and throw him over the cliff so it appears he stumbled in the fog and darkness and broke his neck."

"Yes, sir," replied Dante.

Timothy turned and went upstairs; the time had come to talk to Jennifer. He found her sitting in the library waiting for him. He opened the door sucking in his breath as she was more beautiful than he remembered. She had changed her clothes into a pale gold gown, her long hair hung around her shoulders, her green eyes looking at him. Jennifer wasn't sure how she should react, she had always feared him, but now it was as if he were God-like, having returned from the dead. He crossed the room not saying a word as he poured himself a glass of rum. He wasn't sure how he should apologize to her, and it was important that he did. He stared at her for a moment, drinking in her beauty before speaking, "Jenny, I'm sorry for that afternoon. I don't know what came over me."

"I thought you were dead." Jennifer replied, somewhat still in shock.

Timothy knew she was still reeling from what she went through with Geoffrey and seeing him alive and well, "Can you accept my apology?"

"Can you accept mine? I should have never walked out."

"If you take me back, Jenny, I promise that there will be no more Amandas in my life."

Jennifer rose from her seat, "The question is, do you want me back?" She crossed the room to stand in front of him, "I've been through a great deal, Timothy. In fact, my own cousin is ready to take our children away because he said I was a whore."

Timothy said sternly, "Never call yourself that, Jennifer."

"It might be true, I have to tell you; otherwise, I wouldn't be able to live with myself."

"You don't have to," he took the letter from his pocket and handed it to her, "I just found it this morning and I was coming home to get the stronghold together to come after you."

Jennifer's eyes opened wide, "How did you find this? I put it on the *Lady Liberty*."

"I came home on the *Lady Liberty*." Timothy paused, "The *Moonlight* sunk and Mark and I were captured by Torreya; when we attempted to escape. Mark didn't make it." His eyes began to water.

She touched his arm, "I'm sorry, Tim, I know how close you were to him."

"In many ways he was like my father," Timothy said solemnly.

Jennifer said, "I promise you that I won't jump to conclusions or ask too many questions, I'll do whatever you say. I'll…"

Timothy put his hand over her mouth, "Shush, Jenny. Don't ever change; I love you because you have spunk, and you're feisty." He took his hand from her mouth, his golden eyes twinkling, "Let me tell you a secret. I married you because you were a challenge and so damn unpredictable."

Tears filled her eyes, "I love you, and I thought I lost you forever."

He pulled her to him, looking deeply into her eyes, he said, "Do you know that you kept me alive? The thought of finding you and coming back to you gave me strength to live."

Jennifer looked at him in amazement; he kept her alive as well, "Let me tell you what happened when Geoffrey kidnapped me."

He silenced her with a kiss, "No, some things are better left unsaid," He held her to him, "The important thing is that you're alive, and you are home."

"What about Geoffrey?"

"Don't worry about him, he's had an accident and he'll never bother either of us again. Do you know what I would like?"

Jennifer said, "No."

"I want to take you to a special place that I call Paradise."

"Paradise?"

"Yes," Timothy's eyes twinkled, "it's a little island off the coast of Java, and I owned it."

She was amazed, there was so much that she didn't know about him, "You own an island?"

"I bought it about eight years ago when I was heavily involved in piracy. It was a great hiding place for when I was in trouble," responded Timothy.

She thought for a moment, "Wait a minute, you said you owned it. Does that mean you no longer own it?" The green eyes searched his face.

"That's true. I transferred the island's papers to your name the day we were married. So now it's yours."

"Mine!" Jennifer exclaimed.

"I named it Paradise, but you can change the name if you like."

"No, let's keep it Paradise."

Timothy smiled, "Right now I want to make love to you; however, we need to tell the others that we resolved our problems." He put his arm around her shoulders as they left the library for the sitting room.

Rick Jordan, Prince D'Mattea, Lion, Heather, Maggie and Daphne sat in the sitting room waiting for Timothy and Jennifer; they had been in the library for over an hour. When Timothy and Jennifer entered the sitting room, everyone stopped talking, and Lion ran to his father. Timothy picked up his son and kissed him; the child, desperately hung to his father. "I've missed you, Lion."

"Don't ever leave again, Daddy."

Timothy's golden eyes looked into his golden eyed son, "I promise that I won't ever disappear again." He put the child down. "I have some bad news." He looked at Dante and Rick, "Mark Gregory is dead. He died while we were trying to escape from Torreya."

"Torreya?" questioned Rick.

"Yes, Torreya is the one who sank the *Moonlight*. I now know exactly where Torreya's island is and how to penetrate it."

Dante said, "Are you telling us that the stronghold could penetrate Tortuga, capture Torreya and possibly stop the white slave trade in the Caribbean?"

"Exactly," responded Timothy.

"Then our quest for freedom will become a reality at least in the Caribbean," said Jordan.

"White slavery, yes. But I became aware of a new quest and that is black slavery right here in the United States." He paused, "But we'll discuss that when Jennifer and I return."

"Return?" questioned D'Mattea.

"Yes, I'm taking Jennifer, my three children and a few other people to our island. I don't know how long we'll stay; it might be as long as a year."

"A year? What about the stronghold?" questioned Jordan.

Timothy looked at the two men standing before him, "The stronghold will live on, and I'm placing the two of you in charge while I'm away. When I return, we'll formulate plans to capture Torreya."

"And the stronghold will be successful in at least one area," said Jennifer.

"Maggie, I think you should take Lion to his bedroom, and, Dante," the topaz eyed man stared at Dante, "Sirena must be wondering what happened to you."

"I guess I better get home," Dante said rising to his feet.

"We'll have a meeting tomorrow at noon." Dante nodded at Timothy and Jennifer as he left the house and headed home. Rick Jordan and Heather excused themselves as did Daphne, leaving Timothy and Jennifer alone in the sitting room. Timothy looked at her; she was his life, and she always would be his life. "Why don't you go upstairs and put on that pretty white lacy nightgown."

She smiled, "The one you bought me a long time ago?"

His eyes twinkled, "The very one, and I'll be upstairs in a moment." Before leaving the sitting room, she walked over to him, stood up on tip toes and kissed him. He watched her walk upstairs from the foyer. He returned to the sitting room and poured himself a glass of rum. He sat on one of the chairs and thought about the last few years of his life. He smiled; Jennifer changed him for the better, and he was grateful. He wondered what would have happened if he never met her. He sighed; he probably wouldn't know his son or Yvonne, and he certainly wouldn't have met Torreya. He finished his rum, placed the glass on the table next to the chair and shut the lamps as he made his way upstairs to the master bedroom. When he reached the top of the stairs, he went down the corridor to his bedroom, their bedroom; he paused in front of the door. He was a little nervous; it had been months since he and Jennifer had been together. Only one other time had he felt this way, and that was with

Jennifer also. Taking a deep breath, he opened the door; she was standing in the moonlight like she had the night he asked her to pretend she was married to him. That night seemed like an eternity ago, and now she was his wife. Jennifer deliberately positioned herself in the moonlight so that the white lacy nightgown left nothing to the imagination. She stood motionless in the moonlight as Timothy entered the room and closed the door. He crossed the room, taking her into his arms; he held her, smelling the freshness of her hair and the scent of her skin. He lifted her in his arms like he had so many times before, carried her to the massive bed, and gently placed her on the mattress. Slowly, he began to unbutton his shirt, thinking she had always been beautiful, but today she looked more beautiful than ever except for the first time he saw her on the docks. Jennifer smiled as she watched him undress; she knew deep in her heart that he had always been her destiny from the first moment she saw him on the *Moonlight* in London. As Timothy removed his shirt, he sighed, thinking back to the first day he saw her and knew instantly that she would be his conquest.

ABOUT THE AUTHOR

Charlene J. Centracchio is a native of Rhode Island with multiple degrees from Rhode Island College and Providence College in Education, Social Science, Curriculum and Counseling. *The Pirate's Conquest* was originally written when her mother was sick and later passed from cancer, with the first copyright being January 13, 1983. The book sat in the basement for 37 years while Charlene taught Social Studies and later became a high school Guidance Counselor. During the height of the COVID-19 Pandemic, Charlene decided the timing was right as she was no longer working as a teacher.

Charlene is also an intuitive psychic card reader (www.psychicimpressionslive.com) utilizing a regular deck of playing cards as a tool to connect with the vibration of energy from the person's name. She has been reading cards for 35 years and has many clients that she helps achieve their highest goals for betterment of their lives. She is trained in Reiki Healing, as well as Magnified Healing. Her psychic gift has been passed to her from both sides of her family with the greatest gift and direct lineage coming from her mom's side. Her spirit guides are those who passed on such as her mother and father, as well as various pets and other animals who come to her.

Made in the USA
Middletown, DE
28 October 2022

13633392R00243